MOUNT ROXBY

BOOKS 1-3

AIMIE JENNISON

Mount Roxby: Books 1-3

CONTENTS

FOREVER YOUNG AND BEAUTIFUL

RECLAIMING THE ONE

A NOTE FOR
THE READER

This book has been written using UK English and is set in
Australia. I apologise if there are words or phrases you do not
understand. Please feel free to contact me for further explanation, or to discuss the meaning of a particular phrase or word,
via my email or any of my social media.

PRIDE TO PACK

MOUNT ROXBY SERIES: BOOK ONE

AIMIE JENNISON

Pride to Pack

Copyright © 2014 Aimie Jennison

Cover by Sloan Johnson at Sloan J Designs

Formatting: Aimie Jennison

All rights reserved.

No part of this book may be reproduced or transmitted in any form, including electronic or mechanical, without written permission from the publisher, except in the case of brief quotations embodied in critical articles or reviews.

This is a work of fiction. Names, characters, businesses, places, events, and incidents are either the products of the author's imagination or used in a fictitious manner. Any resemblance to actual persons, living or dead, or actual events is purely coincidental. Aimie Jennison is in no way affiliated with any brands, songs, musicians or artists mentioned in this book.

This book is licensed for your personal enjoyment only. This book may not be re-sold or given away to other people. If you would like to share this book with another person, please purchase an additional copy for each person you share it with. If you are reading this book and did not purchase it, or it was not purchased for your use only, then you should return it to the seller and purchase your own copy. Thank you for respecting the author's work.

DEDICATION

To Nana June.
Thank you for always being my cheerleader.
I will miss you and I will never forget you.

PROLOGUE

"*B*el, get your butt down these stairs now," Uncle Jack bellows from the basement.

"I'm coming. Geez, am I not allowed to even eat breakfast?" I answer, not bothering to shout, knowing he'll hear me clearly, with his were-lion hearing, even if I whisper. Were-animals have extra sensitive hearing.

Aunt Lily pats my back as I pass her, heading to the basement door. "He doesn't want to lose you in this duel, sweetheart. It's your first duel and he knows how strong Jerome is. It has him worried."

I take a deep breath before opening the door and heading down the stairs. The next few hours are going to be painful. Uncle Jack will push me, hard.

Uncle Jack started training me the day after I arrived, at the age of ten. He knew I needed it because as soon as I reached the legal age of duelling—which happened to be eighteen—I would be challenged, time and time again until one of them killed me. The lions just don't think a wolf deserves to be part of their pride. The thing is, I don't even want to be part of their stupid pride.

I just want somewhere to call home.

My home was taken away from me when my parents died. My legal guardian, Aunt Lily, is the only tie I have to my parents. At eighteen, I'm old enough to go off on my own, but my Aunt, Uncle, and cousin Benji, are family. I love them and don't want to leave them.

The basement is set up like any high-end gym, with all the equipment and weights anyone could ask for. The floor is covered in mats to soften the fall when I am sparing with Uncle Jack. I appreciate those mats because I do hit the floor—a lot.

Uncle Jack is standing in the middle of the mats ready to spar. He's trained me in all kinds of Martial Arts, so I'm not limited and won't get stuck if someone fights in some unusual form.

I take hit after hit knowing that this time tomorrow, I will be fighting to the death. This torture Uncle Jack puts me through is for my own good.

The Pride is assembled in the arena, which is basically an open field surrounded by the forests of the pride land. I call it a field but there is nothing there. It's just packed dirt. It has seen many duels over the years; the red dirt the Northern Territory is known for is almost black from all the blood spilled on it.

The lions are circled around the outside of the arena.

Jerome is already waiting in the centre for me.

Humans aren't allowed, it's too dangerous if the fight spreads towards the spectators. Aunt Lily and my cousin Benji are both human so I only have Uncle Jack, who is one of the lions, there to support me.

The crowd parts to let me in.

Uncle Jack gives me one last pat on the shoulder as he stops to stand with the crowd. "You can do this, Bel. Remember your strengths. Forget everything else."

I take a deep breath and face my opponent.

Jerome has a good foot on me in human form. He easily outweighs me. He's smirking at me like he knows he has this fight in the bag.

That's it, Jerome, you keep thinking like that. Let the overconfidence take you that step closer to the body bag.

Grigori Dorfman, the current Leader of the Pride, steps up to stand between us. "Jerome, you have challenged Rosabel to a duel. Does your challenge still stand?"

Jerome nods. "Yes."

"Very well. Rosabel, since you are the challenged party, you have the choice of whether you want to fight in human or animal form."

"Human," I answer immediately. When fighting in animal form, you only need a tooth or claw to connect in the wrong place and you're dead. Fighting as a human may take longer and be harder, but you can control your opponent more. Fighting in animal form isn't a viable option.

Grigori's loud voice booms around the arena. "You both must remain in human form at all times. If either of you shift, or even partially shift, your opponent will be declared winner and you will immediately be put to death. This duel is to the death. Do you both understand the rules?"

"Yes," we answer together.

Grigori throws his arms wide and bows his head. "May the best animal win."

Jerome and I start to circle each other, weighing each other up. Neither of us willing to make the first move.

"Come on Jerome, she's only a little girl," a male voice shouts.

Jerome turns, chasing the voice; I take the opportunity to strike him in the side of the head with a round house kick. He hits the ground and shakes his head. I move in with a kick to his jaw. He seems to anticipate it making a grab for my foot; he was a second too late and only manages to knock my foot away.

I step back and start to circle again as Jerome stands up.

He jabs his fist at my ribs and connects, causing a crack that I have no doubt means something is broken. He follows with a second jab to the same area.

Lapping up the attention as the audience cheers, he smirks. During his distraction I grab his outstretched arm, pulling it against the bend in his elbow. It cracks louder than my ribs, and I see some of the spectators flinch at the sound. I can see the shift cross his face, but he fights it off. Pain can be a trigger to shift, just like it's a trigger for nausea in humans. He did well to fight it off that quick.

The fight goes on for at least twenty minutes, which believe me, when you are fighting to the death *is* a long time. Both of us have been throwing punches and striking with kicks and neither of us is getting the upper hand.

Uncle Jack trained me for at least four hours every day. I have the endurance to handle this fight, but Jerome is getting tired. I can see it and so can the Pride.

"Come on, Jerome. End her," someone shouts.

He tries to execute a roundhouse kick to my face in retaliation to those comments. Fortunately, for me, he's sluggish. I let the momentum in his poorly executed kick take him to the ground before I pounce on his chest and grab his head between my hands.

I snap his neck.

The audience is outraged. Not only have I won, I'm still breathing. A wolf. A female wolf just beat one of their strongest male lions in a duel to the death.

Grigori walks into the arena and states the obvious by announcing me—the only one still standing and breathing breaths that feel like a hot brand being jabbed into my side—the winner.

The crowd gets louder. He tries to calm them down but it's no use. He nods to Uncle Jack, signalling him to come and take me home so he can try to calm the pride without my distracting presence.

I only manage to hobble a couple of steps before Jerome's brother, Daniel, pushes his way through the crowd.

He gives me a murderous glare as the crowd falls silent.

"I challenge the wolf." He steps into the arena and removes his shirt, preparing to fight.

No way can I survive another duel so soon.

I shake free of Uncle Jack's vice-like grip and settle my feet to show I'm not going to run.

"I accept," I reply officially, as required.

Uncle Jack is red in the face, holding his rage back as he rants at Grigori.

Jared Dorfman, Grigori's oldest son and the next in line to be Pride Leader, steps in front of me. I didn't see where he came from, probably because my eyes are swelling shut and didn't spot his stealthy approach. He gently holds my face between his hands, assessing the damage.

I suck in a breath at the concern I see in his golden eyes. My heart pounds a little harder at his soft touch. None of the pride have ever been concerned about me. I start to think I have read him wrong and he's more concerned about the fact that I'm still breathing, that is, until he speaks.

"It's okay, Rosabel. They can't make you duel again so soon. It's Pride law. They have to give you at least a day to heal."

My stomach plummets. As good as a day reprieve sounds, it's nowhere near enough time to heal and be fit enough to win another duel. They are just going to prolong my suffering and death.

My day reprieve passed in the blink of an eye. It could've had something to do with sleeping through most of it. My body's natural urge to heal while I slept took over. I wanted to train but my body was having none of it.

I gingerly walk in the kitchen to give Benji and Aunt Lily a last minute hug goodbye. I'm not feeling very confident today knowing it might actually be the last hug I get to give them.

Aunt Lily dashes across the room the minute she sees me, taking me in her arms, surrounding me with her floral scent. "It's an abomination. Making you duel when you are still recovering from the last one. I feel like storming down to that arena and giving them a piece of my mind."

"You can't do that. It will only cause trouble for Uncle Jack. I've trained all these years. I can handle it." I pull away, putting on my brave face. I need to leave now before I crack, causing her to do exactly what she wants—no doubt writing her own death warrant in the process.

Benji stands from his seat at the table. "Come on, Bel, you don't want to be late. I'll walk you down the road. Uncle Jack said he'd meet you at Grigori's. There was a meeting this morning." He walks straight out the door without making eye contact with Aunt Lily or me. I can smell his tears so I know the reason why. It's the same reason I follow him out silently, neither of us want to make Aunt Lily any more concerned.

Neither of us speaks again until we reach Grigori's drive, both lost in our own heads. I can't help looking at all the gorgeous houses, seeing the picket fences and beautiful flower beds, only to think people passing through this town have no idea the very people who keep these houses so beautiful would be trying their damnedest to have an eighteen-year-old woman killed just because she's another species.

"Bel," Benji's whimper pulls me from my thoughts.

One look at his blotchy face covered in tears makes me pull him into my arms. "Shhhh. It's okay, Benj."

Grigori's door opens. Jared, Uncle Jack, and Grigori file out. Grigori walks out the gate not even acknowledging we are here. But then again Benji is a lowly human and I'm a wolf; we already know what the lions think of me. Why should he bother acknowledging us?

I watch Jared, expecting him to follow his father but he stops in front of us with Uncle Jack.

I release Benji, holding his shoulders firmly with my hands. "Go home and give Aunt Lily a hug. I'll see you in a little while." I don't care that there's no conviction behind my words. It isn't like I can say, 'Have a good life, I won't see you again.' It's probably true but it would just hurt both of us.

Uncle Jack pulls a sobbing Benji into his embrace, looking at me over Benji's dark hair. "I'm going to take him home. You head down with Jared, I'll catch up." With those parting words, he walks off in the direction of home.

I watch them walk away for a second before turning back towards Jared, who's still standing in front of me. In fact, I'm certain he moved in closer because there's barely an inch between us. I can feel his lion's energy crackling against my skin.

"How are you doing, Bel?" He asks as he stares intently into my eyes. The stare goes all the way down to my toes. *Holy hell.* I feel a flush pulsing through my body.

"I'm fine," I answer curtly. Why would I answer any differently when his pride is trying to kill me?

He growls. That growl does something to my body. I can honestly say I have never heard a growl come from a lion before; it's quite disturbing…and arousing.

His hot breath is almost in my face. His nostrils flare as he barks at me. "Now. Answer that again, but without the bullshit this time." I can sense a power blazing from his lion. What's going on?

"Fine," I snap. "I feel like shit. It hurts to move. It hurts to breathe. It hurts to think about the fact that I'm being sent to my death by your whole goddamn pride and no fucker seems to give a shit! There. Is that what you wanted to hear?"

"Not exactly, but it's much better than the first answer." He turns and starts walking towards the arena. "Come on, you don't want to be late."

The closer we get to the arena, the calmer I become. It's like a cloud has descended over me, nothing matters but the fight I'm about to face. No amount of worrying or complaining will change a thing. I've got to duel no matter what; I can't ask anyone else to fight for me.

The pride is already circled around the arena, ready to watch the duel.

Jared grabs my hand and pulls me through the parting crowd.

Great, everyone is going to think I was about to run and needed escorting by the leader's son.

Once we get through the crowd, I pull my hand away from Jared's.

"It's about time you turned up. I thought you must have run off scared," Daniel says snarkily.

That growling noise comes from Jared again but he doesn't follow up with a comment.

Grigori steps between us, stopping any verbal diarrhea from spewing out of my mouth. "Daniel, does your challenge against Rosabel still stand?"

"She killed my brother. Too fucking right it does," he snaps.

"A 'yes' will suffice, Daniel," Grigori says with a smirk.

Is this really a time for jokes? One of us is going to die in a minute. Looking at Daniel's muscular body, I have no doubt it's going to be me.

"Rosabel, choose a form." Just like that, no formal wording.

"I challenge Daniel," Jared shouts from next to me. I had actually forgotten he was there. I flick my eyes to him in surprise and our eyes connect. My heart stutters in my chest at the emotions I see burning in his. Murmurs run through the crowd as people question why. Others are questioning if it's even a legal move on Jared's part.

"Daniel, being the challenged party, you are required to choose a form. What do you choose?"

I'm too shell-shocked to take in what's happening around me after that.

Jared's fighting for me and Grigori is letting him. *Why? Have I been sucked into the twilight zone or something?*

Someone's hand grabs me, pulling me out of the arena and towards the spectators. They're not attacking me, so I assume it's Grigori. I can't tear my eyes away from the two lions in the arena long enough to see who belongs to the hand. All I can see is one mass of golden fur. With the roars and yips I can hear, it's clear someone is winning.

It's only a matter of minutes before it's all over, the fur separates into two. The lion that's moving shifts and a naked Jared is left standing in the centre of the arena.

I manage to breathe a sigh of relief before Grigori drags me back towards the centre. He clears his throat before speaking. "Jared, as the winner, do you wish to take on Daniel's challenge towards Rosabel?"

"No," is all he grumbles, as he picks up his clothes off the ground and stalks out of the arena.

Grigori passes me off to Uncle Jack. I have no idea where he came from, or if he was even there through the fight, but he's here now and leading me home.

The Pride didn't seem to know what to do after Jared took on Daniel. It was a week before I was challenged again. I fought that time, but when I was immediately challenged again Jared jumped in and challenged my opponent right back.

Jared joined in on our training sessions the day after his fight with Daniel, not because he needed the training but so he could help me.

It wasn't long before we became a couple; which really didn't help on the fight front.

They didn't want their future leader married to a wolf.

1

NEW BEGINNINGS

I take a deep, cleansing breath as I pounce off the bus. Twelve hours sitting in a metal container with a bunch of sweating strangers is not the best idea for someone with a strong nose like mine. And that was just the last bus journey. I had been on three more of around the same duration. It takes a long time to drive from the desert of the Northern Territory, all the way southeast to central New South Wales. I could have flown but it's bad enough travelling in a box that's on the ground, there was no way I was going to travel in a big metal box that floats in the air. Were-animals might be extremely indestructible, but I don't think even I could survive a plane crash. My cousin, Benji, isn't like me and even he warned me about the smell.

I should have listened.

Jared will know I have left by now. Uncle Jack promised he would keep him distracted long enough to give me a good head start.

I didn't tell anyone where I was heading because I hadn't really known myself. I'd just closed my eyes, threw a dart at a map of Australia and chose the nearest town that had a werewolf pack. I burnt the map to ashes afterwards so there wouldn't be any clues. So even if he does come looking he isn't going to find me.

I know you're wondering why I left. If I was in love with the man who saved my life by duelling for me for the last six years, why would I up and leave? Well let me tell you, that is exactly why I left. Jared didn't deserve to fight every week to save his mate, or wife, from being killed. He deserves a mate that his pride actually likes and accepts. I didn't want him to resent me and that's all our future would hold; resentment.

I only told Aunt Lily, Uncle Jack, and Benji about my plan to leave an hour before my first coach left. Aunt Lily was heartbroken and Benji wasn't far off, but once I explained my reasons Uncle Jack agreed it was for the best. We managed to calm Aunt Lily and Benji down in the end, but I think it will take them a while to fully come to terms with it.

I am hoping to find a werewolf pack that will welcome me. From Pride to Pack, I'm dreaming of finding somewhere to finally call home.

So here I am in Mount Roxby, thankfully off that stinking bus, with a back pack crammed full of my belongings, two hundred dollars in my pocket, and no idea what to do or where to go.

As I stand on the pavement of the main road, taking in my surroundings, I find myself being drawn to a building across the road. It doesn't look special; it's a corner building and has a midnight blue facade, two double doors of the same colour, and a bright purple neon sign - Misty's. There are no windows that I can see, making me think it's a bar or club of some kind. I can't help but go take a closer look.

There's a piece of paper taped to the door. 'Cocktail mixer needed. Apply within.' *I'm going to need a job.* I had worked in the only bar back home for the last couple of years, so I'm used to the bar atmosphere. *Okay, cocktails weren't ordered very often, but how hard can it be?*

As I push the door open I get a really strong sense of dread. It makes me want to turn my behind around and leave in a rush. I take a deep breath and ignore my senses. Once the door shuts behind me the dread goes with it, as if it's just connected to the door in some way.

The smell of cleaning fluid hits me immediately, along with a whole mix of people's personal scents. In the big rectangular room, the solid wooden floorboards under my feet aren't sticky like you expect to find in a bar. The first thing I see is the bar's counter, which is directly opposite the entrance, stretching about eight metres in length from the right hand corner of the room, to the left. There's a door next to the bar and then there are four booths along the wall; a stage— with a beautiful, glossy black piano on the right-hand side—is positioned in the far left of the room along that side wall.

In front of the stage is a large open area which I assume is used as a dance floor. Covering the rest of the floor space is a mixture of circular and rectangular tables, with booths against the other wall until you come to the door again. Every available wall is covered in floor to ceiling mirrors, which makes the whole place look twice as big. Even though there are no windows it isn't dark and dingy, the lighting is used well. The space between the bar and the door is open apart from a few stools along the bar.

There aren't many customers; a couple sit at the right corner of the bar, a guy sits to the far left side, and another couple sit at one of the circular table's right next to the dance floor. It doesn't look very busy but it is only five in the evening; most people will only just be leaving work. It probably won't get too busy for another couple of hours.

I walk over to the bar where I can see a tall, at least six-foot, slim brunette serving. She looks a little puzzled as she stares at me and I start to panic thinking how bad I must look as I have just stepped off the bus, but as I channel her emotions I sense she is feeling confusion. Surely that can't be related to my looks!

"Welcome to Misty's. What can I get ya?" she says in a cute British accent. I can easily sense the lie. The door must have been warded, that's why I felt the dread. A witch's ward! A human shouldn't be able to walk in and she probably knows all the supernatural beings in town. She must be wondering if it's broken.

"Hi, I'm Bel. I'm new in town. I thought I'd try my luck with the sign on your door," I tell her, whilst holding my hand out for her to shake. She glances down at it warily but takes it in hers as she plasters on a welcoming smile. I know the minute she senses my wolf energy, her smile turns genuine and she raises her brow in question. I nod. "I'm a lone wolf…for the time being."

"I'm Misty, nice to meet ya, Bel. Have ya worked in a bar before?"

I look behind the bar which looks just like any other bar, spirit bottles lining shelves and work surfaces, and fridges with beer bottles and premixes in it. "Yeah, I worked in a little bar back home for the last three years, I can give you a number and name for a reference."

Misty screws up her face and shakes her head. "No, I don't really like getting references; I prefer to see for myself. Are ya free tonight?"

"I just stepped off the bus, I haven't had chance to make any plans yet. So I'm all yours." I grin. How lucky is that, a job from the first place I walk into? Now, let's hope finding somewhere to sleep works out just as easy.

"Okay. Get ya self 'round this side of the bar then and I'll give ya a paid trial tonight. Thursday's aren't very busy, so I should be able to keep my eye on ya." She takes me in from head to toe as if she's weighing me up. I must meet her standards because she walks over to the little flap and raises it to allow me behind the bar.

By the looks of things there isn't much room behind the bar, just enough for three or four people to move around and serve comfortably. There's no shelving with personal items on it, just glasses under the bar, fridges and spirit bottles behind it and the draught levers on top.

"That will be great, thanks. Is there somewhere I can leave my bag?" I show her my backpack as I pull it off my back.

She points to the door between the bar and booths. I notice there is a toilet sign on it, which I didn't see during my observations before. "My office is through there, the code for the door is seven-two-five-nine."

I nod in acknowledgement chanting the code to myself over and over, and head through the door into a small, narrow corridor decorated in wooden cladding on the bottom half of the wall which is finished off with a dado rail. The walls above it are white, but you can tell they are well overdue a fresh coat. There's a door to my left with a beautiful Barbie-like woman painted on the full length of the door, and a couple of metres further up the corridor there is another door with a hot guy painted on it.

I walk over to the guy's door and find myself wondering if he is based on a real guy. *He must have girls coming at him from all angles, if so.* I meet his eyes and decide it can't be a real person because his eyes, they look like emeralds and no one has eyes that green.

On the right hand wall about halfway down the corridor there is a steel reinforced door, which has an electric code panel next to it. *They must get some bad types in here if they have security like this. I didn't see any bouncers.*

The only other door is a fire exit at the end of the corridor, which is painted a charcoal grey and has one of those, press-to-release bars across it.

I enter the code Misty gave me and watch as the light turns from red to green as I hear the lock click.

When I open the door, I see the room is small; one wall is covered in filing cabinets, and there are a few hooks on another wall with a coat and bag hung up. Next to the hooks is another door which must lead to a storage room of some sort because the hallway was too long for there not to be more room.

I place my bag on the floor under the hooks, not wanting the weight of my bag to pull the hooks off the wall.

The office is finished off with a metal desk in the middle of the room with a wooden chair from the bar. The walls are painted a cold grey/blue colour. It isn't a very inviting office.

I go back to the bar to find three more customers.

Misty shows me how things run behind the bar; explaining the customers mostly order cocktails since they're mainly werewolves. I know better than anyone that we find it hard to get drunk. A big mix of alcohol like you get in a cocktail gives a little buzz at least.

The guy from the couple that has been here since I walked in, waves me over to the far side of the bar to take his order.

My first order, here goes nothing.

I give him a big smile as I reach him. "Hi. What can I get you?"

"Can we get two Russian Roses, please?"

I look at him puzzled, wracking my brain to think of what that drink could be, with no luck. *Why couldn't he have picked something simple like a Cosmopolitan?*

Noticing my predicament, Misty shouts the ingredients across the bar as she points each one out. "Shaker, vodka, triple sec, pink grapefruit juice, rose syrup, basil, and the juice of two lime wedges."

"Thanks, Misty. I haven't heard of that one before." Great, my first drink and I don't even know it. What kind of cocktail mixer do I think I am?

"No worries, Bel. You'll probably get a few ya don't know. You'll get used to them eventually. There's a book in the office in case we get a real obscure order but most of the customers know what they are ordering. If in doubt, ya can always ask them. Although ya might get a sneaky customer or two trying to catch ya out on purpose. We have some jokers like that around here," she says, mixing drinks for one of the new customers.

I'm just squeezing the limes into the shaker for the Russian Roses, as I get a whiff of werewolf. I barely get a chance to register the scent before I am hit with a rush of power that can only come from an alpha. The alpha's power wakes the wolf inside me; she starts to stir, making my skin restless and my heartbeat raise. I knew there was a large werewolf pack here but I never imagined I would meet the alpha within the first couple of hours of arriving. *I thought I'd be able to meet a few submissive wolves first; instead I get the most dominant of them all. Great!*

I place the lid on the shaker and start to shake it. I turn around to get a glance at the alpha and can't believe my eyes. He's the gorgeous guy from the men's toilet door painting. I am doing everything possible to not run off to check he's not just stepped out of the painting. He's got a lovely muscular body—but most weres are in good shape—he's about five-foot-eight, with strawberry blonde hair, and he's wearing dark jeans and a baby blue t-shirt.

I pour the drinks out and take the guy's money. I hope he gave me the right amount because I can't concentrate enough to count it, or even think about change. He's started a conversation with a new customer next to him so I don't think he is waiting for change.

I can't stop glancing at the painting guy.

Just as I'm about to take the painting guy's order, Misty beats me to it. "Hi, Theo. How are ya today?"

Smoking hot is how he is! While I'm admiring him I realise he is looking at me, as if waiting for me to answer a question I didn't hear him ask. I look at Misty hoping she can clear it up.

"This is my new cocktail mixer, Bel. You could have warned

me there was a new were in town. I thought the wards were down when she walked in here," she says in jest.

Painting guy—Theo, Misty called him—holds his hand out for me to shake. As our hands meet, a tingling sensation shoots from my hand through every fibre of my body. I jump and try to pull my hand back but Theo is just staring at my hand, like he's never seen a hand before.

What the hell was that? I've felt other weres test power but it's never felt like that before. A test of power feels more like a pressure against your skin but then I've never had a werewolf test my power before, maybe they feel different to were-lions.

His gravelly voice breaks my inner dialogue, "I'm Theo. It's a pleasure to meet you." He lifts my hand up to his mouth and places a gentle kiss on it. I notice his nostrils flare as he takes in my scent. *Okay...Weird!!*

As I look into his alluring emerald green eyes, that look just as much like real emeralds as the ones in the painting did, I distractedly reply, "The pleasure is all mine." *Did I really say that out loud?*

Oh my goodness. Please let the floor open up and swallow me. Any time now would be nice.

He stares at me as he rubs his thumb over the top of my hand and slowly pulls his fingers away from mine. I instantly miss his touch. He smirks, like he knows a secret, and winks at me.

Nice one, Bel. You look like a bloody idiot.

I notice Misty is back at her end of the bar again. Thank the angels she didn't witness me act like an idiot.

Okay. Ask him for his order already. He's only a guy.

"What can I get you?" I can't seem to wipe the embarrassed look off my face. I can feel the flush in my cheeks.

"Do you know what a Johnnie Black Sazerac is?" He's still smirking, like the cat that swallowed that dumb tweety bird.

Thankfully, it's one of the cocktails I actually know. I have made enough of a fool of myself for one night.

"That's Johnnie Walker Black and Pernod, isn't it?" I ask with a questioning look.

Better to be safe than sorry, or embarrassed again in this case!

As I bring my eyes up, I feel the urge to reach out and touch him. I want to feel that power again. I stop my hand before it moves towards him.

"You're good; I usually always have to list that one up when someone serves me for the first time." He seems like a nice guy. I'd expect an alpha to be more serious and commanding. I don't feel at all intimidated by him. I just want to rub myself against him. I'm glad the bar is between us, because it's the only thing that's stopping me.

"The last place I worked was full of men, and that's a man's drink, so to speak."

As I'm mixing his drink, I realise there's a picture of a wolf howling at a full moon on his t-shirt. "That's fitting," I say with a chuckle.

His chin drops and his eyes stare down to where my eyes are looking and gives his own hearty laugh, "I like to state the obvious," he says with a shrug. "Did you put a request in to come into town?" he asks, as I'm admiring the shape of his body through the tight fitting t-shirt.

"Request? I didn't know I had to," I say, with a worried face.

"Any supernatural being that wants to come into town— whether it be for a long or short stay—needs to make a request to me or the leader of the Mount Roxby Vampire's. He likes to be called the King." He raises his eyebrows in exasperation. "I'd recommend me, I don't bite, unless you ask me to," he jokes.

"Oh. I'm sorry; I didn't know anything about it. I'm from a small town that didn't get many newcomers; it's mainly just the pride that lives in the town." I catch the confused look on his face as I say the word pride and quickly clarify, "I was brought up in a were-lion pride."

"A werewolf in a were-lion pride. That's new. I can put you in the system if you want?"

"That will be great, thanks," I say, as I pass his drink over. He gives me some money and I place it in the till like Misty showed me.

"How did they react to you leaving? Being brought up with them; they would have seen you as one of their own, wouldn't they? I wouldn't have thought they'd be very happy to see you leave," he asks.

"Far from it. No, they were glad to see me leave. They had never really accepted me; even though my Auntie was married to one of them." I stare off into space, thinking about how I was treated by the Pride.

"Once I turned eighteen I was challenged every week, and I didn't even want to be classed as Pride. It was duel after duel, I needed to get away." I snap out of my memories, realising I'm telling my life story to a stranger. He's so easy to talk to, I feel like I've known him all my life. Realistically, I've known him ten minutes, if that!

"I'm sorry. You don't want to hear all that," I say, as I shake my head.

"Can I get another?" A customer down the bar waves me over, thankfully before Theo gets a chance to comment on me blurting all that out to him.

The bar seems to have filled with vampires and werewolves whilst I'd been distracted by Theo. I better get back on with the job or Misty will be firing me before I even really got started.

2

UNWANTED ENCOUNTERS

I can't stop staring at Bel, the new barmaid. I can't believe it…But I felt it. The tingle when we touched, my wolf nearly burst out of my skin. That shouldn't happen.

Unless…No.

She can't be.

There's no other explanation though.

I'm dying to touch her again to see if it happens a second time. It's taking every ounce of concentration to stop myself from vaulting the bar to get to her. Her floral scent is making my mouth water and other bodily reactions, completely inappropriate in public.

A heavy hand on my shoulder pulls my attention from my staring. "Who's the hot new barmaid?"

A growl leaves my throat before I can stop it. I catch my energy before it flares. I don't need the whole pack's attention. I turn to face Eddie, who is standing with his hands up in a gesture of surrender.

"Whoa, obviously someone I shouldn't be looking at." He sits on the empty stool next to me.

"Sorry Ed, she's called Bel. New wolf in town," I say, as Bel walks past to serve someone further along the bar. I watch as Ed's nostrils flare when he catches her scent.

"Fuck, she smells good."

As much as my wolf wants to rip his head off for even scenting her, I hold it in. I have no claim over her. I'd only just met her.

My wolf disagrees. *Mine,* is pulsing through my head as he pushes against my skin trying to get to her.

"Did you track the vamp down?" I ask Ed.

Ed is one of my enforcers, or soldiers as some people call them.

Ed grunts. "I couldn't find anything to substantiate the reports we received. Not one person I spoke to has seen any evidence of a rogue vampire. Sorry, boss, but I think it was a time-waster." He waves at Bel as she glances in our direction.

"Hey guys. What you after?" She flashes Ed a friendly smile.

Ed reaches over the bar and offers her his hand. "I'm Ed. It's nice to meet you. I'll have a Jack on the rocks, thanks."

I watch in anticipation as their hands touch, my eyes flashing between them to see if they have a reaction.

"Bel. Nice to meet you, Ed."

I let out the breath I'd been holding when she walks away to get Ed's drink, with no sign of reaction.

"Hey, Theo!" I turn to chase the voice that belongs to someone I usually manage to avoid. Unfortunately, I was too distracted with Bel and didn't even feel or smell her early enough to make a run for it.

I plaster on my best fake smile. "Hi, Chloe. How are you?"

She stops in front of me, trailing her fingers up my forearm. "Much better now I've seen you."

I force myself not to cringe. It's not like Chloe is repulsive—with her beautiful blonde hair, legs up to her armpits, and bright, baby blue eyes—she's far from it. She turns plenty of heads. Unfortunately, she likes to go for the guys that aren't interested, and never takes no for an answer.

I've never casually dated a pack member and I don't intend to start now. Being an alpha, I'm stronger with a mate. A wolf knows his mate when he meets her—I'm pretty sure I found mine tonight. Just imagine the hassle my future mate would have when she joins the pack if it was full of my jealous ex-lovers.

I'm not celibate; I have been in relationships—just not with pack members. I gave up on finding my mate and married a human when I was young, stupid, and wanting to settle down. My marriage ended when she cheated on me. To be honest, the failure of our marriage was my fault. I hadn't told her about being a werewolf, yet I expected her to give me children.

"Can I buy you a drink, Theo?" Chloe asks in a seductive tone.

I glance at my watch to make it look like there's somewhere I need to be. "Actually, I'm just about to leave; I've got a meeting to get to."

Chloe mirrors my actions, glancing at her own watch. "It's a bit late to be having a meeting, isn't it?"

She has no right to question her Alpha, but I don't want her turning up at my house later so I answer her, "Vampires."

Bel makes her way over to us placing a drink in front of us both with a shrug. "I saw you were empty, too."

I pull the glass towards me and pass her some money, making sure to brush her hand with mine. I feel it again; almost like an electric shock shooting from where we touch through my body to my wolf. He jumps up; alert and ready to claim. There is no mistaking it this time. She's my mate. I look into her eyes as they change from chocolate brown to her wolf's amber eyes. She feels it too.

Her wolf knows.

"Thanks, darlin."

She snatches her hand back, looking at it like it was an alien. "Sorry about that. Must be static electricity, or something."

"Or something," I growl, as she rushes off to serve another customer.

After downing my drink, I say my goodbyes and leave

quickly; to make my meeting look genuine. My wolf is antsy enough as it is, I can't handle any more Chloe tonight. He doesn't like that I am leaving Bel behind. He's already calling her 'mine.'

J only get a block away from Misty's when I scent a vampire. They have a bloody scent. Werewolves suffer bloodlust. We love the smell of blood and meat, but vampires don't smell like fresh blood. They have a sickly rotting scent. They have strong noses, too. I don't know how they can handle their own stench.

Hoping the vampire I can scent is the rogue we've been hunting down, I follow the smell. I could do with a good fight to distract my wolf from leaving someone he already considers to be our mate, in a bar full of threats.

It's not long before I realise that fight isn't going to happen. I can feel the vampire now and I recognise this one's energy.

Dominick Draconis. The King.

Yeah, he wishes.

"Well, well, well," Dominick quips. "If it isn't the daddy dog himself."

He may be old and he may act all high and mighty, but he ain't nothing but a mosquito to me.

I tell myself that every time we are in each other's company and I still end up at his throat by the end of the conversation. I'm not going to let him get to me. "Dominick."

"What no happy greeting? No wagging tail?"

Try as I might, I don't manage to contain my growl. My wolf might get his fight yet. "What do you know about this rogue vampire I'm hearing reports about?"

"Touchy. Fine. Let's get straight to business then. I'm following up on the reports too, but none of my men have found any leads. He seems to be good at hiding." His phone chimes in his jeans pocket, he reaches his hand in and pulls it out, but on glancing at the screen he ignores the call by angrily shoving it back in his pocket. "Have your men found anything?"

"Not a thing. My guys are calling it a time-waster, but I have a bad feeling about it and I don't like it."

I'm not a fan of Dominick, but this rogue is his kind and if anyone is equipped to find him, a two-thousand-year-old vampire leader is bound to be better at it than I am.

"You're right to be concerned. He's a threat and we need to find him. I have no doubt that in time we will," he proclaims, with the confidence of a leader.

"Yes, we will," I declare, walking away. I'm not concerned about turning my back on the vampire—even when I know our scent is intoxicating and highly addictive to them. The total opposite of how their revolting stench affects us; werewolves and vampires have a pact, of a sort. We can live comfortably in the same town without a war breaking out. Neither of the species can attack the other without serious punishment. I won't lie and say there aren't 'incidents,' but we stay on top of them and our pact helps keep them far and few between.

I reach into my pocket for my keys, unlocking my Pajero as I approach it. I get in and head home.

My home is the pack's home; which means, any member is welcome at any time. I just hope that Chloe finds someone to entertain her tonight because I'm still not up to dealing with her.

3

VAULTING BARS

I'm distracted as I serve two or three customers. My mind is still on the reaction to Theo's touch. No matter what bullshit I said about static electricity, I know that isn't what caused it. It has to be something to do with our wolves—I'm just not sure what. It didn't happen when I came in contact with the other wolf he was with, so I am leaning towards it being an alpha thing.

I glance along the bar to see if any of my customers are empty. When my eyes reach Ed, I notice Theo is no longer with him. My wolf reaches out to feel for his power but can't. Realising he must have left whilst I was serving; I search the bar for Barbie girl who was coming onto him earlier. My wolf relaxes when I see her plastered all over another guy. *It didn't take her long to move her affection on to someone else.*

It took all my will power not to jump the bar and drag her away from him when I saw her talking to him earlier. I had to remind my wolf that I had no claim over him. I had spoken to him for a few minutes and that was all. He was the local alpha; she was probably pack, and had more right to lay a claim.

---

*M*idnight comes quick and fast. It feels like no time has passed when Misty rings the bell for last call. As the last customer leaves, I head to the office to get my bag, realising a little too late that I haven't organised anywhere to sleep tonight.

Misty enters the office and hands me an envelope with some cash in it. "That's for tonight's shift. If ya enjoyed it, I'd love ya to come back same time tomorrow?"

"Yeah, that'd be great. Thank you," I answer, placing the envelope in my bag. "You don't know any hostels that will be open at this time, do you? I came straight in here off the bus without organising anywhere to sleep."

She looks me up and down, weighing me up. "No. They'll all be locked up now. Ya can stay at mine for the night, if ya want?"

"Really? That'd be great. Thanks. I'll go straight to the hostel in the morning."

"No worries. We'll sort it out. I saw you chatting to Theo. It looked like you got on well." She seems excited at that thought. I'm guessing she's a bit of a matchmaker.

She shows me out of the office, locking the door behind us.

"Yeah. He seems like a nice guy, not to mention easy on the eyes." We both giggle as we leave through the fire exit at the end of the corridor.

There is a top of the range purple VW Beetle parked in the deserted alley. *How come it didn't get stolen or stripped for parts during the shift? It's not as if this alley is a high traffic area.*

As we approach the car I feel that sensation of dread again, which answers my previous question...*Wards!*

I wake up to the smell of bacon, eggs, tomatoes, *ooh* and fresh coffee. My nose is great with smells. It's not such a good thing when the smell is unpleasant, like when I got on that bus full of smelly people. *Ugh.* Times like that I wish I had a human nose. Today? Today I am happy to have an extra sensitive nose. It feels like a week since I had a cup of coffee. I'd even be glad for a bad one at the moment. I can't function without a coffee in a morning, and this coffee smells divine.

I dive out of bed, or should I say off the bed since I didn't manage to get under the covers last night. After quickly washing and changing, I follow the lovely smell of food and coffee; after entering two empty lounge rooms I finally find the source. Sitting at the granite breakfast bar in the kitchen is Misty, eating the best looking full English breakfast I have ever seen. Seeing only one plate makes my stomach grumble and decide I need to find a diner as soon as possible.

"Good morning, Misty. Thanks for letting me stay the night. I'll get out your hair now and see you at five for my shift."

Misty slightly spins her stool to face me. "How'd ya sleep?"

"Great. That bed is fantastic."

"Good. There's a plate of breakfast in the oven keeping warm for ya, and there's some fresh coffee in the pot on the side." She waves her hand in the direction of the oven and coffee.

"Oh. You didn't have to do that. Thank you." I grab the tea towel hanging off the oven door and remove my plate from the oven, sitting at the bar on the stool next to Misty.

After eating my breakfast and drinking the best coffee I've ever had, I reach over and pour myself a second cup from the jug on the table.

Misty puts her cup down for seconds too. "I was thinking, since ya don't have anywhere to stay and there's just me in this big place, do ya wanna stay on a more permanent basis?"

Misty's apartment is actually four apartments knocked into one. She has the whole floor to herself.

"What? Like rent one of the rooms from you? Are you sure? You don't really know me." I can see what's coming; I should have seen it last night when Misty invited me to stay, even though she had only known me for a couple of hours.

I'm an empath. I can feel people's emotions. According to my Aunt, my mum was an empath, too. It's the empathy that's making Misty feel like she can trust me. For some reason, people feel at ease with me. I even get strangers coming up to me on the street and pouring their heart out. Their trust in me isn't false. I'm trustworthy because I feel people's emotions. I don't want them to feel bad, so I do anything I can to make people feel better. I would never do anything to hurt people; for one thing it would hurt me twice as much as it would them.

Misty jumps off her stool and walks over to the sink to rinse her plate. "I know, but I trust ya. I get a good vibe from you and being a witch, I'm all about vibes."

"If you're sure, that would be brilliant. Thank you." I walk over to the sink to rinse my own plate and cup, before placing them in the dishwasher.

The day goes by pretty quick. We just chilled out, drinking coffee and filling each other in on our lives. I got through my life story in no time. I told her about my empathy; which Misty had heard of. Thankfully, it didn't alter her feelings towards me.

Misty has been practising witchcraft for the last ten years. She moved in with her gran when she found out she was a witch at sixteen. Her gran taught her everything she knew. Unfortunately, she passed away last year. She bought the bar and apartment when she was twenty-one with some inheritance money she received from a distant relative she had never met.

*W*e opened up the bar at four in the afternoon and by six thirty it was heaving. There must've been about sixty people spread throughout the bar. When I say people, I mean witches, weres, and vampires. I even think there were a few fae, too. Not a plain ordinary human in sight, thanks to Misty's ward. It's nice to be able to relax and not worry about someone spotting a side effect of a supernatural being. I can see why Misty's is so popular.

I'm having a break in the office at eight when I realise I haven't been in touch with Benji since arriving. When I left he had demanded I ring when I arrived. I retrieve my bag from the cubby hole behind Misty's desk and dig my phone out to find ten missed calls and panicked messages getting more aggressive with each one.

The first text being. 'What the HELL has happened?'

The last text is all caps and I definitely get an urgent vibe from it. 'WHERE THE FUCK ARE YOU, BEL?' He even ended it on a growl that would do any werewolf proud; which is a feat for a human.

I hit call.

When he picks up, I'm expecting a hello to start the conversation. Instead, I just get garbled rambling. I hold the phone away until I think it's over.

It isn't!

It finally goes quiet on his end and I put the phone to my ear.

Now the begging starts. "Benji. I'm sorry I haven't rung sooner, but it's been hectic since I got off the bus. I found a job and a place to rent."

"You should've called, even just to say you're alive. I've been sitting here thinking you must be dead in a gutter somewhere and waiting for the police to come around and ask us to identify your body."

Just then Misty comes in, which means that my break is over and hers has started.

"Look, Benji, my break is over. I have to get back to work but I promise I will send you a huge email giving you a second by second report." I hang up before he can argue about how I don't know how to send email from my phone.

I put the phone and my bag back in the cubby hole, whilst grumbling away to myself. When I look up, I find Misty laughing at me.

"It was, Benji. He was going mental because I haven't rung him to tell him I'm alive," I say, rolling my eyes.

I walk back behind the bar and notice that at least another ten customers have entered since I went on break. The mixture of emotions throughout the room hits me like a brick wall. I take a deep breath and try to focus on my safe barrier that protects me from them. With that breath, there's a smell I recognise from last night.

Theo.

He must be here somewhere. I look around to find him, but come up empty.

"Hey Bel, can I have a Rusty Nail?" yells Theo's lovely gravelly voice from the other end of the bar.

I laugh and nod my head hoping he can see me. I put his drink together—scotch whiskey and Drambuie—walk over to the other end of the bar and place the short glass in front of him.

He takes a test sip. "I'll stump you eventually," he jests as he passes me his money.

"Bring it on."

I serve a few more customers and notice Misty is back out and Lucy, the other mixer, is missing; probably having her break in the back office.

Misty is laughing with some customers when a vampire

comes to the bar. He's the most intimidating vampire I have ever met. The energy coming from him is fierce and wild.

He's at least six-foot-four inches tall with jet black hair in tight curls against his head. His eyes are black and endless. He asks for a Siberian Fizz, which thank my angels I know.

I wouldn't like to ask him how to make it; he's likely to bite me.

I pass him the drink and take the money he offers in payment.

"Are you new here?" he questions

I put the money in the till before answering him. "Yes. I started last night."

As I turn away to look for another customer to serve, he throws his hand in front of me. "I'm Dominick Drake."

As I shake his extremely cold hand, he grins at my shudder. "Do you have a name?"

"Rosabel McGuiness. Nice to make your acquaintance," I say insincerely. I don't know if vampires can feel a lie like werewolves can, and to be honest, I don't care. I just want to get away from him. He gives me the heebie-jeebies.

"The pleasure is all mine, darling," he says rather creepily. He's even looking at me, as if wondering how my blood would taste.

"Quit thinking about what she tastes like. We have a deal—you don't touch werewolves," says the gravelly voice that's becoming ever so familiar. He must have made his way over for another drink, but when I look at his glass, it's still full.

"Oh. Is she a new one of yours?" asks Dominick, looking rather disappointed.

"No. She's a lone wolf. Before you ask, she's on the supe census. I saw to it myself."

"Well. If she isn't part of your pack, she's not included in our deal. I haven't tasted a werewolf for over a century. You taste so much better than humans." He licks his lips while staring at me intently, even hungrier than before.

Brilliant. Why do I have to be something tasty?

With that reply, I feel extreme anger and regret coming off Theo. My wolf bristles at the feel of the alpha energy coming off him. The whole bar falls silent to stare in his direction. I'm guessing it's not just my empathy picking up Theo's emotional state.

Dominick walks off towards one of the tables near the dance floor with a laugh. When he's halfway there, he turns around looks directly at Theo and says, "Hope to have a taste soon, Rosabel."

No chance!

Theo turns back to me. His alpha energy has dulled but I can still feel his emotions through my empathy, and he isn't any calmer. He's obviously trying hard to push down his wolf. The noise in the bar picks up again as if nothing happened.

He downs his drink and slams his glass on the bar, the glass shattering in his hand. I notice he's trembling all over and after hearing a rumbling growl emanating from deep in his chest, I realise he's fighting the change.

Grabbing a bottle of Absinthe in one hand I jump over the bar and grab Theo's elbow with the other. I start dragging him, having no idea where to take him. As I look up, I catch Misty's eye; she mouths the word 'office,' pointing in its direction.

Why didn't I think of that?

I focus on getting him behind that locked door. When I feel that I'm no longer dragging him, he seems to be coming easily and the trembling is easing, too. I enter the code and push the door open and practically shove him inside, slamming it shut behind us.

Taking a deep breath, I remove the lid from the bottle and swallow down a huge swig. I need it. The adrenaline rush is making my wolf twitchy. Theo's energy is running over my skin, it almost feels like his fingers are stroking the fur of my wolf. I pass the bottle to Theo, who's perched his behind on the corner of Misty's desk. He takes an even bigger swig, and although the trembling seems to have dissipated, I can still feel the anger emanating from him.

He holds out the bottle for me to take again. "Absinthe?" He pulls a face, like he has just sucked on the sourest lemon ever grown.

"It was the closest thing to my hand when I jumped the bar. You would have turned furry and no doubt drawn Dominick's blood if I had wasted time looking for something more satisfying." We both laugh, passing the bottle back and forth after taking a swig.

Theo makes a show of eyeing up my height. I can guess what he is going to ask before he even says it, "You really jumped the bar?"

"Yeah," I say, with a shrug as I settle in next to him on Misty's desk.

"How did you manage that? You're only what five-foot? The bar comes up to your chest," he says, nudging me with his shoulder.

"I don't know. It must have been the adrenaline…or something!" We both laugh softly.

We sit in comfortable silence for a moment before Theo breaks it. "I'm sorry for putting you in danger with Dominick. I came over to try and protect you. I never would have told him you were a lone wolf if I didn't think they were part of our pact."

I place my hand on his forearm. "It's not your fault, Theo. Thanks for trying to protect me." His energy feels like electricity entering through the palm of my hand. I can't feel the anger anymore; this is more like the first time we touched. "How are you feeling now?"

He lifts his head and his eyes penetrate mine. "In control again. You stopped an ugly scene unfolding in there. Thanks."

I lose myself in his beautiful green eyes for a second. "I

should get back behind the bar. It will be last call and I'm needed to help clean up. Do you think you can handle going back in there now?"

He pushes himself off the desk and makes a step for the door. "No problem."

I open the door and gesture for him to lead the way through to the bar. The propped open bar door gives us a clear view of the empty room.

Misty stops wiping the bar down and comes straight over to us as we walk through the doorway. "Theo, how ya doing?"

"Much better, thanks to Bel here." He passes her a handful of notes. "For the bottle," he explains.

I walk off, leaving them to their conversation and start clearing the tables. Once the tray is overflowing with dirty glasses, I head to the dishwasher behind the bar. Theo is still leaning against the bar watching me. Misty must be in her office and Lucy must have left while we were in the office. She usually leaves before last call because she has a baby sitter to relieve. It's just him and me in the empty bar.

"How are you getting home?" he asks, before taking another swig from the bottle of Absinthe.

"Oh. I-I'm getting a lift with Misty," I manage to stutter, shocked at the strength of the protection emotion I can feel coming off him.

"When you get home, will you be alone?"

"No. Misty has offered me a room at her place." He must be worried about Dominick following me home and attacking me. I quickly try to ease his mind. "The building is secure; no one can get in without a key. There's a guard on the door and in the elevator."

Theo watches me walk back to the dishwasher and fill it with the last load of dirty glasses. "Good. I'll make sure you get in the car safe, before I leave."

I pause to watch Theo's reaction to my next question. I need to know how much danger I am in. "Do you really think Dominick will want to taste me? As he so nicely put it."

He grimaces. "Dominick doesn't say anything he doesn't mean. So, yes, he will taste you. It's just a matter of when. I'm going to do everything I can to delay the inevitable." He reaches in his pocket, pulls out a business card and hands it to me. It reads: Theodore Wilson, and has contact numbers with an email address TWilson@gymwolves.com. "If you need anything, don't hesitate to call."

I slip the card into the back pocket of my jeans. "Thanks."

4

BLOODTHIRSTY WEREWOLVES

Thankfully, the next few days pass with no sign of the bloodthirsty Dominick. Misty informs me that Dominick is the head vampire—although he likes to be called 'the King of New South Wales'—which is brilliant. I don't have just any vampire yearning for my blood, but the King Vampire of the state.

LOVELY.

I'd much rather have the local pack's alpha yearning for me. Come to think of it there has been no sign of Theo, either.

Misty has been begging me to go to the gym with her. Apparently, she needs a gym buddy because if she goes on her own she can't get in the zone. Me? I'm not a gym person.

A weekly run in the forest as a wolf is usually about it, but I haven't had the chance to find anywhere safe to run since arriving in Mount Roxby. Working from late afternoon until the early hours of the morning and then sleeping until lunch, doesn't give me many hours to explore the town.

I'm not complaining, I love Misty's. I meet lots of people; some of whom come in every night. I get to use my empathy on those troubled and in need. Misty sends me to some of her friends, or regulars, who need it, which benefits me too because the bar ends up feeling like a much happier place once I've helped people. I'd just like to be able to find somewhere that I can run freely.

I have caved and we are pulling into a large car park. There are only two other cars in the empty car park, but not many people will be insane enough to go to a gym at two o'clock in the morning. Did I mention it was a twenty-four hour gym? *Why did I say yes?*

I WANT MY BED.

After filling out the forms and handing the membership fee over to the woman behind the counter; whom I believe wants to be in bed just as much as I do, we walk through the door with a female figure on it. A room full of at least twenty private cubicles. The cubicles surround a large open area, with a few benches, for non-private changing.

We change in the open area, into the crop top and shorts the gym gave us. Even though the clothes were included in the membership, they are kinda cute. There's a little picture of a wolf weightlifting on the leg of the shorts and on the breast of the crop. The gym is called 'Gym Wolves,' so I guess the wolf is their icon. We pick our lockers on the far side wall and dump our stuff. I try not to think of whose sweaty neck it has already been around as I place the key on its dog tag chain around my neck.

I walk into the gym via a door next to the lockers. The equipment is all set up in sections like I imagine most gyms are. Treadmills together, weight machines all together and so on. We head straight for the treadmills with useless TVs on them, it's not like there would be anything on at this time of the night. We choose neighbouring machines and start them up. I put a music channel on my machines TV and crank up the sound so we can both hear it over the noise of the machines and our feet pounding them.

I put the speed up to eight, a gentle jog for me, to stretch. I don't jog for long because jogging just doesn't do anything for my energy level—neither does sprinting in human form—but it's the best I can get in a gym. I up the speed until I'm pushing the machine to find a sprint to satisfy my needs.

Misty is just slowing her treadmill down but I still feel the need to keep sprinting. I suddenly sense someone approaching. I don't bother trying to identify them. It's not like anyone I know will be insane enough to be in the gym at this time of night.

"Hi, Misty. Are you having a good work out?" I can only just make out the male voice over the sound of my blood pounding in my ears and my feet thudding on the treadmill, not to mention the music.

I didn't hear Misty's reply.

"Bel. Why didn't you just go to the bush and shift? It would be a hell of a lot more satisfying." The lovely gravelly voice I hear from right behind me is the last person I expected to encounter here. I'm so shocked, I totally lose rhythm of my sprint and start to stumble, tripping over my own feet.

Brilliant. I'm going to fall flat on my face.

Theo reaches his arms out to steady me, noticing my struggle. Unfortunately, his good intentions only make matters worse, before I can hit the stop button I'm hurtling backwards towards him. He doesn't have enough sense to get out my way and before I know it, I've knocked him off his feet and we're both on the floor, laughing.

Misty is standing next to the treadmill doubled over in laughter. After the laughter passes, Theo gets up and reaches down, offering me his hand. I take it gratefully.

I must have knocked my knee somewhere during the fall because it's bleeding and stinging like a bitch. I'm not too worried about it being hurt. Being a werewolf, small injuries like this heal quickly. It's the blood dripping down my leg and pooling on the carpet that bothers me. I start hobbling towards the locker room but all I manage to do is make more of a mess.

"Where are you going?" Theo asks in a slightly amused tone. "You'll heal in a minute or two."

I glare at the mess I'm making on the floor. "I know but I'm dripping blood on the carpet. I was trying to get to the locker room. At least the tiled floor in there will clean easily."

He reaches his hand over his head, grabs the back of his shirt and pulls it off before throwing it at me. "Here. Press this against your knee."

As I catch it, I get a whiff of his scent and I can't help but hold his shirt to my nose, taking in more of that delectable scent. Misty's giggle snaps me out of it and I realise what I'm doing. I glance around quickly to see Theo's reaction, but luckily he is nowhere in sight. I breathe a sigh of relief hoping he didn't witness that.

I pull the material away from my knee to check if the bleeding has stopped.

Misty gasps jumping back, just as I hear the growl from behind me. I turn around slowly; not wanting my back to the werewolf I can smell behind me, but also not wanting my movements to provoke an attack. I realise it's two nights from a full moon. Mix that with the smell of blood and the young were that's now facing me won't be able to stop the change.

He's on his hands and knees, thankfully still in human form. His growling is not very comfortable in this situation; not to mention that a wolf's growl looks and sounds wrong coming out of a human's mouth.

He's about a metre away from me, slowly crawling closer. Reaching me in no time, he starts sniffing at my knee, which has healed but is still covered in fresh blood. I glance at the bloody t-shirt in my hand. Deciding it's already ruined, I offer it to him, but he's not interested in that at all. Instead of taking the shirt like I hoped, he does something that I really don't like. He straightens up and nuzzles his face against the bare flesh of my stomach.

Why did I pick a crop top from reception and not a t-shirt?

The stomach is the easiest place for a werewolf to rip you apart—no bones to get in the way. I start to panic. If I don't do something quickly, his teeth will pierce my skin and then it'll all be over. Before I come up with a plan I hear the scariest growl, almost a roar, that I have ever heard coming from behind me. Whatever creature belongs to that growl is going be a lot harsher killing me than this pup here.

He stops nuzzling to look around me at the creature. He's not moved away enough for me to escape, the only thing he moved was his head.

Misty is between that scary growl and me. She is only a human. She has no chance of fighting back. A number of options for what I can do run through my head when I hear a familiar commanding voice.

"Leave her alone, Paddy."

"She smells so good," the voice in front of me says, as a rumble comes from his chest. I try to stay as calm as possible, fear will only make him want to rip me up even more.

Theo's wolf's energy runs down my back as he steps up close behind me, making my wolf stand to attention. "Step back from her, Patrick."

Patrick takes a small step back and looks up towards Theo, who's leaning over my left shoulder with his chest pressing against my back. I would probably find it arousing, if we weren't staring down a hungry wolf. Patrick's eyes have no humanity in them. They are the wolf's eyes, not Patricks. He's so close to the change. It will only take a shudder and I'll be dead in a second.

Theo's hands come down on my shoulders making me jump. I feel a rumble coming from him. His energy is leaving him in a wave and going through me. Once it hits Patrick, his eyes are sea blue and so human it's unbelievable. He looks mortified as he realises what happened. "Paddy, you should go home now, mate," Theo orders.

Paddy looks me up and down until he gets to my stomach that has his bloody face print on it. "I'm so sorry."

Theo squeezes my shoulders, silently urging me to accept the apology.

"It's okay," is all I can manage to spit out as the shock kicks in. Hearing my words, Patrick turns and leaves without another word.

Nobody moves until the doors shut. Theo spins me round and leans back to look at my face, still holding my shoulders. I think if he let go, I'd crumple to the floor.

"Are you okay, Bel?" I just stare at him blankly visualising all the bad things that could have just happened.

As he pulls me into his chest and wraps his arms around me, I can vaguely hear talking. "She's in shock." But I can't seem to pull myself into the here and now. I start to come around a bit and realise it must be Misty who he was talking to.

God. Is she okay? She wasn't that far away from me or the almost wolf.

It's then that it dawns on me why I'm in such a serious state of shock, my empathy is feeding it. My own shock has made me lose a handle on my protection barrier causing me to channel Misty and Theo's shock. *Great.*

As I focus and put my barrier back up I notice that Theo is still holding me tightly against his chest. Oh my. His bare chest at that, and what a nice chest it is. Smooth and so toned, and wet? As I pull back wondering why his chest is wet, he wipes a tear from my cheeks. *Oh god, I've been crying. Have I not shown myself up enough in front of this guy, already!*

"How are you feeling now?" Theo murmurs as he rubs my arms with calming motions.

"Like an idiot. Your chest is soaking." I laugh nervously, shaking my head in disbelief at how unlucky I seem to be around this guy.

"Don't worry about that," he soothes.

Misty appears next to us with a tray containing three cups of what smells like very sugary but strong coffee.

Theo uses his hold on my arms to direct me to sit on one of the weight benches, taking a coffee off the tray and handing it to me. He takes a seat next to me, whilst Misty sits facing us on the next one along.

Misty passes Theo a cup and takes the other for herself before leaning the tray against the leg of the weight bench. We all drink in silence. The energy zinging between mine and Theo's touching thighs distracts me from even thinking about making conversation.

"Sorry, I ran off, but Paddy wasn't the only one close to his wolf. I didn't think anyone else was here. If I'd stayed, I might not have been able to control myself because of the pull of the moon. I wouldn't have been as slow as Paddy, I would have ripped you both apart in no time," Theo says, as he breaks the almost uncomfortable silence. His tone of voice says he was ashamed to own up to it. Alphas are known for their control. If an alpha can't control his own wolf, there is no way he can control a pack.

"How come ya came back, if you were worried ya might change?" Misty asks in her cute British accent.

"I felt Paddy's change coming on; it kicked my wolf into gear. The need to protect Bel overpowered the need to feed the bloodlust *with* Bel," he says on an embarrassed chuckle, and shakes his head. "Sorry to talk about you like you're edible."

"That's all right, I'm getting used to it. I've only been in town six days and I've had three people wanting to take a bite out of me," I joke

His face suddenly turns deathly serious, "Have you had any more bother from the good King?"

"No. I haven't seen him since Friday night." I try to sound cheery, hoping to ease his mind.

"Good." He doesn't sound very convinced. But he had warned me it was only a matter of time before the King tries to get his taste. Apparently, when Dominick Drake sets his sight on something, he gets it.

I glance up at the clock and blanch at the time. "Misty, we better get going, it's nearly five." She looks half asleep. I'm just hoping she can manage the drive home.

We all slowly stand. Misty and I stroll back into the changing rooms to get our belongings out of the lockers. Theo goes into the male changing rooms, presumably to get his own belongings.

When we enter the foyer through the changing rooms, we find a shirtless Theo leaning against the wall waiting to walk us to the car. As we reach Misty's Beetle, she shoots by and jumps in the car to start it, leaving Theo and I alone in the empty car park.

"Thanks again for helping with Paddy. I didn't want a death on my conscience after only being in town for such a short time."

"It's my job as Alpha to keep my wolves in line. Paddy is going to be feeling so low for the next day or two. He was looking forward to meeting 'the new hottie.'" He rolls his eyes whist making air quotes. "Eddie's words. And he blew it by losing himself to his wolf's blood lust."

"He's young. He'll get over it. I'll have to remember to thank Eddie for the nice description," I reply with a laugh.

Theo reaches across me to open the car door. I slide into my seat and he closes the door for me before leaning into the open window. "Drive safely, Misty." He shifts his eyes from Misty to me. "Take care."

We manage to get home in one piece thanks to the chilly night air blowing through the open windows.

5

PAIN OF THE PAST

*A*s I walk up to my front door I know I won't be having the quiet night I had planned. I can hear Eddie ribbing Paddy over his disaster first encounter with Bel.

"You wolfed out...That's just..." Eddie can't even finish his sentence through his fits of laughter.

"Fuck off. I didn't turn full wolf."

I walk into the lounge to find Eddie rolling around the sofa and an agitated Paddy sitting opposite.

"Is she okay?" Paddy questions as soon as I walk into the living area.

I sit down next to Eddie, slapping him across the back of the head with one hand, while swiping a beer off the coffee table with the other. "Bel's fine. She's just glad she didn't have to kill you. She didn't want a death on her conscience."

"It was the blood and the moon calling to me. I can't believe I lost control like that. If I wasn't trying to eat her, I would assume it was due to her being unmated and wanting to claim her."

"You want to claim her?" I barely contain my growl. She is my mate. No one but me will be claiming her.

Ours. My wolf is in total agreement with me.

"It doesn't matter if I did! I've blown it now. I've got no chance. Her wolf will think I'm weak, losing control like that," he says, nervously peeling the label off his stubby.

The growl I'd been holding starts to rumble out. Eddie

throws an arm across my shoulders to hold me in place before I can pounce on Paddy. It's a suicidal move on Eddie's behalf because I immediately turn my anger on him. He pays me no attention as he speaks to Paddy. "You had no chance anyway. She's Theo's mate. His true mate." His words calm me. Someone, other than myself and my wolf, was acknowledging that she was mine. I relax back into the sofa and Ed removes his arm from my shoulder and leans forward to grab a fresh stubby, acting as though nothing had happened.

Paddy glances up from the bottle he'd been playing with and his shocked eyes land on mine. "Why haven't you claimed her? She's been in town long enough." Realising his mistake in questioning his alpha, he quickly apologises, drops his eyes to the floor and submissively bares his neck to me. "I'm sorry, I didn't mean any disrespect."

"It's fine, Paddy. I've been asking myself the same question since that first night I left her in Misty's. She's been brought up by a were-lion and his human wife. She hasn't learnt anything about us. I don't think she even understands what our connection, and the physical reactions we get, means." I swap my empty stubby for the last full one.

Ed gets up and grabs another six pack out of the fridge before sitting back down again. "She seems like a bright girl. Surely she would see that it's only you that causes these feelings and reactions. Her wolf would know even if the human doesn't."

"I'm the first Alpha she's met. She is probably putting it down to my alpha vibe."

"You're planning on claiming her though, right?" Ed pops the top off a stubby and passes it to Paddy, who takes it gratefully as he downs the last dregs in the one he'd been holding.

"Of course, I do. I just don't want to force her into it before she realises what it is. My last relationship was a disaster. You know that. It was nothing but lies and deceit. I want this one to go right."

Ed places a comforting hand on my forearm. "Theo. She is your true mate. It won't go the same way as things did with Selena."

"I know, but I thought I loved her. Not only did I lose her, I lost a brother too. It hurt. It still does. Even though I know it wasn't love, not like that of a mate."

"Cain was jealous when you took over the pack. He turned bitter." Ed wasn't around when I took over the pack but anyone could see that Cain was bitter and jealous about me being Alpha—even years after the fact.

"Cain didn't want the pack, though. He's the one who killed Dad. He should've been Alpha after that, but he handed it to me. That's why I don't understand his jealousy."

Wes, my Beta, walks into the room and joins the conversation. "That's not why he was jealous. He was jealous of the pack. The pack took your attention away from him. He was young and he idolised you. He slept with your wife to get back at you for abandoning him. He knew it would piss you off."

I hadn't even heard him enter the house. He must have been working in my office. That revelation floored me, but now that the thought was in my head it made complete sense.

"Why had I not connected the dots?" I mumble to myself, whilst shaking my head. The revelations would do no good. Cain is AWOL now. No one has seen or heard from him in a year.

I stand from the couch and start to strip off my clothes. "I need a run."

Talking about my ex and brother always gets me worked up. A run is what I need to burn off the extra stress it's stirred up. I'd rather a run than hold it in and snap at the wrong person. By the time I make it to the back yard and shift into my wolf form, there's a trail of clothes leading outside and three other wolves standing next to me, waiting to follow my lead.

I lead. I run through the forest with my pack brothers following me. The day's stress runs off my fur as my paws pound into the dirt of the forest floor. The only thought that stays with me is that our mate still needs claiming.

6

WITCHY PERKS

No sooner had I fallen asleep than I was waking up again; time to get ready and go to work. Both Misty and I were so tired when we arrived home after the gym that we agreed to sleep all day, making sure to get up as late as possible, leaving just enough time to get something to eat before work.

Walking through to the kitchen and finding it empty, I pause to listen for any noise indicating that Misty was in the land of the living. I hear nothing other than the humming of the ducted air-con.

"Misty, wake your arse up!" I shout through the apartment. The rooms below could probably hear me but I couldn't care less. I have to listen to the couple in the apartment below my room constantly having sex so they can suck it up!

I start pulling food out the fridge to make us both a sandwich. I'm just plating up as Misty walks into the room blurry-eyed but dressed.

"Coffee. I need coffee."

I point to the steaming cup I placed next to her sandwich. She grabs the cup, mumbles something unintelligible then swiftly guzzles the full cup; slamming the cup on the side as she glances up at me. "Thanks, Bel."

"That was hot. I only just made it." How have her lips not blistered?

"Oh. I did a quick cooling enchantment," she states before tucking into her sandwich.

It's going to take a while getting used to living with a witch.

---

e spot a couple of customers standing outside the doors as we drive by and around the back. Misty pulls the handbrake and dives out the car. She starts chanting something as I follow her and the back door pops open without her even getting her keys out.

"Cool," I announce in awe.

"Oh, that's nothing, honey!" she replies, running to the bar.

She opens the front doors via chant again. That is one cool trick!

Over the next hour or two a steady stream of customers come and goes. A familiar face catches my eye and I make my way over to take his order. He's with another guy I haven't met yet. He's definitely werewolf, I can feel his power, and it's strong. He has to be high up in the ranks.

"Evening, Ed. What can I get you?"

"Hi, beautiful. You haven't met Wes yet, have you?" he queries pointing to the wolf next to him.

I shake my head and extend my hand to Wes. "No, I haven't. It's nice to meet you, Wes. I'm Bel."

He smirks as he takes my hand, "I've heard a lot about you. It's nice to finally meet you."

"All good stuff I hope. What can I get you guys to drink?" I let go of his hand and wipe the bar down with the cloth I keep tucked in my apron, trying to get rid of the nervous thought that people are talking about me.

"Just a Toohey's, thanks," Wes orders. "We're both on patrol, so we best steer clear of the hard stuff."

I grab their beers out of the fridge under the bar and pop the tops off before handing them over.

7

HALF BLIND DATE

Waking up, I realise we made it through the night without any bother. The night was a blur of customers. Then again, we were both on autopilot so a tornado could have hit without either of us paying a blind bit of notice.

I head into the kitchen in need of a coffee fix. I need to function when I get up in the morning. Knowing Misty needs coffee more than I do, I'm not surprised to find her already there with two full cups. What does surprise me is the shit-eating grin she has on her face.

"Good Morning," she says over-enthusiastically. She's definitely up to something.

"Okay. What is it?" I ask, reaching for the cup she offers me.

"You're having tonight off," she practically sings as she leans against the breakfast bar.

I take a sip of coffee before reacting. "Should I ask why?"

"Don't bite my head off, but I've set you up on a blind date. I know you like Theo, but he's being an idiot by avoiding you. Anyone can see the chemistry between the two of you. Your wolves are dying to jump each other. He still hasn't shown you where you can run safely." She has a point. I might like him but he has been avoiding me, apparently before I started working at Misty's he was in there on a daily basis.

"Who is it?"

"One of my friends from the bar last night. He started asking about you so I suggested a blind date. He's going to take you to the cinema." She looks extremely hopeful.

I can't help but complain. "So it's not a blind date. He knows what I look like. It's just a half blind date. *Great!*"

I hate the idea of blind dates. Why would two people who know nothing about each other want to meet up and spend a torturous couple of hours together? Living with a were-lion pride meant there weren't many dating opportunities for me. I guess I dated Jared but our early dates consisted of training to fight so I could stay alive. It wasn't the usual get to know each other thing. I can feel her disappointment press against me when she thinks I'm going to say no.

I find myself agreeing to the half blind date before I really even consider it. Misty has been so good to me since I arrived in Mount Roxby, the least I can do is go on a measly half blind date. "How will I know it's him? When and where am I meeting him?"

"You'll go?" she asks suspiciously.

I nod my reply.

She pushes of the side and pulls me into a huge bear hug. "Thank you. Thank you."

She calms down enough to release me but she's still bouncing on the spot. "He's called Emmanuel. He's pretty hard to miss at six-foot-five and built like a wall. He'd make a great rugby player. He's South African. Dark skinned and believe it or not, bright blue eyes. He'll be waiting for you at six fifteen just in front of the ticket booth at the cinema opposite the bar. You can have a few drinks for Dutch courage before going across."

"Okay. I'm doing this for you," I say, giving her another hug just to try and hold her still. Her bouncing about is starting to make me feel queasy, or is that the nerves?

"Thanks. You won't regret it. He's a really nice guy," she assures me.

I believe her. I just can't help thinking about Theo and how I should be dating him and not this other guy. What am I thinking? Theo isn't interested. My wolf needs to get the idea of him out of her horny mind.

I don't do much for the rest of the day. I hunt for something to wear in my very limited selection of clothes. Misty offered for me to try some of her clothes, but she's a foot taller than me so it's all way too long. I finally decide on my little black dress that never fails me, and some black heels with silver sequins.

I email Benji to fill him in on the last couple of days. He replies immediately demanding a play by play of my date as soon as I get back tonight.

When we arrive at work, it feels strange being all dressed up and showing so much flesh. The uniform I normally wear is black cropped trousers and a tight black t-shirt that has a purple 'Misty's' logo embroidered on the breast and a cocktail list printed on the back.

The customers start coming in. I have to practically sit on my hands to stop myself from getting up and serving them. Every time I move, Misty glares at me and reminds me, "Night off!"

"What do you want to drink? It's on the house. It might chill you out. You are so fidgety it's driving me crazy," says Misty.

"A Johnnie Black Sazerac, please," I say with a laugh.

"Okay. Coming right up," she shouts over her shoulder, as she bounces off to mix it up.

"Make that two, Misty," says my favourite rumbly voice.

I turn to see Theo taking a seat on the stool next to me.

"Okay, Theo, two it is," she shouts back from the mixing counter, pouring the ingredients into a shaker.

Trust him to turn up when I've made plans with someone else.

I flash him my sexiest smile. "Hi, I didn't see you come in." Or feel him. Gee, I must be distracted not to have noticed him.

He returns my sexy smile tenfold. "Hi yourself. You're looking ravishing tonight."

I can feel my face blushing. I hate compliments. "Thanks."

"Aren't you supposed to be on the other side of the bar?" he asks, even though he can tell by the way I'm dressed I'm not meant to be on the other side of the bar tonight.

Misty comes over and places our drinks in front of us.

Theo slips off his stool and grabs his wallet out of his pocket. He's ready to hand some money over when she puts her hands up.

"On the house as a thank you for the other night."

"There's no need for that, but thanks." Theo places his wallet back in the rear pocket of those tight fitting jeans—the ones that hug his perfect butt just right.

"It's Bel's night off. She's going on a blind date with a friend of mine—to the cinema across the road."

For a split second his face drops and anger rolls off him in waves. A customer further down the bar calls out for Misty and she dashes off to serve him.

Theo turns to me. "Do you know his name? I might be able to tell you whether he's a nice guy or not, if I know him." I get the distinct feeling no matter whether he's a nice guy or not, Theo isn't going to be happy about it.

"Emmanuel," I say, shrugging and taking a large swig of my drink. "I'm only doing it to keep Misty happy. She's done a lot for me since I arrived. The least I can do is suffer through a date that I don't want to go on." I don't know why I'm explaining myself. I just feel the need to let him know. *Maybe it's an alpha thing.*

His body relaxes slightly and he takes a mouthful of his drink. "I know Emmanuel. He's not a bad guy, for a witch."

"She didn't tell me he was a witch. Not that it really makes a difference." I look at my watch and realise I'm already two minutes late. I still have to get across the road and traffic is usually a nightmare at this time. I quickly down what's left of my drink.

"I've got to go. I'm already late. Can you tell Misty I've gone and I'll see her later?" I jump off my chair and head for the door.

"No problem."

When I get outside I notice Theo is behind me. I look at him and frown.

He must be able to read the question on my face because before I even open my mouth to ask, he answers it. "I'm walking you across the road. It's dark and dangerous. A woman looking as good as you shouldn't be walking the streets on her own."

I glance at the cinema across the road. "I'm only going across the road. I'm a werewolf, I can handle it."

He grabs my hand, linking our fingers. "I don't care. Dominick has already shown his interest. I'm not taking that chance."

Every man and his dog are driving past leaving us no chance to get across the road. We walk down to the traffic lights on the next corner to cross safely.

"What will Emmanuel think when he sees you and me like this?" I lift our joined hands to get my point across.

"I don't care what he thinks as long as you're safe."

We get to the meeting point five minutes late and as Misty assured me, Emmanuel is un-missable. He's good looking but doesn't make my heart skip like a certain someone holding my hand does. Theo's energy is currently running up and down my arm. It's causing my wolf to pace. She wants to greet him; be it just her energy or full wolf form she isn't fussed.

Emmanuel spots me and waves. I can tell the exact second he notices Theo holding my hand because his emotions have become erratic, and he can't seem to settle them. I have to fight to keep my barrier up.

"Hi Rosabel, Theodore." He nods in Theo's direction as he says his name

I quickly let go of Theo's hand and take a step away. "*Hi!*" I say, a little over-enthusiastically. This is such an awkward first meeting for a date.

Theo throws a concerned look at me before turning his attention to Emmanuel. "Good evening, Emmanuel. I was just escorting your date here safely."

I turn to stand next to Emmanuel and face Theo. "Thanks for the escort, Theo." Then without realising what I'm doing, I lean in and kiss him on the cheek.

"Anything for you, Bel," he says deliberately loud. He then turns and walks back towards the bar without another word.

I turn to Emmanuel, who's still looking at the spot where Theo had been standing. An angry emotion flows off him. *Time for distractions.* The last thing I need is an angry witch putting a hex on one of my only friends.

"So. What are we going to see?" I ask, nodding towards the movie list flashing on the LED on the wall.

He deliberates for a second before answering. "How about a comedy?"

Time passes quickly during the easy going movie. Before I know it the credits are rolling and the lights are slowly coming on. As I stand and stretch, I feel Emmanuel's eyes on me so I glance at him mid-stretch, only to find him staring at the hem of my dress as it exposes more of my skin. As I slowly lower my arms to cover myself, he snaps out of it.

"Sorry," he apologises, realising he's been caught ogling. I don't know how to feel about him watching me like that. I'm a woman and, come on, we all feel sexy when we are being admired, but part of me just doesn't feel right about it. He has my wolf's bristles up, whether it's because he isn't wolf or because he is a witch I don't know, but I won't write him off just yet. She might warm up to him.

I laugh at his embarrassment as he gets up and leads me to the foyer, with a hand against my lower back. Glancing at my watch I notice it's still fairly early and the company isn't that bad, so I decide to prolong the blind date that isn't turning out as bad as I expected.

"It's still early. Do you want to grab a coffee in there?" I offer pointing to the little cafe in the corner of the foyer. "I just need to dash to the bathroom first. That coke has gone right through me."

Emmanuel quickly agrees. "Sounds good. I'll get the drinks while you…freshen up." He struggles to find the appropriate word, but at least he didn't blurt out a pee reference. "What would you like?"

"A caramel latte would be great, thanks. I'll be right back." I dash off in the direction of the little girl's room before he sees me blush.

As I head down the corridor leading to the toilets I can feel someone behind me, and there is a malicious emotion coming off them. I need to try and find out who it is and whether the emotion is towards me or someone else. That's the problem with empathy. I can feel the emotions of strangers towards other people, and it can be so strong as I pass that it feels like it's aimed at me. Most of the time it isn't.

I take a deep breath to see if I can pick up a scent. I smell death—vampire and male. Before I can pick up on anything else, someone grabs my arm and pushes me out the emergency exit near the female toilets.

Once outside he spins me around to face him, pinning me to the wall. I recognise who it is.

Dominick!

He tilts his head and leans in to kiss my neck. I brace myself for the bite but it doesn't come. He stops just as his lips brush against my skin.

"I told you I would taste you soon," his warm breath whispers against my neck, sending shivers over my body. Before I can react or reply to his words, his fangs sink into my throat.

I push with all my strength, trying to move him off me, but

he's far taller and weighs more than me so it's like trying to move a brick wall. I can feel myself weakening from the blood loss. It's pointless! I can feel him pulling at my vein, moaning as he swallows.

After what feels like forever, but is probably only seconds, he retracts his fangs, licking my neck with his tongue, sending another unwanted shiver throughout my body.

"Are you happy now you've had a taste?" I ask snidely, still plastered to the wall by his body.

The amazement is clear on his face. I guess he wasn't expecting that to come out of my mouth. Maybe he thought I'd fall all over myself for more.

"You would have enjoyed it more if I wanted you to, but I expect making you enjoy it would have pissed you off more. I actually like you and would like you to respect me, to a degree."

"Whether I enjoyed it or not, I still won't respect you. You lost any respect I had for you the moment you sank your fangs in me and took from me what I wasn't willing to give," I honestly inform him.

He seems to mull over my remark before responding. "I suppose not. To answer your question, I'm extremely happy. You taste even better than I expected. I don't think I've tasted anything as satisfying in my whole two thousand plus years."

"Wow." I could kick myself for letting my surprise at his age show.

Before he can react to my surprised remark, his phone starts to chime.

"Yes?" he says answering it.

He walks back in the door leaving it ajar for me to get back in, never even looking back in my direction. When I shut the door behind me, he's nowhere to be seen. Charming! He could have at least said goodbye or thanks, after what he just did. After all, I did just give him his feed for the night.

When I get back to the cafe, Emmanuel waves me over from a table next to the window. The last thing I want now is to carry on with this date so I force a friendly smile as I make my way over to him. He stands and pulls out a chair for me. I sit and try to make small talk. It isn't his fault that Dominick just fed from me. We talk about the usual first date things jobs, family, and the like. He tells me about his job as a swimming coach and I just can't help imagining him in his Speedos. The thought makes me wonder if the date might be salvageable after all.

"I'm really sorry to cut the date short, but I have the early shift at the pool tomorrow." He sounds genuinely upset to be leaving.

"That's fine. I've had a great night," I assure him, as we stand and make our way outside.

We swap numbers and as he leans forward to hand my phone back, he goes for the kiss. I have very quick reflexes and manage to turn so his lips make contact with my cheek. I counter with a quick kiss on his cheek. It's not that I wouldn't want to kiss his lips. They look very kissable, but I have had more than enough intimacy for one night.

"We'll have to do it again soon. I'll call you," he says, walking off into an alley down the side of the cinema.

I head towards the crossing. The road is still quite busy and I don't fancy playing chicken. I walk into the bar and find it heaving, which is unusual for a weekday. There must be about twenty customers. We're lucky if we get ten in at the same time on a weeknight.

I spot a couple of empty stools so I sit and wait to be served. It only takes Misty thirty seconds to notice me and come running over. If I didn't know better, I'd think she had the senses of a were.

"I want all the details. How did it go? Are ya gonna do it again?" She's as excited as a kid on Christmas morning.

"Get me a drink first," I say distractedly, rooting through my purse for the ten dollar note I know is in there.

She immediately starts making me a Johnnie Black Sazerac. "Was it that bad? I thought ya'd like him." Her emotions tell me how disappointed she is.

"I like him. He's real sweet. We swapped numbers so we might do something again. It's just something that happened when Emmanuel was getting the coffees." I secretly hope she won't have time to ask me anymore questions. She's passing me my drink and taking my money when a regular named Tommy, answers my wishes by waving her over to be served. I wave her off promising to fill her in when we get home later.

I sit and drink in peace, ordering another off Lucy when my glass is empty.

TESTY WOLVES

I've been sitting in the back corner of the bar for the longest three hours of my life, nursing the same beer and forcing myself not to get up and storm into the cinema complex across the road. I want to find Bel and tear her away from Emmanuel, whether she's having a good time or not.

When the very woman I can't stop thinking about finally walks in the door, my wolf relaxes. He's been pacing for the last three hours so it's a welcome relief.

The other pack members who are also enjoying a drink in the bar glance around; trying to see what has calmed me down. At the beginning of the night they all kept coming over, trying to offer comfort and calm me. But when I almost bit a chunk out of Smithy's throat, they all decided it was better to keep a safe distance.

Those who know about Rosabel, quickly get back to minding their own business. Those who don't, keep watching, searching for any clue as to what might be calming me. I don't care what the pack think. I can't take my eyes off Bel, whether I want to or not.

The little black dress she's wearing hugs her curves and shows off her sexy legs. I want those sexy legs. No—need those sexy legs—preferably wrapped around my waist.

I can see other guys, especially my pack brothers, watching her too, which is understandable. She's an unclaimed fellow wolf. My wolf doesn't like it. Bel is ours but he knows that if any of these guys even try to make a move, we can take them out. They have no chance. Bel isn't leaving my sight for the rest of the night. I will be escorting her home, or following her if need be. My wolf won't accept anything less.

I manage to allow her to finish her first drink. I watch the tension drop off her with every mouthful she takes. Although she's seated, she starts torturing me and every other male in the bar by dancing in her seat. She has no idea how sensually she can move. I can tell by the slight tension still clinging to her shoulders that something must've upset her on her date.

I try to leave her as long as possible, knowing she probably needs the time to herself, but I just can't take the distance between us anymore. I have to touch her. My wolf needs to comfort her. It's his job as alpha and mate.

As I place my hand on her shoulder from behind, I can feel how distracted she is. Her wolf isn't even greeting me by running her energy along my skin, which is unusual. That's one of the reasons I've been trying to stay away from her. My wolf wants to claim her every time she does it, and until she knows what those feelings mean, he can't.

My hand barely touches her shoulder when she spins around and clocks me right on the nose with a mean right hook. I don't even have time to stop her or step out of her reach before I feel my nose crack and the warm blood pour down my face.

I feel the pack members throughout the room bristle, ready to come to my aid. I quickly and silently send out an order with a wave of energy to calm them down, reminding them that I am alpha and I can handle the she-wolf myself.

"Oh. My. God. I'm so sorry. I didn't realise it was you," Bel quickly apologises as she reaches over the bar. She grabs a towel and pulls it over the bar.

"That's a good right hook you've got there. Was your date that bad?" I joke, reaching out and taking the towel from her as I straighten my nose. It clicks back in place and the bleeding pretty much stops. I start healing immediately and if it wasn't for the fresh blood that I could still feel smeared on my face, no one would know she'd hit me.

"No, Emmanuel was nice. It was something that happened when I dashed to the bathroom that has put me on edge. I'm sorry."

Misty takes the bloody towel off me and leans over the bar wiping my face with a wet towel. "There all gone. Have this on the house," she says, passing me a drink that smells like straight whiskey.

I take a large swig of my drink and I lean towards Bel, pulling her into a hug. "Don't worry about it," I say, trying to calm her. As I speak, I take a deep breath and immediately regret leaving her in Emmanuel's care. I can smell Dominick on her and not just his scent. I can smell his saliva. Trust me; saliva has its own scent. If you don't believe me next time you drool in your sleep, smell your pillow. I pull away quickly and spot the bite marks on her neck. Cradling her neck with my hands, I stroke the bite gently with my thumb.

"What happened with Dominick?" I can't help but demand an answer. The alpha in me needs to know. Her mate needs to protect her.

She stares at me blankly for a second. I ready myself to hear her deny it. Surely she knows I can smell him. I see her brain catch up and she explains about him feeding on her in the alley. The whole time I stroke her neck, I'm sending my energy into her wound forcing it to heal quicker. I don't want that blood sucker's mark on her.

As it starts to fade, I know for certain that she is my true mate. I wouldn't be able to use my energy to heal her if she wasn't. I can't help the satisfied rumble that leaves my chest. She is mine, and as much as I want to explain this to her, I can't.

I need to get the problem of Dominick out of the way first.

"Do you know what this means?" I ask, knowing that she

most probably won't have a clue. She wouldn't have had any contact with vampires in Quilpie. Grigori Dorfman runs a tight town. There wouldn't be any vampires stepping foot on his land.

Her frown tells me I'm right before she even opens her mouth. "What? He tasted me. You said he would."

The satisfied feeling I had totally disappears. An angry growl leaves my lips and my energy flares. I'm not surprised one bit when Wesley approaches us.

"Boss. Is everything okay?" he asks, knowing from my energy that it's not.

"No, Wesley." I don't look at him as I answer, I can't. I can't take my eyes off the place where Dominick's fang marks had marred Bel's neck. "Pack meeting in an hour. Do you think you can organise that?"

"Yeah, no problem, boss. What's it about?"

I turn a glare on him. "You'll find out when you get there!" I practically scream in his face.

Wesley leaves without saying another word. He knows full well that he should never question his alpha while I'm in this state.

It takes a few minutes to calm down and address Bel. I can't help but feel sad as I look into her beautiful chocolate brown eyes. "Dominick didn't just taste you, he formed a tie."

When her eyes fill with tears, I realise she must be channelling my sadness.

"What does that mean, a tie?"

"If a vampire drinks from you without draining you or turning you, a tie is formed. Its effects are different with each vampire. It could be that he can read your thoughts, or sense where you are, or even control you to make you do anything he wishes. With Dominick being so old and King, he might be able to do a lot more. Can you see why I'm so upset now?" I can't control the anger in my voice.

"I can see why I should be upset, but why are you upset?" she snaps back.

How do I explain this? Dammit I should have claimed her days ago. Then we wouldn't be having this problem.

"Because he forced you into this, and it complicates things."

"What things?" she asks warily.

I wrack my brain to come up with some reasonable complication that won't make me sound like a crazy, possessive stalker.

"I'm supposed to be helping him find out who's kidnapping his vamps, but the more pissed off I get with him, the less I want to do it." As the lie comes out my mouth I know she's able to pick it up, but I can't do anything to cover it. I just hope my emotions tell her that I'm not completely lying.

"How can someone kidnap a vampire?" she asks, calmly sitting back on her stool. "They're too strong." I can see she's trying to calm me by taking my thoughts away from Dominick.

I want to kiss her for not calling me out over my lie. I refrain and answer her question as best I can. "That's why he's asked for my help. He was convinced it was a vamp, but after interrogating every vamp in the state and coming up blank, he's moving onto the next thing. And the next thing strong enough is a were. He wants me to question the pack."

"Couldn't they have lied to him?" she asks, toying with her empty glass.

I sit down on the stool next to her. "No. You can't lie to Dominick. He's been here two thousand years. He knows a lie when he hears one. When you have extra senses you can pick up on lies when you know what to look for. Raised heartbeat, perspiration, changes in breathing just to name a few."

I catch Misty's eye as she yells out last call and push both our glasses forward to indicate that we want refills.

When she comes over with our drinks, Bel jumps in and

pays her while pushing one of the glasses towards me. "An apology drink."

I can't help but laugh as I accept the drink and the apology.

While we finish our drinks, Misty and Lucy close up. It's not long before Misty comes over with her bag and the keys in her hand.

"Ya ready to go?" she says to Bel.

"Yep," Bel answers, jumping off the stool.

I don't know whether to let her leave with Misty or bring her with me to the pack meeting. By the time I decide I need to bring her, they're both in the car and saying bye.

Before I can say anything Bel's window opens. "You okay, Theo?"

I decide to go with my initial thoughts when I ordered Wesley to organise a pack meeting. I need to fix this and that is what I am going to do. "No. It doesn't feel right leaving you. Will you come with me, please?" I answer honestly.

They both chuckle and Misty shouts through the car. "Are you trying to get in Bel's knickers, Theo?"

Her comment throws me for a loop and it takes a moment to register what made her think along those lines. Not wanting either of them to think I would ever try to get her home just to get in her underwear, I quickly clarify my intentions. "No. I didn't mean it like that that! Not at all." I look directly at Bel. "I need you at the pack meeting, as evidence."

Her face drops and her wolf throws a wave of anger at me. "Fine."

She gets out of the car and slams the door. She drops her head into the open window. "Drive safe, Misty. I'll see you at home in a little while."

Misty drives off without a word.

A very pissed off Bel turns to me and grumbles, "Lead the way."

What the hell have I done?

DECLARATIONS

*A*s he leads me in silence to a very snazzy black car, I realise I may be out of order for being so upset. It's not as if he has ever really made me think he would ever try to 'get into my knickers,' as Misty put it. As much as I want to stay mad at him, I feel like I should apologise. Curiously, my wolf won't let me do it. She's spitting mad at Theo for something.

I try to break the silence. "This car is gorgeous. What is it?"

His face changes from hurt and confused to the sexiest smile as he appraises his car. He gently strokes the bonnet. "It's an Aston Martin, Vanquish. She's my baby."

He unlocks the car with a beep of the remote. It's just as beautiful on the inside—all leather and a new car smell that wraps around me along with Theo's scent.

I'm glad I chose to put my belt on. He isn't exactly sticking to the speed limit as he zooms through the streets of Mount Roxby. I grip the edge of the seat for dear life, trying my hardest not to rip the leather with my claws, which appear as my fear sets in.

"It's okay. I won't crash," he says with a laugh.

"How the hell do you know that? You're driving like a maniac. Do you know how easy it is to crash a car?" I really shouldn't be so demanding towards an alpha, but I can't help it.

He's scaring the shit out of me.

"I'm a werewolf, remember? You know very well we have lots of extra senses and extremely quick reflexes that humans don't."

My claws retract with that reminder, but my grip on the seat doesn't ease much. "Oh, yeah. I didn't think of that. I would still prefer it if you slowed down a little."

He finally slows down, taking a right turn onto a long winding dirt track. It leads into a large opening that holds a magnificent mansion-style house, surrounded by forest. We pull up alongside a dozen cars parked in front of the house.

Theo exits the car and I sit admiring the building and the steps that lead up to it. There are only about eight steps but the way the front entry is designed it is majestic. My door opening pulls me out of my trance.

Theo offers his hand to help me out the car. *Such a gentleman.*

He grips my hand gently in his strong, warm fingers as he leads me into the house and through to the lounge room, which is full of werewolves. Okay. I should clarify that they're werewolves in human form. But they are Pack and I'm an outsider. The full moon is tomorrow night and I can feel the tension in the room as they all turn to watch us enter.

I don't belong here.

Theo addresses everyone as we walk through them, still holding my hand. "Thank you for coming at such late notice and hour."

Everyone nods in unison. It's an extremely unsettling thing to watch.

Once we reach the far side of the room, we stop in front of three chairs that are facing the pack members. Theo stops before the empty middle seat.

An extremely large, scary looking guy, who's dressed in leathers, occupies the seat to his left. He looks like he belongs to a biker gang, not a werewolf pack.

In the chair on Theo's right, is Wes. I had thought he must be high up in the ranks. I can tell by the seating arrangement that he's Theo's second. That makes Biker Guy his third.

Theo directs me to Wes' chair.

Wes stands from his seat and stands behind it without a word. Theo sits me down in the now vacant seat. It's against all my natural instincts to have a were standing that close behind me, but unfortunately I have no choice but to endure it.

Theo releases my hand before turning to the pack. "Please be seated."

The pack drops to the floor.

Once everybody settles into their seated positions, he addresses the room. "First things first. This is Rosabel McGuiness. As you can smell, she's werewolf. Unclaimed and unattached to a pack. She's new to town after travelling from Quilpie; home to a large were-lion pride. Rosabel's been living with this pride since she was a child. She is now trying to find a pack to call home."

"Do I need to put her in the census?" Wes asks from behind me.

"I've already seen to it personally. As you all know Dominick Drake is trying to pin the vampire kidnappings on one of us." A murmur runs through the room.

"I know none of you are guilty, but none of his vampires are either and no matter how hard we try we can't seem to come up with a viable lead. We have been working together to solve this mystery but now Dominick has taken something without permission. It belonged to me and was under my protection."

I look across to Theo in surprise. *Surely he isn't talking about me and the bite. I'm not his.*

"What did he take?" a guy with a buzz cut seated near the front asks.

Theo explains and when he finishes, the guy still isn't satisfied.

"But she isn't pack. She doesn't belong to anyone. The pact we have with the vampires only protects the pack, not lone wolves. I don't understand how this affects us, or why it bothers you."

Theo's gaze penetrates my eyes with concern flowing deeply from his emerald green eyes. Through my empathy I feel a wave of guilt coming off him. "I'm bothered because she is everything to do with me. She is *mine*." He ends his statement on a possessive growl.

My wolf instantly stands to attention. *Finally!* Happy to hear him talk about me in a possessive way. *Ours.* My wolf sends the word through my mind.

The tension in the room doubles. Ninety percent of the wolves in front of me are extremely irate.

"She's your true mate? Why haven't you claimed her? True mates are always claimed at that first meeting between them; from both sides. I'm sorry but Ms. McGuiness looks just as surprised on hearing this information, as the rest of us here," suggests a beefy looking guy in the back.

Theo slips from his chair and kneels in front of me. He leans in and presses his body between my legs. My heart is pounding in my chest. I want this badly, but I am terrified. His left hand squeezes my thigh as his right hand slides up to the back of neck. He pulls my mouth towards him. I feel his hot breath against my lips right before he presses his mouth hungrily to mine; devouring my lips, tongue, and breath in a deep, 'owns me, my wolf and my soul,' kiss.

My eyes close and my hands roam around his strong neck, through his soft hair, gripping the back of his neck. He groans against my mouth. We break apart, panting. I have been owned, in front of his pack. I open my eyes, once again seeing the room full of werewolves before me.

"Yes. That is exactly what I am saying. I will spell it out just in case some of you still don't quite understand. Rosabel McGuiness is my true mate, and I am claiming her."

His wolf's energy brushes against me, covering me in his spicy scent.

That's when I feel my wolf's energy reciprocate by releasing her sweeter scent and brushing it along his body. I close my eyes and concentrate, feeling every inch of him as she touches him. It feels just as it would if I was touching him with my own fingers. He feels divine. Audience or not, with the feel of him under my wolf's energy and his wolf touching every inch of me, I'm just about ready to pounce and take him right here.

I think it's safe to say he feels the same. If the bulge I see him trying to hide as he stands has anything to do with it.

As he steps away and turns to the furious pack, I can smell our scents have combined making the most amazing fragrance.

I have so many questions going through my head.

Are we mates?

Does this happen to all mates or is it just a typical werewolf thing, between two wolves?

An angry scream pulls me away from my questions.

"That is ridiculous! She hasn't even been in town two minutes. You have plenty of females in the pack to choose from. You can't choose her." A brunette female is standing in the middle of the crowd demanding everyone's attention.

"I AM ALPHA!" Theo shouts. His Alpha power spreads throughout the room making his point. I can feel it prickling against my skin and I'm not even part of the pack. I dread to think how bad it hurts those he is forcing it onto.

"Bel is my true mate and I have claimed her." There's a deadly calmness to his voice. It sounds scarier than his previous statement.

A beautiful long-legged blonde parts the crowd. She stops in front of him, reaches out and trails her hands down his chest. It's the same Barbie that was coming onto him in the bar a few nights ago.

"You haven't finalised the claim. We all saw she was willing to do it in front of us all, but you didn't." She's referring to my reaction during our kiss. Her hands go lower towards his waistband.

"I can satisfy you—now and always," she whispers, before planting a huge kiss on Theo whilst her quick and nimble fingers work on his belt.

I release a ferocious growl, as I pounce towards her. I rip her hand from his belt and launch her across the room.

She hits the wall with a loud thump and drops to the floor, moaning—right before a large piece of plaster falls, lands on her head and knocks her unconscious.

I turn away from the crumpled Barbie to find everyone watching in stunned silence. It's then I realise what I've done. I have attacked a pack member in front of her whole pack—one night before the full moon.

To top it off, I was unprovoked.

I'm a dead wolf.

I turn to Theo in a panic, "Oh god, Theo. What have I done? I—"

Before I can finish my sentence, Theo cuts me off with a monstrous laugh. Everyone gasps as he throws his arms around me and sighs into my hair. "Oh, Bel."

Once Theo's laughter settles and silence fills the room, Wesley speaks up. "Now that that's all cleared up. What are we going to do?"

Theo releases me. "I have been thinking about that."

He sits me in his chair and starts to pace the floor. "The only way to break a tie with a vampire is through said vampire's death. That's going to be tricky. We're talking about Dominick after all."

Wesley nervously clears his throat. "No. I mean, what are we going to do about the elusive vampire kidnapper?"

"Oh, yeah, that. Well your guess is as good as mine. What I

do know is we have to find them, if only to clear the pack," he says, still pacing the floor.

"The Pack isn't responsible, and according to Dominick, neither are the Vamps. Could there be a rogue were doing this? One we're not aware of?" Biker Guy suggests.

"It's a possibility, Billy. There have been reports of a rogue vampire, but for now we should all keep our eyes, ears, and noses open for any evidence of a rogue of any kind. We'll discuss this more at Saturday's meeting. Stay safe tomorrow. Make sure you're all at your designated places. Good night."

Without a word they all stand and start to file out the front doors.

"Can someone get Chloe out of my house on the way out?" Theo asks, pointing to the still unconscious leggy blonde laying in a heap on the floor.

A young guy, who was just about to go out the door turns, walks to Chloe and effortlessly hauls her over his shoulder, "Do you know where she lives?" he asks as he turns to look at Theo for an answer. It's then I recognise him as Paddy from the gym the other night.

Billy 'Biker Guy,' whom I have decided must be Theo's third, pats his pockets before pulling out a pen, a crumpled scrap of paper and jotting down what must be her address.

Paddy glances at it as he takes it from Billy's hand. "Cheers, Billy," he says, heading out the door with Chloe bouncing over his shoulder.

The room emptied, leaving Theo, Wesley, Billy, and me. I watch from my seat on the chair as Theo leaves the room through another door, Billy and Wesley both follow. Not knowing what to do, I rest my head back against the chair and close my eyes. *I could really do with getting to bed soon.*

"It's much comfier in the other room, you know." Theo's gravelly voice makes me jump.

"I didn't know if you were discussing pack business. I

thought I'd just close my eyes until someone told me different," I confess.

He slides his fingers around my wrist and pulls me to my feet, leading me towards the doors to the room he had been in. It must be a dining room. I can now see a beautifully restored antique twelve-seat table pushed against one of the walls. It matches the three chairs Theo, Wes, and Billy were using in the meeting.

Billy and Wesley are now sitting on a red L-shaped sofa when we walk into the lounge room.

Theo pats the seat next to him, suggesting I sit there. When I sit down, Theo throws an arm around my shoulders and pulls me against his chest, and puts his feet up on the solid oak coffee table.

Once everyone is comfortable, the brain storming starts.

The three men go over ideas on how to find the rogue vampire. I lose interest pretty quickly and close my eyes, listening to the strong heartbeat under my ear, and it's beating in time with my own. I can feel his voice vibrating through his body and in no time I feel myself drifting off to sleep. Try as I might, I just can't stop myself.

***

*A*n incessant twitch in my thigh wakes me from a deep sleep.

I try to move my arm so I can slap the offending body part, only to find it tangled with an arm that doesn't belong to me. I only have to use my nose to work out who it belongs to. I can feel Theo's energy pulsing off his body, and his scent is everywhere.

"If you don't stop that phone from buzzing, I won't be held accountable when I break it," Theo grumbles as he burrows his head under the pillow.

With that, I realise it isn't my thigh twitching; it's my phone vibrating in the pocket of my dress. I take note of the time, quarter past five in the morning, and the caller ID, Misty, before hitting answer.

"Misty, I am so sorry for not calling," I apologise, thinking she must have been worried that I hadn't made it home yet.

"Theo called to let me know ya'd fallen asleep and he wasn't waking ya."

Theo places his arm over my middle and pulls me towards his body. His energy running along my skin comforts me and I relax into him.

"I'm not calling about that. Ya've got a visitor. I can't get out of him who he is. He's in a bit of a state."

I sit up immediately.

Jared has found me. I bet he's drunk. I hope he doesn't get aggressive with Misty. He isn't usually violent unless he needs to be. He isn't a bad guy.

"I'll be right there, Misty. If he gets violent you lock yourself in another room, you hear me?"

"He doesn't seem like he'll hurt me but I'll keep that in mind," she says before disconnecting the call.

I grab my shoes from the floor alongside the bed and pull them on. The bed moves as Theo gets up. My mind is running away with me imagining all the damage Jared could cause while I'm on my way.

God. I hope he stays human.

Theo appears in my line of sight, crouching before me. He rubs my forearms with his warm hands. "Everything is going to be okay. Let's go and see what's happening."

Instead of going through the front entrance like I expect, he leads me through a door that brings us into a garage. I hear the click of a car unlocking and look around the array of cars. It isn't the black car from last night that flashes its indicators; it's a 4x4 of some kind. I'm not much of a car junkie. The badge tells me it's a Mitsubishi and that's about it. It's white, if that helps.

It doesn't take us long to get to Misty's. Theo pulls up outside her apartment block and starts to exit the car. I lean over and grab his arm to stop him. "Theo, wait."

He closes the door and sits back in his seat.

I release my hold, allowing my hand to relax against his arm. "You can't come up. If it's who I think it is, all hell will break loose if you do."

He gives me a worried look. "If there's a threat I don't want you going up there without me."

"He isn't a threat to me. He'd never hurt me. But he will be a threat if he sees you. Please Theo," I plead. I need him to let me go up alone. I don't know if Jared will recognise my change in scent, but if Theo goes up too he'll flip. He'll attack Theo and I can't have that on my conscience.

"Okay. But I will wait down here, until I hear that you're safe. If I hear anything that sounds violent I won't be able to stop myself from coming up there."

Knowing it's the best I'm going to get, especially from an alpha; I grab his face and give him a quick kiss before exiting the car.

"Thank you," I call over my shoulder as I dash into the building.

I walk into the apartment, expecting the worst. A fight with Jared or worse yet, a bloody Misty if he'd lost it, in my absence. My brain takes a minute to catch up to what my eyes are seeing. My cousin Benji is sitting on the sofa. A suitcase is by his feet and tears are streaming down his bruised and battered face.

"Oh, Benji," I whisper, dashing to crouch before him.

"I'm sorry…he made me…made me tell him," he says between sobs, as I pull him into a hug.

Misty comes into the lounge from the kitchen with a tray

loaded with coffee and cookies. She gives me a worried smile as she catches my eye.

"Don't cry, Benj. Did he do this to you?" I ask pointing to his face. Neither of us needs to say the name, we both know who we're referring to. Jared.

Taking a few deep breaths he calms down and reaches for a coffee and a cookie. "Yeah, I tried not to tell him. He didn't want to hurt me, I could tell. But he wanted to know where you were and he knew I could find out. I pinged the GPS on your new phone. I'm sorry."

I'd bought the new phone a few days before leaving so Jared couldn't get a hold of me or ping my GPS. Looks like my purchase was pointless.

"It was all pointless. I should have just stayed; he wouldn't have done this to you then." I reach out and stroke his bruised face as I try pushing away the feelings of guilt.

Benji smiles at me but it's sad. "No. You needed to leave. You don't belong there. You need a pack. You always have."

My phone starts vibrating in my pocket. When I look at the ID and see Theo's name I jump up from my seat and pace to the window.

"Oh shit," I say to no one in particular before hitting answer.

10

HUNT

I barely hold back from storming into the building. I'm an Alpha, the leader, the protector. Allowing my mate to go upstairs alone to face an unknown danger goes against all my natural instincts. I last five minutes before I can't take it any longer.

I reach into my pocket and manage to pull out my phone without crushing it in my hand.

Bel answers fairly quickly. "Theo."

The relief of hearing her voice causes me to lose control, leaving my phone a crumbled mess in my hand.

"Dammit!" I yell, throwing the useless pieces of phone across the cab.

I try not to slam the door as I get out. I don't need a busted truck to go with the busted phone.

Once in the apartment block, I take one look at the elevator and know I won't be able to handle waiting. I storm straight for the stairs, taking them two at a time.

I hear the security guy calling me.

"Sir, you can't go up there. You need to be signed in. Sir!" It doesn't sound like he's following me up the stairs. His lazy arse probably took one look at the stairs and decided to leave me to it.

I barge into Misty's apartment, only calming down when I see Bel standing unharmed in front of me.

"Theo? The call's not going through," she says, waving the phone in her hand about.

"Yeah. Technical glitch with my phone. I thought I better just come up." I look around the room and find Misty on the sofa.

"Sorry for just barging in Misty. I wanted to make sure you were all safe." That's when I notice the visitor next to Misty. His face is battered and bruised and he looks like he's been crying too. Bel and Misty might be okay but this guy isn't. The Alpha in me wants to jump in and help.

"Everything is fine, Theo. This is my cousin, Benji." She gestures towards the black and blue stranger on the sofa. "He's been in a spot of bother but he's safe now."

I watch her saunter towards me. The sexy sway of her hips makes things stir beneath my jeans.

"Thanks for checking on us." She leans up on her tiptoes and kisses me on the cheek. If that isn't a dismissal, I don't know what is.

"Always," I reply before taking her mouth with mine. I'm not leaving without tasting her. "See you tonight at the hunt?"

"Oh, no. I won't be hunting."

"Not hunting. Why?" It's unheard of for a wolf not to join in a hunt on the full moon. Even a lone wolf will hunt alone. We feel closer to our wolves on a full moon because she sings to us, begging us to change. Nothing but pregnancy will stop us from changing on a full moon and sometimes even that doesn't stop us. That's why miscarriage rates in werewolves are so high. Sometimes the wolf just takes over and the change is too violent for a foetus to survive.

"I've never hunted. The pride would never allow me to hunt with them and they made sure to run their hunts in time with the full moon, no doubt out of spite. I'll just shift here. I'll be fine." She reaches around my neck and pulls me down to whisper in my ear. "I don't feel comfortable leaving Benji in this state. We've only just stopped him crying."

I hold her waist as she drops back down on her feet. "I'm

not happy about it. A wolf in my town should be able to hunt. But I understand your reasons. How about I take you on a special hunt on Monday—just the two of us? I'll pick you up about noon."

She smiles gratefully and steps out of my arms. "Yes, that would be great. Monday at noon it is."

I nod and say goodbye to both Benji and Misty as I head for the door. I can feel Bel following behind me, her energy brushing against my skin. I turn to find her standing in the doorway.

As I reach to pull her into my arms again, the lift dings and the doors open behind me. Glancing over my shoulder I see a security guard with a face like thunder barge out.

"Sir, you need to leave. You can't just storm into the building like that. We have a security system to keep the residents safe." He dismisses me and turns his attention to Bel. "Ms. McGuiness, I'm sorry about this blip in our security. I will escort this man out and personally make sure nothing like this happens again."

"It's fine, Bob. He's a good guy." Bel starts to back away out of my reach. "Thanks again, Theo. I best get back in and see to Benji." She reaches for the door and closes it without even a goodbye kiss.

The lift behind me dings. The security guard must have already called it back.

"You need to leave now, sir."

Holding my growl in, I turn to the security guard. My wolf is unhappy with being ordered around by this man. He's just a human. He doesn't realise the dangers of giving me orders. I keep telling myself that I can't attack a defenceless human as he glares at me.

I place my hand on the doors and wave him in—my wolf can only take so much. He might not consider the guy a threat, but that doesn't mean he will give him our back.

It doesn't take the lift long to make it down to the ground floor, making me think he must have stopped to check all the lower floors before getting to Misty and Bel's floor.

I head straight for the front door, ignoring the guard behind the desk whom had decided to take it on himself to give me a lecture about signing in and calling up to the residents before going up. I close the door behind me while he's still mid-rant.

I walk around the house when I arrive and head to the back yard. I can hear the pack members fooling around.

Wes is flipping burgers on the barbie. Alyssa, his mate, is lounging on the grass with a couple of other females; Rachel, Chloe, and Delly. Eddie and Matthew are throwing a football around. The only member missing is Paddy.

The rest of the pack are all in groups at other locations. It's too dangerous for us to hunt together. We can be noisy on a hunt. Humans would notice large groups of us, making our existence harder to keep from them.

There are already dangerous groups of humans who grow up knowing that fairy tales and monsters are real. They like to call themselves 'the Cleaners.'

Their mission is to cleanse the human race of all supernatural beings. They're trained generation after generation to destroy us. If we hunted in one large group, we would be giving them the opportunity to wipe out a whole pack at once.

We rotate locations and members so we all get a chance to hunt together. It's safe and it works, so we stick to it.

I reach out for the footy, grabbing it as it soars straight towards my head. "Nice try Eddie but you know I'm too quick for you. I don't know why you bother."

My comment doesn't stop me from throwing the footy back in Eddie's direction at full pelt, aiming for his arse.

He easily catches it with a laugh and carries on his throwing game with Matthew. It's virtually impossible to catch a wolf off guard. Our reflexes are just too quick.

"Is Paddy on his way?" I ask no one in particular.

Everyone looks at me but not one of them offers a reply.

I turn my attention to Ed and head for Wes at the grill. "Ed. You two are pretty good mates. Why isn't he here? He's usually one of the first to arrive, he loves the hunt."

"I haven't heard from him today. I just figured you'd sent him to track for the rogue vamp or whoever is kidnapping the vamps. He often goes silent when he's tracking." Ed makes his way towards me, digging his phone out of his pocket. He taps the screen and holds it out. We can all hear it without even putting it on speakerphone. The seven of us crowd around as we listen to it ringing out before Paddy's voicemail finally kicks in.

"You've reached Paddy. I'm either ignoring you or I can't answer the phone right now. Depending on which category you fall in, leave your number and I might call you back."

I speak up knowing he'll call back immediately on hearing my voice. "Paddy, call me."

Ed wanders off, redialling his number.

I close my eyes and feel for him through the pack bonds. I find him in no time, agitated and scared. I open my eyes.

"Something's…not right. He's scared. We need to find him, retrace his footsteps." I think back to the last time I saw or heard from him. The pack meeting. He left last night with Chloe over his shoulder.

I focus my sights on Chloe. "What happened when he dropped you off last night?"

"I'd come around by the time we arrived at my house. I thanked him with a peck on the cheek and left him in his car.

He didn't drive away until I closed the door behind me. Was I the last person to see him?" she asks, sounding devastated at the thought.

"Fuck! He's still not answering. When I got home and he wasn't there I thought he'd gotten lucky with Chloe. I should have fucking called him. Some mate I am," Ed says, pacing around the yard with his wolf riding him. I can feel the energy flowing around him.

Delly steps up to him, placing a comforting hand on his arm. "Don't beat yourself up, Ed. You won't be any help to him if you turn wolf now. You know turning so close to the full moon means you won't shift back until morning. We have a few hours before we have no choice but to shift so let's make the most of it."

He nods his agreement and they all look to me for direction. The problem? I have no fucking clue how to find him. He was in a car; meaning there's no scent trail to follow.

"Wes. Can you call the rest of the pack and make sure no one else saw him after he dropped Chloe off?" Wes wanders off with his phone in hand.

"What if the person taking the vampire's has him? Are we safe? Could it be the Cleaners?" Alyssa asks, with a trembling lip.

I pull her petite frame into my arms. "He's alive, sweetheart. It's not the Cleaners. We all know they wouldn't keep him alive. Whoever has him, we'll get him back. To make sure everyone is safe tonight, we'll bring everyone here for the hunt. It will just have to be a quiet one."

"What about the Cleaners?" Alyssa gasps as she steps out of my arms. We all know the dangers of hunting in the full pack.

"It's a last minute decision. Even if they find out about it they don't have the time to organise an ambush. We'll just have to be extra alert. Do you think you could organise getting everyone here?" Giving her a job will take her mind off worrying about Paddy and the pack's safety. Alyssa doesn't need to worry about those things. That is my job as Alpha.

"Sure." She nods and runs into the house, probably to use the phone in my office.

"We'll get some food together for when the pack arrives," Delly offers, taking Chloe—whose sole attention is on Ed and his phone calls—by the arm and heading into the kitchen.

Matthew and Ed are the only two left in the yard.

"We'll go see if we can pick up anything at Chloe's. It's the last place we know he was so it's our best option."

I look closely at Eddie. "Do you feel like you can handle coming with us? Your wolf was riding you pretty hard a minute ago; we can't have you shifting in the middle of Chloe's street."

He takes a solid minute to weigh up his wolf and whether he will be calm enough to allow him to join us. "I'm all right now, boss. He's settled down."

Taking him at his word, I turn and head for the truck, hoping for everyone's sake we find Paddy and this is all some silly mistake.

If someone has taken him, all hell is going to break loose.

11

CONS OF A TIE

hen Theo left, the three of us spent the day catching up. Because it's a full moon, I need, the night off to change so Misty heads off to work alone, leaving Benji and me to have a movie night.

"What do you fancy watching, Bel?" Benji asks, flicking through Misty's DVD collection.

I make my way to the bedroom to shift.

"Surprise me," I shout, before shutting the bedroom door behind me. I can normally wait until later in the evening before shifting, but I haven't had the chance to shift since moving here, and my wolf is antsy and ready to come to the surface.

Hoping to ease the shift, I remove my clothes and drop down to all fours. Shifting is not a nice feeling. Essentially your bones are all breaking, realigning again within seconds. The whole process is over in a matter of minutes but it's painful. If you haven't changed in a while, it hurts more than normal. Once I release my wolf she practically pounces out of my skin. I can't help the grunts of pain coming out of my mouth. The grunts soon turn to a howl. I shake out the last tingles of pain just as the door opens.

"That sounded painful." Benji winces at the thought as he holds the door open for me to exit, making sure to stay clear. After a painful shift, your skin stays sensitive for a while.

I trot to the lounge, curl up on the floor in front of the sofa. I'm not sure where Misty stands on the animals on the sofa front, so I feel more comfortable sticking to the floor. My eyesight has changed with the shift but I can still see the TV; it's just colourless. I can smell the sage Misty has been burning. She's always burning something. This morning it was sage for protection against Jared apparently.

Benji follows behind me, plonking his butt down on the floor next to me. He grabs the popcorn off the coffee table and presses play.

Benji chose the movie Rent, which is one of our favourites. We like to sing through the whole thing. It's not something I can do in wolf form but I won't enjoy it any less.

Halfway through the movie my wolf starts getting agitated. I get up and pace through the apartment, finding myself stopping and staring at the front door every time I pass. She wants out. She wants to join Theo. She feels she should be hunting with them because she has some insane idea about Theo being *ours*.

"Bel. You aren't normally like this. I don't know what to do for you. If you don't stop whining, someone might come up to see what's happening."

Whining? I didn't even realise I'd been whining.

"We don't want them to find you. They might not believe you're a dog and you know I can't lie for shit," Benji says, crouching down between me and the front door. He smooths his hand over my head and down the fur on my back. It does the trick and calms me enough to stop my whining.

Benji stands and heads back to the lounge and the TV. "Come on, let's go put another movie on. I'll even let you drool over Brad Pitt in World War Z."

The day after the full moon I find myself walking into work carrying Benji in my arms. He can't pass Misty's ward because he's human. He keeps wanting to turn and run away, even after she mutes it enough for him to go through without dying.

When we open the front doors to the bar, Tommy is waiting. He's like a piece of furniture. The bar wouldn't feel right if he wasn't propping it up.

As the night goes on I notice it's nowhere near as busy as it usually is. We actually find ourselves standing around between serving customers.

I wipe the already clean bar down for what feels like the fiftieth time. "It's so quiet tonight."

"It always is after a full moon. The werewolves are all recovering from their wild night." Misty's voice sounds muffled as she answers while cleaning out one of the fridges behind the bar.

The only customers we have are Tommy, Vera, and Mike; all witches. I give them all fresh drinks.

Misty moves on to the last fridge. "Why don't you and Benji pick a few songs on the jukebox and have a boogie. It's not as if we're rushed off our feet."

We choose a few silly songs to dance to. The first one that starts to play is 'Stop' by The Spice Girls. We both know the dance off by heart so we're pretty entertaining.

Misty, Tommy, Vera, and Mike are all whooping and cheering until from out of thin air Dominick appears beside me.

My protective instincts kick in, but not before I jump.

"Here. Get a drink. Stay at the bar. I'll be there in a minute," I say, pushing some money into Benji's hand. He practically runs to the bar without argument.

"Rosabel. Your little friend is safe with me. I'm not interested in his blood after tasting yours."

"What do you want, Dominick?" I grumble. I am pretty sure this isn't going to end nicely, especially if past encounters are anything to go by.

He grins, reaches out and trails his fingers down my neck. "Isn't that obvious? You. I want you to become my feeder; my servant."

"Not a chance, Dominick. I will never be yours. I want you to remove this damn tie, too," I growl, stepping back from his touch. My wolf may want to find a pack to join. When you join a pack you are connected to each and every member. You can feel them. It's comforting. It's not that I can feel a connection to him but even the idea of being connected to a vampire is just all kinds of wrong.

"Oh. You know about the tie?" He sounds disappointed, until he speaks again. "The tie can't be removed. I'm sorry."

I glare at him, hearing the lie in his apology. "You're not sorry, and a friend informed me it can be removed with *your* death."

He laughs. "Is that a threat, Rosabel?"

I try to be as serious and intimidating as possible, when I open my mouth next. "If that's the only way to break it, yes." Being intimidating to a King Vampire, who is two thousand years old, is virtually impossible, at least I thought it was but Dominick's face is telling me something else. Maybe I did manage to intimidate the good king a little.

"You meant every word of that. You would kill me. I can feel it." He looks puzzled for a moment.

"Are you an empath?" I ask. It would be the only way he could feel my emotions like that.

"No. But you are," he says in surprise. "It seems the tie has given me two gifts that I know of. One, I can materialise wherever you are by just thinking your name. And two, I can use your empathy against you." His words make me want to punch him. How dare he!

He smirks, stepping towards me again. "Now, now. Don't get angry."

"STOP THAT!"

Laughing sinisterly, he leans in and kisses me on the cheek and before I can get a punch in, he leans away licking his lips.

Cocky bastard.

"The friend that told you how to break the tie wouldn't happen to be Theo, would it?"

"It was your intention for him to find out. That's the main reason you did it." The taste of a werewolf may be enticing for him, but he wanted to get at Theo and biting a werewolf because of a loophole was always going to rub the alpha the wrong way. Dominick seems to get off on it. Even I can see that and I haven't been in town long.

"Of course, it was. Has he worked that out already? He's smarter than I gave him credit for." He leans forward, inhaling my scent. "You've mated."

I nod as I lean away. "He chose me in front of his pack."

"And you chose him in return, I can smell the scent. But you're worried about it, why." It was a statement not a question, "You haven't sealed it yet. That is why it's not so dominant, and I can't let you seal it." He's worried. He might be able to use my empathy against me, but I could still use it against him too. *Why would he be worried about us sealing our mating?*

I glance over to see Misty and Benji huddled together in deep conversation at the bar. "You can't stop us, Dominick." When I don't hear a reply, I turn back to find that Dominick's nowhere in sight.

When I get back to the bar, Misty pushes a glass of what looks and smells like my usual towards me. "Looks like ya need it. What did he want?"

"Just to rub it in about the tie. I hate him," I mutter before taking a nice large mouthful of my drink.

Misty gasps and drops the glass she'd been drying. It smashes at our feet. "Don't say things like that, it will get you killed."

We both bend down and I start picking the big bits of glass

up. "If that's the case, my name will already be on the execution list. I told him I'd kill him if that's the only way to break the tie. He knows I meant it too. He could feel it through my empathy. And thanks to the tie, he can now use it against me."

Misty grabs the dustpan and brush, sweeping up the smaller shards as she speaks. "You have to tell Theo. He is the only person that could protect you against Dominick."

Our three customers leave during our clean up so Misty decides that since we've only had the three customers all night, we may as well close up early.

*J*wake up Monday morning grateful for our early close the night before. It meant I could actually wake up on the first alarm at eleven o'clock, instead of hitting snooze three times.

I quickly get ready as my nerves start to kick in. I'm excited to be going for a run with Theo but I'm nervous of how he will be with me. I don't really know where we stand with the whole mating thing. *Was it just an act or was it real?*

When the clock reads three o'clock, I accept that I've been stood up.

Relief washes over me when the phone rings half an hour later.

I can hear Benji answer it in the lounge room. "Hello." I'm not close enough to hear the person on the other end. If I was in the same room as him I would hear them no problem, but I'd been sulking in my room.

I dash through the apartment.

"Yes. You've got the right number. I'll just get her for you." He holds the phone out towards me, mouthing the name. 'Emmanuel.' I can't help feeling disappointed.

I take the phone and try not to sound as disappointed as I feel. "Hi Emmanuel. How are you?"

"Good thanks, Rosabel. I just wondered if you wanted to go out again. Misty told me it's your night off."

Another date? Part of me doesn't want to. I can't stop thinking about Theo. I should accept that Theo doesn't want me and see where things go with Emmanuel? "Yeah, that sounds good. Do you mind if we just go to Misty's though? It wasn't busy last night and I feel like I had a night off. I'd like to be there to help if things get busy."

"That's fine. I was going to suggest Misty's anyway. Seven thirty sound okay?"

"Perfect, I'll see you later."

"Bye," he says before disconnecting the call.

I place the phone back in its cradle on the sideboard.

"Ooh, a second date," Benji teases, taking a seat on the sofa.

Misty walks in from the kitchen, practically jumping up and down. Obviously she's been earwigging on the phone call. "I'll entertain Benji at the bar. I might even let him help me out behind it."

"Sorry, Benji, but Misty you might not want to do that. Benji has two left hands. They just don't seem to coordinate," I warn her, deadly serious.

12

SECOND DATES

I have to carry Benji into the bar again. I think we might have to figure out how to get him in without the wards affecting him at all.

I offered to work until seven o'clock. That gives me half an hour to get some Dutch courage.

Seven o'clock comes around fast.

Benji takes my place behind the bar as I take a seat on his vacated stool. He experiments on me with his first drink. It tastes just right. It's a shame he smashed three glasses in the process. I get the feeling that poor Misty won't have any left by the end of the night.

Emmanuel walks in the door at half past seven on the dot, catching me off guard with a kiss on my cheek. He orders a drink from Benji, who manages to make it without breaking a single glass.

We sit at one of the smaller circular tables to chat for a while. I start to think it could be great if something comes out of this between us. He's sweet and attractive but then I remember he isn't what I want.

Emmanuel jumps. "How did you do that?"

"Do what?" My questioning frown disappears the second I hear the unwanted voice behind me.

"He's talking to me, my delicious, Rosabel. Not you."

I turn to face Dominick. Trying out my intimidating expression again. "Unless you have come to remove the tie, you might as well just disappear again."

"Rosabel. You know Mr. Drake?" Emmanuel asks.

"She knows me intimately."

I feel rage coming off Emmanuel in waves and wonder why he's so mad. This is only our second date and we haven't even come close to discussing exclusivity.

"Tell him the truth, Dominick," I order. "Tell him that on our last date, you trapped me in that alley behind the cinema and drank from me without my consent."

"Oh. You do spoil my fun," he whines. "Do you really want me to leave you with this witch? He's not worthy of you. You deserve so much better. I thought you're mated with Theo, anyway? If you're not, you might like to try dating me."

I feel resentment coming from Emmanuel. Which quickly changes to happiness. *Odd. Out of Dominick's last sentence, what would make him happy?*

"My private affairs are none of your concern, Dominick." I grab my drink and take a sip as I try to calm my wolf down. She wants nothing more than to take control of my body and rip Dominick to shreds.

"Well. I came here to do you a favour but if you don't want me to give you the warning, I'll just let you find out by yourself." He turns, making a show of leaving.

I stand and grab his arm, forcing him to look me in the eye.

"Are you threatening me?" Funny how Dominick asked me the same question only yesterday and yet they sound so different. He'd been amused. I am far from it.

"No. I would never threaten you. I had a were-lion come to me requesting a living order today. He was asking for your address."

"Jared." I sigh, slumping out of my threatening position.

"Yes. I believe that was his name. Should I have withheld your address?" He actually sounds concerned.

"If you hadn't, it would have only been a matter of time before he followed my scent. Thank you for the warning. I appreciate it." I sit back in my seat and down what's left of my drink.

Dominick grins. "See. I'm not as bad as you think."

I beg to differ.

Dominick leans in and presses his lips against my neck, forcing me to lean away until the table presses into my ribs.

My heart starts to race, knowing that his fangs will sink into the skin any second now. I feel the short sharp scratch as they break the skin. I'm surprised when they don't sink deeper and he dematerialises into thin air. I touch my neck and see the blood on my fingers before turning back to Emmanuel.

"You're bleeding. Did he—"

I cut him off. "No. He was just showing me he can feed off me if he so desires. Can we just forget about it?" I am really getting sick of Dominick and his controlling ways.

Emmanuel grants my wish. Changing the subject, as he reaches for his own drink on the table. "So. Jared has found you."

"How do you know? Misty. Is there anything she doesn't tell you?" I joke, playing with my empty glass.

"Don't blame her. I was digging for information."

"I'm not going to have to worry about you stalking me as well, am I? Dominick and Jared are too many stalkers as it is. I don't need another one." Even though I say it with a laugh, I'm serious.

We both laugh and enjoy some more easy conversation over a couple more drinks.

As the last call is announced, he offers to walk me home. It's a nice fifteen minute walk. Misty and I usually use the car as it's the safe option. Two women walking the streets at two or three in the morning is a little dangerous. Walking with Emmanuel, I am pretty sure nobody will bother us.

Our conversation still flows well on the way home.

Emmanuel pulls me to a stop outside the apartment building, "I had a really good night."

"Me too," I reply honestly.

Before I know it. He quickly takes my mouth with his.

I won't deny him anymore. I like him. This might actually lead to something if I can stop my wolf thinking about Theo. I fist my hands in the front of his shirt as I deepen the kiss.

He lets out a moan and pulls away.

Wow. What a kiss.

"I was thinking the same thing," he says, with a laugh.

Oh good god. Did I say that out loud? What is it with men and me making a fool out of myself in front of them?

He brushes his thumb over my lips. "I better leave before I kiss you again."

We say our goodbyes and he leaves without any more kisses.

I enter the apartment building in a happy daze, still thinking about that kiss.

My happy mood disappears when I step out of the lift; thanks to the sight of Jared sitting on the floor against our apartment door. He looks like he's been there a while. God only knows how he got past the security guards. *Am I ever going to catch a break?*

Looking dishevelled, he jumps up as soon as he sees me. His usually well-styled blonde hair is a mess; no doubt from running his hand through it every two seconds, exactly like he is doing as he stares at me.

"Bel." He sighs, leaping towards me, trying to take me in his arms.

I manage to push him off before he gets a hold. "Jared, don't. I've had a week full of annoying, pushy men and I'm not in the mood to deal with another. I shifted on the full moon but I haven't run since arriving in Mount Roxby. I don't want to have a forced shift."

"I just want to talk, baby. I've missed you so much."

I let him have his moment. I really don't have the energy to argue about it. I open my mouth to reply, and close it again, having no idea what to say.

The lift pings and Misty and Benji step out from it. *Saved by the bell. Thank you, angels.*

"Look, Jared, it's late. If you really want to talk, meet me at work tomorrow. My shift starts at five o'clock. It's a bar called Misty's down Main Street. Have you seen it?" A big public place is the best place to meet him. Misty's is perfect.

"Yes. I saw it earlier. I'll be there. Thank you."

I step around him to unlock the door and gesture for Misty and Benji to enter before me. I daren't look back at Jared. I might just break my resolve and fall into his arms. I have missed him. I love him. Of course, I have missed him; I just know we shouldn't be together. We're not right for each other.

I need a pack, and he needs his pride.

"He's a bit intimidating—alpha level intimidating," Misty mutters as we make our way through to the kitchen. She opens a cupboard and takes out three glasses.

I run the cold tap and fill the glasses one by one, we all like to take a glass to bed with us. "Yeah. He'll be taking over as Pride Leader when his father steps down. I hope you don't mind me telling him to meet me at work, I just figured it would be better meeting him in a public place."

"Not at all. It's safer that way. You'll be able stick to your guns about not being together easier in public."

13

WOLFING OUT

*W*aking up the next day my wolf is practically crawling out of my skin. I really wish Theo had turned up to show me where to run. I am desperate for a good run, but because I don't know anywhere safe to go, the gym will have to suffice.

The gym looks busier than the last time. I head straight through to the lockers and dump my stuff; taking a towel and bottle of water with me and placing the locker key around my neck.

Just as I place my bottle in the holder on the treadmill, Wesley stops beside me.

"Rosabel, hi. Theo isn't here today."

"Hi." I frown. "Why would I think Theo was here?"

"He owns the place, I thought you knew," Wes says.

I remember the card I memorised, the one Theo gave me with his number on it. His email did have the gym's name in it. *Why hadn't I put two and two together?*

"I didn't realise. I'm just here for a workout. I don't know anywhere safe to run so this treadmill will have to do." I step on and crank the speed up. I really shouldn't take my anger out on Wes but I can't hold it back.

As I start to run I expect Wes to leave, so I am surprised when the next question comes out of his mouth.

"You haven't seen Paddy have you? The guy who almost wolfed out on you?"

"I know who Paddy is." I laugh, remembering how embarrassed the poor guy was. "No. I haven't seen him since he left Theo's after the meeting. Why?" I step off the treadmill so I can give Wes my full attention.

"He hasn't been seen or heard from since he dropped Chloe home after the meeting. It looks like the kidnapper has moved on from vamps to werewolves."

"Oh, no." I didn't know what else to say. What can you say to someone whose pack brother is missing?

"I know."

Looks like I am not the only one who's short for words. His phone rings and he digs it out of his shorts pocket. He glances at the screen before speaking again. "I have to get this. Enjoy your workout, Rosabel," he says as he walks away to answer the phone.

I work out for an hour before deciding it's pointless. My mind is too busy thinking about poor Paddy—not to mention the equipment just isn't doing anything for me. My wolf wants out, to run and nothing less will suffice. She feels more on edge than before I started.

When I arrive home Misty and Benji have already left. I quickly change into my uniform, having showered at the gym.

I arrive at work at the front entrance just as Misty opens up.

"Hi, Tommy. Looks like ya have company today," Misty says, laughing at her own joke.

Tommy walks through the doors heading straight for his stool. "Sure do, Misty."

"Sorry I'm late. The gym was a waste of time. I don't know why I even bothered," I grumble, following Misty through the bar.

"I bumped into Wesley. One of the pack members has gone missing. They think it's the vamp-napper moving on to were-wolves." I go into the office and offload my bag before joining Misty behind the bar.

"Who's missing?"

"Paddy. The one that nearly turned wolf on me last week."

"Poor thing, he's a nice guy. I hope they find the kidnapper before anyone else goes missing." Misty starts making Tommy his usual.

Benji's sitting in his usual seat with a drink in front of him. He's starting to become like Tommy. "How did you get in here today?" I can't see Misty carrying him in, not with the way he thrashes about trying to get away.

"I walked right in. Misty made me a bracelet that negates the ward for me." He holds his wrist up showing me the bracelet. The ordinary looking piece of leather cord suits his bony wrist. I reach out to touch it hoping to feel the magic, but I can't feel anything. It just feels as ordinary as it looks.

A group of seven witches come in together, and just as I hand the last one his drink Emmanuel walks in. He heads straight to my side of the bar and sits next to Benji.

"Sorry, but I couldn't stay away from you," he says with a grin.

Oh what the hell! I lean over the bar and give him a peck on the lips. Only, when our lips connect, I get a lot more than a peck.

I hear a growl coming from the door and I pull away, expecting to see Jared. When I get far enough away from Emmanuel's scent I catch the spicy scent from the other night and I realise too late that the growl belongs to Theo. I don't need to be an empath to know that he's sad and angry, when I catch sight of his beautiful face. The mix of emotions coming from him is so overwhelming; I can't even pinpoint one of them confidently.

He takes slow, sure strides towards me. "Bel, we need to talk." He glances at Emmanuel before adding, "In private."

"Use the office," Misty says, sidling up beside me. The last thing she wants is the alpha to go wolf in her bar.

I head to the office without saying a word. I have no idea what to say to him. Part of me feels guilty about being with Emmanuel, yet another part keeps reminding me that he stood me up.

He follows me to the office in silence. He closes the door and rests his forehead against it.

I can feel his energy pushing at my skin. "What's going on, Theo? I've already told Wesley I haven't seen Paddy."

"It's got nothing to do with Paddy." That spicy scent coming from him is getting stronger by the second. He takes a deep breath and spins around to face me. "There is a were-lion asking about you. He wants to reside here. I sent him to Dominick so I would have time to warn you." I could tell that isn't what he wanted to say.

"You're too late. He turned up last night, not long after Dominick warned me he'd passed on my address. But that isn't what you really wanted to say though, is it?"

"Yes, that's it. I guess I could have told you in the bar after all," he lies.

"Theo. I'm an empath and a werewolf. If I couldn't feel your emotions through my empathy, I'd still know you are lying. My wolf can tell. What do you really want to talk about?" I slam my hand on Misty's desk to emphasise my impatience. I really don't want to be pissed, but he's blatantly lying and I can't stand it.

"An empath," he repeats, stunned. That's not exactly a good sign. Maybe I should have told him before. "Why were you kissing the witch? We're mated."

"Theo." I sigh. "You haven't said two words to me since leaving Misty's on Saturday morning. You promised to show me where it was safe to run on Monday but stood me up. I assumed everything said at the meeting, must have been bull-shit, or at least the full moon causing you to do it. So when Emmanuel asked me out again, I said yes."

Theo finally steps away from the door, coming to a stop when I'm within reach. He reaches out and brushes my hair behind my ear. He doesn't crowd me. He can probably tell that I'm angry and fighting my wolf for the change. I may not be part of his Pack but he is an alpha. He'll be able to sense my wolf and how much she wants to get out.

He takes a deep breath. "I'm sorry. Paddy going missing hit the pack hard. I've not had two seconds to even think since then. I know it's no excuse. I came here tonight to beg for your forgiveness and to see if you would go on a date with me, since we pretty much skipped that step."

My anger dissipates with his words. How can I be angry with him when he has so much on his plate? "Theo. I forgive you."

Before I can say more, he grabs my face between his hands, and takes my mouth with his. As he runs his tongue along the seam of my lips, begging for entry, I pull away.

"Wait. What about Emmanuel? He's a nice guy; I can't just trade him in."

He's looking at me with such adoration that I can feel his love wrapping around me.

I'm kissing him again before I even realise that I've moved. My hands are around his neck, fisting his hair. Our scents mix and Theo lifts me by the hips and places me on the desk, knocking papers to the floor. As his hands roam my body, mine take a journey over his muscular chest and down his abs. As I reach his belt and start to undo it, his nimble fingers work at my zipper.

"I can't let you do this," Dominick says from behind me.

Theo jumps away from me startled. "Where the fuck did you come from?"

"Didn't Rosabel tell you? One of the gifts I received from the tie gives me the ability to materialise wherever she is at just the thought of her name." He smirks as I get off the desk and face him.

"Why the fuck are you here, Dominick?" I ask him pointedly.

"I told you the other day. I can't let you seal your mating," he tells me.

"What does our mating have to do with you?"

Theo and Dominick answer my question at the same time.

"Death isn't the only way to break the tie."

"Sealing our mating breaks the tie," Theo adds with a smirk.

I glance between them both, not knowing who to address. I focus on Dominick. "Is that true? When Theo and I seal our mating, the tie between the two of us will be broken?"

"I believe so, yes," Dominick states as the door opens and Misty comes in.

"Sorry to disturb ya but I need ya out there." She hooks a thumb over her shoulder indicating the bar. "Jared and Emmanuel are both getting anxious. I can't serve and keep them calm." She glances at Dominick as he dematerialises. "What the hell?"

I dismiss the empty space with a wave of my hand. "He arrived the same way. He's a pain in my arse. Sorry about leaving for so long. I'll be right out."

Misty closes the door again leaving the two of us alone.

"I need to go. Neither of us wants Jared losing control. He'll cause a lot of damage and probably take a number of people out before anyone can subdue him."

Just as I reach the door to the bar, Theo spins me by the shoulder and pins me against it. His mouth descends on mine without warning. I kiss him with everything I have. How could I not? We were about to do a hell of a lot more in that office before Dominick dropped in. Theo pulls away from my lips resting his forehead against mine.

"It might be a while before I get to do that again. It sounds like you're going to be busy. I love you." I stand there taking in his words as he pushes the door behind me open, giving me no option but to exit.

I work my way back to the bar, without reacting to his words.

I love you.

Did he even realise he said that? I walk behind the bar in a daze, watching Theo join Wesley and a beautiful, petite redhead at Lucy's side of the bar.

I shake myself out of my stupor and make my way to Emmanuel. "Sorry about that. We had some crossed wires we needed to sort out." I'm not going to dump him in the middle of a packed bar.

He grabs my hand and presses his lips against it. I smell the spicy scent and turn to see Theo watching. I give him a smile to let him know everything is fine as I pull my hand from Emmanuel's grasp.

I hear the beginnings of a roar, a rumble coming from the back of a throat. It's coming from beside Emmanuel. I glance over to spot Jared.

Here comes World War Three.

I tap Misty on the shoulder as she pushes the drawer back in on the cash register. "I'm sorry I've been a pain in the arse tonight, but do you mind if I take Jared to one of the booths so I can get this chat over with?"

"Don't worry, ya can't help it. As long as war doesn't break out in my bar, I won't dock ya wages," she says with a grin, before heading off to serve another customer.

After hearing my conversation with Misty, Jared gets up and walks towards the tables.

I follow him to an empty booth, ignoring half a dozen eyes I can feel watching our every move. Not only are Emmanuel and Theo watching, but so are the pack members who are scattered throughout the bar.

"Okay. Jared, you wanted to talk, so talk!" I say before my butt even hits the seat. Once I'm sitting and my eyes connect with his. I can see the heartbreak in his eyes. Who am I kidding? I feel it too. Jared was the first person not related to me that actually loved me. He stood up for me when everyone else wanted me dead. He put his life on the line for me.

"Why did you follow me Jared? You know we can't be together. Your pride wants me dead. They won't let you lead if we are together. You were born to lead. I can't be the reason you don't."

He reaches across and wipes a tear from my cheek before grasping my hand on the table. "I love you, Bel. I needed to make sure you were safe. We're meant to be together. I would've left with you."

My wolf starts to pace inside me, agitated. She doesn't want him. She's always liked Jared. He protected us. I don't understand her change in heart.

I knew Jared would act like this. Putting his life on hold to protect me is what he does. "As you can see, I'm safe." I let go of his hand and lift my arms to gesture at my unharmed appearance. "You need to go home, Jared, back to your pride."

"Bel, we have been through this a million times. It's my father's Pride, not mine." His voice rises and everyone in the bar looks our way. The werewolves are no longer pretending not to be listening.

Seeing red, I stand up. *"Dammit Jared!"* Before I can even finish berating him, my wolf takes my temper and uses it to come through. I'm suddenly no longer a human but a wolf. I hadn't even felt the usual pain.

Growling at Jared, my front paws on the table and my snout in his face; I can see he's trembling, no doubt fighting his own change. But that doesn't stop me snarling.

Theo's calming energy alerts me of his presence.

"Rosabel. You're not going to rip Jared's throat out, are

you?" I can feel his alpha energy pushing at me to obey. As much as I don't like the thought of him being able to make me obey an order, it pushes my wolf back enough for my human half to realise the mistake I'm making. I don't want to rip Jared's throat out, especially not in Misty's bar.

I look into his concerned emerald eyes and rub my head against his hip. I jump down off the bench seat and lay down on the floor next to the table.

Theo sits in my vacated seat and begins talking to Jared in a hushed voice. I can feel the tension throughout the room—even though everyone has returned to their own conversations. Emmanuel is blatantly staring in our direction but not making a move to approach.

"Jared. I understand that you have protected Bel for a long time."

I growl, insulted at the fact that Theo is insinuating I needed protecting.

Theo ruffles my fur to calm me down. "We know she doesn't need protecting, but I'd like to thank you for keeping my true mate alive."

Jared's anger dissipates within seconds. I look at him to see defeat in the slump of his shoulders.

A whine leaves my throat as I rub my snout against his shin.

"Your true mate?"

Theo nods his head as he rests his chin on his steepled fingers. "If you choose to pursue her, I will have to take it as a challenge."

"If you really are her true mate, I have no right to challenge you. I love Bel. I wouldn't hurt her by challenging her true mate." Jared glances over his shoulder towards the bar before leaning further across the table towards Theo. "Why was she all cosy with the witch?"

Theo laughs. "Let's just say things have become a little complicated."

14

STALKER STATUS

*T*hings sure did get complicated.

My plans for tonight involved making it up to Bel for not being around since Paddy's disappearance, and relaxing with my mate.

As I sit opposite Bel's ex, I thank my lucky stars he's deciding to back off. It's not that I don't think I could handle taking him out in a duel but seeing us fight would be hard for Bel.

"I won't pursue, Bel, but I'm taking a break from the pride for a while. Both me and my father believe I need to see more of the world before I take over as leader so I'd like to stay in town if you'll allow it?"

He'd kept Bel alive for years. I owe him. I give permission with a nod.

Without a word, he stands and starts to leave. As he moves, I catch Paddy's scent in the air.

Within seconds I am up and have Jared pinned to the wall with my arm across his chest. Bel is growling beside me but I don't have time to deal with her. I need to find out why Jared has Paddy's scent on him.

"What the fuck?" Jared spits, looking at Bel; who is growling and baring her teeth to him. She would have caught Paddy's scent too.

I reach into my pocket and pull out one of the missing person flyers Alyssa had been pasting everywhere.

"Where did you see this guy?" I ask, shoving the flyer into

his chest. I quickly release him, needing to stay calm. I can feel the pack crowding in around us and I don't need them ripping into him before we get answers.

I watch with bated breath as Jared looks at the flyer closely before answering. "I've never seen this guy."

"You have his scent on you. Can you explain that?"

"I swear. I have never seen this guy. Maybe he brushed past me in the street. I've been knocked by so many people today, maybe it was transferred from someone else." I can sense the truth in his words.

I step back allowing him to exit.

"If you do see him, I'd appreciate it if you could let me or one of my wolves know."

"Of course." Jared exits the bar without glancing back at any of us.

After watching him leave, I crouch down and take Bel's head in my hands, making sure to scratch behind her ears. "As much as my wolf wants to come out and play with you, you really need to change back. You're putting the pack on edge." Her tongue darts out to lick my cheek. I stand and she stretches out but doesn't shift.

"You might want to take her somewhere private. She isn't keen on a public naked parade," Dominick announces from behind me. God. This guy is pissing me off; I shouldn't need a fucking vampire to tell me what my mate needs. If he hadn't stopped us earlier I would know what she needs and what she is thinking.

As I look apologetically at Bel, ready to lead her through to the office she silently shifts before my eyes.

I can't contain the growl leaving my throat. I didn't think this through. I don't want all these people seeing my mate naked, pack members or not. We may be used to nudity and don't always look at it sexually but I don't care.

I don't want them seeing her.

Billy must have read my mind because before her change is complete he hands me his full-length leather trench coat, which I cover her up with.

"Thanks," Bel says with a grin, as she pulls the coat around her.

I silently fasten the buttons and tie the belt saving her sensitive fingers the job.

Ed approaches, his eyes on the door Jared had just exited. "Should I follow him, Boss?"

I step back from Bel and turn towards Ed as I answer. "He was telling the truth. There's no need to follow him." Seeing the sadness in Eddie's eyes is tearing me apart. I reach out and pull him into a hug to comfort him. "He's alive, Ed. We can all feel him. I promise you we will get him back."

Emmanuel pushes past us and throws his arm over Bel's shoulder and pulls her in close to his side.

I release Ed and don't hide the fact that I'm listening to what Emmanuel has to say.

"Misty told me to take you home. Before you complain about leaving her in the lurch, Benji is going to work the rest of your shift."

Bel steps out from under Emmanuel's arm and wraps her arms around my waist. "Theo thanks for stopping me from losing it with Jared. He would never have let me live it down if I'd drawn blood."

"I'm Alpha; it's what I'm here for."

Standing on her tiptoes she stretches until her mouth is to my ear. "It was something a mate would do, too." Brushing her lips against my earlobe she lets me go, she leaves the bar without another word. Emmanuel follows closely behind her.

My wolf growls at the sight. She's my mate. Why am I standing here watching her leave with another guy in tow?

Fuck it. I'm not.

I leave Misty's in a rush, not caring what anyone thinks

about my rude departure. Once outside, I follow Bel's scent, sticking to the cover of the shadows from the buildings I pass. I feel like a stalker following them home but it's all I can do to keep my wolf calm. I'm not far behind them when I pick up their conversation.

"What is it like to shift?" Emmanuel asks.

"It varies. Depending on the situation. If you choose to do it, it can be great, therapeutic even. It's always painful to a degree, but again it varies depending on how much you need to change. Tonight for instance, I didn't feel a thing. My wolf was riding me too hard. Changing back can be embarrassing if you are in front of a crowd. It's not so bad if they are all weres. We see naked people all the time. We hardly ever notice it. But tonight I was in a bar full of witches and vampires too."

"How did Dominick know what you wanted?"

His mother fucking tie, that's how. Thankfully, I didn't say that out loud. My stalker status would be revealed if I had. I really don't need that getting out.

"When he drank from me, we formed a tie that gave him certain abilities. Materialising wherever I am is one, feeling my emotions is another. I am pretty sure that isn't all he has up his sleeve."

It's a quiet night out tonight and we seem to have the street to ourselves. I watch in the darkened doorway of the building next to Misty's apartment as Emmanuel kisses Bel. It isn't a lingering kiss but, nevertheless, my wolf doesn't like it.

Emmanuel waits, looking at the door expectantly.

Bel, you better not invite him up.

My wolf will not allow him to cross that threshold. My stalker status would well and truly be blown. Bel will already know I'm here. She'll be able to feel my energy. If the wind is blowing in the right direction she could probably catch my scent too, but Emmanuel will have no clue he's being watched.

"It's really not safe for you to come up tonight. My wolf is still on edge, she could easily take over at the slightest provocation."

More like I would kill the bastard.

"It's okay. I can control you."

I'm not at a good enough angle to see his face so I don't know what context he's saying it in, but regardless, I don't like the thought of him controlling my mate in any way, shape, or form. I force myself to stay still and calm.

"What do you mean? How can you control me?" Bel sounds wary.

Emmanuel looks around taking in his surroundings. He looks edgy. I don't know what he senses. I'm not picking anything out of the ordinary up. He's not happy about it—whatever it may be. "Forget I said anything." He glances at his watch before adding, "I've got to go now but can we meet for lunch tomorrow?" He's already retreating.

"Sure. Text me the details," Bel shouts after him.

I watch Bel walk into the building before pulling my new phone out and hitting the buttons to dial her number.

"Hello," she answers breathlessly. She must've run up the stairs.

"I thought he'd never leave."

"Same here, until something spooked him, that is."

"You caught that too?" I ask intrigued.

"I couldn't sense anything. Could you?"

I reach out once again, feeling for anything unusual that could have spooked him. Once again, I feel nothing.

"Not a damn thing," I reply as I start to pace on the pavement. No longer having the need to hide. My wolf is torn between needing to claim his mate and protecting her against whatever dangers lurk in the dark of the night.

"He's lucky you didn't invite him up. He wouldn't be breathing right now if you did. In fact, if I go solve that breathing problem, you could go out to lunch with me instead of him." If I am being honest that isn't a joke. I'd willingly kill him just so I could be with my mate.

"Be good. I need to go out with him to let him down gently. But if you come into Misty's tomorrow night you might get a repeat of our earlier kiss. A treat for being so good." The giggle I hear through the phone makes blood flow to what's beneath my zipper.

"Oh, well, that's me sold. I'll behave. That means I have to get off the phone though, because if I don't, I can't guarantee I'll deserve that kiss tomorrow." I know full well she can hear the arousal in my voice.

"Night then," her voice sounds all breathy before she cuts the connection.

I place my phone back in my pocket and force my feet to walk away from her building and back towards the bar.

I have a pack member to find.

15

FRIENDS

*A*fter waking up and getting dressed, I am ready to face the day. I walk through the apartment to the kitchen in the hope of finding some coffee. I can't believe I shifted in a bar full of customers. I'd taken Jared to the booth to save the customers from the dangers of anyone shifting, but I never thought I would be the danger. I'm usually calm and in control. It must be Theo and this mating thing that has my wolf in a tizzy.

I stop in my tracks when I see Benji on the couch. His bags are packed by his feet; his eyes are red and swollen indicating he's been crying for some time.

"Benji. What's wrong?" I dread his answer.

"Oh, Bel." He jumps off the couch and dives into my arms. I give him the hug I can see he needs—until he pulls away—all while wondering what the hell has him in this state. He sits back on the sofa as if he'd never moved.

I take a seat next to him before he speaks.

"Mum rang during the night. The Cleaners ambushed the pride during the hunt. Dad was injured. He's out of danger now but Mum needs me. She wants me back in the protection of the pride. I have to go home."

I can't stop the tears running down my cheeks. Uncle Jack has always treated me like his own. If it wasn't for him teaching me how to fight once he took me in, I would never have survived my first fight. Jared may have helped keep me alive by fighting for me, but Uncle Jack is the original hero.

"When do we leave?" It's not a question of whether I go. Aunt Lillian and Uncle Jack need me. I might not be pride, but my family is, and they need all the help they can get.

"*We* don't. I do. You have too much here. You have to stay. You've found your home with Theo and his pack. Claim it. If the Cleaners are still hanging round the pride, it's too dangerous for you to return. You know the pride would trade you in for their safety in a heartbeat."

Knowing he's right, I won't argue. "I'm going to miss you. Sorry we haven't been able to do much while you've been here. I promise, when you come back I'll show you everything this town has to offer. You are coming back aren't you?"

"I'll come and visit again, but it was never going to be permanent. I love you, but you need to find out who you are—what it means to be a wolf. I don't belong in that life," he says sadly.

"I love you, too, Benj." I can't say anything else without bursting into tears, but I don't need to add more. He knows everything I'm unable to say.

We walk down to the street and find a taxi already waiting for him. I give him one last hug as the driver puts his bags in the boot.

"Thank Misty for me. I'll ring you when I arrive," he says, turning his back to me and getting in the car.

"Of course. Give Aunt Lil and Uncle Jack a hug from me," I say, closing the door on him.

I glance at my watch and wave to the car as it drives into the distance, noticing that I only have ten minutes before I'm supposed to be at the cafe Emmanuel text me last night. I dash upstairs to grab my purse, phone, and shoes.

Finding the apartment quiet and seeing no sign of Misty, I decide to leave her a quick note explaining about Benji, telling her where I am going and that I will see her at work, if not sooner. There are people going missing left, right, and centre.

You don't need to be a brain surgeon to realise it's best to have someone know where you are heading and when you should be back.

I close the cafe door behind me and look around the greasy spoon cafe for Emmanuel. There are fifteen booths on either side of a narrow aisle and it doesn't take me long to notice him sitting at the furthest booth on the right. I recognise the Motown music playing quietly. Uncle Jack is a huge Motown fan. Being lunchtime, there are only a couple of free tables.

Probably thinking I haven't seen him, Emmanuel waves. It's pretty hard to miss his big frame, but I guess he might forget that.

I take a deep breath to ground myself, preparing for what I need to do. As I start to make my way towards him I get a strong whiff of Paddy's scent. I glance around. One of the customers must have been in contact with Paddy recently. One of them could be the kidnapper. There must be twenty people in here plus staff. There is no way I can pinpoint the culprit without an interrogation.

Taking another deep breath, I focus on my empathy to I see if I can pick up any suspicious emotions. I don't hold much hope because unless they are focused on the kidnapping at this very minute they are probably feeling happy about their food, which means I won't be able pick up on the bad stuff.

As expected, I find nothing.

Thinking the scent could be cross-contamination, I decide to focus on one thing at a time and get this thing between me and Emmanuel finished.

Ever the gentleman, Emmanuel stands as I reach the table.

He leans over and kisses my cheek and we take seats opposite each other.

"Rosabel. Is everything okay? I can't help but notice you looked a little distracted."

"Benji left this morning. There has been an attack on the pride. That's playing on my mind," I say, plastering a reassuring smile on my face. It's only partly a lie.

The waitress comes to a stop at our table, halting our conversation. Her pen poised on her pad ready to take our orders. "Whatchahaving?" she asks, mashing her words together. Next time someone complains about Misty's accent I'll remember to send them here to Trudy.

I quickly look at the menu that Emmanuel pushes across to me.

"I'll have a hamburger and tea, please," he says.

I order the first thing I see. "Chicken salad and a coffee for me, please." Coffee is no-brainer since I didn't get one this morning.

Once the waitress leaves, Emmanuel reaches over the table and grabs a hold of my hand. "You should've told me you were being bothered by your ex. I could have warned him off."

I don't want to make him feel insignificant by reminding him that Jared is a were-lion and wouldn't take a blind bit of notice of a witch. I decide to brush it off. "It's sorted now. Don't worry about it."

"Yes. He won't be bothering you anymore," Emmanuel says, grinning up at me. Anyone looking at him would think he chased Jared off, not Theo.

My mobile starts vibrating in my pocket. I pull it out of my pocket and look at the screen to see a number I don't recognise. I glance at Emmanuel apologetically. His sort of smile and barely nod don't deter me from answering it anyway. It could be someone from the pride about Uncle Jack.

"Hello?" I answer warily

"Is that Rosabel?" If it wasn't for the pure fear I could hear in the person's voice, I would suspect it was a stupid telesales call.

"Yes. Who is this?"

"Wesley. Have you seen her?" He's so anxious, my empathy doesn't work over the phone but it's pretty easy to pick up from his tone. I have no idea who he is talking about.

I put as much authority into my voice as I can muster. "Wesley. You need to calm down and explain what is going on, slowly and clearly."

I can hear him take a deep breath and then the line is silent.

I give him a full minute of silence before speaking again. "Welsey. Are you still there?"

"Yes," he says, sounding unbelievably calm. It's like he's a different person to the one who called. "It's Alyssa, my mate. She's gone missing. Have you seen her?"

"I don't think so. What does she look like? I don't think I know who she is."

"MY MATE!" His yell is loud enough that even Emmanuel hears him. He reaches for my phone but I swat his hand and lean away. I can handle being yelled at by a distraught werewolf.

"Shouting at me won't help, Wes."

I can hear Theo in the background. "Who are you shouting at now, Wesley? I was sure you had scared everyone in the pack as it is."

"Wesley, put Theo on the phone. He'll be able to explain the situation better."

I hear a few noises as if the phone is changing hands, along with Wesley's muttering to himself. "My fucking mate is missing. That's the goddamn situation."

"Hello." I would recognise that gravelly voice any day.

"Hi, Theo. What does Alyssa look like and how did she go

missing?" Wes doesn't seem like the type to let his mate out of his sight if he didn't think it was safe.

"Bel." He sounds surprised to hear my voice. "I told him you wouldn't know who she was, let alone what might have happened to her. She was at Misty's last night. She's about your height with long, red curly hair. Sometime during your time as being a wolf, she went to the ladies room and never came back."

"Sorry. The only time I saw her was when we came back from the office. She was at the bar with Wesley. I didn't see anything on the way home."

"I know. I followed you remember? I didn't see anything and told him as much. There was no need for him to bother you." I can hear the anger in his voice.

"It's okay, he's just worried. Do you think it could be the person that took the vamps and Paddy?" I smile apologetically at Emmanuel, assuming he must be pissed that I'm on the phone on our date. He doesn't even acknowledge my smile. He's too engrossed in my side of the conversation to notice.

"Unfortunately, it's looking that way. She wouldn't just leave and not be in touch with anyone by now. Even when they argue and she storms out she always tells him where she is going." Theo's voice is full of concern.

The waitress arrives with our food and drinks. Emmanuel tucks straight into his burger.

"God. I hope you find her." If it is the same person that took the others someone needs to do something about them. They can't be invisible. Someone has got to have seen something. I would hate to be Theo right now. As alpha, it all lands on his shoulders.

"We will find them all. I won't have it any other way! In the meantime, will you make me a promise? Ring me every hour to check in. I need to know you're safe. I couldn't bear you being taken," he says, with a voice full of honesty.

"They won't be interested in me, I'm not pack." I stab a piece of lettuce with my fork and slide it in my mouth as I listen to his reply.

"You are my mate and that makes you pack. If anyone is trying to get to me that makes you on the top of their list. The tie to Dominick could make them interested too. They've taken two of his vamps so they could be trying to get to him too. I don't like the thought of that. Maybe I should put a guard on you." The last sentence was said more to himself.

I agree quickly. "I promise. I will check in every hour."

I don't want a guard on me.

"WESLEY!" he shouts away from the phone. "Bel, I've got to go, Wesley is picking a fight, with Chloe, of all people."

"Bye," I say to the dial tone. I place my phone on the table and have a large swig of coffee.

"I'm guessing another pack member has gone missing," Emmanuel states.

I chew a mouthful of chicken before answering. "Yeah, last night. I don't know what Theo is going to do but it isn't going to be good for whoever is taking them—not when he finds them."

He turns the conversation to mindless banter as I finish the rest of my meal. The waitress collects our empty plates. "Can I get you anything else?"

I need to end this with Emmanuel—whatever *this* is.

"Another coffee, please?" I reply, with a nod.

She looks at Emanuel for his order. "Nothing for me, thanks."

I wait until the waitress places my coffee in front of me and leaves again before talking. "Look, Emmanuel. I don't know how to say this, or where to start, so I am just going to be blunt and honest, okay?"

"O-k-a-y?" He sounds wary.

"I think it would be better if we are just friends. You know about me and Theo being true mates? Well—"

He cuts me off before I can finish my sentence. "That's just your wolves. They're only a part of you. Not all of you."

"That's not how mates work, Emmanuel. We are meant for each other on all levels. We are the missing piece of each other. I didn't know any of this until yesterday. I just can't feel anything other than friendship towards you and you deserve more than that from a relationship."

He stares at me dumbfounded.

I don't know what else to say so I offer him my hand in a handshake over the table. "So…friends?"

He glances down at my hand. I can feel anger emanating from him but he takes it with a false smile. "Friends."

This is, no doubt, going to bite me on the arse later but for now, I'll take it as a win.

16

ALLIES ATTACK

s we open up at work I fill Misty in on Benji leaving, and my decision about Emmanuel. I was worried about how she'd react because he is her friend, but thankfully, she agreed that I'd done the right thing by him.

I was just going out the back door with my arms full of rubbish bags when I get hit by a wall of anger. I can't see over the bag so I use my other sense, smell. Taking a deep breath, I pick up three scents; Dominick's, Paddy's, and a female werewolf I don't recognise.

Letting the bags down as quietly as possible, I slowly creep out deeper into the alleyway. It takes me a moment to comprehend what exactly I'm seeing. Paddy and Alyssa have both jumped Dominick. Alyssa is on his back and Paddy is attacking him from the front.

Dominick grunts as Alyssa claws at his neck with her nails. He flings her off and she hits a bin with a thud. He then turns his focus on Paddy, pushing him away. I can see he's trying not to hurt them. He could easily kill them if he wasn't holding back. He isn't the King of the New South Wales vampires for nothing.

Within seconds, there are no longer three people in the alley before me. There are two great big wolves and Dominick. They both pounce at him again, but he's still not fighting back. I watch as they both start tearing chunks out of his limbs.

I can't just stand and watch this.

I quickly remove my clothes, not wanting them destroyed

as I shift. If I get through this fight in one piece I don't really want to have to walk into Misty's naked. Once my wolf comes forward, she takes me through the shift fairly quickly. I don't have time to get hung up on the pain. I need to help Dominick.

I run at Alyssa and sink my teeth into the fur on her back. I manage to pull her off Dominick, flinging her a good three feet away. I take a second to hope Dominick can handle Paddy on his own before readying myself in a crouch to pounce at her.

I watch as she mirrors my crouch. Her back legs brace to pounce only she doesn't. She freezes and just stares at me. I reach out for her emotions hoping to get some clue as to why she hasn't followed through the attack, only to feel nothing. She isn't feeling one single emotion. As I'm staring her down trying to decide what to do, she turns and sprints away.

I watch her run until she is out of sight. I don't want her changing her mind and coming back for a surprise attack while my back is turned. Happy that she isn't returning, I turn to help Dominick against Paddy, only to find Dominick in a heap on the floor and Paddy tearing at his body as if it was a delicious deer. Surely vampires don't taste *that* good. Their stink makes me gag enough I don't want to attempt tasting them.

I growl to get Paddy's attention as I stalk towards him. He'll probably think I am after his meal and defend it, taking his attention away from what's left of Dominick and focusing solely on me. We are very territorial over our food. Only once he sees me, he chooses to leave his meal and retreat in the same direction Alyssa had.

I trot over to Dominick and nudge his face with my muzzle.

"I'll be okay once I feed," Dominick mumbles.

I lick one of the wounds on his arm and regret it instantly, *bloody animal instincts*. I was correct, vampires taste as bad as they smell. I feel a grip of steel around my left flank. I turn and get a glimpse of another vampire before I am soaring through the air.

"*No!*" yells Dominick.

There is nothing I can do to stop the momentum. I hit the side of a building with a thud and a loud crack sounds in my ears as I'm propelled into darkness.

I slowly start to come around. I can hear a mumbling but can't make out what exactly is being said. I concentrate trying to recognise the voice. Dominick.

"She saved me you idiot! I'd be dead if not for her, and what do you do? Thank her by throwing her at a brick wall." I feel hands roam my body, looking for injuries.

"Sorry, boss. Look. She's waking up," says a voice I don't recognise.

"Rosabel. Can you hear me? It's Dominick." The hands on my body stop roaming to gently cradle my face.

I slowly open my eyes and find Dominick centimetres away from my face. All I can see is the deep endless pools of black that are his eyes. I know you're not meant to look a vampire in the eyes because they can take over your mind and enslave you, but I can't seem to tear my eyes away. His eyes are just so beautiful.

"You need to change back to your human form so we can see what injuries you have," Dominick says with surprising concern.

I close my eyes and try to ignore the pain in my head. I concentrate with everything I have to push my wolf back and return to my human form. Thankfully she doesn't fight and the change is fairly painless. I open my eyes and can no longer see my furry snout.

Dominick is standing with his trench coat spread out around me. I stay tightly curled to try and hide my nakedness. He nudges a pile of clothes towards me with the toe of his shiny dress shoes.

"Here. I got your clothes. Get dressed. No one can see." I

look at him with a frown, "Okay. No one except me, but I've seen it now so there is no point in turning around."

I guess he has a point.

I slowly sit up, which is not a good idea. Everything starts to spin and the nausea hits. I *need* to get dressed. I try to ignore the spinning and nausea, but have you ever tried to get dressed when the world is spinning? It is such a hard task to get your limbs into the right holes in your clothing when they won't stay still. Somehow, I finally manage to get fully dressed.

Dominick drops his arms and secures his coat once again. I see the vampire that threw me at the wall standing behind Dominick. He's tall, lanky, and wearing a neon yellow t-shirt under a black leather waistcoat with black leather trousers that leave nothing to the imagination. I'm surprised the lack of circulation doesn't cause permanent damage. His short bleached blonde hair and blue eyes remind me of Spike from the TV show Buffy. The more I stare at him, the more I realise he is attractive in his own way.

"I'm sorry about that." He shrugs, pointing to the wall that's now decorated with a nice crack in the mortar. "I thought you were attacking, Dominick."

I suddenly remember the state Dominick was in before I hit the wall. I glance at him, now standing tall and looking as strong as ever. If I hadn't just witnessed the fight and seen the state he was in, not to mention the tears in his clothing, I wouldn't believe he'd been in a fight.

"How do you look so good? You looked like death warmed up a minute ago." Realising who and what I am talking to I quickly add, "Well, you know what I mean."

Dominick looks over to where he had been in a heap on the floor. My gaze follows his and falls upon a woman who seems to be staring at Dominick, smiling as though she is getting high just looking at him. The sight of her is quite disturbing.

I quickly look back at Dominick. "Where did she come from?"

"When Chomp saw the state I was in, he extracted her from the street." I'm guessing Lanky Leathers is Chomp. Interesting name choice.

I can't stop myself from glancing back at the woman. "Will she be okay? She looks a little…high." I couldn't think of a better word, maybe star-struck would have been more fitting.

"She's fine. It's the compulsion. I didn't have time to let her go; I needed to check on you. Chomp, you may release her now."

Chomp follows his order immediately, kneeling down in front of the woman. I watch as he turns her face from looking at Dominick, when their eyes meet she gazes at him for no longer than thirty seconds before becoming a normal person. She takes Chomp's hand, politely thanks him and walks away without a glance in our direction.

Dominick's hand appears in front of me and I reluctantly take it. I don't think I would manage to get up otherwise.

My head pounds. I put my free hand to my head hoping I can't feel my brain falling out. Satisfied it all feels normal, I pull my hand away to see it covered in blood. That means I'm not going to be able to go straight back to work. At the very least, I need a shower and change of clothes first.

The three of us walk in the back door of Misty's. Dominick is practically holding me up, my jelly legs aren't much use. Not only is Misty going to kill me for having to go home for a shower and change, but she's going to dance on my grave for bringing customers through the back door.

As we walk through the door leading into the bar, Misty catches sight of me and gasps.

"Bloody hell! What happened to you?" she asks.

The whole bar suddenly falls silent and I know without

looking around, that every eye in the bar is on me. I must look as bad as I feel.

Theo comes running over from the far end of the bar.

"LET HER GO!" he yells. "What the hell did you do to her?"

"If I let go of her, she will probably fall down and I didn't do anything to her. You need to speak to some of your wolves. She wouldn't be injured if they hadn't attacked me." I hear the smugness in his voice. No doubt his face looks just as smug.

Theo gently pulls me away from Dominick and into his own embrace. "What the hell are you talking about?"

"Theo, he's right. I was there." Turning in his arms, I tell him everything that happened in the alley.

While Theo takes it all in we move to a booth, and Dominick gives us his theory. "It looks to me like your wolves have gone rogue, oh mighty alpha."

"Dammit Drake. Now is not the time for jokes," Theo chastises. "Alyssa wouldn't be able to go rogue. She's mated to Wesley. When you're mated you have that other wolf's energy connected to your own. The only way a mated wolf could go rogue is if both of them go rogue."

As if summoned by the mention of his name, Wesley charges into the bar, aiming straight for our table.

"ALYSSA! What's happened to Alyssa? Her scent is all over the two of you," he growls accusingly.

"Wesley. You're lucky they didn't do anything to her. She attacked them." Theo's voice is full of authority, making it hard to argue with.

"No. She wouldn't do that," Wes says unbelievingly, yet defeated, his Alpha wouldn't lie to him.

"Whether she would or she wouldn't, she did. We need to find out why? Go see if you can track her scent out the back. That's where it all happened. Billy, go with him," Theo orders.

Billy appears out of nowhere, but more-than-likely he was

somewhere else in the bar, listening in to the conversation, like all the other wolves were.

As they exit through the back of the bar, a grief-stricken Emmanuel enters through the front doors. He glances around looking for someone. His eyes land on me, widening in horror. He barges through the pack members surrounding the table all while muttering, "I'm sorry."

Please don't let him be here to beg for us to try again. I really don't need that while my head is pounding, especially not in front of the bar full of the pack.

He crouches down beside me and reaches for my face, gently caressing my head wound.

"I just heard. You shouldn't be hurt." Turning his attention to Theo, who is still holding me against his warm body. "What good are you as her mate if you can't protect her? Let alone from your own wolves."

"Emmanuel!" I jump to Theo's defence.

"No, Bel. He's right. You should never have come to harm and from my own pack members. Forgive me," Theo says, placing a kiss on the uninjured side of my head.

"There is nothing to forgive," I say, giving him a peck on the lips and not caring who sees. "Paddy and Alyssa didn't hurt me. I can't say the same for Dominick though."

"But your head, and all the blood?" Emmanuel asks, drawing my attention back to him.

"That's my fault," Chomp admits, stepping up to the table beside Dominick. "She's lucky the new law came in saying only Dominick or Theodore can kill another supernatural being because I would have killed her otherwise."

Theo's hand, resting on my waist, gently squeezes. "I'm taking you home; you need to get cleaned up."

I look towards Misty who is still serving behind the bar. She is just hanging the phone back on the wall bracket. "I'll be real quick, Misty."

"Don't even try it. You can't work with a concussion. You're not coming back in tonight. Lucy is on her way." I return the smile she is giving me and Theo gently lifts me into his arms.

"I can walk," I complain, not sounding too convincing. I quite like being held in my mates strong arms.

"Don't argue!" he demands, making his way through the bar doors and towards his gorgeous car. He opens the car door while holding me with one arm. That's werewolf strength for you. We can bench press a car. He's not going to have trouble holding me in one arm. He places me in the passenger seat and buckles me in. I don't complain, knowing his wolf will need the reassurance.

Just as he indicates to pull away from the curb, the Bad Boys theme song starts playing. He turns the indicator off and puts the car back in neutral before reaching into his jeans pocket and taking his phone out. He answers it without looking at the screen. "Hello."

I stare straight ahead out the windscreen, trying my hardest to give him privacy and not listen in on the conversation. With my hearing I can hear the other side of the conversation, no matter how hard I try, and he knows it. His hearing is just the same.

"Theo. I'm scared. I think someone is outside." The sexy female voice on the other end of the phone makes me forget all about not listening. If he wanted a private conversation, he would end the call and ring back after he has dropped me off at home.

"Chloe. I've told you that place has the best security system invented, so even if someone is outside, they won't be getting in."

"Oh, okay. How long are you staying out? I'll feel safer once I'm not alone."

He sighs and glances at me. I don't know what he is trying to read in my face but it makes me feel uncomfortable.

I quickly turn away and look out my window.

"I'm just taking Rosabel home. I won't be long."

"Thank you. I'll see you soon," she sings through the phone.

Theo hangs up with no goodbye, putting his phone back in his pocket. Expecting him to put the car in gear and pull away from the curb I get a shock when he just sits there, rubbing a hand over his face. I feel a wave of sadness coming off him.

"Sorry about that. Some of the pack members are worried about the kidnapper. Chloe lives on her own. My home is the pack's home. They're all welcome to come and go as they please. She's staying until things become safer."

I start to feel a bit jealous, I don't like the fact that Chloe, of all people, is staying at Theo's, especially since she's the one that said she should be his mate. I hear Theo chuckle and realise the car is full of my mating scent.

Great. Could that have not been kept a secret?

"Don't worry, she's got no chance. I'm yours, remember?" He says as he leans across the console and gives me a chaste kiss. I can smell his arousal and realise he's aroused by my jealousy. His body starts releasing his mating scent too.

We both laugh because it looks like we are both as bad as each other.

17

POTENT STEAM

I can't help but be aroused by her jealousy. When Emmanuel made the comment about me being no good because I can't protect her from my own pack members, I didn't think her wolf would forgive me. I know she said she did, but to know that she's jealous makes me believe it that much more.

This beautiful woman sitting next to me in my car is actually my mate.

Mine!

I pull back from the kiss, not too far. I might want to take her lips again in a more passionate kiss. "Tell you what, why don't you come back to mine? You can shower there and I am sure I can find some clothes for you to wear," I suggest, grinning.

"Will I need clothes?" she asks with a cheeky smile, knowing exactly what her words are doing to me.

"Be careful. I might hold you to that," I warn, unable to hold the rasp in my voice back.

It doesn't take me long to drive us home.

We walk in the door to be greeted by Chloe in a lacy number that doesn't leave much to the imagination. How dare she prance around my house wearing that? I have a mate. What does she think will come of her meeting me at the door wearing something like that?

I smell Bel's mating scent and can't contain my anger.

"PUT SOME CLOTHES ON!" I shout.

Bel squeezes the hand she is holding and rubs her thumb over the back of my hand in a calming gesture.

I quieten my voice. "I don't appreciate you walking around my home half-naked, Chloe."

She turns and storms upstairs without another word, but not before giving Bel a deathly glare.

"Well. I give her a ten for trying," Bel jokes. If she can joke about it I can calm down.

I remind myself that this is the first time Bel and I have had some time together. With people going missing left, right, and centre, we need to make the most of it. It will only be a matter of time before something comes up. Hopefully one of my guys will get a lead on the damn kidnapper because my wolf sure does want someone to pay.

I lead Bel into the one room I know we won't get disturbed in—unless it's an emergency. Let me tell you, if someone does disturb us, someone better be dying. I lead her to my bedroom. I am not wild in my paint taste. It's just a good ol' cream. I like the bed being a focal point. That's what a bedroom is all about, after all. Glancing at the bed I am grateful for the clean black satin sheets I put on this morning but I'm starting to regret bringing her in here. My wolf wants to claim her. He always wants to claim her but seeing the bed is making him ride me harder.

I close the door behind us and show her straight to the bathroom trying to ignore the bed and my impatient wolf.

"Wow. That is some spa bath," Bel says, looking at my extra-large spa bath. It takes up most of the left hand side of the room.

I shrug at her comment. "I'm a large guy and I like a big bath."

I walk over to the two-headed shower and turn it on. I renovated this bathroom after my ex left, always keeping the idea of a mate in mind. What good is a shower if you can't fit two people in it?

"I'll just get you some clothes while that warms up," I say, heading back into the room to go through my chest of drawers and find a t-shirt and some boxers that will be suitable.

I can feel Bel's eyes on me, as she watches me while leaning against the doorjamb.

Once back in the bathroom, I grab a towel from under the sink and place the items on the bench next to the sink. Steam is filling the room and my wolf is getting antsy thinking about her being naked in the shower. I can smell her arousal so I know she is thinking along the same lines as me. I need to get out of here before I pin her in the shower. I try to remind myself she has had a knock to the head. It's not the right time to be pinning her anywhere.

"I'll be just outside. If you need anything, give me a shout," I say, quickly escaping the steam and the smell of her arousal.

I pace the room, having way too much energy to sit still. I chant to myself. "You will *not* go in there."

She deserves more than a claiming in a shower.

She deserves romance and sweet gentle love making.

"You will *not* go in there."

Bel's mating scent comes out from the crack under the bathroom door.

Oh fuck it!

I can't hold back anymore.

It's time to claim my mate.

18

VANISHING ACT

I look in the mirror and see what a mess I am. I remove my clothes, wondering why Theo wasn't aroused by Chloe when we came in. She is gorgeous, and as much as I hate her, I can't deny it.

The room fills with my mating scent. It mixes with the steam of the shower, making it even headier. I step under the shower head and close my eyes, enjoying the feel of the water running over my face and body.

I feel a slight draft and open my eyes to find I am no longer alone. My eyes hungrily take in a very naked Theo before me.

"Do you mind if I join you? I thought I could scrub your back." He reaches around me for the soap with the cheekiest smirk on his face, knowing full well from my scent there is no way I'm going to say no. I am even more turned on now by his naked body pressing against me.

I pull the bottle of shampoo from behind my back and wiggle it in front of him. "You better start from the top and work your way down."

"Of course," he remarks, as he takes the bottle and pours some into his hand.

He carefully works the shampoo into my hair so he doesn't hurt my injured head. The shift helped it heal a little and with every minute that passes it is healing more. It will be fully healed by morning. The water turns a rusty colour as it runs down my body and into the drain.

He lathers his hands with the soap. Knowing he's going to

be rubbing them over my body makes it look erotic. I bite my lip in anticipation. I don't have to wait long. His hands start at my shoulders and work their way to my chest. He bends his head and latches onto a nipple. A growl comes from deep within me. My wolf's energy pounces out of me and latches onto Theo's wolf.

Theo straightens and I follow my wolf, pouncing at him. He catches me and I wrap my legs around his waist as my hands go to his hair. The feel of his hard arousal pressing against the exact spot I want him sets me on fire. He takes my mouth with his not caring about finesse, biting my lip to gain entry.

I can't help grinding myself against him. I can't believe I am acting like a hussy, but I need him. He's my mate and I need to claim him. He spins us around and presses me against the shower screen.

Everything starts to spin and I feel dizzy. The room passes by in a blur of colours, which start to change slightly as the spinning starts to slow, until it's normal again.

Only it isn't normal, because I am no longer in Theo's arms.

As I look around the strange room I find myself in, I start to panic. The arousal I had in the shower is long gone. It's obvious by the grand heavy wood desk in the middle of the room and leather chair behind it that it's someone's office. Someone with very expensive tastes, if the magnificent wall tapestries hanging to cover the stone walls are anything to go by.

As I get closer to the desk I can see what looks like a robe with a note on top. Reading the exquisite handwriting and seeing my name I pick up the note and read the rest.

My Saviour Rosabel,

I thought you would appreciate the robe, so you could be covered before I enter.

Forever in your debt.

— DOMINICK FILIOUS DRACONIS

Of course, Dominick would be at the root of this.

Just as I am tying the robe closed the door behind me opens and Dominick barely enters the room before I start demanding answers.

"How the hell did I get here and what have you done with Theo?" I shout as I poke him in the chest.

"Calm down, my saviour. I have done nothing to your lover. He remains where you left him. All be it, he may be slightly concerned about your whereabouts." He pauses and I open my mouth to yell some more, but he carries on, "You teleported here because I called you here. I wanted to tell you that I will allow you to claim your lover, even though it will break the tie between us. Think of it as a gift for saving me tonight."

"You pompous ass! Why didn't you just leave us to it?"

"I wanted you to know it was a gift. I thought you would prefer me to do it before rather than during the afterglow," he says, with a smirk that I would love to slap off his face.

I pace away from him trying to rein in my anger. The pacing helps me think.

"You wouldn't have been able to do it after because the tie would be broken. That's why you did it now."

"Oh, Bel. It isn't the tie that enabled me to call you here. You have turned out to be a very interesting creature indeed. You see, Chomp has a very specific taste in blood. He loves a Druid and you have druid blood in your veins. As a druid you can teleport and be called upon, once you learn how to control it you will be able to choose whether or not to go when called."

"Bullshit! I don't know any druids. My parents were both werewolves." I storm back towards him.

"I know nothing of your kin, but I trust Chomp's word and

to have druid blood you must have one somewhere in your ancestry."

"Fine. I'm a druid werewolf. You have informed my about the gift. Send me the fuck back. NOW!" I scream.

Dominick steps around me and casually takes a seat behind his desk. "I can't send you back, only you can do that. I *can* talk you through it though."

"Let me get this straight. You brought me here knowing I knew nothing about these druid abilities and how to harness them?" I ask in disbelief.

"You are forgetting I can teleport myself, too. It may be from a different source but essentially it is the same ability. You just have to visualise where you want to be. See every detail, smell every scent, and will yourself to be there."

I take him at his word and do as he says. Closing my eyes I try to visualise Theo's room but I'm so angry, the only thing I can manage to picture is me slogging Dominick with a good left hook.

Taking a deep breath and clearing my mind, I try again and again with no luck. My mind is now too blank.

I can do this.

I once again close my eyes and picture the steamy bathroom —the two man shower along one wall and the huge Jacuzzi in the corner. I smell Theo's scent filling the room and mingling with my own. I feel the steam in the air caressing my skin, and finally I will myself to be there.

I know I am there before I even open my eyes. I can feel the smooth slate tiles under my feet and I can actually smell Theo's scent. I can't believe it, there was no spinning this time around. Excited to be back it takes me a moment to notice that the shower is no longer running and I'm the only person in the room.

I run through his empty bedroom and down the stairs, in a panic, screaming his name.

"THEO? THEO!"

I come to a halt as I enter the dining room, which happens to be jam packed with Theo's pack. Every head in the room turns to face me as Theo barges through the crowd wearing nothing but sweatpants. He doesn't give me long to take in the sight. He reaches me in a heartbeat and pulls me into his bare chest.

"Bel. Am I ever glad to see you. One minute you were in my arms, the next you were just…gone. I thought…" he didn't need to finish, I can imagine what he thought. *The kidnapper.* He squeezes me harder. I breathe in his scent. It feels good to be back in his arms. My wolf wants to dig her way under his skin. She wants to become part of him.

"What happened? Where did you go?" His fear fading with me in his arms, I can now hear and feel the anger behind it. So much anger, not knowing who is to blame must be hard for him. He is an alpha. He's meant to protect his people. Someone just ripped me out of his arms and he needs to punish them.

I pull back a little to look in his eyes. "Can I speak to you in private?"

I let my eyes roam the room full of pack members to get my point across. I don't really want to tell him everything I have just learned in front of the whole pack. I'm back where I started in Quilpie with Jared. I'm the odd one out again, not worthy of him. The minute they find out, they will push me out. I won't be good enough for their alpha. Some of them already think that due to my upbringing with the pride, essentially Chloe. Chloe is going to love this bit of news.

He leads me back to his room with a hand on my lower back.

Once in his room I gesture towards his bed. "You might want to be sitting for this."

He follows my suggestion without argument and I recall everything that occurred since I left his arms in the shower. I wait for him to take it all in. I start to fiddle with the hem of the robe. He's taking too long to answer. I'm going to have to walk past the pack, humiliated.

Just as I am about to go and get the clothes he was lending me from the bathroom, he speaks.

"A druid werewolf? Okay." It sounds more like a statement to himself but I answer him anyway.

"Yes. If you just give me a minute to get dressed, I'll leave." I head towards the bathroom willing to wear my blood stained clothes, as long as I can just get away quickly. I only manage two steps before he grabs my shoulder and spins me to face him once again.

"Why do you want to leave?" I can feel the worry coming off him in waves. It matches what I see in his eyes.

"I don't want to leave but I understand you will want me to. I'm part druid, I'm not werewolf enough for you," I say, as I try to pull away from his hold.

"There is nothing I want more than to throw you on that bed and make love to you. You are my mate, my other half. I always thought that was a corny thing men said to women to keep them happy, but the second I met you I just knew. It doesn't matter what you are. You were made for me. It means you are more than enough for me."

He cups my face and presses his lips against mine. My wolf pounces on that kiss, her energy pressing for more. I kiss him like it's the last kiss I will ever have. His hands move down my body to my waist. He picks me up and throws me on the bed. I bounce once before he lands over me.

Are we finally going to do this? *With the Pack downstairs.*

"But the Pack?" I say, unsure about whether we should be keeping them waiting.

He gives the tie on my robe a tug and I can feel the cool air caress my skin as I become exposed. He grins down at me. "The Pack can wait."

19

LOYALTY

*L*ying next to my mate—my well and truly claimed mate —I could easily get used to being curled into his side, stroking his chest hairs as he plays with strands of my hair. I don't think my wolf has ever felt this calm or content.

Theo's energy suddenly changes from the blissful energy that was just flowing through the both of us to something that feels like fear. Before I can break the silence to ask him about it, he clears his throat.

"I was terrified earlier. I thought the kidnapper was behind your disappearance. I ran around the house like a lunatic. When you were nowhere to be found I thought I had lost you before I'd even really had you. I have never felt like that before. I have never been that terrified. Not in battle facing death myself. Not when my father was killed, not even when I became alpha. Never." He holds me tighter against him and I squeeze back hoping to comfort him and decide to get my thoughts about the kidnapper off my chest.

We could be looking at the wrong suspect.

"I've been thinking. Why are you so sure the kidnapper is a vampire or werewolf? Couldn't it be any supernatural creature, maybe a druid or a witch?" I ask, leaning up to look at him.

"It could be a druid but we haven't had any around town for a long time. I still can't see how a witch could overpower them if they are controlling them in some way? I don't know of a spell that could do that. They would have to be channelling something dark to be able to strip people of free will. It's not a white witch power like most of the witches in town practise."

Discussing the kidnapper and the pack reminds me that they all remain downstairs. "Do you want to go and deal with your pack? We've kept them waiting a while." I giggle, picking my words carefully so as not to sound like an order. No one gives orders to the alpha.

"*Our* Pack. We are true mates. You are the Alpha female. And you're right, they have waited long enough. We should go put them out of their misery," he says, patting me on the butt.

I shift, allowing him to get out of the bed.

He pulls on the sweatpants he removed earlier and grabs a t-shirt out of a drawer. He throws another at me along with a pair of shorts. They hit me in the face and I hear Theo laugh as I breathe in the scent on his shirt.

We both pad down the stairs barefoot, hands entwined. The bond from our mating is like nothing I could ever have imagined. I can feel him deep within me, like a comfortable blanket wrapped around my soul. I'm aware of his feelings, his contentment somewhat like my own, but it's nothing like my empathy; it's more internal than that. The pack are there, too. I can't pick out any specific members but I can feel them as a whole.

We walk through the lounge with the L-shaped sofas and I glance at them longingly. Theo must notice because he stops, questioning me by just the look on his face.

"Maybe I could just stay here while you talk to the pack?"

He shakes his head and smiles. "No. You *are* Pack remember. You have to face them eventually."

"Oh, fine," I concede.

I tug his hand for him to lead me into the dining room where the pack await us. Before opening the door, he pulls me into his arms and kisses my forehead, giving me time to take a calming breath. The deep breath I take is filled with his scent;

calming me even more. I love how he can read me now and know exactly what I need.

"Thank you," I say, pecking him on the lips. I reach around him and open the door.

In our absence, the pack has gathered in groups to chat. Some sit, some stand, and some lean against the furniture that is in the middle of the room. Theo stops and stands in the doorway.

Everyone turns to look in his direction, curiosity written all over their faces. We had been gone for at least an hour. I can understand their curiosity.

"Thank you for coming tonight. I apologise for the late notice and the delay," he says, addressing the pack. "The reason I called you here no longer remains. As you all can see, my beautiful mate is no longer missing."

The pack immediately starts clapping, startling me into taking a step back and banging my back against the door frame.

Wesley steps forward. "I'd like to say, on behalf of the pack, congratulations. It's an honour to have true mates as our alpha pair." He kneels before the pair of us and bows his head. "Loyalty to my pack, loyalty to my alpha pair, for as long as I may live."

Theo steps forward bringing me with him and places my hand on Wes' shoulder and places his on the other. "Loyalty to my true mate. Loyalty to *our* pack for as long as I may live," he says, giving me a nod as he glances in my direction.

I stare at him blankly. I know I should say something but I'm not really sure what. My wolf pushes to the forefront of my mind, and with her she brings the knowledge and natural instinct. The words just flow out.

"Loyalty to my true mate and *our* pack for as long as I may live."

With that, the whole room drops to their knees. "Loyalty to my pack, loyalty to my alpha pair for as long as I may live."

The feel of the pack inside me starts to pulse, and with a snap I feel it solidify. I can feel every member. I can distinguish every member even the ones I have never been introduced to. I know who is mated and who isn't.

I am pack; there is no doubt about that now.

"Rise," Theo commands. Once every member has risen he proceeds, "Now that we have dealt with the formalities it's time to get our pack members back."

The room erupts with a chorus of agreement.

"As most of you know, Paddy and Alyssa attacked Dominick Drake earlier tonight. If Rosabel hadn't discovered the attack in time Dominick would have been killed; which would have resulted in an instant war. Rosabel brought up a valid point just a short while ago. She brought it to my attention that we may be looking at too narrow a suspect pool—that a druid or witch may be kidnapping and stripping them of their free will. The fact that neither of them would attack Dominick of their own accord makes me believe that Bel just may be right.

I think the best way to find this person is to start patrols. Alyssa went missing at Misty's and this most recent attack was there too, making me believe the suspect may be connected to that area. I suggest we start there and work our way out. Since he has two wolves, I want you in groups of three. Billy, I'd like you to take the first patrol tomorrow night. Who would you like to take with you?"

Billy, the biker, steps forward in his leather trousers, a black muscle tank and heavy boots. No jacket.

Shit his jacket is still on the sofa at home.

"I'll take Phil and Darren if that is okay with you, boss?"

"Yeah. I'm happy with your choice. Phil. That okay with you?" He nods to a guy in front of us who wouldn't be my first choice.

He's tall and so thin that if a gust of wind hit him he'd snap in half. He has a dark crew cut but it's his fashion sense that makes him stand out the most. His red and blue check shirt matched with beige trousers look great, until you look at his Jesus sandals with socks.

"That's cool."

"Darren. How about you?"

"I'm all yours," says a gruff voice. Now this guy I would choose. He's freaking huge in all directions. Honestly, he must have come through the front door sideways. It looks like it is all muscle, too. His shaved head has a nice shine to it. He's wearing a navy wife-beater with white-washed jeans and what look like steel-toe capped safety boots.

"Good. I suggest all three of you meet around the back of Misty's at half past five. I'm going to speak to Dominick and see if he will send some of his guys on patrols, too. Every man helps. I'll meet the three of you when Misty's shuts. If you see anything unusual before then call it in." All three guys nod and Theo looks around taking in the rest of the pack.

"You may all leave now, but be sure to stay safe and stick in groups. Thanks again."

I step away from the door as everyone moves to file out, many stopping to say a few words to Theo on their way. A few of them even greet me with a smile and welcome me to the pack.

Theo is so attentive to his members. I smile as I watch him deal with them all. This wonderful and gorgeous guy is my mate. When I left Quilpie to find a Pack never, in my wildest dreams did I imagine finding my true mate. A guy I can actually love. It hits me like a sledge hammer as I watch him follow Wesley and Billy out of the room whilst chatting. I have only known him a short time but I do…I love him.

I am just about to follow him when I sense someone behind me. I quickly spin around uncomfortable with a stranger at my back. I find Chloe in skinny white jeans and a fitted fuchsia pink singlet with her long blonde hair straightened to perfection, to match the perfect heavy make-up. I try not to think about what I must look like after my hair had been left to dry wild and that all my make-up washed off from my shower. I don't think any woman could help but feel slightly inferior when standing next to the beautiful Chloe.

"Looks like it's just you and me now, Rosabel. They could be a while in there chatting pack business. Maybe we should take the time to get to know each other a little?"

I know, without a doubt, I am allowed in there with Theo and the others, and as much as I feel bad to think about leaving Chloe to her own devices, I haven't forgotten how she feels about Theo and I mating. She made it perfectly clear with the outburst at the last Pack meeting—not to mention the way she greeted Theo earlier this evening.

"There you are?" Theo says, popping his head around the doorway. "I was starting to worry you might have vanished again," he adds, jokingly.

"I'm coming," I say, as I turn towards the door.

A wave of jealousy from Chloe almost bowls me over. It's so strong I actually stumble. I was right to remember where she stands in regards to me and Theo. There is no way she is going to just move aside and accept this.

Glancing back at her I decide I need to keep my enemy close. "Sorry Chloe. Maybe we can get to know each other another time. Grab a coffee and have a manicure or something?"

She looks at me, the shock is written all over her face. "S-sure that sounds good," she stutters, as I leave the room.

I find Theo and Wesley in the lounge, sitting in the same place they had been last time. It's the first time I have really looked at Wesley tonight. He looks miserable. His sadness pouring off him and filling the room.

As I sit next to him, he looks at me with a puzzled look, probably wondering why I'm sitting next to him and not Theo. I ignore his look and put my arm through his, stroking his forearm in a comforting gesture.

"We'll bring Alyssa home. She looked well tonight. She didn't have any injuries. I promise we'll get her back." I give him a reassuring smile, which he surprisingly returns.

"I know we will. Thanks, Rosabel. You really are going to be a great addition to the pack."

I stand up and kiss him on the top of his head.

Shit! Maybe I shouldn't have done that in front of Theo.

I glance up at Theo, dreading seeing the look on his face, but he's giving me a heart-warming smile.

As I sit next to him he leans into my hair and whispers in my ear, "Thank you. That's the first smile I've seen on his face since Alyssa went missing."

Billy suddenly appears with five mugs on a tray. He hands us all a coffee and places a tea on the table for himself. We all give the fifth mug a curious glance,

"I thought Chloe might be joining us. What with her staying here and all. Shall I take it up to her or just leave it here, boss?"

Theo grabs the phone out of its cradle on the coffee table and dials a number.

"Hello," Chloe answers.

"Hey, there's a coffee here for you if you want to join us?" He hangs up without giving Chloe a chance to reply.

Chloe arrives in the room so quickly she must have been in the other room still. She sits on the floor leaning next to Theo's legs.

"Thank you," she says, taking a mouthful of her drink. She really is grateful for us letting her join us. Her emotions are so strong.

We all enjoy our coffees in silence.

Looking at Billy reminds me that I still have his jacket.

"Billy. I forgot your jacket. It's still on the sofa at Misty's apartment."

"No worries, Rosabel. It's not like I really feel the cold anyway. Just leave it at the bar tomorrow and I'll pick it up."

I could try my newfound trick. I suppose now is as good a time as any. "It's okay; I'll get it for you now."

As Theo and Billy both go to protest I put my hand up to silence them. I shuffle my bum in the seat to get more comfortable making all four of them look at me with puzzled expressions.

This will be so much more fun if I don't tell them what I'm going to do.

I close my eyes, take a deep breath and concentrate on breathing in and out. When I feel totally relaxed, I picture Misty's huge lounge, the cream leather sofa in the middle of the room with Billy's jacket on the back, the wooden sideboard with the telephone and answering machine on top, the three tall floor lamps; the one next to the sofa, the one next to the sideboard and the one in the far corner by the brown suede beanbag. I feel the thick, luxurious cream carpet under my feet and smell the lavender scented candle that Misty always burns before bed.

I open my eyes and see all that I just pictured behind my eyelids. I can't believe it worked first time. I grab Billy's jacket, pulling it on. I quickly pull a pen and paper out of the sideboard drawer to write Misty a note, too.

Misty,

   I'll be staying at Theo's tonight. I promise I will fill you in on everything tomorrow.

— BEL

Leaving the note on the sideboard for her to see, I place the pen back in the drawer and step into the middle of the room. Again, I take a few deep breaths as I close my eyes. I picture Theo's two red suede L-shape sofas; one opposite the other with the solid oak coffee table between them. I feel the cold slate floor under my feet. I smell Theo's lovely scent—Billy's, Wesley's, and Chloe's, too. I open my eyes to find myself standing behind the sofa.

Billy and Wesley are both staring at me stunned.

I walk around the sofa to Billy, while sliding the jacket off and pass it to him.

"There you go, one jacket. Thanks for the loan!" I turn and sit down next to Theo. Both he and Chloe are equally stunned.

"Wow. That really was something—minus the fear," Theo says proudly, sliding his arm around me and pulling me against his side.

"I figured I might as well try my new trick out," I say, with a shrug.

Billy finally remembers how to speak. "How the hell did you do that?"

Wesley and Chloe still seem to be struggling to pick their jaws off the floor.

I suddenly realise the consequences of my actions. *I'm going to have to tell them about the druid in me.* I hope this doesn't change how Billy and Wesley feel about me. They seem to have accepted me. It can't really change the way Chloe feels. She already hates me. I look at Theo and he seems to understand the inner debate I'm having. His reassuring smile gives me the courage to bite the bullet.

"When I disappeared earlier, Dominick called me to him. I thought he was able to do it due to our tie. He informed me that I actually have druid blood in me, giving me the ability to teleport just now and earlier when Theo called the meeting, although it was Dominick controlling my dematerialising earlier, not me."

No one speaks; they just stare at me like I have two heads. I am squirming. Theo can probably tell I want to bolt.

He stares at me intently. "Don't even think about leaving!"

It's an order. I stare into his beautiful eyes. My vision blurs as my eyes fill with tears.

He gently strokes my cheek with the back of his knuckles. "Okay. Now that you're staying put, you're going to listen to me."

I can only manage to nod, being too choked up with tears to speak.

"First things first. The pack has no decision in the matter of who I choose as a mate, they will respect you whether they like you or not. Secondly I love you, druid or not." He leans forward and kisses me on the forehead, pulling me in to hug him.

Once I get my tears under control I make a move to pull away, only to feel Wes and Billy both join in on a group hug. "You are our alpha's true mate, making you our alpha female. We all stated our loyalty earlier. We have accepted you just like Theo said, druid or not," Wesley says, making his feelings clear as we all take our seats once again.

"What is wrong with you three? Are you insane? She's a druid werewolf? She can materialise wherever she wants! What else can she do? She's playing you all. Druids are dark and evil. Well, I'm not falling for whatever spell she's put you all under. I do not trust her," Chloe hollers, as she stands.

The sofa vibrates with the growl coming from deep in Theo's chest. I grab for Theo's hand to try and calm him, but before I can get a hold on it he snatches it away.

Billy speaks first—probably trying to give Theo time to calm down before he bites Chloe's head off—and I mean literally bites it off. His eyes have already gone the deep black of his wolf's. The anger filling the room is stinging against my skin.

"Chloe, not all druids are bad. There are some that focus on the dark magic but not all. Some are healers. Before you ask, no we don't know which Rosabel is but I can sense and so can you that there is nothing evil about her. You're just jealous that Theo doesn't want you as a mate. If you accept that, you might notice there are plenty of others in this pack that actually would take you as a mate and be worthy of it, too. But you are too blind to see that."

"But—" she starts to argue before Theo cuts her off.

"No buts, Chloe. You need to apologise to Rosabel and you will respect and accept her. Do you understand?" His eyes are back to his human emerald green but if she doesn't agree they won't stay like that for long. His anger is still stinging against my skin. It hasn't even gone down a notch.

"Yes, I understand. I'm sorry, Rosabel," she says, bowing her head in submission. Her tone makes it blatantly obvious that she is anything but sorry.

"Get out of my sight. I don't want to see you again until you apologise and mean it," Theo demands.

Chloe turns on her heel and short of stomping her foot like a child, storms off.

"I'm sorry." The disappointment is clear in his voice.

"You don't need to be sorry. Like Billy said, Chloe wants you and no matter what or who I am, I don't think she will ever like me."

"Theo, I'm going to head off, if that's okay?" Wesley stands, looking at his feet.

"Goodnight," Theo snaps. *I think someone is still grouchy.*

Wesley walks out of the room and we hear the front door open and close.

I quickly jump up, realising that if I was in his shoes, there is no way I would want to go to an empty home with Alyssa missing.

Just as I rush past Theo I sense his concern. "I'll be back in a minute," I shout, running out the front door, hopeful of putting his mind at rest.

"Wesley. Where are you planning on going?" I ask, just as Wesley is unlocking his car door.

"I don't know. Our house is going to be so quiet and empty without Alyssa." He stares off into the distance with glazed-over eyes.

He isn't going anywhere.

"Lock your car! You're staying in one of Theo's spare rooms. If he can let Chloe stay, even after he got so mad at her, I'm sure he won't mind you staying! Come on. Let's go find you a room."

He locks the car and takes the hand I offer him as we head back into the house. I lead him up the stairs that are off to the left of the front door. They lead to the wing that Chloe is staying in. *At least I think they do.*

We reach the top of the stairs that lead into a narrow corridor. The walls are white with no photos, paintings or windows, just doors spread about seven metres apart on the left, and three doors right next to each other on the right wall. The first door on the left has some very strong anger seeping out so I think it's safe to assume that's the room Chloe is staying in. The three doors to the right must be some sort of storage; I'm guessing linen cupboard, since they're right near the spare rooms.

Once we reach the next door on the left, I open it door and find a larger room than I expected. It's been painted in a lovely lemon colour, which makes me smile. It's a happy colour. There is a king-size brass bed opposite the door with a window on either side of the headboard. It's neatly made with white satin sheets and has a lemon knitted blanket folded at the foot.

There is a white painted chest of drawers against the left wall and hanging above that is a beautiful painting of a view of a sunset off the top of a mountain. *I will have to ask Theo where that was painted. That is a place I would love to visit.*

I check the bathroom for towels, toilet paper, and soap. "Is this room okay for you, Wes? Chloe is in the room next door. You don't want move further down the hall do you?" I say, knowing he can hear me from where he is sitting on the bed.

"No. This room is fine. I can ignore her," he replies. I can hear the smile in his voice.

Not finding any towels in the bathroom I head back out to what I hope is a linen cupboard in the hall. If I am wrong, I might have to ask Chloe where the spare towels are. *I really don't want to talk to her, if I don't have to.* Thankfully my guess is correct. I take a couple towels back to the room and place them on the end of the bed.

"There's a couple towels; if you need more there is plenty in the cupboard out in the hall." He probably already knows all of this, no doubt having stayed over before.

"Thanks, Rosabel, for everything. You are going to make a great alpha female," he praises.

"You're welcome. I am sure Theo would have offered you the room himself if he wasn't so worked up about Chloe. Now. You get some sleep so we can find Alyssa tomorrow."

20

HEART TO HEART

Having heard Bel enter the house again a few minutes ago, I decide to go track her down. I know Chloe is down at the front of the house. I don't want her to be causing any trouble while I'm not there. I know Bel would be able to handle herself against Chloe. She has lived through numerous duels after all, but Bel doesn't need the hassle or guilt if she injures Chloe.

I head towards the front of the house with Billy following behind. It doesn't take me long to realise that I made the right decision. I can clearly hear Chloe and Bel at each other's throats.

"Are you threatening me?" Chloe demands. I have no doubt that she probably threatened Bel first.

"I hope there aren't any threats being thrown around in my house," I command from the bottom of the stairs. Neither of them could have heard me approach because I watch helplessly as they both stumble around at the top of the stairs, grabbing opposite walls to steady themselves.

"Theo you surprised us both so much we nearly toppled down the stairs one after the other. You might have had two dead women to deal with." Bel chuckles nervously. The fear I can feel in her makes me think she very nearly did do just that. I should have been more careful. They were in a heated discussion. Of course, they wouldn't have heard me.

"Sorry," I grumble, still thinking about what I could have caused.

"There are no threats here, are there Chloe?" Bel asks as she glares at Chloe. She can no doubt sense that I can't handle much more tonight before my wolf comes out to play.

"No," she replies, before going into her room and slamming the door.

Bel jogs down the stairs to join us by the front door.

"Night, Rosabel. I'm going now! I'll probably see you tomorrow at Misty's," says Billy.

"I have the night off, so maybe not. Then again, I can't seem to keep away from that place so you're probably right," she says, with a laugh.

I open the door and my laugh falls flat when I spot Wes' car. "I thought Wes left. Why is his car still here?" I give Bel a questioning look.

"Oh, yeah. Erm...you were mad, but I didn't think you'd mind. He's in the lemon room. He didn't want to go home without Alyssa. He wouldn't have been able to handle the emptiness. I'm sorry," Bel rambles, with her head bowed in submission. She is my mate. She doesn't need to show me submission like that.

I tilt her chin up with my hand until her worried eyes meet my stare. "Thank you." I pause, not hiding how mortified I am. "I can't believe I didn't think of that. What kind of an alpha does that make me?"

I shouldn't be allowed to call myself Alpha if I can't even care for my pack members like I should.

"Come on, boss. You have a helluva a lot on your mind at the minute. You were furious when Wes left. You had Chloe's shit in your head and fighting your wolf wasn't helping you with being considerate and compassionate," Billy says.

I catch the worried expression he throws Bel's way. I know what that expression means. The last thing the pack needs is the alpha to be feeling weak. It will cause the whole pack to weaken. The pack is weak enough at the moment. I need to find them. We can't go on without clues much longer.

Bel's voice brings me out of my internal musing. "Billy is right, Theo. I only thought of it because of my empathic ability. I could feel Wesley's emotions. I couldn't let him leave feeling like that."

Billy looks at Bel, clearly astonished. "You're an empathetic, druid-blooded werewolf?"

We all laugh.

"Let's just say I'm unique!"

I gaze at her admiringly. "You certainly are, but in a good way."

"Right. I'm off before Little Miss Unique Wolfy here decides I'm not fit to leave and sends me to the pink room," Billy jokes as he steps out the door.

I laugh. "Have no fear; Chloe is in the pink room."

We both stand and watch as Billy walks to his bike, straddles the saddle as he turns it over and speeds off down the drive.

As I lead Bel back to the lounge I can feel her energy changing by the second. She is worried about something, no longer laughing and joking. I can't leave her to worry like that. We are mates now. She has me to talk things through with.

"What are you thinking about? You feel sad and worried." I sit on the sofa opposite her. She seems to be staring into space and my question jolts her back to the here and now. She looks around the room as if she doesn't even remember getting here. She stands up and picks up the tray with the mugs from earlier on it.

"Do you mind if I make another coffee?" she asks. Not exactly what I was hoping for, maybe the coffee will relax her enough to talk to me.

"Go ahead. Help yourself." I watch as she goes into the kitchen to make her coffee.

I have a bad feeling that she is trying to delay something and, from what her feelings through our bond is telling me, I'm not going to like where this conversation is going.

She walks back to the sofa with two mugs, placing one in front of me and then sitting down opposite me again. "I don't know how you take it or even if you wanted one. I hope it's okay."

"I'm not fussy. It'll be fine," I say absentmindedly, as I reach through our bond hoping for some insight into her thoughts.

"You regret what happened between us earlier?" I ask. "Upstairs?" I quickly clarify. I can't stop the sadness escaping me. The bond might not be telling me what exactly she is thinking, but her regret and sadness are coming through loud and clear.

She takes a calming breath before speaking. "Yes, in a way I regret it, but not because I didn't enjoy it, or want it, or because I don't think we are true mates. We are, I *know* that. I love you, Theo. I want to be able to do what we just did every night. I want to be able to wrap my arms around you and fall asleep cuddling you like my personal teddy bear." She stops to catch her breath and I take the opportunity to ask the most important question.

"But we can do that, every day. So why regret it? I can feel it's the truth you speak, but I can feel your regret too. I don't understand why you regret it?"

"Please. Let me finish. It might take a while but when I'm finished you'll understand, I promise." Her begging does me in. I nod for her to carry on, imitating zipping my mouth locking it with a key. I lean over the table to pass her the imaginary key.

Her laugh is magic to my ears. It wipes the sadness from the room, if only for a second. "Thank you," she says, just before the sadness creeps back in. "Okay, the reason I regret it is because it has complicated things. It's made this conversation and decision so much more painful." Her eyes fill with tears but she doesn't break down. She steels herself and carries on. "When I started seeing Jared, we were eighteen and totally besotted with each other." She chuckles and I can't help but frown wondering what her past with Jared has to do with now.

"His pride wouldn't accept me. Jared wasn't leader, but he would be. One day his father would step down and he would takeover. The pride loved him. He had a happy life. When I came along it all changed. I'm not a lion. I'm a wolf—a predator. That makes me a threat. I came here to find people like me and I really thought I had found that in you and your pack. But I'm not just a wolf like you. I'm druid as well and that makes me a threat again. Chloe, and no doubt some others of your pack will feel that way."

I open my mouth to speak but remember my promise to allow her to finish, so I close it without speaking.

"We were together for six years and not a week went by without one of us being challenged. As besotted as we were, he would only end up resenting me for turning his happy life into a constant battle. You know his feelings haven't changed; he is still as besotted as that first day we met. Having to fight day after day made us miserable, we couldn't enjoy each other. I finished with him in the end because he deserved better; to find a mate that the pride accepts. At first I thought they would give in and accept me, but I was kidding myself. I got over him. I guess knowing now that I have a true mate made it easier. I loved him but maybe I was never really in love with him, especially not as much as he was with me. I knew he would never accept us not being together, that is why I left Quilpie. I thought once he knew it was over and that I had left with no trace for him to follow, he'd move on. But we both know I was wrong."

"I still love him but in a sibling capacity, like I love Benji. You met Benji, didn't you?" she asks, looking at me with her sad eyes.

I nod, but again, I don't speak. I need her to get to her point.

"I can't live like that again, Theo. Challenge after challenge. I'm not going to be the cause of your pack's destruction. I'm not destroying your life, Theo—not yours. You deserve so much more. You deserve love and if we end this before it starts now, you'll get that. There are plenty of people in this town that would jump at a date with you. One of them is upstairs in the pink room." She stops talking as the tears stream down her face.

I can't hold my tongue anymore, whether she has finished or not.

"But what about you, Rosabel? Don't you deserve the love you want—the love that wants you?" I make my way to her, kneeling before her and holding her shoulders in each hand. "It won't be like that with us. I am alpha, it *will* be different." I give her a pleading look, hoping she can feel the hope I am sending through our bond.

I see it in her face as she rides my hope but within a second it's gone and the tears come thicker and faster. "Chloe has already challenged me, Theo. We've been together properly, what, a couple of hours? And the challenges have already started. That's the first of many. I could feel the hatred towards me in that meeting and it wasn't all coming from Chloe. Once news of my druid blood comes out there, will be more that won't accept me."

The hope I had disappears instantly. If this is what she really wants I need to accept defeat. I'm her mate and I can't even make her happy.

"You're right, but they won't all challenge you. Only a few of the more dominant will. The submissives will accept defeat and welcome you. Don't forget some of the most dominant already accept you, like Wes and Billy. You said Chloe has already challenged you. What did she say exactly?" Even I can hear the hope creep back into my voice.

"She said you might have mated with me but she'll make sure you change your mind and I'll get thrown out. And when that happens, killing me will be right at the top of her to-do list." Threatening death is a challenge no matter when you plan on doing the deed. Chloe has challenged her. There is no getting away from that unless Chloe revokes the challenge.

"Chloe is strong," I say, pulling her close as my concern gets the better of me. Earlier I had thought Bel could handle Chloe without a problem, but that doesn't mean she won't get hurt in the process. Chloe is one of the most dominant females in our pack.

Bel pulls away with a laugh. "You think she'll beat me!" she says, sounding astonished.

"Like I said, she's strong. She's on par with Billy and she often likes to bring it up. I'm not sure who would win between the two of them. It would be close."

She grins from ear to ear. "If she really is as dominant as you think, we could make this work." Having no idea what she is getting at I frown.

"You and me, a couple," she adds. I feel my smile mirror hers.

"What are you planning?" I ask a little dubiously.

"We will have to take it slow. Don't force me on the pack like you have been. No more meetings. I know they've already officially accepted with the words but they need to feel it, too. I can feel through the pack bonds they don't all feel what they said. They need to get to know me as just Bel, fellow pack member, not alpha female."

"But what about Chloe and her challenge?"

"She said she will kill me. I have to take it as a challenge. But that might help us if she is as dominant as you say. If I win, others won't be willing to challenge me. So we fight." She shrugs nonchalantly.

"Yes, that will work." I cringe at the excitement I can hear in my voice. I sound like a kid on Christmas Day.

I move my hands to cradle her face and lean in to kiss her. My mouth brushes against hers as my tongue licks at the seam of her lips. She grants me entrance by parting her lips slowly. Her hands grip the hair at the back of my neck before she pulls away, leaving us both gasping for air. Our arousal is thick in the air. I stroke her cheek with my thumb, unable to keep my thoughts away from sadness and worry.

"What are you thinking about? You look sad and you shouldn't—not after that kiss," Bel queries.

I drop my eyes to the floor. "That I am in love with you, Rosabel, I have only just found you and I don't want to lose you to Chloe."

She mirrors my movements from earlier, tilting my chin so my eyes meet hers, stroking my cheek with her thumb. "I am dominant and I am strong. I have duelled and beaten stronger than Chloe. If I went up against Wesley I wouldn't be able to bet on a winner, but Chloe I can handle."

I struggle to keep the shock off my face. "Really?"

"Yes! I'll beat Chloe, trust me," she says confidently.

21

TAKEN

We both pull away to look at our watches when the doorbell rings. *It's four in the morning, who would be at the door at this time?* I glance up at Theo who looks just as uncertain as I feel.

We both walk to the door. Before opening it, we both close our eyes, trying to sense who it is on the other side.

"I can't smell any scent through the door. It's too thick. They don't feel like Pack, familiar but not Pack." Theo confirms my own thoughts.

"Whoever it is they're scared, hurt, and female—young too," I say, using my empathy.

Unlocking the door, he opens it cautiously.

A girl that looks about sixteen, give or take a year, pounces at Theo shouting, "Ted." between sobs. She throws her arms around him and hangs off his neck. She is just a bit shorter than me—although Theo isn't tall, she is hanging a good ten inches off the floor. Theo is hugging her in return so I relax, assuming he must know her.

As I take her in, I see a similarity in her. Her long ringlets down to her waist are the same colour as his and her eyes are the same shape only more sage green not emerald. I can see a nasty looking bruise on her right cheekbone.

"Rubes, what's happened? Why are you here?"

She lifts her head and looks up at him giving him full view of the bruise.

The anger leaves him in such a strong wave that it actually

knocks my feet from under me, leaving me sprawled on the floor like an idiot.

"That bastard!"

She buries her face into his chest and sobs even more.

"Theo, she needs some ice on her cheek. Have you got any?" I get up and shut the door, hoping to calm him by making him realise he needs to care for her, not get angry at someone who isn't even here.

He pulls her against his side, leading her to the kitchen.

I can feel Wesley following behind me. "You okay, boss?" He sees the girl then, "Ruby? Hi."

She turns to look at him, but before she replies he sees her bruise.

"Oh shit! Are you okay, sweetie?" He strides over to them. By the feel of his anger, I'm guessing the whole pack would be willing to rip someone to shreds for Ruby.

Ruby sits on the counter top in silence with the ice pack pressed to her cheek and the two men hovering in front of her like bodyguards.

I walk over to Theo and touch the small of his back with my fingers. He must have been somewhere else with his thoughts because the touch catches him by surprise. He spins around on his heels and the anger in his eyes terrifies me so much I take an involuntary step back.

Never back down too easily from a werewolf.

They find it fun and will probably tear you apart!

"I'm sorry. I didn't mean to surprise you," I practically whisper.

He shakes his head like trying to shake a vision from his sight.

"I'm going to head home. You're busy and we have sorted our problem. It's my night off tomorrow but you know what I'm like. I'll be at the bar anyway just on the other side of it for a change." I stand on my tiptoes and kiss his soft lips with a gentle brush of mine. He returns my kiss and I pull away smiling. "I know you are going to be busy so I'll understand if you can't make it to the bar. Don't worry."

He nods and turns to Wesley. "Wes. Can you give Bel a lift home?"

"I'll go 'teleport' in the other room," I remind them both with a grin before Wes can reply.

I walk into the dining room and close the door behind me. Closing my eyes, I picture my room at Misty's and open them to find I am there. *This teleportation is getting easier with each attempt.*

The room feels empty and lonely without Theo. He's my mate I should be with him. I'm missing a vital piece of myself when he isn't around. At least I know where he is. I don't know how Wes is managing with Alyssa missing.

I go to the bathroom but decide to skip changing into my pyjamas. I climb into bed in Theo's shorts and t-shirt so I can fall asleep feeling safe and secure as I breathe in his scent.

A startled cry wakes me up. I instantly dive off the bed into an attacking stance before even opening an eye.

"I'm sorry. I got ya note. I thought ya'd be at Theo's? I've just done some washing, I was going to put these clean clothes on ya bed. Ya scared the crap outta me," Misty says, clutching at her chest with an armful of folded clothes.

I quickly straighten up and sit back on the bed. "I forgot about the note. I only got back just after four, I should have left you a new note."

I look at the little alarm clock on the table next to the bed, it's one o'clock in the afternoon. I can't believe I slept eight hours straight, I usually get up at least once to use the bathroom through the night.

"Thanks for the washing," I add, as she places the pile on the end of the bed.

"I've just made a fresh pot of coffee. Do ya want me to bring you a mug?" she asks, turning to leave the room.

I stand up and head for the bathroom. "No, thanks. I'll be out in a second. I'll just get changed and join you." I really don't want to change out of Theo's clothes. They're a comfort to my wolf, but I need to act like a normal human being and not be hung up on someone's scent, mate or not.

It doesn't take me long to get washed and changed, and find myself walking into the kitchen.

Misty greets me with a steaming mug of coffee, and a bacon and egg sandwich.

"Thanks, Misty. Do you realise you'll never get rid of me if you keep spoiling me like this?" I joke.

"That's my point. I don't want ya to leave. I love your company. Now tell me everything." Misty loves gossip.

Who am I to keep of it from her? I fill her in on everything that happened after I left work last night.

"Wow. Nothing is boring when you're around, is it?" We both burst into laughter at how true her statement is. I've been here only a short time, yet so much has happened. I'm turning into quite the drama magnet.

"Do ya think he'll meet ya at the bar later?"

"I'm only guessing that Ruby is his sister, but the state she was in when I left, I don't think he'll leave her home alone to come and see me," I reply. If I was in his shoes I wouldn't leave her.

"Ya said Chloe was staying at his. She might be happy to keep Ruby company for an hour or two."

I laugh at that comment. "Did you hear me when I mentioned that Chloe challenged me because she wants Theo for herself? There is no way she would make my life that easy."

Before we know it, it's time to get ready for work. Even

though I'm not working I decide to go in with Misty and help her open up.

As soon as the customers enter she demands that I get on their side of the bar. I'll comply for now but if it gets too busy I'll be jumping over to help out.

Emmanuel comes in and sits on the stool to my left. As awkward as I feel, it's a small town and we need to be civilised with each other.

"Hi. How has the last twenty-four hours treated you?" Emmanuel asks, breaking the silence. *Was it really only in twenty-four hours? It feels like days.*

"Hectic. How about you?" I ask.

"Yeah. It's been pretty busy for me too."

I feel a hand on my right shoulder. "How's our Little Miss Wolfy doing?" I didn't need to look to see who the voice belonged to. The scent and accent, along with the pack bond, told me it was Billy.

Evidently Emmanuel did have to look and he gives Billy such a glare that I think if looks could kill a were, Billy could possibly be dead right now.

"I'm fine thanks, Billy, but I thought I was Little Miss *Unique* Wolfy? Am I not unique anymore?" I pout.

"Don't be silly." He chuckles. "You'll always be unique. It was too much of a tongue twister for me."

"So. Are you here to tell me that Theo is standing me up?"

Panic crosses his face. "No, no. He's just running late. He's outside talking with Dominick, trying to persuade him to send some of his men to help us out. He's not too keen but I don't blame him. They are the ones that keep getting attacked, we are just the ones that get kidnapped and controlled." He rolls his eyes.

Realising I have just made it sound like Theo is my new boyfriend in front of Emmanuel, I turn to make sure I haven't upset him, only the stool is empty. I look around the bar but he is nowhere in sight.

Billy looks at the stool too and shrugs before sitting on it himself. "Weird guy!"

Misty comes to a stop in front of us. "What do you two want to drink?"

"I'll just have a bottle of something low-strength, thanks Misty. I'm patrolling and Theo won't be happy if I do it drunk. What do you want, Wolfy?" He looks at me with such a serious face.

I burst out laughing. "Little Miss too much for you now?" I shake my head at his laziness, "I'll have a Cosmopolitan, thanks."

"Coming right up." Misty turns to the mixing area to make my drink.

"How come you have a night off anyway? You only worked half a night last night?" Billy asks.

"I know. I'm such an unreliable employee. Misty has a heart of gold. She still thinks I deserve a night off." Misty places our drinks in front of us.

"Keep the change," Billy says, handing Misty some notes.

Misty gives him a flirtatious smile, which he returns. *I think I may have a cupid-style job coming up in the future.*

Billy finishes the bottle in two swigs. "I better get off. It's time to meet my men." He gets up and kisses me on my cheek before turning and walking towards the door.

I suddenly get a bad, gut feeling deep within me. I don't know what it is that unsettles me but I don't think tonight is going to be without violence. "Billy?"

He spins around to look as he pushes the exit door open. "Angel?"

"Be careful." I give him a smile, which he returns with a confident one.

"I will…*Shit!*" I watch his face change from confident to pure fear.

"What's wrong?" I shout. I can feel it deep inside the pack bonds. Something is seriously wrong.

"Trouble," he says, running out the door. He moves so fast I don't even see him leave, not even a blur. His voice just comes from the empty air.

I only sit there for a second wondering what to do before deciding to follow. I'm a werewolf and I have a pack now. That pack is in danger and I need to do anything I can to help.

I don't make it two steps before Dominick falls in the door. "Rosabel they took Theo and killed Chomp," is all he manages to spit out before collapsing in a heap on the floor.

A female vampire rushes in after him shouting. "Someone needs to feed him! He'll die without the blood." Not one person in the bar steps forward to offer their blood. They all just stare at Dominick's lifeless body in silence.

"Misty, ring Wesley. Tell him they've taken Theo and he'll need to call a pack meeting. We have to find them!" *Listen to me being all calm and rational. I'm usually the rambling mess in an emergency.*

Unwilling to let Dominick die, I walk over and put my wrist towards his mouth, only to have his female vampire push it away. "You're a werewolf. He can't feed from you. You're alpha won't allow it. He'll retaliate with war."

"That alpha is my mate. He'll understand my decision."

"You are the 'saviour' he talks about? You taste too good and he won't be able to stop. He'll end up draining you. He'll never forgive himself, or me."

"You said he'll die if he doesn't get fed. Your compulsion won't work in here and no one is willing to offer. You won't be able to drag anyone off the street in through those wards. Their hearts will give up before you get them in. I'm not letting him die so I'll have to take the risk of him draining me." I put my wrist to his mouth but he's so far gone that he doesn't do anything. He needs to taste the blood before he'll drink.

I shove my wrist into the female vampire's face. "Bite me so he can taste the blood."

She looks uncertain for a split second but she leans forward and I feel her fangs pierce my skin. *Fuck it hurts!*

She's looking directly at me but isn't pulling away. She isn't drinking either. I look into her eyes. "Dominick will die you need to release my wrist. NOW!" She immediately follows my command.

I rest my wrist on Dominick's mouth once again. He's still not reacting to the blood. *Please, don't let it be too late.*

"Dominick. Come on babe you need to feed." I can't suppress my panic. "You're getting five star here. Feed dammit!"

My eyes fill with tears as I start to give up, when I suddenly feel his mouth close against my wrist and his fangs pierce the skin again. He starts to pull at the vein and as much as it hurts, it's the best thing I've ever felt because it means he's going to live. I'm not sure why him living bothers me so much because I don't really know him. I shouldn't care, but for some reason I do. He's only been feeding for a minute or two but I'm starting to feel dizzy!

Shit! She was right!

He is going to drain me!

"Dominick, you've had enough, you need to stop now!" I shove at his face with my free arm.

Fuck!

I have black spots dancing before my eyes, the spots are getting bigger by the second.

"Dominick, you greedy bastard. You're KILLING ME!" I scream. Managing to keep my eyes open long enough to see Dominick's eyes open. I catch a glimpse of recognition cross his face and I feel him release my arm as I fall to the floor.

"Rosabel, I'm so sorry." I can hear Dominick repeat it over and over, again his voice is getting more distant. Focusing solely on his voice pays off. It slowly becomes louder.

"Someone get her some orange juice," he demands. "She needs fluids and sugar."

I don't hear anyone move but when I open my eyes there is a glass of juice being held in front of my face. I sit up slowly leaning against someone's leg as the hand holding the glass carefully feeds me.

When I've drained the glass, I look up to see that it's Dominick's hand. He passes it back to the female vampire.

She takes it away and before I can blink she's back with the glass full once again.

Taking it in my hand this time I realise too late that I should've made him feed off my left wrist, the glass drops to the floor because my hand is drained and sore. As I watch the glass fall, I thank the gods I'm a quick-healing werewolf. I don't think a human would've survived that feed. I was too close to death.

Dominick catches the glass a second before it smashes on the floor.

"I am so sorry, Rosabel." I can see the regret in his eyes, hear it in the tone and feel it in his emotions. With vampires being dead, I would have never thought they would feel emotions like humans. I always thought emotions were for living things, but I guess I've just been proved wrong.

He points his finger at the female vampire. "You should have never let her feed me, Patsy. I nearly killed her and you should have known that was a strong possibility." He may be chastising her with his words but there's no conviction behind them. I think he blames himself more then he blames her.

"I told her not to—"

I quickly cut her off. "She tried to stop me. If anyone is to blame, it's me. No one else offered and I wasn't going to just stand by and watch you die."

"What? You were willing to die to save me?" He actually sounds touched.

"To be honest, not really. I didn't think you would actually drain me, especially if you knew it was me but you were so out of it, I couldn't make you see what you were doing. It was a close call."

Too damn close.

"You're not just a Lone Wolf anymore, you have a pack. You could've stood by and done nothing. Thank you for having enough faith in me to risk your life."

"I couldn't live with myself if I allowed someone to die if I could save them, but thanks for not killing me."

We are still sitting on the floor, directly in front of the door when Billy runs in and stumbles over us.

"What the hell? I left you for five minutes and you manage to get yourself in trouble?" he says, as he shakes his head.

I open my mouth to explain but he cuts me off before I can get a word out.

"There isn't time to explain. I've come to let you know that after I felt Theo's pain and left here, I followed his scent for five blocks, but the napper must've somehow managed to totally erase it after that point because it just stopped dead in the middle of the path. I couldn't pick it up again. So, what do you want me to do now?"

"Why are you asking me?" I ask, frowning.

"You're Theo's mate, which means you, my dear, are in charge until he gets back."

"Wesley is his second. Shouldn't he be in charge? He'll know better than me what to do," I retort back.

"No. Theo is just missing, which leaves you our alpha female and the highest ranking pack member. If he'd died, Wes would automatically become Alpha until someone challenges him for the position," Billy explains.

"But the Pack don't really know me. How can I expect them to take—or even respect—my orders?"

"They will do it for respect to Theo! What do we do now?" he asks.

How the hell should I know? I have never even been in a pack before, let alone led one.

"Misty has already called Wesley. I assume he will be organising a meeting to make a plan of action."

"Sounds like a good place to start to me," Billy praises me.

"If you could help organise that I'll get Dominick's side of the story and meet you there. I assume it'll be at Theo's still? If not, I'll need a lift because I won't be able to teleport there."

"Theo's place is pack headquarters. We'll all gather there. I'll check in with Wes and see what he needs me to do. Tell him to pull the pack together. I'll spread the news in here on my way out." He offers me his hand to stand, which I happily take because I've realised I'm still on the floor leaning against Dominick's leg and start to feel silly for being here.

"Catch you in a bit," I say.

I stand and look around for the first time since Dominick fell in. I suddenly notice everyone is frozen. "Wait a minute. Why is everyone frozen?"

Dominick, Patsy, and Billy all look around just as shocked as I am.

"I did it," says Misty, as she walks out from behind the bar. "I thought it would be better to freeze them, than having the werewolves trying to stop you feeding him," she adds, when none of us say anything.

"Good thinking," Dominick praises her with great sincerity. If she did it early enough no one will have seen him nearly kill me.

"That's a cool trick. What else have you got up your sleeve?"

I joke, as Misty laughs she clicks her fingers and everyone unfreezes and acts like nothing happened. *I hope no one looks at their watch and wonders where the time went.*

"Okay. Now everyone is moving again. I'll go start organising things. See you in a little while." Billy doesn't wait for me to reply, he just walks off. I watch him tap a few people and lip read him saying three words. "Pack meeting now!" Once he's given the order, they immediately leave and he moves onto another pack member.

I feel bad for Misty. All her customers are leaving. Where are all the witches when you need them? Oh, that's right, there is one out there somewhere controlling the werewolves. I have no doubt about it being a witch now. Not one pack member would attack Theo unless they weren't in control of their own actions.

Dominick, Patsy, and I find an empty booth near the wall. Patsy gets in one side and Dominick sits next to her, leaving the seat opposite for me. Unfortunately, it leaves my back to most of the room. I shuffle into the corner and sit against the wall. I can see anyone approaching. Just as I get comfy, I spot Misty walking over with a bottle of bourbon in one hand and three glasses in the other.

"Hey. Thought ya might need this to calm ya nerves. It's on the house," she says, placing the bottle and glasses on the table.

"Well, thank you very much, Misty. Although, I'd rather you let me pay since you are losing your customers to a pack meeting," Dominick says, taking a couple of notes out of his pocket and tucking them into Misty's jeans pocket.

"Thank you, Dominick." She has a strange sparkle in her eye as she smiles at him, along with the flirtatious smile she gave Billy earlier; makes me think there's going to be a love triangle happening sometime soon. She heads back to the bar but when she gets a couple of steps away she glances back at Dominick over her shoulder.

We really don't have time for romance at the minute.

"Dominick. What happened outside?" I ask, making him tear his eyes away from Misty's direction.

He opens the bottle and fills all three glasses before answering me. "Well, as you know, Theo arranged to meet me. We were standing out the front and Theo was asking if I could send some of my men on the patrols with his wolves. I wasn't too keen because it would put my men in danger of attack. The wolves are getting taken but seem to be in good health. We hadn't been alone long; Billy left us to see you." He's staring off into the distance as if he is picturing the scene.

"He was trying his hardest to persuade me when we were ambushed. Neither of us fought back. Theo tried to command them to stop but he just couldn't get through. He didn't want to hurt them because he knew they weren't in control. It was then the lion jumped on me. I didn't see anything else. I had to fight back, it was me or him."

"Did you just say a lion jumped you?" There is only one lion I know of in town and that is Jared.

"Yes. It looks like he's controlling your friend too…Jared, wasn't it?"

I nod in agreement and take a mouthful of my drink as I let him carry on.

"Chomp sensed my distress and joined us in the fight. There was one fighting each of us but no matter how much I injured Jared he didn't act like he felt it. I don't know if it was just because they weren't in control, or if he's got some protection on them and they can't actually be injured. I never saw any blood on them. I'm Chomp's maker. When he died, I felt it. It was then that Jared left me, which turned out for the best because I wasn't far off death myself, as you saw. I just saw them drag Theo away. He looked like he was in a bad state. He wasn't moving. I can't tell you if he is dead or alive." He looked really concerned. "That's when Billy came out and I fell in."

"He's alive," is all the lump in my throat would allow me to say. He has to be alive. Besides, I would have felt it if he'd died.

Dominick pulls me away from my thoughts. "I guess we now need to come up with a plan to find them. Billy said the scent was gone so tracking is no good."

"*We* need to find out who is controlling them? I can tell a liar through my empathic ability but I can't interrogate every witch in town." I pause a second to think. "They have attacked you twice, so it's safe to say they want you dead. Do you know a witch that hates you enough to want you dead?"

Dominick laughs, spraying the table with the mouthful of bourbon he'd just had. "A number of people want me dead, Rosabel. Not everyone is as nice to me as you are."

"You saw for yourself that no one would offer to save him," Patsy adds.

"What if we set them up?" They look at each other then back to me, without saying a word. I explain the plan that just popped in my head. "It's safe to say they won't attack again tonight. He's got too much to deal with. Theo being injured is going to cause him some problems. If he was just another pack member he'd maybe be okay, but Theo is Alpha and no one can control an injured alpha. You need a stronger alpha or to lock him up until he starts to heal and calm down. He'll probably try again tomorrow night. Theo should be calmer by then. We need to set a trap."

They look at each other for a minute. It almost looks like they are having a silent conversation. *It's actually making me feel out of place.*

"What kind of trap?" I can tell from Dominick's emotions he's uncertain about something.

"We'll have to use you as bait." I look at Dominick hoping he doesn't disagree; he nods for me to carry on. *A good sign.*

"If you hang out in the back alley, make it look like you're meeting Wesley to plan what we're going to do next. I don't think he'll understand pack politics enough to know Wes isn't acting leader. Obviously we'll have pack members, and whichever of your men, there, watching from a safe distance—close enough to jump in when they attack, but far enough away to not be spotted beforehand. Paddy, Alyssa, and Jared shouldn't be able to pick up any scents because they're not in control of their own actions. They won't be thinking anything but what the controller is telling them; which will be to kill you. The controller has to be at a good vantage point with a clear view so he can see what's happening. My guess is a roof or fire escape of one of the surrounding buildings. As soon as the controlled wolves arrive, we look for him. If we can't see him and they attack, we get you out." I leave it at that, hoping he agrees.

"What time and where do you want me?" he asks.

I'm too shocked to answer immediately. I stumble over my words. "I-I guess first dark. If you meet Wesley by the bins near the back door of the bar. Send your men in and I'll tell them where to go. In the meantime, I'll look for some good places to put everyone."

"I'll be there but my men won't be. I can't put them in danger—not after losing Chomp."

"I understand. That's not a problem. I'll make sure we have plenty of pack members."

Patsy looks scared. "He controls the weres. What's to say he won't take them all over in the back alley and kill you immediately?"

"We just have to hope we get him before he gets them," Dominick says, as he stands to leave. "Thank you for earlier. I'll be there at first dark," he says, addressing me.

I stand and lean in to kiss him on the cheek. "I won't let them kill you, I promise. Even if I die saving you."

He laughs as we break away, "I know you are my 'saviour' after all. I can feel the truth through our tie."

After a smile, I close my eyes and teleport to Theo's.

22

CONTACT

I appear in the drive, deciding that is the better choice because if I enter through the front door like the rest of the pack, they might respect me that bit more. They will probably all know about my druid blood by now. Chloe will, no doubt, be spreading the word hoping for more haters to join her hate-on-Bel group.

I walk up the steps to find my least favourite werewolf playing bouncer at the front door. I can hear numerous footsteps behind me leading me to think there are at least three or four pack members behind me. *Surely she won't make a scene in front of them.*

"Hi Chloe," I say politely, as I pass.

She deliberately plants her feet and stands in front of me, denying my entry. She smirks. "Pack only."

I really don't have time for a fight. I need to find Theo.

"Chloe, you know full well that Theo has claimed me for his mate and I've been introduced to the pack as alpha female. Let me in so we can plan how we are *all* going to help find Theo and the others."

She doesn't move.

I sigh. "I haven't forgotten about your challenge. I told Theo about it and he agreed. I do accept. As soon as he's back, we are good to go."

I glance over my shoulder and count at least eight pack members watching and waiting to get in.

It looks like they're going to get a show after all.

Deciding my only option is violence, I turn my body slightly. To Chloe, it might look like I'm going to just walk down the steps and leave but I'm not. I'm just getting momentum. I swing my body back around with as much force behind my right fist as possible. When it makes contact with her jaw, she flies backwards and smashes through one of the closed, beautiful front doors. *Great I'll have to pay a fortune to replace that. It's got to be custom-made.*

The small audience behind me gasps. I can feel a small amount of anger coming from them. To stand my ground, I turn to address them. "Does anyone else want to waste more time questioning my position?" No one says anything or makes any move in retaliation. I turn back to the doors. I start to step over Chloe, who is out cold on top of the door when I hear Wesley shouting.

"WHAT THE FUCK IS GOING ON HERE?" He catches sight of me and bows his head, probably in apology for his tone of voice. "Rosabel?" He questions as he glances down at Chloe, still on the floor.

"She wouldn't let me in. I told her once we find Theo we can deal with the challenge she offered me, but she wouldn't step aside."

"Whoa. Back up a minute! She's challenged you? When? Does Theo know?"

"Yes. Last night after I left you in your room. I assumed you must have heard with it being right outside your door. I told Theo. He agreed we need to duel."

"Okay. We'll deal with that another day. Are you ready to sort this lot out?" he asks, gesturing with a sweep of his arm at the werewolves.

I step into the room and hope that is answer enough.

We head to the dining room. It has been arranged just like the first meeting I attended with the furniture pushed to the edges of the room. We get to the front of the room and stop in front of the three chairs.

"Wes, do we need to wait for Chloe to come around and join us before we start?" I whisper, hoping the rest of the chatting throughout the room covers my words. I don't want anyone else knowing I have no idea what I am doing here.

He shrugs. "No. She isn't of rank. She can join us when she's ready. It serves her right if she misses out on knowing the plan."

I nod in agreement.

I turn and face the crowd, looking at each pack member standing before me. There are a number of faces I recognise. Darryl and Phil, who Billy had picked for his patrol tonight—the one that got cancelled the second Theo went missing. I have no idea how to start this meeting? *How does Theo start them?*

I force a friendly smile on my face. "Hi."

They all immediately stop chatting and nod in unison. They remind me of freaky programmed robots.

Wesley gives me a reassuring smile and Billy moves next to me, reaching out to stroke my arm in comfort.

I need to be honest with them. "I'm not sure how to start this, but I'll try to make it as quick and painless as possible."

There are a couple of friendly chuckles through the crowd. It helps to relax me; if just a little.

"First things first. I've spoken to Dominick and he's told me everything that he saw happen earlier tonight. He's also agreed to act as bait since he has been attacked twice now. I'm assuming that's the reason the kidnapper is taking pack members. He can control animals so that is his best weapon to kill a vampire! He's controlling a were-lion too!"

A guy in the front of the crowd speaks up. He looks like a cowboy from the boots with spurs, to the jeans, checked shirt and hat. I bet he even wears chaps some days. "If he's controlling Theo, all hells going to break loose. There is no one who will win against him. He's too strong."

They all seem to stare at me awaiting my response.

"I thought that too, but Dominick said Theo was hurt, badly hurt, and only dragged away once he was unconscious. I can feel Theo's pain. I don't think he will be able to calm Theo enough to control him for at least another couple nights. He'll have him caged up or locked away somewhere until he can control him. If we can pull together a good trap, with Dominick as bait tomorrow night, we might come out of this alive."

Numerous voices throughout the crowd shout out. "Yes!" I watch as others nod their agreement.

"We'll come up with the details tonight, and then call those we will need tomorrow. I'm not sure who or how many of you we will need so don't make any plans," says Wesley.

I feel a wall of anger drift through the crowd. It takes me a second to spot her but the minute I see Chloe, I know the anger is coming from her and being aimed directly at me. *Lucky me.*

"NOT NOW CHLOE! Theo will be furious enough when he gets back and hears about you playing bouncer earlier. You'll be lucky if he doesn't kick you out of the pack for this," Wesley commands. He's very dominant, thinking back on my words to Theo last night. I'd bet on him to win if we fought.

Chloe looks from me to him. She immediately turns and leaves without a word.

The rest of the pack slowly file out of the house.

After the pack leaves, Billy, Wesley, and myself head to the lounge. It's like the meeting after the meeting. Billy goes straight for the kitchen to make the drinks; which makes me think that is his usual job. Wesley and I sit on the sofa.

"You did real good in there, Bel. Theo will be as proud as punch when he hears about it," Wes praises me.

"Thanks, Wes. I just hope this plan works and we get them all back soon. He's only been gone a couple of hours and I'm already feeling edgy. I don't know how you've managed to get through the two days Alyssa has been missing," I say truthfully. My wolf seems to be pacing constantly and there is no calming her.

"Neither do I. Just keep telling myself we'll get her back. We have to," he admits.

Billy comes in with three drinks. "We'll get them all back tomorrow, try not to worry." Wesley and I both smile at Billy's words. I have a feeling that none of us are as confident as Billy sounded right then. When there's a bunch of werewolves going against someone that can control werewolves, there are a number of things that can go wrong.

"Right. Let's get down to business. What did Dominick tell you about tonight?" Wesley asks.

I tell them everything about the fight; from when Billy left Theo and Dominick alone in front of Misty's, to when Billy returned after I saved Dominick. I take a sip of my coffee and look up to find Wesley looking livid.

"Did you just say Dominick fed from you again, *and* nearly drained you in the process?" he demands. I won't call him up on his demanding tone. He's concerned about his missing mate. He deserves some slack.

"Yes," I say cautiously. When he doesn't say anything and just stares at me, I feel the need to say more. "He did drain me, to the point that if I was human I don't think I'd be here now, but I'm alive and that's the main thing. It wasn't Dominick's fault. He was nearly dead himself and I taste good. Ask Paddy later, he'll agree—I'm hard to resist." I laugh nervously, unable to stop my rambling. "He couldn't stop, but thankfully he stopped in time. I didn't think he'd drain me, or even come close but he was so out of it…I was wrong."

"I'm glad I'm not the one who has to tell Theo when he gets back," Wes says, thankfully sounding slightly calmer.

Thinking about Theo being protective brings Ruby to my mind. "Oh my god! How is Ruby? Is she still here? Does she know what's happened?" I can't believe I had forgotten about Ruby. She must be so worried.

"Yes. I'm here and I know," says a voice from behind me.

I turn around to see her standing out from behind the sofa I'm sitting on. Her red eyes and wet cheeks tell me she's been crying for some time. How did none of us notice her? How long has she been there?

"What are you doing down here? I told you to stay upstairs." Oh great. Angry Wesley is back.

Ruby cowers slightly but stands her ground. "No one would tell me anything! I needed to know. Theo wasn't here," she points at Wes, "and you guys were holding a meeting and running around looking all worried. I knew something bad had happened." She breaks down into heaving sobs.

I get up, put my arm around her shoulders and bring her back to sit on the sofa. She shuffles into the corner of the cozy sofa.

"I'm Bel. I don't think we were introduced last night," I say.

"Yeah. I asked Ted about you after you left." She bursts into tears again and I stroke her knee for a second to comfort her. Weres are touchy feely creatures. We use touch to comfort each other. Sometimes we even sleep in piles. Being the outsider of the pride I had never been privy to one of these piles but I have heard plenty about them. Ruby is only human but having grown up around a pack, I'm sure she's used to touch and comfort as any were is.

"He'll be back tomorrow." I try to sound confident.

Wesley looks at me. "What did you and Dominick agree on as the plan for tomorrow night?" He still sounds mad but I can tell he's trying to sound calmer. He probably doesn't want to upset Ruby any more.

"We didn't come up with anything in great detail. Dominick will be in the alley out back of the bar and some of us will be hiding in the shadows to protect him when they attack. But before we jump in, we have to find the controller. He has to be somewhere with a view of the alley. He'll need a view of them to be controlling them as well as he is. He must be at a vantage point. I'd suggest a fire escape or the rooftop of one of the surrounding buildings. You two would be best to decide who and how many of us go. I think it would be safest if we make it look like you're meeting Dominick, Wes. As second to Theo, everyone except pack will think you're in charge. Do you think you'll be able to handle being in the line of fire when Alyssa attacks?" I hold my breath hoping his answer is what I want to hear.

"I'd actually prefer that over hiding. I'd want to run out when I see her so if I was meant to be hiding, I would ruin everything. That all sounds great. You are going to make a great alpha female," he says with a smile.

"Billy, you have a think about who you think is best for the job overnight. We can discuss your choices tomorrow and then start with the phone calls."

"No worries! I've been thinking already. The boss can communicate with the two of us when we are in wolf form. Do you think if we tried now he could tell us where he is and we could go get him?"

Wesley looks serious for a moment before a huge smile spreads across his face. "That might actually work. He's badly injured so he should still be in wolf form. Only problem is, we can't talk to him and he won't know to communicate with us if he doesn't hear us." His face is solemn but suddenly hope dances behind his eyes. "Bel, you're his mate. It should work between the two of you. Dammit! Why didn't I think of that sooner?"

"Do you really think that could work? I haven't even met his wolf yet." I knew that wasn't exactly true as soon as it left my mouth. I know his wolf. He's there with Theo all the time. He's part of him just like my wolf is part of me.

"Alyssa and I can do it and we're not true mates like you and Theo are. Your bond is one of the strongest bonds I've seen. Everyone in the pack can feel how much he loves you. When Theo falls, he falls hard." He rolls his eyes. "What have you got to lose? You might as well try it."

All three of them stare at me, hopeful. How could I let them down? Plus, if I can get Theo back tonight that would be wonderful.

"Okay. You'll need to talk me through it. Remember. I've never done this before."

"All you have to do is shift and talk to him in your head. If it's going to work he'll hear you and you'll hear him reply, his voice in your head…It's odd at first but you'll get used to it," Wes informs me.

Here goes nothing.

I stand up and crouch behind the sofa. I don't like the idea of getting naked in front of Wesley and Billy, let alone Theo's teenage sister, Ruby. I strip with great difficulty; the dress is the easy bit. It's the underwear that causes me trouble. You try taking undies off while crouching down!

Naked as the day I was born, I take a calming breath to relax. I don't even need to call my wolf to come forward. The instant my defences are down, she's there taking over my body. Her anxiety over Theo isn't helping my pain during the change. I can't stop myself from grunting. Once I feel the change is complete and the pain starts to ease, I open my eyes and see furry paws in front of me. I try to shake out the remaining tingles before I walk around the sofa into the view of Billy, Wesley, and Ruby.

A gasp comes from Ruby and I whine in response. I don't want her to be scared of me. Her gasp confuses me, being brought up with werewolves, surely she has seen plenty of them in the fur before.

"She won't hurt you, Ruby. You don't need to be scared," Wes calmly reassures her.

"I'm not scared."

She is telling the truth. I smell no fear. Billy and Wesley should sense that too.

I start to walk over to her slowly, so she can touch me if she wants to. That might make her feel more at ease.

She moves to sit forward on the chair and reaches out to stroke me, starting with my shoulders. "Theo hasn't let me be around you guys in wolf form for such a long time. It was a shock to be so close to the beauty of you," she says, as her stroking hand works its way behind my ears. She knows how to stroke a wolf. That's the best spot to scratch. She could scratch me there all day if she wanted to.

"Our Bel here is some beauty," Billy says. He's the sweetest, scary biker, werewolf I have ever met.

"Let's find Theo. Focus people." Wesley sounds anxious.

He's right!

I lie down on the floor in front of the sofa and close my eyes.

"Theo, can you hear me?" I ask in my head, feeling like an idiot. Nothing. I knew this wouldn't work.

"Theo…Theo…It's Bel."

"Bel…you're…here?" He gasps and grunts and pauses between each word, like it is taking a great effort to speak.

I'm suddenly hit by an immense wall of pain. Great. My empathy even works this way. I suppose it's all through telepathic connection in a way so I don't know why I am so surprised.

"I…can't…see…you." I feel his hope; no doubt at the thought of rescue. He must think I'm there and not realise I'm only in his head.

"No. I'm not in the room, Theo; I'm in your head, like when you communicate with Billy and Wesley in wolf form."

I feel him deflate as the hope in him vanishes in a split second.

"We're coming to get you. You just need to tell me where he's keeping you," I say quickly, hoping to lift his mood.

"Was unconscious, don't know," he stumbles.

"What can you see around you now?" I ask hoping he can pick something, anything, up.

"Black. No eyes," He's not making much sense.

I reach through the bond hoping to pick up something better, but I get the shock of my life, he's so close to death.

"Theo, baby, we have a plan—a trap for whoever has you. We'll have you back tomorrow night." I hope he can hang on until tomorrow.

"Danger. Can control pack. Can't confront him," he warns.

"It's okay. The Pack will be safe, I promise."

I hope!

"Why aren't you healing? You shouldn't be in this much pain now." He should have been healing. If anything, he feels like he's getting worse as I talk to him.

"Need meat." His anger hits me like a physical punch to the gut.

"What? He's not given you any?" I can't believe he'd starve an injured werewolf. He must be insane. Wolves are dangerous as it is but an injured wolf is even worse. All they can think about is healing and meat gives us the energy to heal.

"N…" I take that as a no.

"Please stay with me. Hang on until tomorrow night. We'll

come and get you. I need my Teddy bear to hug remember?" Nothing.

Oh god, please!

"Babe, you're my mate. I've only just found you. Don't leave me now. I need you."

"Bel…I…love…you!"

"I love you, too. You're going to hang on for me, aren't you?" I beg.

"I'll try." He feels uncertain. "He's coming."

"Can you smell him?" I feel a sharp pain in my neck.

"Tran." He disappears. I can't feel him anymore.

Tran? Tran? Tranquilliser!

My anger and sadness fills me.

I open my eyes and the scene before me is really confusing. I am standing at the bottom of the stairs, growling at Billy and Wesley, who are guarding Ruby half way up those stairs.

Chloe barges through the door to the hall on my left shouting, "What is going on d…" the second she sees me, she changes her tone to a whisper, "Wes. What's happening?"

My attention instantly changes from the three on the stairs to Chloe. My wolf has been dying to tear her apart.

Wes doesn't answer her and addresses me instead. "Bel. Did you talk to Theo?" I can feel him coming back down the stairs.

I stalk closer to Chloe. She is backing up against the wall. The fear coming from her is making me enjoy this all the more. I growl at her.

The terrified scream behind me catches my attention.

Ruby.

"Bel. Where's Ted? Let's go get Ted." She sounds terrified.

Ted, my Teddy.

I instantly shift back to human. I'm naked in front of the four of them.

Wes grabs my clothes and brings them over warily.

"I'm sorry about all that. I didn't realise it was happening, I wasn't aware of the things here. I was with Theo. Did I hurt anyone?" I look at each of them inspecting for injuries.

They all stare at me in silence.

I can still feel Chloe frozen in fear behind me as I slip the dress over my head. I shift the position of my body slightly so that my back is to the sofa and Chloe is to my side; in case she decides to attack. She has her head down in a bow towards me.

"No, Bel. You just scared us for a minute, that's all." Ruby sounds shaken.

"Ruby. I'm sorry I didn't mean to scare you," I plead.

"It's okay."

"What made you so angry? Is Theo okay?" Wesley asks, even he sounds shaken.

I look at Ruby wondering what to say? How much can she take? It doesn't take her long to guess what I'm thinking.

"Just tell me. I need to know, even if he's dead. Please just tell me." I hope she really means what she's saying.

"He's not dead, but he's in a real bad way. I'm not sure he'll last the night."

The whole room fills with everyone's sadness.

"He wasn't making complete sense, but he knows we are coming for him tomorrow night and he said he'll try to fight, to hang on until then. He's not getting any meat and he isn't healing."

They are all listening in silence but their emotions are speaking loud and clear. They've all gone from sadness over his imminent death to raging anger over the controller not giving him any meat.

"He can't see anything. I don't know if his eyes are injured or he's blindfolded. He just said black, when I asked him what he could see. He was unconscious between Misty's and getting there so he doesn't have any idea where he is. The controller just shot him with a tranquilliser dart and that's when I lost contact with him."

They are still staring at me in silence, but the rage is speaking loud and clear.

Billy is the first to break the silence. "Fuck! I can see why you became so aggressive."

"Okay. So tonight's rescue mission is a no-go but we still have tomorrow's plan of attack." I think Wesley is trying to reassure us all so we keep our hopes up, but maybe he is just reassuring himself out loud.

"Since I know we're not being ambushed and the growling has finished, I'm going back to bed, good night." Chloe turns and leaves out the same door she just entered, shutting it behind her.

"I'm off to bed, too," I say. "We'll need as much energy as possible for tomorrow. It's going to be physically and emotionally draining. Billy. You're staying here the night, aren't you?"

Billy nods in response.

"Bel, you might as well stay, too. There are enough rooms. You're acting leader. It would probably be best to be where the Pack can get in touch with you," Wes suggests.

"Plus, the more weres in here the safer since someone broke the door and deemed it unlockable." A smarty-pants Billy adds, making us all laugh.

"I'm not sure. I need to eat." Shifting takes energy and makes me hungry. "I don't have any other clothes here and I can't really sleep in this," I say, gesturing towards my dress.

"Ted has heaps of food. He's always eating. I'm sure we can also find you a spare t-shirt and sweats. Please say you'll stay," Ruby begs, with an eager look on her face.

"Okay. I hope there is a lot of food because I'm going to be shifting a number of times over night to check in on Theo; remind him to hang in there. Where are you sleeping Ruby?"

"I'm in the room next to Ted's. You could sleep in the room on the other side of mine," she offers.

"Okay. Sounds like a plan," I agree, with a smile.

"I guess that means I'm your next door neighbour, hey?" Billy says, as he nudges Wes in the ribs.

"Ow, Billy. If you're scared of sleeping downstairs on your own, you can be my neighbour. I'm off now. Do you want me to walk with you, Billy, to keep you from getting scared?" Wes jokes making us all burst into laughter.

"Fuck off, mate," Billy says.

"We can ring the pack members we decide would be best for the job after breakfast; about ten o'clock. All three of us will need to be down here to discuss it at eight thirty," Wes says more seriously.

I frown. I'm not sure if it's the fact that Wes wants me in on the decision or if it's the fact that he was referring to eight thirty in the morning. I haven't seen that time of the day in years!

"Why do I need to be here that early? I wouldn't have a clue who would be good for the job." I complain.

"You need to ring and give the order to do the job. It comes with the role of the alpha's mate. Well in this situation, it does anyway."

"Then I can come down at nine forty-five," I suggest, more cheerful at that thought.

Billy starts to laugh. "Are you not a morning person by any chance, Wolfy?"

"Are you kidding? I've not seen that side of noon for the last two years," I say, shaking my head. *It's too bloody early.*

"Eight thirty," is all Wes says, as he opens the door leading to the hall.

Billy waves bye to us and follows Wes, closing the door behind him. Leaving me and Ruby alone in the lounge room.

23

REUNION

*H*earing Bel's voice gave me a boost. I don't know how she knew but I was desperate for something to cling on to—to make myself live. She reminded me that I have a pack, a mate, and my baby sister relying on me. I need to get through this. The tranquilliser wasn't fun, but it's wearing off now. I need to focus.

"Look, he's coming around." Is that Alyssa?

"Don't get too excited. He might be too out of it to recognise us. He might attack us." That is definitely Paddy.

He must have knocked me out so he could bring them in here.

"At least he might recognise you. I've only met him twice. He'll eat me first," says who I can only assume is, Jared. Since I saw his lion attacking Dominick earlier I know he's under the kidnapper's control.

I need to shift back to human. I can't exactly talk to them in my wolf form. They are right. An injured werewolf is dangerous. I rein the wolf in. He comes willingly, knowing it's the best thing for all of us. He may be injured but he knows I would never put us in danger while we're so vulnerable. It's one of the most painful changes I have ever made. The intensity of the pain takes my breath away. I lay as still as possible once I'm human, not wanting to irritate my already sensitive skin and nerves.

"Theo, it's Alyssa. Can you hear me?"

"Yes," is all I can manage. The shift took it out of me. I will heal better in wolf form. The sooner I can talk to them and get back, the better. I honestly don't feel like I am going to make it until tomorrow night.

Someone covers me with a blanket.

"Someone needs to take those bullets out of you. You're never going to heal if those stay in you," Alyssa says, rubbing at a sore spot on my upper arm.

"Bullets?" I ask, trying to inspect my arm.

"I'm betting silver by the way you're not healing," Jared says, as he steps closer.

I can't control the warning growl that comes out of my mouth.

He holds his hands up in surrender and takes a step back. "Sorry. You're injured and your wolf doesn't know me. I'll stay over here."

"I can smell your lion. My wolf doesn't like that you are a predator. I'm sorry. I'm not normally so grouchy."

"It's understandable. You have at least three silver bullets in you and numerous injuries that aren't healing," Jared admits.

"I have your blood on me. I can smell it. Did we do that to you?" Alyssa asks, sounding distraught.

I sit up, ignoring the pain that rolls through my body, and pull her into my arms. "Alyssa, you did not do this. You may have been the weapon but whoever has us was wielding that weapon. Do you hear me?" I command.

"Yes," she whispers against my chest.

I look over at Paddy and he must see the pain on my face. He walks over and pulls Alyssa against his own chest.

"Go sit with Jared whilst I try removing the bullets out of Theo," he says, guiding her towards Jared.

Paddy turns back towards me and starts poking at my arm. "If I could shift just my claws, I could probably dig them out, but I can't do that. They're too deep. I need something…" he says, as he looks around the room for anything that could be of use.

I look around, too. The room is sparse. Three camping beds against different bare walls and a bucket in the corner. I guess the kidnapper doesn't want us to find anything we can use as a weapon.

"Can you shift just your claws, Jared?" Paddy asks, as he looks at Jared.

"I can but Theo's wolf won't let me near him as it is. There is no chance in hell he will let me near him with my claws out," he says, from his seat on one of the beds, with Alyssa tucked into his side.

"It's okay. I'll be able to hang on until tomorrow night. I spoke with Bel before he knocked me out." I tap my forehead to clarify how I spoke to her. "They have a plan."

"Bel is always the one with the plan. You're a lucky man," Jared says.

I am feeling weaker by the second. The silver isn't doing me any favours. I need to get it out. I shift just my hands, hoping to be able to dig them out myself. I reach around to the one Paddy was poking at and I can just reach it. I cut a cross through the wound to make it bigger and then dig my claw into the newer larger hole. I feel the silver. Not only does the arm it's in sting like a bitch, but it stings the claw that touches it too. Trying to ignore the pain, I keep digging. I add another claw to the wound hoping to pincer it out. It works! I drag the bullet through the wound and drop it to the floor with a grunt.

Feeling slightly faint and nauseous, I give up any thought of removing the other bullets and lay down where I am sitting. "That will have to do. I can't do anymore."

"You did good, mate. I honestly don't think I could have done that if I was in your shoes," Jared praises. "If you shift, I will watch over your wolves whilst you sleep."

I don't even bother thanking him. I give my body over to my wolf and fall into a deep sleep.

24

SEEKING CONTACT

"*O*kay. First things first. Where's the food?" I ask Ruby, as my stomach grumbles in agreement.

Ruby leads me to the kitchen and starts pulling food out for a sandwich. I manage to stop myself from eating the ingredients before the sandwich is made. But once that sandwich is in my hands, I eat in total silence, enjoying every mouthful.

Once I'm finished we both head up to the bedrooms. Since I have to get up so early, I should get as much sleep as possible. I also need to ring Misty and Benji; he should be home and I haven't heard from him yet. I understand why he was so mad when I didn't ring him after arriving here.

We get to Ruby's room and say our goodnights before she enters and closes the door behind her.

My door is painted a lovely lavender colour. The bedroom is laid out the same as all the other rooms I've seen. There's a brass bed with the head against the far wall, which has bedside cabinets on either side. There is a dresser on the side wall that has a plant pot with a lavender plant in it. The other wall has two doors—I'm guessing an ensuite and a wardrobe. The room has a really calming feel to it. Not that it will help calm my wolf at all, she's too edgy. The only thing that will put her at ease is having our mate happy and healthy in front of us.

I take my phone from my clutch bag and call Benji. It rings for a long time making me think it's going to click over to voicemail.

I'm just about to disconnect the call when Aunt Lily answers.

"Hello. This is Benjamin's phone."

"Hi Aunt Lily. It's Rosabel. I'm just ringing to make sure he got home safely. Is Uncle Jack okay?"

"Jack is doing fine. He's complaining about being cooped up so it seems he is back to his normal self. Benjamin is trying to distract him with a game of chess at the moment, but you know Jack. He won't be fooled for long. Shall I get him to call you back?"

"It's getting late now. I'll try him again tomorrow. Thanks, Aunt Lily. Pass my love onto Uncle Jack and you take care."

"Thank you, Rosabel. Good night."

"Bye," I say, disconnecting the call.

I don't bother putting the phone away. Instead, I scroll through my contacts and call Misty.

"Hello?" she answers with a sleepy voice.

"Misty, it's Bel. Did I wake you up? I'm sorry."

"It's okay. I wasn't in bed. I dozed off on the sofa with the candle burning, so it's a good job ya called or the candle could have burnt the apartment down. How's the pack coping without Theo?" she asks, sounding more alert.

"They're doing as good as can be expected and surprisingly they're letting me lead them. I only had a little trouble from Chloe, but that wasn't anything new. She wouldn't let me in. I knocked her out and ended up breaking Theo's front door in the process." I'm still dreading the cost of that door.

"You knocked her out?" she asks, surprise clear in her voice.

"Yeah. In my defence I just wanted to get past and I did try asking first. We have a plan for tomorrow night. The only thing is, with me falling into the leader position it means I need to be there. Do you think Lucy will be able to cover for me?" I ask, dreading her answer. If she can't do it, I have no idea what I will do.

"I guessed ya'd need a few nights off. She said she can do the next three nights."

"Oh, Misty. You are a star! I'm so bloody unreliable. I'm surprised you haven't fired me yet," I say, only half joking.

"The reasons you've been unreliable have been through no fault of your own. I'm not firing you for that."

"Thanks anyway. I have to go now. Wesley wants me up at eight thirty. Can you believe it? I think he's mad. I'll try and pop in the bar before all hell breaks loose."

"No problem. Sleep tight. I'm glad I won't be up that early. He's definitely not sane," she jokes, before disconnecting the call. I didn't even get to remind her to blow out the candles.

I quickly type up a text before setting my alarm for eight thirty and placing my phone on the cabinet by the bed.

I head into the bathroom to clean up. I find a towel and a towelling robe hanging on the back of the door so I decide to take a shower. The hot water running down my body is calming and relaxing but I start to remember my last shower with Theo. Before I know it I have tears streaming down my face. I don't want Theo to be torn away from me before I really get to have him.

Once I'm dried with Theo fresh on my mind, I decide to drop in on him to check he is still okay. I close my eyes and pray he's there.

"Theo. It's Bel. Can you hear me?" I wait for a reply but it doesn't come. I try again.

"Teddy baby, keep fighting. I'm coming to get you." I still don't get a reply but I can faintly feel his hope. He must be in a deep sleep, hopefully healing. Either that or the tranquilliser hasn't worn off. I'll hope for the former.

I open the door of the bathroom to find Wesley sitting on my bed. Glad I decided to wear the robe; I pull the tie making sure it's secure.

"Oh. Hi Wes." To say I'm surprised to find him here is an understatement. The look on his face tells me how worried he is. I have no doubts it's about Alyssa.

"How's Theo? Is Alyssa with him?" He blurts out.

I make my way over and take a seat next to him. "I'm not sure. I couldn't get a response from him maybe the tranquilliser hasn't worn off. I think he heard me because I could feel his hope, faintly. The good news is he's still alive. Sorry if I woke you up. I didn't think I'd be noisy."

"No. It's okay. At least we all know it's just you and we're not under attack. You need to keep checking on them to make sure they're all okay." His voice trembles as he speaks. I don't blame him.

I'm worried and I haven't been mated anywhere near as long as he has. I'm surprised he hasn't tried communicating with her since she's been missing. "Did Theo order you not to try and communicate with Alyssa?"

He tilts his head to the side with a stern look on his face. "Yes. He said I'd get lost in the communication and wouldn't leave her. It's been killing me knowing I could talk to her but I'm not allowed. I know he's right but it's still hard." He turns his eyes back to the floor before standing and making a move for the door. "I suppose I better let you get to sleep before you want to contact Theo again."

"I'm not sure I'll be able to sleep," I admit.

"I know," he says as he closes the door behind him. Just before it shuts he sticks his head back in. "Thank you."

I smile in return, but it's too late I'm left staring at a closed door. Getting into bed is easy. Laying there and trying to fall asleep is harder than I expected. I can't stop thinking about Theo and how if he hadn't been taken we would probably be in his room right now, snuggling up in bed amongst other things. Thinking about snuggling with Theo makes me crave his scent. I quickly pull on the robe and go to his room.

I open the door to Theodore's room and see Ruby sitting on the bed with her back against the head board, cuddling one of the pillows in a death grip. If that pillow was a person they would be struggling to breathe. The room looks different from how it looked last night and I can't quite place what's causing the change.

"I'm sorry. I didn't think anyone would be here. I'll leave you to it." She looks up at me in shock like she hadn't even heard me enter.

"No. Stay." She pats the bed next to her in a gesture for me to join her. "You miss him too. You need to be here just as much as I do." That's what's different; the bed has fresh sheets on it. A deep blood red satin set is replacing the black set from last night.

I sit on the bed next to her and we both slide down under the covers and sniff the sheet at the same time trying to breathe in Theo's scent. We look at each other and laugh.

"I know it doesn't even smell of him because I helped him put them on fresh this afternoon. How stupid am I?"

"As stupid as me because I know they were black sheets last night." We both chuckle in unison.

"Do you like the red? He put them on especially for you. He said red is the colour of passion. It reminds me more of blood than passion but, hey, that's my opinion," she says with a shrug.

"Well to be honest, I thought of blood, too, but don't tell Theo I said that. I do like it though, now I know what he meant by it." I admit.

"I heard you growling not long ago. Were you talking to him? How is he?" All the happiness she just had in her face vanishes with her words. I can feel nothing but sadness coming from her.

"He's still in a deep sleep. I didn't get a reply from him but I could feel him. He's still alive," I say cheerily, hoping to give her something to cling on to. "Will you tell me about him? I haven't known him for that long; I'd love to hear some stories," I add. Hearing about him will make me feel closer to him, and hopefully talking about him should do the same for Ruby.

ONE TRACK MIND

"*R*osabel! Wake up!" Wesley's shout wakes me up. It sounds like he's pounding on the bedroom door, the one I was meant to be staying in anyway.

"I'm coming in," I hear him announce.

I stifle my laugh; he's not going to find me in there.

"DAMN IT," he yells.

I stay quiet. He can wait for me to get dressed. He sounds mad and I don't really fancy facing a stressed out, angry werewolf first thing in a morning.

Ruby and I talked for most of last night. She told me about their upbringing, which sounded just as hard as mine but for different reasons. Their mother and father split up when Theodore was nine years old, and his mother was pregnant with Ruby. Their dad was high up in the pack. He couldn't divide himself equally between family and pack. Ruby mentioned another brother called Cain, who is two years younger than Theo. Apparently he's a lone wolf, who doesn't get in touch often. The werewolf gene skipped Ruby; which she finds disappointing.

Unfortunately, just because you have a were as a parent, does not mean you will be a were, too. They have human genes, as well. It's just luck of the draw. I'm not sure where the luck lies though. Are you lucky if you do become were or you don't? I suppose that is up to the individual really.

Once Theo changed for the first time when he was sixteen, his father took him under his wing and introduced him into the pack. Doing the same thing with Cain two years later. With Ruby being human, their father wasn't interested in her.

Ruby turned up on Theo's doorstep because her mother's latest boyfriend is a sleaze ball—Ruby's words. He came on to her and when she turned him down, he told her mother she came on to him. Her mother hit her and threw her out. I don't know how a mother could do something like that to her daughter.

Once the sun came up we decided we needed to go to sleep before we lost the chance for sleep altogether. We ended up sleeping next to each other in Theo's bed.

"ROSABEL! Where the hell are you? You better not have teleported home to get more sleep!" Wesley sounds like he's ready to tear my head off. I better face him now before he actually does tear it off.

"I'm coming, keep your hair on." I didn't bother shouting. He'd be able to hear my voice downstairs with his hearing. Only Ruby wouldn't be able to hear anything out of the room she's in, being the only pure human in the house.

Wes storms into the room and takes in the scene before him. He looks mortified at the sight of us both in bed.

"You don't seriously think…" I can't even finish the question. I know what he is thinking. I can't believe he's jumping to that conclusion.

Ruby must catch onto our train of thought because she burst out laughing. "Look at his face," she manages to get out, before another fit of laughter takes over.

"Have you managed to wake sleeping beauty up yet? I thought you might need a prince to do it." We can hear Billy taking the stairs two at a time. He must have felt Wesley's horror because he suddenly becomes very serious. "Wes. What's wrong mate?" He walks around Wesley to see what he is looking at. Us! "No way!" He sounds excited. He seems to be taking the scene better than Wesley had, but he's jumped to the same wrong conclusion. He seems more excited than I'd like; especially since Ruby is involved. She is only seventeen. Too young for him to be thinking about like that.

"You are not serious." Ruby sounds astonished by two guys coming to the same conclusion after seeing two girls in the same bed.

"Ruby. You must know by now, especially since you hang out with Theo's pack a fair bit," I say, as I get out the bed in my underwear—they've already seen me in my birthday suit, underwear is a step up. I walk over to Theo's chest of draws. I start raking through it to find something to wear. "Men have a one-track mind. Especially when faced with two women in bed together, no matter how wrong they are."

I find some t-shirts in the top drawer and take one out. It's the one with the werewolf howling at the moon, that he'd been wearing the first night I saw him. I find some sweatpants in the third drawer and pull out a grey pair.

"Do you think Theo will mind if I borrow these?" Billy is still staring at me; Wesley's eyes are averted to the floor, with bright red cheeks. I stand waving the clothes in the air but no one is answering me.

When I glance over at Ruby, she is getting out of bed and grabbing the robe off the foot of the bed to cover herself, being careful not to flash her underwear to us.

"Billy, what are you staring at?" I ask, hoping to keep his eyes on me.

"Sorry, but you were both in there in just your underwear!" he says, as if we don't already know.

"Yes. We both had the same idea of being close to Theo by being in here. We talked for a while and went to sleep when the sun came up," I clarify.

"Together!" Wesley still sounds stunned.

"I'm going to use the bathroom now. That's if I'm allowed?" I don't wait for an answer. Instead, I go straight in to the bathroom and lock the door, hoping Ruby can manage to escape without a Spanish inquisition.

Before I even bother getting dressed, I shift, calling my wolf forward so we can check on Theo again. "Theo. Can you hear me?"

"Bel. You're okay? I was worried the tranquilliser had hurt you when he shot me." It's great to hear his voice.

I can't help but giggle at his words. "You're the one on deaths door, and yet you're worried about me? I'm fine. I tried to communicate with you again before I went to bed, but you were out cold. I could feel you faintly so I knew you were still with us," I explain.

"I'm glad you're okay." I feel him relax through our mating bond.

"Has he given you any meat yet? You sound and feel much better."

"Yes. He gave us some meat during the night. It won't keep me going long. It was enough to let me draw some energy from the pack. It should keep me going until you get here, later."

"Ruby and Wesley will be glad to hear you're better. You said us. Are you with the others?"

"Yes. They were in the room when I came around from the tranquilliser. They're both well. Alyssa was a little distraught at the thought of having hurt me but I think I managed to talk her out of that. Jared is here too. How is Dominick and Chomp? They were both in big trouble when I fell unconscious?" He asks.

"Chomp is dead, well dead dead; you know what I mean. Dominick wasn't far from following him but I donated a bit of blood, and he's fine now." I hold my breath as I wait for his reply, wondering how he will take the news about Dominick feeding from me.

"I bet he enjoyed that, the donation. So that means we have

a tie to break again when I get back. That could be fun." His cheery reply helps me relax.

"Hey, cheeky. You might not be up to it." I can hear the laughter through our connection. But feeling through the bond, I can tell he's been pretending to feel better than he actually is. He feels extremely tired and he's struggling to keep up the act. "Theo. You can't fool me. I'm an empath and your mate. I can feel how tired you are."

"What? Your empathy works even like this?" He sounds as shocked as I was when I discovered it too.

"Yes. You're feeling guilty now for lying to me. Actually, you're probably only feeling guilty because I found out. You didn't feel guilty when you were actually lying."

"Sorry. I'm just trying not to worry you." I can feel the truth to his words.

"I know you're going to hang on for us, no matter how bad you feel. You're not one to give up. I better go before Wesley rips my head off."

"He better not." He sounds mad; his anger flowing through the bond confirms it. I'll take it as a good sign that he has the energy to spare on emotions like that.

"Oh, he's mad because he told me I had to be up, ready and downstairs by eight thirty. Have you heard of such a stupid idea? That is way too early for me to get up. He had to come in the bedroom and wake me up just before I came to talk to you. I'm only guessing because I haven't seen a clock yet, but it feels like lunchtime, but that could just be the hunger from all these changes confusing my biological clock," I try to explain.

"He can't give you orders," Theo demands. Did he even listen the rest of what I had said?

"I know. I had to lead a pack meeting last night. That was so fun." Sarcasm at its best.

"Did you have any trouble?" he asks, sounding nervous.

I really shouldn't worry him, but he'll be able to tell if I keep it from him. "Not really, except I owe you a new set of front doors. Don't worry. It's secure enough with all the top dogs staying there," I joke, hoping he doesn't ask for more details.

"Oh great. I dread to think what else can get broken before I get back tonight," he says with a laugh.

"I better go rally the troops so we can prepare for your rescue."

"I love you, Bel." It isn't just words. I feel the love being sent through the bond.

"And I love you, Theo." I could spend all day talking to him but I know I can't so I tear myself away by pulling my wolf back.

I get dressed as quickly as I can.

I head down the stairs and in my haste I lose my footing about halfway down. I reach out trying to grab the wall or something to stop my fall but there is nothing I can grip.

"SHIT!" I scream as I fall head first down the stairs.

Billy appears out of nowhere, at the bottom of the stairs, stopping my decent before my face smashes into the slate floor. "Jesus, Bel. Are you okay?"

"Oh my god, Bel!" Ruby cries, her voice sounding closer as she gets nearer.

"You caught me just in time, thanks Billy. You appeared out of nowhere. How did you know?" I ask.

"I felt you through the pack bond, not to mention heard you thudding down the stairs. I'm a werewolf. I've got good speed. I'm just glad I was quick enough. We can't have you damaging that beautiful face of yours." He leans to kiss me on the head but Ruby pushes him off me trying to help me up; which would be easier if my feet weren't still halfway up the stairs.

If Ruby had just left it to Billy to help me up, he would've been able to support my weight no problem. Hell, he'd be able to bench press a car, one-handed at that. That's a good bonus to being a were, super strength, and like Billy already said, speed. Unfortunately, Ruby doesn't have the strength of a were.

After watching us struggle for a second, not to mention seeing my face almost hit the floor once or twice, Billy barges Ruby out of the way. "Move it, Rubes, I'll get her. You go make Bel a coffee. I have a feeling she needs one to function in the morning."

Ruby disappears into the kitchen, hopefully to make that coffee. Billy is right. I'm ready for one.

Billy picks me up without a problem and carries me across the room to the sofa.

"Thanks Billy," I say, as he sets me down on the sofa.

Wesley is sitting opposite me with a face like thunder. *Thanks for your concern.*

"Sorry it took me a while to get down here, but I checked in on Theo while I was in the bathroom."

"We heard you. How is he?"

Ruby passes me a mug of coffee and it smells perfect. I take a sip, burning my tongue; I do that so often you would think I'd learn my lesson and wait for it to cool before drinking it, but the smell draws me in every time. I set the mug down on the coffee table before I do it again, as Ruby takes he seat next to me.

All three of them watch me with anticipation written over their faces.

"He's okay. He didn't realise my empathy worked through the connection so he tried to pretend he was better than he is by acting all happy and normal, but I could feel how tired he was. He became a bit more truthful after I called him out on it. He's keeping his hopes up and knows we'll be there soon. He said he's been taking energy from the pack, which is helping him."

"So that's why you have been so grumpy, Wes." Billy nudges him in the ribs playfully.

"I thought Wes was always grumpy." giggles Ruby.

"Well there is my excuse. Now tell us the rest." He tries to give me an order.

I don't know what comes over me but I'm not standing for it.

I stare him in the eyes, I wouldn't normally stare a werewolf down unless I know I could kill them in a fight, like Chloe for instance. Because if you won't back down and they won't back down that is what a stare contest will lead to—a death match. Wesley is really dominant and so am I. I'm honestly not sure who would come out alive between the two of us. Since I'm Theo's mate, I'm pack leader in his absence so the orders should be coming from me alone, not Wesley. I can hold my wolf back and only show the dominance I am willing to show. I'm not really sure how I do it and I've never heard of anyone else that can do it. But I made the mistake of showing my full dominance to Jared's pack and I have learnt not to do that again. I usually try to make it so I sit in the middle of a pack, not too dominant to be considered a threat and not too weak to be abused. There is only Wesley and Billy here, so I pull out my dominance to make Wes come to his senses and back down.

As I strip down emotionally to bare my animal, I feel Chloe come in the room. Her fear starts to grow along with my dominance.

Neither Wesley nor I look away from each other. It goes on for what feels like a long time, neither of us wanting to give in. Thinking on it, I don't even think he really meant it as an order in the first place, but I am not backing down and Wesley obviously feels the need to stand his ground too.

"Come on guys, there's no need for this." Billy tries to stop us.

"Billy, keep out of it!" I order with every bit of dominance I have. I guess my point gets across because he doesn't speak again.

My order must make Wesley realise something too because he looks down to the floor before dropping to his hands and knees and crawling over to me. He stops before me and turns his head, baring his neck. It's an animal thing, to offer a vulnerable body part in apology to the more dominant giving them the choice to rip you apart or chastise you.

I choose the latter by leaning forward and biting his throat, not hard enough to draw blood or even hurt; a nip more than a bite. But it's a chastisement, which is needed. As weird as it feels, I know I have to do it, it comes with the job. Maybe it was Theo's anger over Wes and his orders still residing in me that caused me to stand my ground.

We both sit back in our seats without another word.

By now Chloe has joined us, sitting on the floor at Billy's feet. She's dressed extremely conservatively for Chloe; wearing a fuchsia pink hoodie and sweatpants, with hardly any flesh showing at all. I guess Theo isn't here to impress.

They all look at me in silence, waiting for me to carry on.

Before I can open my mouth, Ruby breaks the silence. "Does someone want to explain what just happened?"

Billy looks at me questioningly.

I nod allowing him to answer.

"Dominance games. Pack stuff, sweetie." He smiles at her reassuringly.

"But she bit him," she says, sounding astounded.

Wesley turns his neck to show her that there is no wound, just a pink mark which will fade to nothing in five minutes. "It wasn't hard," he admits.

She shrugs dismissively.

Billy is watching me. I can feel through his emotions that my dominance arouses him. I don't know whether to feel flattered or creeped out by that.

Chloe has fear rolling off her in waves. I'm not the only one who can feel it. Billy reaches out and rubs her shoulder in comfort.

Wesley is concerned, no doubt about Alyssa.

"Theo said the others are safe and well. They were all together after he came around from the tranquilliser," I say, realising I have made them wait long enough.

They all stare at me in silence so I speak again, hoping we can get back to more normal conditions. It's all too tense after the stare down. "So who are we taking tonight?"

Wesley hands me a piece of paper over the coffee table. "Billy and I picked a few guys we think will be best for the job. Their names and numbers are on there," he says, pointing at the piece of paper in my hand. "Obviously, if you think someone is better for the job, by all means change it."

"No. It's okay, Wesley. You both know the pack members better than me. You know who is right for the job." I glance over the list and notice Chloe's name isn't on it. Theo had told me she was one of the most dominant, and a good fighter, which made me think she'd be pretty useful. "How come Chloe's not on there? She is one of the strongest in the pack."

Chloe looks at me, gobsmacked.

I tried to sound as friendly as I can but I'm still showing too much dominance for my liking, with me shifting so much recently, I'm finding it hard to push it back into hiding. My wolf likes being out at full strength.

"Yeah. We were going to put Chloe on but we thought she'd be better staying here with Ruby. We know how good you are, Chloe," says Wesley. He sounds a lot calmer. We might be getting back to normality now.

"I don't need a babysitter, I'm seventeen," Ruby complains.

"No. She's not staying to babysit you. Think of it as more like a bodyguard. Especially, with the front doors in the mess they are in. Theo left you with me when he went out and I can't let anything happen to you while you're in my care," Wesley says.

"Fine," Ruby snaps back, clearly not happy but willing to let it slide.

I pick up the phone from the coffee table and call the guys on the list. They all listened to my instructions silently with no arguments—just like the three wolves in the room with me. Each of them assured me they would be at Misty's on time.

Billy manages to get us all joking and laughing in no time. He's got a heart of gold that one. He soon takes Ruby and Chloe in to the kitchen to help him make sandwiches for lunch, leaving me and Wesley alone in the lounge. I think he did it on purpose since there is still a little bit of tension between us. Maybe he hoped we'd be able to sort it out in private.

Wesley speaks up first. "About what happened earlier, I didn't mean it as an order. I was just grumpy and didn't think before I spoke."

"I know. I don't know what came over me, I think it might be something Theo said to me," I admit.

"You had every right. I shouldn't be giving you orders."

I feel the need to explain. "Theo said that too. I think with his words fresh in my mind and my wolf close to the surface with all these changes I have been doing, my animal instincts took over."

"How did you become so dominant and then just let it disappear again? You only feel mid-pack dominant now, but you were a hell of a lot more a minute ago?" He asks.

"To be honest. I'm not sure how I do it, or what I do. The best way to describe it is that I bury my dominance deep inside me and only leave a mid-level amount on show. When I was younger I had it all on show and had so much trouble with Jared's pride feeling threatened. I was always being challenged. That was probably just as much to do with being a wolf and didn't belong with the lions, as it was to do with my high dominance. One day it just happened. I could hide it, not that it helped with the lions. They already knew my full strength. I don't ever want to be treated like that again, so I keep it under wraps now."

"I never realised it would be hard being a lone wolf. Does Theo know about your strength?"

"I've never let it out since I originally hid it a couple of years ago. I don't think he knows, unless he has a way of feeling it without me showing it," I say, with a shrug.

The others come back with three big plates full of sandwiches and mugs of fresh coffee.

"I can't believe you two thought me and Bel were, you know…this morning," Ruby says, between bites of her sandwich.

"Come on. You were in bed together," Wesley says, grabbing a sandwich.

"And only in your underwear," Billy adds.

"What were we meant to think?" Wesley finishes.

"Chloe. What would you think if you saw me and Ruby just waking up in Theo's bed together?" I ask, just to prove a point.

"That you both needed to feel close to him," she answers, proving my point perfectly. *Men!*

"What? You wouldn't think they'd been together? Not even if they got out in just their bras and undies?" Billy seems astonished that she hadn't jumped to the same conclusion he and Wesley had.

"No. I guess it's a girl thing. My best friend and I used to sit and talk to each other while we had baths when we were growing up. Hell. We still do if we are getting ready for a night out together," She informs him, rendering Billy speechless.

"Besides. Rosabel is mated to Theo, and you both know I've had a crush on Paddy and Eddie, for like forever," Ruby says, blushing as she realises me and Chloe had no idea.

"Aw, Paddy is a sweetheart. Eddie is a player, I'm not sure

he's suitable for you Ruby," I say, getting nothing but an eye roll from her.

"Yes. Stay away from Ed. He'll end up breaking your heart," Wes warns Ruby. "I bet you weren't calling Paddy sweet when he was trying to make you his meal not so long ago," he says to me, with a smirk.

Ruby glances from Wes to me with a worried look on her face; probably concerned that her crush might have a habit of eating people. "*What?*"

"It wasn't really his fault. I was bleeding my delicious blood all over the place, right in front of him two days before the full moon. What did I expect?" I say, making everyone laugh at the thought.

26

UNEXPECTED GUEST

"Hubby. I'm home," says a stranger's voice from the front of the house, followed by a really irritating cackle of a laugh.

"Oh. God help us. The bitch is back! That's the last thing we need right now," Billy announces, obviously recognising the voice or more likely the cackle. That cackle isn't one you will forget in a hurry.

A blonde walks through the door looking like she's raided Chloe's wardrobe. She's wearing a baby pink tank top and a denim mini skirt, or belt whatever you prefer to call it, she's matched it with black knee high boots to finish off the look. Her mannerisms are just like Chloe's. She's almost like a twin.

"Oh great," Ruby whispers, as she gets up and heads for the kitchen.

"Wesley. What are you lot doing in my house? Where's Theodore?" She sounds just like Chloe too.

I bloody hate women with an attitude.

"Ruby is living here now. Theo asked us to stay and look after her while he's away with business." That was quick-thinking Wes. Well done.

"What? All of you? There are four of you looking after a seventeen-year-old?" she asks, sounding slightly perplexed.

"Yes. Safety in numbers and all. As you probably noticed, the front door isn't quite intact," Chloe throws out there.

"Ok. I'm going to get changed. If Theodore isn't here, his

room will be free. I'll go in there," she says, before heading for the stairs.

This strange woman is not sleeping in Theo's room. I don't care who she is. "No! That room is taken. Any of the downstairs rooms are free," I clarify.

I hear Billy chuckle and start to wonder what he's laughing at, until I catch a whiff of my bonding scent. Jealousy will do that to a girl.

"And who might you be?" she snaps at me with attitude that could give Chloe's a run for her money.

I look at Billy, who looks at Wesley, who looks back at me with a shrug.

Ruby comes back from the kitchen and perches next to me on the sofa. "That's Rosabel. She's Theo's girlfriend and that's why his room is taken."

"His girlfriend? Oh, well. I'll go in the baby pink room down the hall near the front door. My case is through that way. It saves me carrying it far," she says, sounding put out as she walks off. I don't feel one bit of guilt.

"Who is that?" I ask no one in particular.

"She's Theo's wife, Selena. They've been separated a year. She cheated on him," Wesley answers, clearly not wanting to.

I'm floored by his answer. No one has mentioned a wife to me. "His wife," I whisper to myself.

"Aw. Didn't he tell you he was married?" Chloe asks smugly. So much for thinking she was starting to like me.

"We've not really had a chance to have the getting to know you conversation, yet." That wipes the smug smile off her face; I don't need to tell her what we have done. She already knows. I quickly dismiss Chloe and look at Wesley. "You said she cheated on him. Is she insane? He'd kill the guy."

Wes glances nervously in the direction Selena had disappeared. "She doesn't know about any of us."

"What? He married her without telling her what he is?

Where did she think he went every full moon?" I whisper, so she doesn't hear me if she decides to come back—not that I couldn't feel or hear her coming. Sometimes when you know something is a secret, you can't help but whisper when talking about it.

"Exactly. She isn't really bright. She just believed he was away on business," he explains.

"Well, fuck," is all I can manage. I can't imagine Theo deceiving someone like that.

Selena comes back in the room, halting the conversation. She sits down and starts chatting to the others, as if she has never been away.

I manage to sneak off unnoticed and go back up to Theo's room, to get away from her. I need some time alone with my thoughts. I've got more than enough things to think about right now.

27

EXECUTIONER

I am only alone for about half an hour before Wesley knocks on the door to tell me we should think about going to find the best places to hide in the alley behind Misty's. He's right, of course. I tell him I'll meet him there after teleporting to the apartment, so I can change into more suitable clothes.

When I open my eyes, I find myself in my bedroom at Misty's. I can't help but notice how strange it feels being here. I don't belong here anymore. I go through the few clothes I have, hunting for the black hoodie and matching pants I know are there. I quickly pull them on with the black Nikes I have from my uniform at 'the Chief,' glad I had thought to bring them; considering I never wear them. It looks like they'll be my mission sneakers now.

Walking through the house looking for Misty, I come up empty. She must have gone to the bar early knowing we will be heading that way early as well.

I take a slow stroll to the alley to meet Wesley and Billy. I take the fifteen minutes it takes to psych myself up. I'm nervous about giving orders to all these guys. They all seemed compliant on the phone but they could always change their minds when they are face-to-face. We all need to do everything we can to get Theo and the others back. I feel down our mate bond, hoping for an insight into his well-being. He's still there but I can't get much else from him. Maybe he's blocking me from feeling him again.

It doesn't take us long to scout out some good hiding places. We decide to head in and grab a drink while waiting for the other guys.

We have chosen five of the of the most dominant pack members, thinking or more like hoping, the controller will have more trouble taking over the more dominant members. The only problem with that way of thinking is he's controlling Jared and he's alpha material. Wesley is adamant Theo's pack has some of the strongest wolves in Australia.

They all turn up one after another, not one of them a second late. The first to walk in is Darren from Billy's patrol the night before. We told everyone to wear black so it would be easier to hide in the shadows. He's wearing a black skin tight tank top and black slacks with his steel-toe cap boots. I still can't believe how huge he is. He had to open both doors to get in the bar.

Phil is next to come in, the other guy from Billy's patrol. He's wearing a black shirt, slacks and shoes, not his sandals and socks like he had on the other day. Although he looks like he's dressed for a party rather than an ambush. When I asked Billy earlier why he picked him, his answer was that he's reliable, fast, and loyal. 'He's the one person I'd want at my back in a fight,' he told me. I'm still not sure what good he'll be if all hell breaks loose, he doesn't look like the fighting type. I suppose if the plan works, we won't need any of the guy's. The only reason they are here is for plan b! I suppose if all hell breaks loose he'll be able to run away, *Fast!*

Greg is the next. He's one of the older pack members. He looks like he's in his mid-forties, although looks aren't much to go by with weres. We age slower than humans so we could be a lot older than we look. That being said, a human could look ten years older than he is and be bitten at forty. He'd still only look forty. Were DNA could cure a disease you carry but it won't make you look younger. He's five foot six, or thereabouts, with dark greying hair and hazel eyes. His camouflage consists of black jeans and black t-shirt with white sneakers.

Our fourth man to enter is Eddie—again, in an all-black ensemble. He's only twenty-two; I say only, but that's just two years younger than me. I think I feel older then I am because I had to grow up quick without my parents. He's got ginger hair and freckles with bright sky blue eyes. He's a similar build to Theo, not big but not small. He's cute, too. I can see why Ruby has a crush on him.

Our fifth and final man to turn up is, Dave. I recognise him as the cowboy guy at the meeting, who spoke up about my plan. Only today he's minus the cowboy gear. I don't think I would have noticed it was him if he hadn't given me a really mean look as he walked in. It's funny how you can remember who doesn't like you more than you can the friendly or silent ones. Without his cowboy hat, I can see a blonde ponytail and brown eyes. He is easily six feet tall.

They all greet us with a nod and wait for instructions; except Eddie, who decides to barge past everyone, grab me by the waist and give me a wet, open-mouthed kiss on the cheek. I push at his chest to get him out of my personal space. "Hi beautiful. Where do you want me?" he says, with a wiggle of his eyebrows. Yep. I was right. He's too much of a player for Ruby.

"Stop flirting, Ed, or Theo will kill you," Wes admonishes.

"Theo isn't here," he says, as he follows my step back.

"He'll hear about it, whether he is here or not. Now stop messing around. We need to focus on getting our pack members back," I order, having had enough of him wasting time. I quickly follow up with everyone's instructions on where they need to be and what they need to do.

It doesn't take us long to assemble into our designated positions; leaving us to wait for full dark to arrive along with the vampires. I'm hiding in a shadow at the entrance of the alley. I can smell Dominick so he must be nearby.

"Are you all here?" his voice says in my head, just before he walks around the corner.

How the hell did he do that?

He tells me, with two words, "The tie."

Brilliant. What other tricks does he have up his sleeve, thanks to that bloody tie?

"I'm not too sure myself, yet, Bel," he replies in a serious tone.

I wasn't talking to you. I think it managed to come over as a yell in my thoughts—I hope it did anyway.

"Sorry." I even hear the chuckle in his voice. It doesn't take Dominick long to reach Wesley.

I have a great view of them. I picked this position for that reason, plus the werewolves will have to pass me before they reach Dominick. That's when I need to turn my attention on our surroundings for the controller. I have a pretty good view of most of the buildings, thanks to the alley being nice and wide.

I hear a thud behind me so I turn quickly, hoping we didn't get all this wrong and I'm the one under ambush in the shadows where no one can see me. But I don't find an ambush.

I find Patsy facing me with a satisfied smile. "I scared you!"

I look her up and down, stunned that she's not wearing her usual attire. She's got her hair tied back and she's wearing sweatpants with a hoodie identical to mine.

"Patsy. I wasn't expecting you." There is no way I'll tell a vampire they scared me, true or false. "Dominick said he didn't want any of you here being put in danger."

"I'm not good with rules and orders. Especially in this case. I can't sit back and wait around while he's in danger. I'm not letting him be killed." I can feel her anger creep over my skin.

"I won't let him get killed either Patsy. Dominick knows that. I'll put my own life in danger before allowing his death."

"Yes, Dominick trusts you. But I don't. You have druid in you and they are not all to be trusted."

Alyssa, Paddy, and Jared come into view; thankfully they are all still in human form. I suppose that's a good thing.

I wonder how that thing works between me and Dominick. Maybe I can warn him. I was only thinking before. "Domini—"

His voice in my head cuts me off before I can say anymore. *"I heard, thanks."*

I turn my thoughts to looking for the controller by focusing on the roofs of the surrounding buildings. I can't see anyone on any of them. Why did I assume he'd be on a roof? He could be in one of the buildings looking out a window. If he's in the dark, we have no hope of seeing him.

Shit!

Panic flows through my body. If that's the case all hell's going to break loose and we won't all make it out alive, especially if he manages to take over the others I brought when they come out of the shadows!

"Rosabel. Feel for his emotions; vengeance or anger." Dominick's voice brings me out of the panic.

Yes. Okay. Calm down, Bel. Use your senses!

I reach out to see what emotions I can pick out. Everyone's emotions have an individual feel to them. People I've met once or twice like the guys, I can start to recognise their individual feel. I can ignore those emotions coming from our guys like, Wesley's sadness and concern, most probably over the sight of Alyssa. I can feel strong anger bordering on rage, but that's coming from Patsy next to me. I'm not going to be able to feel anyone else's anger while she's so close to me.

"Patsy. You need to either get rid of the anger or move away from me. I need to sense his anger. Yours is blocking me from it," I practically yell at her. If I was thinking straight I would have maybe asked her a little calmer.

Understanding what I meant and not taking offence to my

tone, she does as I ask. Her anger eases almost immediately and is replaced with pure happiness.

I wonder what she was thinking to get that happy so quick, from such a dark angry place.

Aha. Now we are getting somewhere! I can feel some anger and a lot of resentment coming from the building I'm standing next to. He must be directly above me. That's probably why I couldn't see him. I'm surprised Dave couldn't. He would have a good view from his hiding place.

Found him, Dominick. I think to alert him as I run around the corner to the fire escape we checked out earlier. We had made sure we knew each fire escape and where it led, since we had no idea which building he'd choose. Luckily, it's only a four-storey building.

I can feel Dominick and Wesley getting tense. The controlled weres must be ready to engage.

"Hurry. We won't be able to hold them off long without someone getting hurt." Dominick confirms my thoughts. A bit of pressure is always helpful to give you the power to get up four flights of stairs in seconds.

I pull myself onto the roof and can't believe what's in front of my eyes. I take a deep breath to catch his scent because I just can't trust what I'm seeing.

"Emmanuel, Why?" is all I can manage to say.

I must have startled him—he hasn't got senses like me. He spins around and glares at me with a shocked look on his face.

I'm hoping that means the action down below has stopped.

"They needed showing they're not better than us just because they are stronger and faster," he spits out between clenched teeth.

"Who?"

He nods his head in the direction of the alleyway. "The werewolves and vampires. I took Stephen and Mary at first, thinking kidnapping the vampires would make a war break out between them, but for some reason Dominick never thought Theodore was behind it. Instead, he asked for his help. I couldn't control them, and I couldn't let them go because then Dominick would kill me. I had to kill them!"

Stephen and Mary. No one ever told me their names. Knowing them now makes them real people. Emmanuel killed them?

"Not long after that, I found out I could control domestic cats and dogs, just a freak accident. I found Paddy drunk one night leaving Misty's and thought 'what if?' And, it worked. I used him to attack Dominick. That way he'd have to blame Theodore. Paddy is one of Theo's wolves, after all. The opportunity came to take Alyssa, so I did. The more werewolves I could use, the more damage I could do."

"Jared? Why did you take him? He isn't Theodore's pack." It just doesn't make sense.

"After he caused you to change in front of the bar, I had to punish him. He seems like a person who likes to be in control and if he isn't, well that sounds like good punishment to me." He has a smirk on his face, which I'm not too keen on. The Emmanuel I'm looking at now isn't the Emmanuel I dated.

"Theo. Was that planned?"

"No. That night I thought God must be looking down on me because I was so lucky! If I could control the alpha, I might be able to control the whole pack. It will save me taking them one by one. But it didn't work. Theodore's too strong. He wouldn't succumb to my control." He pauses for a second staring off into the distance. I can feel his rage strengthening. "With the alpha missing, the pack should have fallen apart, but Wesley took control making sure that didn't happen." The way he said Wesley's name was a concern. I think if he could cast a hex, poor Wesley would be in trouble right about now.

"It wasn't Wesley that led the pack. It was me! As Theo's mate that job fell on me. I'm highest in the pack, after Theo, of course," I admit, hoping to disperse some of that rage he's aiming at Wes.

I hear a noise behind me and watch as Emmanuel's eyes dart around behind me. I don't need to look; my nose is telling me it's Dominick and Billy.

Dominick chooses that moment to enter my head again. *"Rosabel, it's only Billy and I. You need to persuade him to release his control."*

"Emmanuel. You can't control them forever. Please let them go and tell us where Theo is so he can go home," I ask him in my most persuasive voice, while slowly and continuously walking towards him. I try to come across as friendly as I can in this situation. I'm not worried about him hurting me because I know Billy is behind me, and he's quick. If Emmanuel tries anything Billy would be there before Emmanuel could cause me any severe damage. Billy won't let anything happen to me. That fact, I'm certain of.

He looks at me sadly and shakes his head. "I can't. If I tell you where I'm keeping Theodore, he'll kill me. The only way I can stay alive is to keep him."

"You can't do that!" Billy and I both shout in unison.

"He's right! If he lets Theodore go, he'll be against a death sentence. He's attacked pack. Theodore has to retaliate, it's law," Dominick says out loud, directed at me. "But Emmanuel, you seem to have forgotten you killed Stephen and Mary; who were my people. Therefore, I can retaliate." I hear the smile in his voice.

Emmanuel steps back away from us all. "You can't. You'll never find Theodore if you kill me."

"That is none of my concern."

"WHAT?" I spin around and glare at Dominick and find Billy staring at him just as perplexed as I am.

Dominick doesn't say anything out loud, he just stares at me with pleading eyes while addressing me in my head. *"Ros-*

abel. He'll have kept them in the same building, if not in the same room. He'll have had to have been close to them all. They'll be able to tell us where that is when he releases them."

"So, you're playing bad cop?" I think back at him, wondering whether I should believe him. He is a vampire after all. Why would he care if we get Theo back or not?

"Trust me, Rosabel," he says in my head.

Billy is looking back and forth between the two of us; something on my face must be showing that we are having a conversation somehow. Dominick's face has shown no emotion the whole time, actually come to think of it; he very rarely shows emotion on his face at all.

I turn my attention back to Emmanuel to find Wesley standing next to him. He must have come up another fire escape somewhere behind Emmanuel. "Bel. You or Dominick need to kill him so we can get the others back. I would love to do it, but unfortunately it falls on you." He really did sound like he was disappointed that he couldn't do it.

I step up to Emmanuel, close enough so that I could kiss him, although what I am about to do is far worse than that. He has tears streaming down his cheeks. *I suppose imminent death could bring the strongest of men to tears.*

"I'm sorry, Bel. I wish it could have worked between us. You're the one for me."

I can't kill him!

"You have no choice. You're doing this for Theo!" Dominick says out loud. I don't know if he is warning the others about what I was thinking or if he has forgotten to say it silently.

You might be used to killing people but I'm not a murderer!

"Any of us would make it a long and painful death. That is our nature. You cared for him; you can make it easier for him. You can make it quick." I've been staring into Emmanuel's eyes through this whole conversation and now I realise I have matching tears running down my face.

How do I kill him quick without a gun? That would the quickest way, I think to myself. I feel Dominick is about to answer me, so I jump in before he does. *Yes. I know what I have to do. You don't need to answer that.*

I lean to whisper in Emmanuel's ear. "I'm sorry," I say on a sob.

"Thank you, Rosabel," are his last words.

I place my hands around his neck and with a quick sharp twist, he drops slightly. I expect him to hit the floor with a thud because as soon as I heard the crack, I had to let go. I look around to find Wesley had caught him and is lowering him gently to the floor. I drop to my knees and place my head in my hands.

Someone lifts me up and walks me back towards the fire escape I came up. The voice that speaks belongs to Billy. "Let's get you out of here." He leads me down the steps but my legs are too shaky and I keep stumbling.

There is no way I'm going to make it down four flights, without falling!

Dominick appears next to me. There is only room for one on this fire escape so he must be levitating or something. He turns his back towards me. "Climb on," he commands.

I don't argue. He wouldn't offer if he couldn't do it, plus I have just murdered someone I was dating only a few days ago; if I fell to my death I probably deserve it.

I put my arms around his neck to hang on, trying not to picture Emmanuel's neck and how easy it was to snap. Dominick is a vampire, so at least I can't snap his by accident. It will take a lot more than Emmanuel's did, plus I don't know if that would actually kill Dominick?

The shock starts to wear off as I find myself sitting in the back of an open van that wasn't here when I went up on the roof where I...*Oh god. Did I really just do what I think I did? Think about something else.*

The others are huddled together about five metres away. It's good to see Paddy and Jared back to themselves. I feel a lot of tension coming from them. I focus my hearing to hear what they are talking about.

It's Billy that is talking. He's rubbing his stubble on his head with his hand in a motion from back to front. It looks like an anxious habit he must have. "So you don't remember anything? None of you?"

I shoot off towards the van and barge through the group in a split second. I don't care who I'm shoving or what they are. If a human was watching, I don't even think they would pick my movement up. I would just vanish from the van and suddenly be with the group. The guys here might catch a blur with their supernatural eyesight but I'm not sure and I don't really care.

"Did I just hear that right? They don't know where they were kept?" I'm glaring at Dominick and ready to stake him right now. Even if that makes it my second murder within minutes of my first. I guess once a murderer always a murderer. A second won't really make much difference. He just made me kill the only person that knew where Theo is.

"I'm so sorry, Rosabel. I had no idea they were hypnotised. I thought they would remember everything." He is sorry. I can feel his regret. I can even see it on his face and in his eyes. I know I shouldn't look a vampire in the eyes because they can make you do things just by meeting their eyes, but I trust he won't try anything. I'm not sure why but I do. Even after seeing the regret in his eyes, I can't calm down.

"You're sorry? I just killed the only person who knew where he was. On your word, that they'd be able to tell us. How the hell are we going to find Theo, now?"

I can feel aggression run through the pack members in the alley at what I've just said.

"Angel. You need to calm down. We've all been worked up

tonight. Your tension could make us all change and that won't be useful to the boss, will it?"

I look at Paddy and Eddie; both their eyes are no longer human. I don't need to look at any of the others to realise what Billy said was right.

"Okay, sorry," I say through gritted teeth, as I take a deep breath and reach out to find someone happy. I find Wesley and Alyssa, who must be in Misty's and pull their happiness into me. With that happiness clearing my head I get an idea.

"Dominick. Theo mentioned a census for all the supes in town. Does it contain home addresses and other property addresses?" I can feel the hope run through everyone—that my idea might actually lead somewhere.

"Yes. But there are a lot of us in town. It could take days to find Emmanuel's entry. I'll get Patsy on it straight away, but if you get one of your men on it too they can start at opposite ends. If someone knows his last name that will help." Patsy leaves immediately after he says her name.

I look at Billy, having no idea who would know where the census information is kept. "I'm on it. Darren, you take everyone to Theo's shed and give Doc Patel a call; best to get everyone checked over. Don't forget Selena. Don't let her see any of you. Dave, can you go let Wesley know what's happening and ask about for anyone in the bar who might know Emmanuel's address?"

"No. I'll do that. Dave you go with Darren. Emmanuel was Misty's friend, I feel like I should break the news to her. I'll find out what she knows at the same time. Dominick, do you mind helping by asking about in the bar too?"

"It's the least I can do," Dominick says, as his guilt flows off him. I feel even guiltier now that I have just realised I killed one of Misty's friends.

"Rosabel, do you want me to stay and help you too?" Eddie asks. His eyes back to his human sky blue. Thank God!

"That will be great. Thanks, Eddie."

He beams at me in delight.

Everyone heads off in different directions. Billy is going for his bike. Darren, Dave, Phil, Paddy, and Jared all get in the van I found myself sitting in not long ago, leaving Dominick, Eddie, and myself in the alley.

I look up at the roof. *Is he still up there? Oh my god! What did I do?*

"Rosabel, he gave you no option. Greg has taken him to the morgue. He'll make sure everything is dealt with. Let's get inside and focus on finding Theo," Dominick says, making his way to the back door that Misty must have left propped open for us.

28

FACING DOWN
THE WOLF

e enter the bar to a round of applause. Wesley has already spread the news. Ignoring the applause, I immediately look around for Misty but only find Lucy behind the bar on her own; which is really unusual for a busy night like this one.

I lean over the bar and shout over the crowd, "Lucy. Where's Misty?"

"No idea. When Wesley announced that Emmanuel was dead, she ran off through the back. If you didn't see her outside, I'd guess she's in the toilets or office." I nod with a smile, to let her know I heard her over the rowdy crowd and turn to go find Misty.

I nearly fall over Eddie, who had been standing directly behind me. "Oh, Eddie. Will you do me a favour and ask about in here for an address? Let Wesley know what everyone else is doing, too."

As I look around the bar to make sure Wesley is still here, I see Dominick is already asking people questions.

"Yes. Consider it done," Ed says, slipping away into the crowd.

I go straight through the back hoping to find Misty. I check the toilets as I pass but she isn't there. I just hope she hasn't slipped out between us entering the bar and now. As I open the door to the office, I get hit by a wave of sadness. It doesn't do my guilt any favours. I killed one of her close friends.

"Misty. I'm so sorry." I have no idea what else I can say. Nothing will make her feel better.

"It's okay. Ya had no choice. Wesley explained everything. I just wish everyone wasn't so happy about it. I feel so guilty that I set ya up with him. I had no idea he was like that," she manages between sobs.

"I went on dates with him and I had no idea either. He hid that side of him well, but he wasn't all bad." I start to cry. "I actually cared for him and if Theo and I weren't true mates, who knows, I could have fallen in love with him. And yet I just killed him."

Misty comes over pulling me into a hug. "It's okay. Don't live ya life blaming ya-self, ya had no choice." she consoles me, making me giggle at the situation.

"I came in here to console you not the other way around. I need to ask you something, too. Do you know his address? He didn't tell us where Theo is and the others don't remember anything about what they've done, or where they've been," I ask, hoping for some good news.

"I'm sorry, no. We always met up away from our houses. He never knew where I lived until he walked ya home," she says frustrated. Probably because she can't help.

"It's okay. Patsy and Billy are both checking the census, and Dominick and Eddie are asking in the bar, too. I'm sure we'll find it soon." A shocked look washes over her face.

"Oh. Poor, Lucy. I left her alone and the bar is packed tonight." With those words she dashes out of the office, leaving me staring at the door as it closes behind her.

I look at the chair behind the desk and think how nice it would be just to sit down for two minutes. But I don't have the time. I need to find Theo and the only way I will do that is by finding an address. It's like finding a needle in a haystack.

I open the office door and walk straight into Eddie, again.

"We'll have to stop doing this," I say, whilst rubbing my nose after bumping it on his rock hard chest.

"I don't know. I quite enjoy it," he says, with a cheeky grin.

"No one knows anything in there. We're going to have to wait on Patsy and Billy," Dominick announces as he walks up behind Ed. He doesn't sound happy at the prospect of waiting.

"I know this might sound obvious, but can't you just teleport to him? Billy said you can just think of somewhere with your eyes shut and be there when you open your eyes," Ed enquires, sounding eager for his plan to work.

"I can do that, yes, but I need to be able to smell, see, and feel the place in my head to get there. Not knowing where exactly he is means I don't have those senses about the place. I've never seen him in his wolf form, so I can't even try and do it by looking at him," I say, furious at myself for not being able to do it. Eddie's eagerness fades within a split second.

"But you know his scent. If you focus on just that, it might work. What have you got to lose?" Dominick always seems to know just what to say. Eddie gives me the loveliest, encouraging smile. How can I say no to that? I guess it's worth a try.

"All right. I'll give it a try."

I close my eyes and focus on nothing except Theo's dark spicy scent, letting it surround me like a blanket. On opening my eyes I find myself in Theo's room with a shocked Ruby staring at me with her mouth dropped open.

"Sorry. I'll explain later," I say, before closing my eyes and trying again. I would rather keep looking for Theo than waste time explaining what I'd just done.

This time I open my eyes hoping with every ounce of my being to see Theo in front of me, only to find myself in his lounge. *Crap*! At least Selena isn't in here. I don't think I'd be able to escape without an explanation if she was.

I go back to the alley feeling totally defeated.

"Did it work?" Eddie was so excited at the thought of me

actually finding Theo. It's such a shame to fill him with the disappointment I feel, too.

"No, sorry. I just ended up in his bedroom and his lounge. I scared poor Ruby half to death," I say, trying to lighten the disappointment by adding that bit about Ruby. "If only he'd not stood me up the day he was meant to take me on a run, I'd be able to picture him, too." Now I'm mad at Theo; which isn't really fair considering he's the one trapped alone somewhere that no one knows about.

"What colour fur does he have, Eddie?" Dominick asks.

"It's a rusty colour. Why?" We both eye Dominick with the same questioning look.

He answers me rather than Eddie, "Because if you picture a wolf with that colour fur while doing what you just did with his scent, you might find him."

I close my eyes and picture a rusty coloured wolf, just like Dominick suggested. I wrap Theo's dark spicy scent around me. I feel the swirl that I felt when Dominick called me to him that first time, and as I open my eyes hoping I'm not at Theo's house again. I find myself faced with a big rusty wolf. I did a good job with the colour. It's just as I imagined. It's just the size I was off on; he's easily double the size I imagined—absolutely huge! And he's growling at me. I didn't imagine that.

"Theo. It's me, Bel! I've come to take you home!" I approach him cautiously, but when I am about a foot away, I realise he's not here with me.

He's delirious. His fur is matted with blood; obstructing my view of any actual wounds. I reach deep into our mate bond hoping to get through to Theo.

The wolf before me pauses and weighs me up.

I don't move. I can't tell if he recognises me or if he is wondering if I taste good. It's much scarier being faced with Theo ready to eat me than it was being faced with Paddy. He's making a rumbling growl deep in his chest as he slowly starts to edge towards me. I hold my hand out for him to sniff and hope he recognises my scent.

It doesn't take him long. He's barely sniffed it when he drops to the floor with a whine. His whole persona changes. He's extremely weak. It must have taken so much out of him to pretend to be so fierce.

When I fall to my knees and reach out to feel for injuries, he doesn't protest. I rub my hands over his head and neck, which all feels normal. I find the first wound on his shoulder. He doesn't even flinch as my fingers probe it.

What the hell is wrong with him? He should at least be reacting to the pain.

"Jared just informed me that Theo has at least two silver bullets in him. He clawed one out himself last night." Dominick's voice answers the question I was asking myself. I don't complain this time.

Thanks.

In the blink of an eye, I shift my hand to claws and slice into his shoulder making the wound bigger, once I get it deep enough so that I can see the bullet, I shift my hand back and grab the bullet between my fingers. I grit my teeth against the burning on my fingers where the silver comes in contact with my flesh, and drop it to the floor the second it's out.

"Theo, one down. Let's see how many more you have in you," I say, running my hands over his body. I find numerous bites but I can't find another wound that looks remotely like a bullet. I'm about to give up when I find it lodged in his front leg. It's not too deep but I still need to use my claws again to make the wound big enough for me to get a grip on the bullet. I'm throwing that bullet across the room in no time.

"I think that's it, Theo. Now we could do with some meat to get your energy back up." I regret my words as soon as they leave my mouth.

Mentioning food to a hungry wolf. Clever idea, Bel!

His eyes flash from the black of his wolf's to emerald green. Theo must be fighting his wolf for control.

I slowly back away looking for an exit, catching sight of the reinforced steel door with no handle. I realise I have no chance getting out of that so I give the rest of the room a quick glance. All blank solid walls and not one window to be seen.

Brilliant! There isn't even a wardrobe I could lock myself in.

"Rosabel, don't worry. We're on our way. I can sense you," Dominick says through our link; the panic clear in his own voice.

I turn my full attention back to Theo. "They know where we are. They're on their way. Just hang on a little longer."

His eyes are fully black now; telling me his wolf is back in full control. I have to have faith that he won't harm his mate. Normally that wouldn't be a problem but he's been confined and left injured for twenty-four hours. To make things worse, I just pulled out two silver bullets that had been stopping him from healing and taking all his energy. He's not exactly in his right mind right now.

"We're two minutes away Rosabel!" Dominick tries to reassure me and fails miserably.

It won't take him that long to devour me.

"Calm down. The fear will make him want you all the more." Dominick suggests.

How helpful, Dominick. It's not like I already know that, being a wolf and all.

Shifting into my wolf would only serve to make Theo feel more threatened, therefore, pushing him to attack me. I find myself backed into the corner of the room; I must have been backing up whilst arguing with Dominick.

Theo is stalking me. He nuzzles his snout into my stomach trying to get to the soft flesh he could tear into. Thankfully my hoodie is in the way. I hear the material rip.

Nothing like jinxing myself.

His teeth brush against my skin as I am wracking my brain for something to say to stop, or distract him but I can't think of anything.

I hope you are bringing some fresh meat with you, Dominick.

At that moment, the door bursts open three feet away from me.

The noise is not distracting Theo one bit. There is no way I can get to the door. He has me pinned to the wall.

Dominick and Ed appear from around the door.

"Eddie. You need to get out of here, Theo is full wolf. It will force the change on you. We don't need two wolves in here!" Panic once again floods my body.

"It's okay, I can fight it. If I feel like I can't, I'll leave. Theo you need to leave Bel alone. Come to me. I have some meat for you." He throws a dead rabbit in the room. It's freshly killed and dripping with blood. God only knows how he got one so quick.

Theo doesn't even bat an eyelid. "Theodore. You don't want to hurt, Rosabel. I nearly killed her yesterday. I know what pain it would cause you if you killed her. You don't want to feel that pain."

Both Ed and I give Dominick a perplexed look.

Are you insane? That's only going to make him angrier, Dominick.

"*Yes. That is my plan. If we get Theodore mad enough, he might take control.*"

Yes. Control enough to want to kill YOU!

I look down at Theo. I have to find something to say to ease the situation. When I see Theo's emerald eyes looking at me my fear subsides and relief washes over me.

"Theo. Ed has lots of those rabbits for you. Please go eat them," I say, pointing to the dead rabbit on the floor. I'm hoping Ed has more, at least.

Theo rubs his head against my leg, probably in apology at

almost eating me. He walks over to the rabbit and starts to devour it.

I walk by him, slowly, hoping not to make him feel like I'm trying to steal it from him. Animals get extremely territorial over food. Once I reach Dominick and Eddie in the doorway, I can't believe how much safer I feel now that I am standing next to another werewolf and a vampire.

The three of us stand there, watching Theo thoroughly clean up the rabbit. Once he starts licking the blood off the floor, I nudge Ed. He gets my hint and leads Theo to a van, which looks like the one from the alley earlier. The only difference, this one is blue not white. They both jump in the back with a mountain of rabbit bodies.

God knows where he got all of them from.

Dominick gets behind the wheel so I climb in the passenger side.

It doesn't take long to get to Theo's house. We drive around the back of his house where he's got a big shed on the land there. I call it a big shed but it's a huge eight-bay workshop. Eddie called it 'the shed.' I had to add big and that still isn't a good enough name to describe it.

I get out of the van and walk in to 'the shed,' leaving Ed and Dominick to help Theo out. The floor is covered in gym mats. There are a couple punching bags and a weight bench, with weights. He must use this as a training area. There is also a couple hospital beds on the far wall set up with what looks like up-to-date medical equipment around them. The training room doubles up as a medical room.

Jared is sitting on the edge of one bed, and Paddy is on the edge of the other.

Wesley is cuddling Alyssa in the corner of the room. I don't think he'll be letting her out of his sight for a while. Just like I won't be letting Theo out of my sight for a while either.

Billy is standing with a woman of Indian descent, whom I

don't recognise. She has a black, chin-length bob, and wearing a white doctor's coat with a stethoscope hanging around her neck.

As I approach Billy, he turns his attention to me. "Hey, beauty. You did real good tonight," he says, pulling me into a quick side hug. "This is Dr Patel. Dr Patel this is Rosabel."

She reaches out and shakes my hand. "Call me, Zainab."

"Nice to meet you, Zainab. I'm Bel. How are these guys doing?" I ask, waving my hand, gesturing to the three that had been taken.

"I've just finished checking them over and they are all perfectly healthy."

"That's great news. We have one more patient for you to look at. He's not in as good a condition as these three though. He should be in any minute, now."

I turn to look at the door and see Eddie walking in with Theo trotting in alongside him. His eyes roam the room looking for something. When they land on me, he heads straight for me. He stops in front of me so I crouch down.

"Bel, be careful," Billy warns me.

Wesley appears next to me ready to protect me if he needs to.

"It's okay. He won't hurt me!" I say confidently, before putting my arms around his neck, cuddling into his fur and filling my lungs with his lovely scent. My wolf is itching to get out. I can't stop myself whimpering in his ear. "My wolf will join you when you've been checked over, if you want?" I think it was her telling him that not me.

A rumble comes from deep in his chest, which I take as yes, along with the excitement I feel emanating from him.

I stand up and Theo pads over to the empty bed that Jared had been on a few minutes ago.

Jared is now standing behind me in a protective stance.

I notice Dominick is missing. "Eddie. Where's Dominick?"

"I need an invite from Theo. He's not got the ability to give one at the minute." Dominick's voice says through our link. I turn and head for the door before Eddie could answer.

"He's outside. You seem to know that already. How?" His curiosity rushes over my skin.

"We've got a blood tie. He answered me before you did, in here," I say laughing, while pointing to my temple.

"What?" Jared's anger hits me like a wall. I thought he'd be jealous when any other guy is involved, but he's angry like he's concerned for my protection. But then again, why would he be jealous? Dominick is a vampire. He's dead. I don't think he'd be capable of love. I don't think I'd be able to fall in love with someone that is dead either.

"Am I?" Dominick asks in my head. I'm kind of getting sick of not being able to think without being interrupted.

"Can't you just listen to me when I'm actually talking to you? Rather than butting in on my personal thoughts. I can only hear what you want me to. How come?" I take a few steps out the door before Dominick walks into view from around the other side of the van.

He speaks out loud this time, "If you want to drink some of my blood, then you'll be able to listen in on my thoughts whenever you wish, too." He tilts his head in a gesture to offer his neck to me.

"Eww. No thanks." That thought totally grosses me out. *Although I'm not sure why? Because when I'm in wolf form I hunt and eat animals; fur, bones and all.* It's probably because Dominick's cold and dead that it freaks me out so much.

"I have blood running through my veins and a heartbeat. Am I really dead?" He grabs my hand and places it on his bare chest through the opening of his dress shirt, right over his heart. I feel the thud, thud. It's slightly out of time compared to a human's. It has an extra faster thud, thud in between the normal thud, thud. Werewolves run to a slightly different beat too.

I move my hand away and force myself not to wipe it on my sweats.

"I don't know," is the only answer I can give him.

"I must leave now, Rosabel." He kisses me on the forehead before I even have the chance to think about dodging it.

"Thanks for your help tonight," I say, pulling away.

He smiles. "We are even now." He disappears with a pop before my eyes. How come he can make noises if he wants?

I turn back to go inside, only to find Jared standing in the doorway. I feel his concern tickle against my skin. "I don't like you having this tie with him. I don't trust him."

"He's not too bad, if you didn't nearly kill him the other day. I wouldn't have had to donate my blood and I wouldn't have a tie at all."

His face drops into a look of sadness as his guilt brushes against my skin.

"I'm sorry, Jared. I shouldn't have said that. It wasn't you. It was Emmanuel." I lean in and give him a big hug and he squeezes me back hard. He was always great to hug.

"I miss you baby Bel, I really do." The truth of his words is evident in his emotions. His love is just as strong as it was when we first got together all those years ago.

"I know." I stay in the hug to hide that I am crying. I don't want him to get the wrong idea if he sees so it's a good job he seems happy enough to still be hugging me. We hear a fierce growl coming from inside the shed causing Jared and I to break apart and run inside.

I can't see a problem with the scene before my eyes, except Theo was looking directly at me, growling. I look back at the door. He would have seen me and Jared cuddling but I can't feel jealousy coming from him.

The room fills with his bonding scent.

"Jared. Stay there," I warn as I put my hand behind me to stop him coming any closer.

"Yeah. I get the point," he replies as Billy, Paddy, and Alyssa walk over to where we're standing. I head for Theo, who is still growling quietly.

"Come on. You need to get out of here," I hear Billy say to Jared behind me.

"But, Bel?" He's worried that I'm going to get hurt.

"It's not her he wants to hurt," Billy tells him as Theo pounces in front of me facing Jared, growling fiercely once again.

Jared puts his hands up above his head like you do to the police to show them you have no weapons. "It's okay mate. I'm going," he says, backing up and out the door.

I start taking my clothes off. Wesley has seen me naked and I'm sure Dr Patel has seen plenty of people naked before. I need to get into wolf form so we can communicate better.

I've just pulled the bra off my arm, to be fully naked, when Eddie emerges from the cupboard with what looks like some medical supplies in his hand, "Is this what…" he looks up midsentence, "…you. Wow."

I instantly smell his arousal and so does Theo.

He spins around and growls at Eddie in warning, just as the room fills even more with the bonding scent. For Eddie's sake this time.

Billy comes running back in as I finish the shift into my wolf form; *I guess he heard the growl.*

He takes in the scene. "Eddie. What have you said?"

"Oh, Eddie. For god's sake. You've seen plenty of naked people before." He must have caught on to the scent of Eddie's arousal.

I trot over to Theo and wiggle my behind at him in a flirty way to distract him. *"I'm all yours, Theo."* It seems to get his attention.

"I never doubted that. You were crying. Jared upset you." He was trying to protect me. I can't help but smile at that thought.

"No! He didn't upset me, not really. He was telling me he missed me. I could feel how much he loved me still and I cried because I can't return those feelings."

Theo rubs his head against the side of mine and I notice a mass of matted blood on the back of his neck, making me think there must be a serious wound there.

"Has Dr Patel looked at this wound on your neck?"

"Yes. It's all healed. I just need to wash the blood off my fur, that's all. There is one on my stomach, too. I'm healed enough to change back now, but I'd rather have you to myself like this for a while first, or maybe for the rest of the night. I'm sure the pack can cope without talking to me until morning." Theo strides over to the corner on the gym mats. He turns around a couple of times to get comfy.

I make the same move curling up next to him.

"I love you, more than I knew it was possible to love someone," he blurts. The love flowing through our bond. He meant it with all of his heart.

"Ditto."

I feel him chuckle in a wolfy way against my side. *"Has somebody been watching 'Ghost' too much?"*

"Sounds like I'm not the only one since you knew what I meant."

We both chuckle at that. It's great to feel him so happy, not to mention, healthy.

"Has anyone filled you in on who the controller was?" I ask him. I guess he should be told and since I was in charge. I should be the one to fill him in.

"No. Not yet. I guess I'll have to bring him to justice tomorrow. Where is he?" He sounds as though he hates that part of being alpha. *I don't blame him, I do too!*

"No. You won't. It was Emmanuel. He wanted to cause a war between the werewolves and the vampires."

"I know you dated him, Bel But I have to serve a death sentence.

It's the law." He thinks I said no because I didn't want him to hurt Emmanuel.

I wish that was the case.

"No, it's already been done. I k-killed him." My voice cracks in my head and tears well in my eyes. I don't know if I'll ever get over killing someone I cared for. Killing the pride members that duelled with me was a completely different thing. It was them or me. I could live with that. Emmanuel, though. Emmanuel was different.

"Oh, Bel. I'm so sorry you had to do that. It must've been hard for you." I can feel his regret through our connection. He nuzzles his snout against my fur.

"It was. But I had no choice."

"Why didn't you just leave him to me?"

"He knew he had a death sentence. He wanted to hold you hostage so we wouldn't kill him."

"Thank you for taking over and coming to rescue me." He gives me a toothy snarl that I think is meant to be a smile. It's hard to tell on a wolf's face.

I snuggle into his fur, breathing in his scent. It's so relaxing after such a long twenty-four hours.

We both lift our heads as we hear the door open, to see Billy rushing in and closing the door behind him. "You guys need be quiet. Selena thinks we have a pack of wolves on the property. She's talking about setting traps." I start to giggle in my head. There is a pack of wolves on the property, well a quarter of a pack, not to mention the lion.

Theo changes into human in a second flat. "What is Selena doing here?" He's fuming. I don't need to be an empath to know that.

I quickly shift to human form while Theo strides to the cupboard and pulls out some sweats and a t-shirt, yanking them on quickly. He wets a towel and rubs at the visible blood on his neck and face.

I quickly gather my clothes and throw them on.

"She turned up this afternoon. She hasn't said why. She just booked herself a room. Didn't Bel tell you?"

"No. Bel didn't tell me," he snaps, aiming his anger at me.

Now wait a minute. Why are you mad at me?

"It totally slipped my mind. I have had a lot on it tonight. I did just kill someone for god's sake. I'm terribly sorry she wasn't on the top of my list." Sarcasm at its best. On the defensive, I go.

"Sorry, I snapped. I'm mad at her not you. She has no right to just turn up." He comes and kisses me on the top of my head. "Come on. Let's go kick her out." Grabbing my hand and interlocking our fingers, he pulls me out of the shed after Billy.

Just as we step out the door, I pull his body back towards me. "One thing first." He turns to look at me.

I reach up and put my hand behind his neck and pull his head towards me, brushing my lips against his. He reciprocates by working his mouth over mine. I pull away and press our foreheads together as we both catch our breath.

Breath caught, we step away and find Billy standing nearby waiting for us. The three of us head for the house and enter through the glass doors in the lounge without a word. I'm too busy thinking about how great that kiss was to bother speaking.

"No wolves on the loose out there, but look who I found making out behind the bushes." I'm sure Billy added that last bit for Selena's sake.

"TED!" Ruby screams as she pounces on him, throwing her arms around his neck and her legs around his waist. "You're okay?" she adds as she drops her legs back down to the floor.

He gives her a squeeze before breaking away. "I'm fine, Ruby."

Ruby turns to me pulling me into a hug. "Thank you so much, Bel."

"You're welcome." As soon as she lets me go, Theo grabs my hand again.

I look around the room for the first time since entering. It looks so small compared to normal. I realise that's probably because it's full of werewolves; Wesley, Alyssa, and Paddy are all squashed together on the sofa facing the stairs. Selena and Jared are on the other one, Ruby is next to Jared. Eddie and Chloe are sitting on the kitchen bench top leaving Greg, Darren, Phil, and Dave all standing around leaning against the walls through the room. Billy walks to the kitchen and leans against the side next to Chloe.

Everyone seems to give Theo a little nod. I think they all probably want to come over and welcome him back just like Ruby had, but I'm sure Selena would ask why everyone was so pleased to see him. Ruby's reaction looked suspicious enough! Ruby goes back to her spot on the sofa next to Jared, who ruffles her hair as she sits down. *Typical Jared.*

"Selena. What are you doing in my house? I thought I made it clear, you are not welcome anymore."

Theo. Just cut to the chase why don't you?

She stands up, walks up to us, and actually tries to cuddle him. Before she manages to get a hold of him, he takes a step backwards dragging me along with him.

"Can we talk in private?" she asks, giving me a pointed look.

"Anything you want to say, Selena, can be said in front of everyone here." He waves his hand around the room. She follows his hand with her eyes falling on everyone, one by one.

She stares down at her feet. I can see the contemplation on her face, deciding whether she should tell everyone her business. She must have decided to go with it because she opens her mouth to speak; only nothing comes out for a second while she lifts her eyes and looks at Theo. "I thought we could give our marriage another go."

Theo sighs shaking his head "You're too late. A couple

months ago maybe I would've been stupid enough to take you back, but I'm with Bel now. I'm not giving up what we have, for you. If that's all you wanted, you can get your stuff together and leave."

Tears fill her eyes, but she doesn't move. She takes a deep breath. "I'm pregnant! The dad chucked me out. I thought you..." She doesn't finish her sentence.

Theo's body goes tense next to me before I hear Eddie's whisper.

"Oh, fuck." If I had human ears, I wouldn't have heard it.

Theo squeezes my hand, too hard. I'm actually glad I have super strength or he might have broken something. Then again, if he carries on squeezing much longer he might just do that.

Selena is once again staring at the floor.

Theo glances at me with his wolf eyes as he releases my hand before storming up the stairs. We all hear the door slam behind him, leaving me to wonder if it's still going to be intact when I go up there.

"Theo?" Selena shouts as she makes a move to chase after him.

For the second time in a few minutes I find myself extremely grateful for being a were. I reach the bottom of the stairs first and manage to block her way. There is no way she wants to go up there when he's as angry as that.

"Just let him calm down. He'll come down when he's ready to talk," I say forcefully.

I watch the thoughts cross her face whilst she decides whether to tell me to get out of her way or just listen to me and wait. She chooses right, going for the latter; turning and sitting on the sofa without a word to me.

I sit down on the stairs, not wanting her to try and sneak up to him when I'm not paying attention. I don't know why he got so angry. His anger appeared before she mentioned the father so it can't be because he kicked her out. I'm so deep in thought that I jump a foot off the step as I feel someone's hand rubbing my knee. I look to my left to see Billy sitting on the step beside me.

"Penny for your thoughts?" he asks.

I shake my head and shrug. "Just wondering what got him so mad. It's still escalating, I can feel it."

"We all can. You should go talk to him. It might calm him down. Just be cautious," he warns me.

"Do you think he's that angry at Selena, that he might attack me?" *I really don't think he'd hurt me no matter how angry he is, not after he managed not to attack me tonight when he was so hungry and injured.*

"I don't have time to explain everything, Theo's mood is affecting everyone, and we can't risk exposing ourselves in front of Selena."

I look around the room at the others and he's right; everyone is tense. Paddy is really struggling at fighting off his wolf.

"The main cause of Theo and Selena's arguments were because he wanted kids like, yesterday, and she never wanted them. Now she turns up pregnant. The one thing he wanted from her, she gave to someone else."

I have a really bad feeling in my gut. "What are you trying to say, Billy?"

I finally place that look he had in his eyes before he ran upstairs. Regret.

"I honestly don't know. I just figured you deserved to have a heads up."

I quickly kiss him on the cheek. "Thanks Billy."

I race up the stairs needing to know what Theo is thinking because my brain is coming up with too many scenarios I don't like.

Theo's door has a crack running right down the middle and

the frame is loose, but it's intact enough to be serving its purpose. I knock on the door before opening, just to be courteous. He'll have been able to sense me coming, not to mention hearing my footsteps. I open the door before he has time to reply to my knock and close it behind me.

He's pacing back and forth across the room.

I decide to steal Billy's line. "Penny for your thoughts?"

He sighs and carries on pacing.

I sit on the edge of his bed ready to wait for him, but to my surprise he joins me, putting his head in his hands. We sit in a silence that I'm not willing to break. If he wants to talk, he can. He came up here to think and calm down. I haven't joined him to make him more tense, if that's even possible, by asking him stupid questions like, 'are you okay?' when it's blatantly obvious he's not.

He lifts his head out of his hands and stares at me with his beautiful emerald green eyes that are filled with nothing but love and regret. "Bel, I'm sorry," he says, giving me a bad feeling this is a conversation I don't want to be involved in.

"Billy is right, isn't he? You're going to take her back." It's a statement, not a question. There is no need for him to beat around the bush to tell me what Billy already has. There are tears running down my cheeks as I look at him making him a blur. I can't read what his eyes are saying, but I can feel his emotions loud and clear, the love, regret, and guilt.

He's made his decision.

"Bel. I…"

I don't need to listen to him tell me his decision, not when I can already feel it. I close my eyes so I can let my body take me wherever it wants to.

God only knows where I'll end up!

29

PRIVATE
CELEBRATION

I see Bel prepare herself to teleport whilst I'm mid-sentence. Her eyes close and her body relaxes slightly.

I am not letting her disappear on me.

"Don't you dare!" I yell, as I grab a hold of her, hoping to distract her enough to make her hear me out. Her eyes open as I'm kneeling before her and I quickly plead my case.

"He's wrong, Bel. How could you think I would do that to you? You are my true mate. You were made for me. I couldn't love anyone else, no matter what. You have my heart and it's not going anywhere. It belongs to you. Do you hear me?" I ask as I let my hands cup her face and roam around to her hair.

"But I felt your regret and guilt."

"Being an empath, you should know not to jump to conclusions about what people's emotions mean. I was feeling those things because I was planning on asking you if we could help Selena out, give her a roof for a while. I felt bad for even thinking about putting you in that situation," I explain.

"Oh," she says clearly embarrassed. "I thought—"

I don't give her a chance to finish her sentence. I take her mouth in a searing kiss, full of my passion for her. She relaxes into the kiss, I lay her back on the bed.

"What about everyone downstairs? They'll want to celebrate with you," she says as our mouths part.

"We can all celebrate together, tomorrow." I pause to peck her pretty pink lips. "Tonight, I'm celebrating with my mate," I say, before showing her exactly how I plan to celebrate.

FOREVER YOUNG AND BEAUTIFUL

MOUNT ROXBY SERIES: BOOK TWO

AIMIE JENNISON

Forever Young and Beautiful

Copyright © 2015 Aimie Jennison

Cover design by: Sloan Johnson at Sloan J Designs

Formatted by: Aimie Jennison

DEDICATION

To anyone who feels like the black sheep of the family.
This is for you.

Considering I'm only seventeen-years-old, I've seen some unspeakable things in my life. You'd probably put it down to having an alpha werewolf for a brother, but you'd be wrong. Humans can be monsters too.

Waking up with a hand making its way up my thigh is nothing new. Sadly enough, I've become accustomed to my mum's boyfriend of the day, or week—if they last that long, trying it on over the years. They always give up attempting to get their sexual appetites fulfilled by my mother, she constantly passes out before they get down to the nitty-gritty. Instead, they prefer to come into my room when I'm asleep and try their luck with me. I guess sleepy is better than comatose. It's not something a seventeen-year-old should have to deal with, but it's been my life for so long now. Just me and my mother. The only reprieve I get is when I spend my holidays with my brothers and their pack.

It takes me a minute or two before I'm fully awake enough to register what's happening. Terry's hand is at the apex of my thighs when I throw my arms out and shove him off the bed and onto the floor. I won't let him take me, her last boyfriend caught me when I had no fight in me. The memory of the smirk he gave me when he realised he'd taken my virginity spurs on the fight in me today. I'll never allow a man to take from me without permission again.

"Get off me, you perv," I yell, not caring whether I wake Mum up or not.

He hits the floor with a grunt, before pulling himself up and coming at me again, the look on his face turns my stomach.

"Come on, sugar. I've seen the way you've been watching me when you don't think anyone is looking."

"I swear, you touch me again and I'll break your nose." I form a fist to show him how serious my threat is, but he laughs and keeps coming. My brothers have both taught me how to look after myself over the years. Living with a werewolf pack can be dangerous, if you don't know how to handle yourself in a fight. Werewolves are short-tempered creatures, so altercations are always breaking out when you're surrounded by them. In saying that, I've never had to use my fighting skills against a werewolf opponent. It's always the humans.

His hand reaches out to touch my breast and I throw a punch without a second thought. I don't know whether Terry was more surprised that I threw the punch, or that it had actually connected, causing blood to pour from his now broken nose. Forgetting my breast, he cups his hands around his nose and glances up at me; the surprise in his eyes suddenly changing to fury.

"You little bitch," he screams, as he doubles his efforts to get to me. Just as his body wrestles me to the bed, the bedroom door bangs open and my mother storms in.

"What the fuck is going on in here?"

I pause under Terry, taken by surprise that she can even get a full sentence out, let alone see straight, knowing the amount of drugs she's injected into her veins only a short while ago. Seeming just as surprised at my mother's appearance, Terry loosens his grip on me and I quickly take advantage, pushing him away enough to scoot out from under him.

"He was trying to rape me," I say, as I work my way over to my mum. "Just like all your previous loser boyfriends."

"I was not raping *you*. You were trying to seduce me." Terry sounds astonished that I would even suggest such a thing.

"You were in *my* bedroom. You were on top of *me*. And you have a busted nose, how can you say I was seducing you?" I glance at Mum to make sure she doesn't believe the shit he's spewing, only to find her giving me a glare that says she believes every word he's said. "Mum, you don't believe this bullshit? Surely you can see through it, even if you're still high," I plead.

She walks towards me, and I relax thinking she's going to pull me into her embrace. I don't notice the fist by her side until it's too late to block it. I stumble back with the force of her uppercut to my cheek bone. It starts to throb almost immediately. "Mum…?" I whisper, too astonished by her actions to even finish my question.

"Come on Terry baby, let's get you cleaned up," she says, dismissing me as she guides him out of the room.

I drop to sit on the bed, unable to process that my mother just took that sleaze ball's word over mine. If it weren't for the throbbing pain in my face, I'd think it was all just a dream. The knowledge that she hit me spurs me into action. I can't live like this anymore. I dash around the room filling my backpack with anything I can't bear to leave behind, knowing full well she'll sell anything I do leave.

Once I'm packed, I stare at my closed door and wonder how I'm going to leave without another confrontation. I turn and seeing the window, I decide it's the best way to avoid my mother and Terry. Once I have the window open and push out the fly screen, I throw my backpack to the ground and climb over the sill, feeling somewhat grateful for being in a single story house.

Picking up my backpack and throwing it over my shoulder, I slowly creep around the house practically holding my breath as I pass the kitchen. I know they're in there, I can hear them. Listening to the noises, I discern she's giving him what he tried to get from me. My anger at my mother doubles as I walk away from the house, knowing they're too preoccupied to hear me leave.

I make it to the end of the street before I realise that although I know where I'm planning on going, I have no idea how I'm going to get there. My brother, Theo's house, is my safe haven. I might be surrounded by dangerous werewolves there, but at least I'll be protected. No one would ever hurt me, not intentionally. Just as I'm passing the bus stop a bus pulls up to let someone off, I jump on board.

I stay on the bus until it reaches its last stop, which luckily, happens to be a short walk from a roadside café and petrol station. The café is a frequent stop for truckies since it's situated nicely on one of the main highways across the country.

As I walk into the café, I take note of three trucks parked outside. The drivers are all in the café. Two guys are sitting on the main bench that runs the length of one wall, with a good space between the two of them. There's a woman paying for fuel at the counter, if it weren't for her steel-toe cap boots and high visibility vest, I wouldn't have guessed she was the third truck driver.

"Thanks, Vera, I'll see you in a couple of days when I come back up," she announces, as she walks away from the counter. If she'll be coming back up, that means she's going south. If I don't pluck up the courage to ask her for a lift, I'll miss the chance altogether. The other drivers could be heading north.

"Excuse me," I call out nervously.

She pauses in the doorway, sucking in a sharp breath and wincing as she glances at me, reminding me that my face must be bruised up pretty good by now. "Jesus, have you been in the ring with Tyson?"

Her joke eases my nerves and I can only assume that was her aim. "Yeah, something like that," I answer, before asking what I called out to her for in the first place. "Is there any chance I can grab a lift? I'm heading to Mount Roxby, if you are going anywhere near there?" I hope she'll take pity on me.

Her smile answers me before her words do. "I drive right past Mount Roxby, I'm happy to have a bit of company for a change. I'm Jules," she says, offering her hand.

"Ruby," I reply, taking her hand.

We'd made good time. Only three hours have passed as Jules pulls to the side of the road just at the entry into Theo's driveway. She insisted on dropping me off at the drive and if her truck were smaller, she would have dropped me at the door, but the trees are too close to the edge of his driveway.

Opening the cab door, I grab my bag off the cab bed behind the two seats. "Thanks, Jules. You really did save me tonight."

"You've been great company, and you have my number so you can always call if you ever find yourself in a similar situation. Don't just jump in anyone's cab, that's a dangerous game to be playing."

"I don't plan on being stuck in that situation again, but I promise I'll call if I am," I reassure her, jumping from the cab.

My feet hit the gravel with a thud, forcing a cloud of dust to rise around my feet, visible only because of the truck's headlights.

The walk up the drive takes me a good ten minutes. Theo has a large acreage of land surrounding his house. He doesn't want prying neighbours when he has a pack of werewolves coming and going; which is pretty understandable. When I reach the door, I straighten my backpack and push the little button that is the doorbell.

I see the silhouette of two people approach, but they don't

open it immediately. When the door finally opens, the sight of my big brother with his caring green eyes before me causes the floodgates to open. I can't hold back the sobs as I pounce into his arms and call him the pet name I've always used. "Ted."

AN UNEXPECTED
ARRIVAL

I'm humming to myself as I make my way down the stairs with the dirty sheets from Chloe's bed. It took two months for Theo to persuade her that since the Controller was dead, she was safe in her own home. I think she was just lonely and enjoyed the company here, but no one seems to care what I think.

I'm not one of them so my opinion doesn't matter.

Getting my criminology degree online via Open Universities Australia isn't good enough for Theo. He thinks I need to be working, too. And since I can't find a job in town that will allow me to have a bodyguard following me around, he decided to employ me as a cleaner.

In my own home.

I prefer waitressing to cleaning. Back home I worked in a little café, working all the hours I could, mainly to stay clear of Mum and her boyfriends. She knows how to pick an arsehole —then again she doesn't exactly deserve any better. I enjoyed it, though, chatting with the regular customers and sometimes even flirting with them. It's not like I can flirt with the couple of pack members I find cute, Theo would kill them if they so much as breathed in my direction.

Just as I'm about to turn into the laundry, there's a knock on the front door. Throwing the dirty sheets in the laundry, I quickly turn and run for the door, wondering why Theo hadn't unlocked it this morning. No one knocks unless the door is locked, and when it's locked, they will turn the handle until it breaks. *Damn werewolf strength.*

I yank it open, surprised to find that it's not locked. "What's with the knock—" The words die on my lips when I find myself face to face with my mother.

"Have you got a hug for your mum?" she asks. I glance behind her for any sign of her boyfriend. "Terry isn't here, I left him," she says, wiggling a suitcase in her right hand.

Oh God, no.

"Don't just stand there gawking, give me a hug and let me in." I can tell she's annoyed now, even though she's clearly trying to hide it behind a playful tone.

I relax, feeling the heat that only comes off a werewolf's body, as one steps up behind me. "Is everything…" It sounds like Theo is surprised to see Mum, too. Gently reaching out, Theo pushes me aside as he steps forward in one smooth movement. "What the hell are you doing here, Mum?"

She drops her suitcase and her eyes well up as she takes my brother in. "Theo?" Reaching out, she strokes a shaky finger down his cheek. "It's really you?" she asks, before bursting into tears.

Theo glances at me looking as disturbed as I feel. I shrug my shoulders. I really have no idea what's gotten into her. In a resigned gesture, he pulls Mum into his arms and inside the house.

Picking up the suitcase, I close the door and follow them into the lounge. Placing the case on the floor behind the L-shaped sofa, I head into the kitchen and flick the switch on the kettle. We're all going to need a cup of tea to get through whatever conversation is coming. We'd probably rather something stronger, but with Mum being an alcoholic and nasty when she's drunk, it's not a good idea to crank out the good stuff.

By the time I make it to the coffee table with three cups of tea, Theo has Mum comfy on the sofa opposite him. She's wiping at her cheeks with a handful of tissues.

"Thanks," she says, as she reaches out taking one of the cups and bringing it to her lips for a quick sip.

Finding my voice, I speak up as I take a seat next to Theo. "What the hell are you doing here, Mum? Do you not remember that you *hit* me last time we were in the same room together?"

I haven't taken my eyes off her the whole time. I wouldn't believe it if I didn't notice the wounded look appear across her face as clear as day. She's not putting it on either, it seems completely genuine.

"It's something I'll never forget or forgive myself for. It's no excuse, but I was high and when I came to realise what I'd done…it was too late. You'd already left. I needed to get straight. I haven't touched a drop since that night, and I've seen a therapist daily."

Seeing a therapist daily? Yet here she is out of reach of her therapist? She'll have a drink again before this day is out. That's how she works. Beg for forgiveness and then fall back in the bottle again, or even worse—the needle. It's a vicious circle and I've had enough of it. That's why I came to Theo's.

I can't believe she followed me. I stand up ready to leave because I cannot bear to be near this woman.

"Wait, let me finish explaining everything. If you still want nothing to do with me when I'm done, then I'll walk out the door and you'll never have to see me again. I promise."

I glance down at Theo, hoping I'll see something in his face to give me the courage to stick to my guns and leave. Tugging on my hand, he gestures for me to sit back down next to him.

"Give her a chance. I'll throw her out myself if she goes back on her promise to leave. Okay?"

I sit with a sigh. "Fine, you've got five minutes."

"Thank you," she says, reaching out to grab my hand.

Evading her hand, I grab my tea and bring it up to take a sip. The thought of being all loving and holding Mother's hand, makes my skin crawl, and in return that makes me feel sick to the stomach because a daughter should love her mother. A daughter should want that kind of affection from her mother. What a fucked up mess we are.

"Speaking things through with my therapist has helped me see more clearly where my issues stem from. You're father had his faults, but I loved him dearly. Unfortunately, he always put the pack before me. I was only a human, I wasn't strong enough for him. He never really wanted me as a mate, but when I fell pregnant with Theo and carried him to term, he felt the need to claim me as his mate. He put up with me because I could give him children, and hopefully they carried the were-wolf gene. You should understand something about that Theo. You never did take Selena as your mate, did you?"

Out the corner of my eye, I see Theo nod his agreement.

She quickly picks up where she left off. "He wasn't a gentle man and he hated that he had to hold back when he was with me. I knew he fucked other women; women who could handle his strength. I didn't kick up a fuss because I didn't want to lose the small part of him that I had. Theo came along, you were my baby and nothing else in the world mattered." The smile on her face was like nothing I'd seen before. It made her look ten years younger and so beautiful. Like a mother that could have been loving, had she'd chosen that path.

I can't help but wonder what the hell any of this has got to do with her hitting me?

"Cain and Ruby came along and I felt blessed. Truly blessed, I couldn't care what your father did anymore. I was glad he left me with my babies so he could run the pack. I didn't need him. I only needed you three. My life was bliss, but then Theo you hit puberty, and I realised you were a werewolf like your father. I already had an idea that was the case because you were never sick, not even with a head cold. I denied it for as long as I could, but your father saw these things and once it was time, he took you away from me." She wipes at her tears with the back of her hands before blowing her nose into a tissue. "It was painful, God, so painful, but I had Cain and Ruby relying on me. So I carried on, only allowing myself to feel the pain when I was lying alone in bed. Most nights I cried myself to sleep, but by morning I was back to being the best I could be. When he came back for Cain, he broke me. I couldn't pretend like before, even though I knew Ruby needed me. I'd lost two of my babies, and in the process I lost myself in the booze. Being numb to it all was all I cared about." Reaching out, she takes my hand in hers.

I can't sit here and listen to this.

Watching the tears stream down her face is going to break me.

I want to stay angry at her. Damn it!

I pull my hand away from hers. "You lost two of your babies and then you pushed the only one you had left away. What did I do to deserve that? Was it because I was a girl? It felt like you hated me for being the only one there. It wasn't enough that my father hated me because I wasn't a werewolf. No, my mother had to hate me too." The lump in my throat's starting to become painful, making me acutely aware that I either need to leave or break down in front of her. Hearing the crack in my voice, Theo tries pulling me into his side. I almost go, but I quickly come to my senses and remember how pissed I actually am.

Running from the room before I can break down anymore, I leave via the front door, without looking back.

Am I really so unlovable?

2

SEEDY BARS

*P*ulling my car to a stop on Theo's drive, I spot Ruby as she storms out of the house slamming the door behind her. Removing my seatbelt, I open my door ready to go and find out who's upset her. I can clearly hear her sobbing as she runs off blindly down the drive. My phone starts to ring in my pocket and I dig it out as I follow slowly behind her.

"Yo," I answer.

"Eddie, I need you at mine now. Ruby's run off upset and I can't go after her. I need you to find her. It's too dangerous for her to be out there alone."

"No problem, boss. I'd just pulled up as she stormed out. I'm following her now, I won't let her out of my sight."

"Thanks, Eddie." The silence in my ear told me that Theo had hung up after his parting words.

Ruby slowed while I was on the phone, making me only a step behind her as I put it back in my pocket. "What's happened, Ruby?"

"I just want to be alone," she complains, wiping at her eyes before turning to face me.

Seeing the streaks of black makeup on her checks I rub them away with my thumb. "Who's made you cry, Rubes?"

"I can't...I don't want to think about it."

She wants a distraction and I'm up for that. I'm good at distractions. Throwing my arm over her shoulders I pull her into my side and start to lead her to the car. "Let's go find a seedy bar to drown our sorrows in."

It didn't take long to find the seediest bar in town. Bob's Tavern is one of two human bars in town; it's situated on one of the back streets and looks just as seedy as it is. It may be dirty and full of old men, but no one will bother you while you drink yourself into oblivion. I glance across the table at Ruby, she looks like she has the weight of the world on her tiny shoulders.

"Are you ready to talk yet, beautiful?"

Downing the rest of her drink she waves her empty glass at Bob behind the bar to bring another. "My mum turned up at Theo's…with a suitcase."

Rage races through my blood. I'd seen the state she arrived in. Her bitch of a mother had hurt her. *How could Theo even let her in the house?*

"She's claiming sobriety and begging for forgiveness," she explains, not even noticing my rage.

Taking a deep breath, I calm myself before speaking. I almost let a growl slip out. "Why are you upset?"

Her eyes well with tears, she looks up with a trembling chin. "She explained losing Theo and Cain broke her. I wasn't enough to keep her going. I know my father has always hated me because I wasn't—"

"Here you go, sweetheart," Bob interrupts, placing a fresh vodka and coke in front of Ruby and taking the empty glass back to the bar.

"He hated me b…because I wasn't like you all." My wolf is becoming restless hearing her sad tone. I stretch out my hand and squeeze her fingers.

"He couldn't have hated you, beautiful, he probably just didn't know how to connect with a human. I don't believe anybody would be able to hate you."

Giving me a grateful smile, she squeezes my hand. "Thanks

Eddie. That's a nice thought, but I guess we'll never know. It's not like it really matters now, he's dead anyway."

"I'll prove it to ya, drink up!" I nudge her glass in front of her on the table. "You need a night out with the boys, and then you'll know that no one can hate you. Are you up for it?" I challenge.

She stares at me, shocked. I can practically see her inner debate. A big, beautiful smile crosses her face as she picks up her vodka and downs it. "Bring it on," she says, slamming the glass on the table.

3

BOSSY BROTHER

s we pull into the drive and Eddie parks his car next to Jared's Subaru, I spot Theo standing by the front door with his arms folded across his chest, and I *know* I'm not going to get past without a fight.

"Great, he's got his dad head on. I seriously wonder if he forgets he's my brother and not my dad?" I mutter, getting out the car.

"He's alpha. He only wants you to be safe."

I turn to Eddie. "I'm human, I'm not even pack," I argue.

He gives me a serious look. There's not even a hint of humour in his blue eyes, which is unheard of for Eddie. "You are pack. Anyone of us would die for you, just like we would any other pack member." His last word finishes on a growl.

Knowing I've upset him I feel the need to apologise. "I'm sorry, I didn't mean to piss you off, too." Looking at the storm in his eyes, I know it wasn't good enough. His departing grunt only clarifies my thoughts.

Taking a deep breath, I face the inevitable and head over to Theo. After giving me a murderous glare, he turns and walks in the house. Knowing I wouldn't dare do anything but follow wherever he's heading. Probably his office.

I take a long moment to close the door of his office behind me as he takes a seat on the edge of his desk.

"Running off like that was dangerous. There's a rogue vampire out there leaving dead girls on Dominick's doorstep. Just because he's a vampire doesn't mean you're safe during the day. He could have a human working with him. What the fuck were you thinking, Ruby?"

I have no option but to be completely honest with him. He's a werewolf and can sense a lie, I turn to face him and mumble the last thought that came into my head as I ran off this morning. "Am I really so unlovable?"

Opening his arms, he loses the anger in his body with a sigh. "Come here, sweetheart."

I let him envelope me in his big arms, the feeling instantly relieving my fears.

"It was dangerous, Rubes. You're my baby sister; I don't want anything bad to happen to you." He pauses to kiss the top of my head. "You need to promise me that while the rogue vamp is still on the loose that you won't leave this house without having a pack member with you?"

"I hate being a freaking human," I complain into his chest. "It's a good job I've already planned on going out with the boys tonight."

Pushing me away from his body he looks at my face. No doubt, trying to ascertain if I was being serious. "You're not going out with those guys."

"Eddie invited me and I said yes. It would be rude to go back on my word now." I grin, knowing my brother is a man of his word. He would never ask me to go back on mine.

"*Eddie!*"

The door instantly flies open. Eddie must've been standing on the other side the whole time. If he were a human I would accuse him of eavesdropping, but he's a werewolf, so he could eavesdrop on this conversation from most of the rooms in the house with his acute sense of hearing.

"I can't believe I'm agreeing to this…You do *not* let her out of your sight at all!" Theo orders.

Eddie nods his agreement.

"Wait a minute. What if I need to pee?" I ask in a panic.

"You pretend to be a couple and sneak into the toilets for a quickie. Ed, you turn your back while she pees," he informs me, evidently having it all worked out.

"No way," I demand.

"Then you hold it in because those are my conditions. It's up to you, if you don't agree, you don't go." Turning to Eddie he dismisses any argument I could have. "Who else is going with you?"

"It's just me and Paddy tonight." Eddie shrugs. "We're the only ones not on patrol," he quickly adds.

The frown that crosses Theo's face convinces me he's going to change his mind. I slump into the sofa against the wall.

"I'll pull Matthew and Jared off patrol. The rogue vamp is Dominick's mess, he can send more of his guys out to make up for the loss of my two."

I perk up at his words, offering some advice. "You don't have to lose the use of your guys. Eddie is one of your strongest wolves, I'll be safe with both him and Paddy."

"That's not happening, Ruby. Quit, while you're ahead," Theo says, his fists tightening against his thighs, his brow furrowed, and his jaw set firm with determination.

Taking in both his and Eddie's determined looks I know I'm not going to get a better offer. "Fine," I quickly agree. I give Theo a quick kiss on the cheek and run off to get ready before he can change his mind.

4

BOYS' NIGHT OUT

I stare in the mirror as I smooth down my skirt, wondering for the umpteenth time whether it's too short.

"You look gorgeous, Rubes."

Looking up, I meet Bel's eyes in the mirror's reflection, leaning on the doorjamb. "It's not too short?"

Striding over to me, she shakes her head as she stops behind me. "You're going to have every hot-blooded males' eyes on you tonight. It'll make the guys' *job* of watching you a nightmare." She laughs.

I slump down on the bed. "I hate this. I wanted to go out with the guys and have some fun, not turn their night out into a job. I hate being a human. If I were a werewolf, I wouldn't need watching. Maybe I should just tell the guys to go without me."

"Rubes." Bel sits beside me, puts her arm around my shoulders and pulls me into her side. "Ed is high up in the ranks, he knew taking you out would mean watching over you and he asked you anyway. You need a night out, if I wasn't working I'd be joining you."

"Are you ready, Rubes?" Hearing Eddie's voice, I jump up and quickly apply some lipstick, taking in my outfit and smiling. I'm going to have fun, even if it kills me.

"Have fun and drive those boys mad," Bel says with a wink, before glancing at her watch. "I'm going to be late for work if I don't leave now. I want to hear all about your night out, tomorrow." She suddenly disappears before my eyes.

Teleportation would be a fun ability to have.

Making my way down the stairs, I slow my pace as I come to the bottom hoping not to seem too eager. Paddy whistles as I come into view.

"It's about time," Matthew grumbles. Matthew has never really had any time for me; another wolf who feels humans don't deserve the time of day, no doubt. He would've loved my father.

Jared shoves at Matthew's arm. "Shut the fuck up. You wouldn't even have the night off if Ruby wasn't going out."

"I don't have the night off. We're on babysitting duty," he spits out, with a slightly disgusted tone. Now I am really wondering if he is related to my father. *Ass.*

Grabbing him by the shirt, Jared shoves him across the room. "You know what? We don't need you. Fuck off, go do your normal patrol."

Matthew stares Jared down. He has no hope of winning and he knows it. Looking away, he silently storms out of the house. Jared's an alpha werelion, of course, Matthew had no hope of winning.

"Theo isn't going to like this." Paddy worries, looking at the door Matthew just exited.

"I'll explain things to Theo," Jared reassures Paddy, as he gives me a hug. "You look good, kid," he whispers, kissing my cheek.

"Thanks Jared," I say, before he walks off heading in the direction of Theo's office.

Jared has been staying here at Theo's since the night of the rescue. Getting to know him has been great. It's not hard to see the knight, Bel once fell for. His blond hair, blue eyes, and lean physique are an easy turn on. He calls me 'kid,' so I'm pretty sure he's never seen me more than as a sister; another brother to add to the ever-growing list of brothers.

*T*he club is packed. The guys prefer Misty's over night clubs, but my one hundred percent human status won't allow my entry into Misty's without a specially warded bracelet to negate the entry ward. So taking that into account, it's no wonder the guys have done nothing but complain as we barge our way through to the bar. The complaints flow right over my head. All I can concentrate on is my sweaty hand wrapped in Paddy's as he pulls me through the crowd.

Getting served within a minute, Eddie hands me a drink before handing a bottle of beer to each of the others.

Spotting a table become empty as someone walks away, I point in its direction. Nodding his head, Jared leads the way. It's one of those high tables you can either stand at or perch on a stool. Choosing to stand, I push my stool aside, Eddie and Paddy do the same. Jared is the only one who prefers to use the stool.

Placing my purse on the table with my drink after taking a healthy swig, I make my way to an empty spot at the edge of the dance floor. I'm here to party after all and I'm only about a foot away from the guys, so they could quickly reach me if they felt the need for safety reasons.

I lose myself in the music, but it isn't long before someone tugs me back against their hard body. "Hey baby, can I take you on a ride?" He leans down and licks the side of my neck in one long stroke of his tongue. I try to pull away from his iron grip with no luck. "I can give you the best night of your life, all with one little dance."

Judging by his words and actions, he must be a vampire. That meant with one dance and an endorphin-filled bite, I'd be high as a kite and having a blast. I quickly decline his offer, all while doubling my efforts to break free of his grasp.

Suddenly Eddie is beside me, shoving the vampire away with enough power to push a human across the room. Luckily for me the vampire uses his strength to brace himself, or I may have flown across the room, too.

Standing his ground, the vampire releases me and turns to face off with Eddie. "Who the fuck do you think you're shoving, you furry fucker?"

"I'm shoving a bloodsucker who has his dirty claws all over a pack member."

Leaning in, the vampire makes a show of sniffing me. "She may be covered in your wolf scent, but she smells all human to me. No trace of a mating to any of you," he says, grinning smugly.

Ed growls and yanks on my arm, pushing me behind him. I'll probably be left with bruises in the morning. "She's the alpha's sister. So you tell the rest of your bloodsucker mates To. Stay. Fucking. Clear," he emphasises each word through gritted teeth.

Raising his hands, the vampire slowly backs away, disappearing into the crowd. "She didn't taste that good anyway," he replies, leaving his words floating around us.

"Fucker," Eddie grumbles as he turns to face me, reaching his hands out to cup my face leaning in close. I lick my lips, unable to take my eyes off his. His other hand touches my neck and I close my eyes, pursing my lips for a kiss. I startle as I feel his fingers brushing over my pulse.

"He didn't bite you?" The question pierces through the lust fogging my mind. I quickly pop open my eyes, pulling back from his hold.

"No, he didn't," I say, with a shake of my head.

"Are you sure? You seem..." breaking off mid-sentence, I

watch as he inhales. I've been around wolves long enough to know that he's trying to scent something.

Oh God, he's going to pick up my lust. Please let it be mingled in with everyone else's.

"I'm fine, just a little shook up. I could do with a shot or two," I say, hoping to distract him.

A smile graces his face making his dimples pop. "That's the best idea I've heard all night. Shots coming right up," he says, taking me to the others at the table before heading to the bar.

I knock back my drink and tug at Paddy's hand. "Come and dance with me!" I plead.

He shakes his head, causing a strand of his dark hair to fall across his forehead, giving me the urge to brush it back into place.

"I don't dance," he says stoically, as his eyes roam the club.

I shrug at his rejection and quickly make my way back to the dance floor before I can follow through on the urge to straighten his hair. I'm on a boy's night out; I can't act like the needy girl coming onto one of them. I'll never be asked to join them again.

"Your loss," I mutter to myself.

I find an empty space and start to sway, losing myself in the music. I can feel bodies brushing up against me, but no one is being inappropriate with their hands. They're probably only too aware of the three sets of eyes on me. They have all been following Theo's orders of not taking their eyes off me all night.

When I feel a set of hands grab my hips, I don't worry about it being some pervert. I know the guys wouldn't let anyone like that touch me, not after the Vampire. It has to be one of them.

Probably Eddie. He's been dancing most of the night with one chick or another.

Turning to find a familiar face, I can't hide my look of surprise. "I thought you couldn't dance?"

Grinning mischievously, he tugs me closer against his body. "I said I don't dance, not that I can't dance. After watching those dickheads grinding all over you, I thought I'd better show them how to dance with a lady."

For the rest of the night, Paddy shows me exactly how well he can move.

THE GREEN-EYED
MONSTER

Seeing that bloodsucker with his hands on Ruby had me seeing red. I still haven't managed to calm myself completely down, having her face between my hands I wanted to lean in and kiss her. When I scented her lust, Jesus…my hard-on still hasn't gone down. She was probably lusting over the thought of the vampire bite. We all know how good they can make it feel. I shouldn't even be thinking about her that way, she's only just turned eighteen. Being twenty-two, Theo would have my balls if I ever make a move on her.

I couldn't stand watching her dance with the fucking humans, so I sent Paddy to dance with her. She likes him and he'll look after her, he's strong enough to protect her and Theo will be happy because Paddy isn't a ladies man. He's nineteen, much closer to Ruby's age than me.

He's better for her.

It doesn't mean I can stand watching it, though. I've left it to Jared to watch over them as I keep an eye on the exits from the dance floor, while dancing with some of the chicks in the club.

The lights in the club flick brighter and then back to dim, indicating last call. I brace myself as I catch Ruby's scent, knowing she must be coming up behind me. Her hand touches the small of my back, slipping under my shirt and brushing my skin. A rumble leaves my chest as I release the chick I'd been dancing with.

"Are you going to dance with me tonight? Time is running

out, even Jared had a dance with me," she speaks near my ear, her breath giving me goosebumps.

Wishing right now I'd kept a chick around so I'd have an excuse not to dance with her, whilst telling my dick to behave, I turn and hold her at arm's length. Having none of that, Ruby stumbles and plasters herself to me. "Jesus Rubes, are you drunk?"

"No. I've only had as much as you guys," she says defensively, her pout makes me want to kiss it away. *Fuck!*

Masking my lecherous thoughts, I laugh. "Yeah, but you don't have the metabolism of a werewolf." Holding her steady against me, I start to sway with the music. "Where did Paddy go?"

"To get me another drink," she slurs. Water is the only thing she'll be drinking from now on. The song finishes and the lights come on.

"Drink up," shouts one of the security guys.

Ruby stumbles in the direction of the table, keeping one hand tight on her hip, I help her along.

"We can't take her back to Theo's in this state. He'll kill us," I state to the boys.

"How the hell did she get this bad? She's been dancing all night," Jared asks, taking in her inebriated state.

"She's been keeping up with us. We should've stopped her." I'm pissed at the three of us for letting her get into this state. It's too easy to forget that humans can't hold their liquor like we can.

Reaching into his pocket, Jared pulls out his phone. "I'll message Theo saying we're staying at your place. I'll spin some story about not wanting to wake Selena and Trudy coming in this late."

"Don't mention that woman, dammit," Ruby grumbles with a deadly glare aimed at Jared. Putting his arm around her shoulders and kissing her temple, Paddy deftly distracts her.

"Come on, Princess, let's head to the car. These two can catch us up," he says, leading her out of the club.

Tearing my eyes away from their backs, I turn to look at Jared.

"Follow those two out and get the car started," he says, throwing me his car keys. "I'll give Theo a call, he'll be waiting up for us."

I step out the club to find Ruby and Paddy playing tonsil tennis next to Jared's Subaru.

What the fuck?

Storming over, I pull Paddy off her by the scruff of his neck and shove him against the car with a growl. "What the fuck, are you doing? She's plastered and you're taking advantage of her, you fucking dick."

He lowers his eyes in submission, no doubt realising how wrong he was to be caught in that position.

Ruby tugs at the back of my shirt. "We were just making out. You've been doing it with chicks all night. Get over it, Eddie,"

"Come on, sweetheart, let's get in the car and leave these two to their little fight," Jared says, as I feel him pulling her away from us.

"She's having my room tonight. You're not going anywhere near her until she's sober, even in the car." I push away from him, not caring how hard I do it.

"Anyone would think you have a thing for her," he mutters, as he opens the passenger door.

They'd be fucking right.

Ignoring his comment *and* the voice in my head, I slide into the back of the car next to Ruby; who's snoring with her head leaning against the window.

Only a few minutes pass and Jared pulls to a stop outside our two-bedroom duplex. Paddy exits the car silently and heads straight to unlock the door, as I walk around the car and pick up our sleeping beauty.

Carrying her into my bedroom, I place her gently on the king-size bed. Stepping back, I stare down at her. She looks so small on my bed but so perfect; like she belongs there. My wolf is more than happy with her being there, he's nudging me to join her. It takes all my willpower to ignore him and turn away from her.

It surprises me to find Jared standing in the doorway with his arms folded across his chest. "You want her!" His words are a statement, not a question.

"I can't have her. I'm too old for her, no one would let me near her," I say, hoping to end the conversation.

He shakes his head. "You're a good guy, Ed, and you're only what…four years older? That's not too old."

"She has a thing for Paddy, so it's pointless even discussing it." I edge forward to leave the room, forcing Jared to step back in the hallway to give me space to close the door behind us.

We hear Ruby moan through the closed door. "Eddie, I think I'm going to be sick."

"Look after her, she's going to need it. Is there anything I can get you?" Jared offers, as he starts down the hallway.

"No. We don't have any paracetamol. We never need the stuff," I say, as I quickly grab a bucket from the bathroom; which is just across the hall from my room.

Paddy likes to try and save water by placing it in the bottom of the shower when he uses it. It just pisses me off and gets under my feet. I usually end up kicking it over, so he hardly ever gets to pour it on the plants like he means to.

Placing the bucket beside the bed I sit down. Holding her hair back with one hand, I rub gentle circles on Ruby's back with the other as she vomits over the edge of the bed and into the bucket. Once she's emptied her stomach, she lays back and closes her eyes with a whimper.

I watch her for a minute and when her breathing evens out, I get up and pick up the bucket to clean it out before she needs it again.

"I like you too, Eddie," she mutters.

6

UNWANTED GIFTS

Closing the door to my private quarters, I breathe a sigh of relief. Today has been a harrowing day. Being the King has its drawbacks some days. Thankfully, once the younger vampires die for the day, I finally get a reprieve before I have to turn in myself.

A knock on the door tells me I'm getting no respite today. "I hope it's important because you know your life isn't worth anything less," I call through the door.

"I'm sorry to disturb you, sir. But there's been an unexpected delivery," Niko my head of security announces, as he opens the door and enters, carrying what looks like a young girl's body hung over his shoulder. The lack of heartbeat tells me she's dead. It's the third body I've been gifted in as many weeks.

I sigh and ask a question I already know the answer to. "Let me guess, nobody saw him?"

"Not a thing," Niko answers, with a shake of his head.

"What's he getting from this?" I ask, not really needing an answer because it's obvious. He's getting a kick out of pissing me off.

"He's getting a nice fill while he drives you crazy as he disrespects your laws," Niko answers me regardless, dropping the body to the floor with a thud.

We don't have many laws but not killing for food is one of our oldest and most important ones.

"I wasn't in need of an answer, Niklaus."

"Sorry."

I dismiss his apology with a wave of my hand as I crouch over the body. A single bite to the artery; completely drained, late teens, blonde. I pull her eyelid back to see her eyes are green just like the others. I don't know why I even bother looking.

"I think we can officially say he has a type."

Leaning as close to the wound as possible, I try to catch his scent hoping to recognise it so he can be stopped before another innocent life is ended. I know how addictive it is to drain a body completely, there's nothing like drowning in someone's life force, and when you hit that point of no return…The laws are there for a reason. Could you imagine if we were all free to kill when we feed? We'd start to run out of humans in no time.

"Do the usual. Disguise the wound and put her somewhere she'll be found." A beautiful young thing like this is bound to have someone missing her. It is better they find her and be placated with some explanation of what happened to her, rather than be searching for a missing person and digging for anything they can find.

Niko picks up the girl with a nod and leaves without a word. He still has a short time before he's dead for the day. The older we are, the longer we can last, but like humans we need sleep to recuperate. He'll most likely do the job himself leaving his feeder to just dispose of her. He's one of my most loyal men. I didn't sire him, so he has no real tie to me but he's as loyal as any vampire I've turned myself. Even more so. Niklaus has been by my side for a long time. He's never left, even after he turned his lover over one hundred and fifty years ago.

As I close the door behind me, I pull my phone out of my pocket and make my way to my desk perching against it. I hit call on the relevant number and put the phone to my ear as I wait for an answer.

"To what do I owe the honour that the head bloodsucker

called me himself?" Theo answers, as snarkily as ever. I thought our recent fight against the Controller had brought us closer together. I guess I was wrong.

"I'm in no mood to bite, Theo. He's killed again. Same MO. And I'm no closer to finding him. He's good at covering his tracks, but he's getting braver and dumping them closer. Someone is bound to catch him soon," I explain, getting right to the point.

Theo's voice thunders down the line. "Soon isn't good enough, Drake!"

"What have your wolves found, Wilson?" I snap, addressing him by his surname as he had me. I take a moment of his silence to calm myself down. Not enough to stop myself making a remark. "I thought as much."

He sighs. "Fine. Just because neither of us is close to pinning him down, doesn't mean we have time to waste. The longer this takes, more innocents die. That is unacceptable," Theo admonishes, as if I don't already now this.

"Do you think I don't care about that?" I don't give him time to answer, pausing for just a second before carrying on. "Just because my morals are different to yours, it doesn't mean I'm completely heartless."

"Huh…" he pauses, as if not knowing exactly how to reply, before carrying on without acknowledging my previous statement. "Thanks for updating me. I'll make sure my guys search harder." He hangs up without saying goodbye. *And people call me rude. I deserved an apology there.*

Throwing my phone on the desk, I make my way to the king-size bed, getting comfortable before calling my feeder in. "Sam, send Gerry in now." I don't raise my voice knowing Sam will hear me well enough with her acute vampire hearing.

Only a couple of minutes pass before my tall, dark, and handsome feeder and lover for the night enters the room. Closing and locking the door behind him.

7

HANGOVER AND FLASHBACKS

*S*omeone's going at my skull with an ice pick. I try to lift my head off the pillow and instantly regret it; the ice pick becomes even more persistent. Grabbing my head to secure it in my hands, I can't help but groan.

If I survive this, I'm never drinking again.

The door bursts open and I turn my head to find Eddie barging into the room, wearing just a towel around his waist and shaving cream on his face. His ginger hair looks almost brown, wet from the shower.

"Jesus. I thought you were dying."

Even the sight of him practically naked doesn't take my mind off the hammering in my skull. "I am," I complain, as I squeeze my eyes shut hoping to ease the pain.

"How are you feeling, beautiful? Do you need some painkillers?" he asks from beside me. I feel the bed dip as he sits beside my legs. He's almost naked next to me on the bed and he's as cool as a cucumber.

Freaking werewolves and their immunity to embarrassment over nudity.

Taking a breath to calm my hormones. I gulp in the smell of food coming through the now open door. "Oh my God! What's that smell? I think—" My stomach heaves at the smell, stopping me mid-sentence.

Seeing my predicament, Eddie pulls me to the edge of the bed where I can see a bucket strategically placed on the floor. I lose what little I have left in my stomach while Eddie holds my hair and strokes my back. I vaguely flash to something similar happening throughout the night.

Did he really look after me all night?

"Do you think you could keep some painkillers down?" he asks, still stroking gentle circles on my back. I grimace at the thought of swallowing anything.

"I think I have some *Alka-Seltzer* in my handbag. They should settle my stomach and ease my head," I answer, as I close my eyes and enjoy the comfort of him rubbing my back.

His hand stops and his weight lifts off the bed. "I'll see where your bag got to. It might have been left in the car." I hear his footsteps pad through the room before the door closes with a click and all goes quiet again.

I shuffle just enough to lay my head on the side of the bed, rather than having it hanging over the edge and close my eyes as I wait for Eddie to come back.

I wake up to find a glass of water and a double packet of *Alka-Seltzer* on the bedside table. I have no idea how much time has passed since Eddie left. Moving slowly, trying not to set the ice pick to the skull again, I sit up and mix the tablets with the water, drinking it down when it stops fizzing.

Feeling marginally better, I decide to find the others, after a visit to the bathroom. I really need to brush my teeth even if it's only with my finger. It doesn't take me long to freshen up, and soon I'm walking into the lounge to look for the guys.

"Eddie? Paddy?" I call out as I walk through the duplex. Seeing no sign of anyone. Looking at my watch, I notice it's ten in the morning. I open my mouth to call again as Paddy comes in through a door leading outside from the kitchen.

"Hey, Sleeping Beauty has woken up," he says, as he reaches into the fridge, pulling out a bottle of orange juice.

"How're you feeling?" Jared asks, as he enters through the same door and stops to lean his back against the worktop.

I grimace at the sight of the acidic orange juice. "I'm okay.

It's nothing a glass of lemonade and a packet of plain chips can't sort out. I guess Mum managed to teach me a few things in her drunken predicaments." It's ironic really; in my anger at my mum I went and did one of the things I hate her for. Turned to the booze. I don't think I could feel any more disgusted with myself.

Obviously putting two and two together Jared pulls me into a hug. "You're not a drunk, sweetheart, you just had a night out and let loose. We all need to do it sometimes." Kissing me on the top of my head, he releases me.

"Where's Eddie? I think I owe him a thank you for staying with my vomiting arse last night," I say, as I peer around, thinking his name will conjure him. Werewolves tend to turn up when they hear their names, even if they've been in an entirely different part of the house.

"He had to go to work. He'll probably turn up at Theo's later, you'll be able to thank him then," Paddy says distractedly, as he roots through the fridge. "Aha! I knew we had one in here somewhere. Here…" he says pulling a can of lemonade out and holding it out in front of me.

I take the can and tap the top before popping it open. "Thank you."

"There're some chips in the pantry if you want some. The plain ones never get eaten."

Looking in the pantry I see plenty of plain bags. Grabbing the bag that's closest to me, I shut the pantry and sit at the breakfast bar settling in to try and cure my hangover.

Jared talks over my munching. "I called Theo last night and spun some shit about not wanting to wake up Trudy and Selena. That's why we slept here. I don't think he believed a word of it so be prepared for the papa-wolf lecture."

"I'm always prepared for one of those. He gives me one on a daily basis," I say, with a laugh.

Jared laughs. "Yeah, I've noticed he likes to father you," Jared admits. He's been living with us since he arrived in town. He'd have to be blind not to have noticed.

"I think he's trying to make up for our father not wanting anything to do with me. He's just attempting to be the father figure I never had. Unfortunately, he forgets I'm eighteen. I've managed so far, I don't really need a father now." I stand as I finish my last mouthful of chips.

Paddy takes my rubbish and throws it across the room and into the bin. "He's the alpha, he fathers us all," he says nonchalantly,

"Let's go face the music then," I state, walking out the room, heading for the front door and car; knowing now is as good a time as any.

*P*addy reaches past me to open the car door, giving me an eerie déjà vu moment. *Oh, shit!* Scratch that, it's a flashback from last night. I kissed one of my crushes hours ago and I'm only just remembering it now.

Our mouths coming together in a kiss before my hands roamed over his chest and around his neck.

"We kissed?" I ask stunned.

He reaches his hand up and rubs at the back of his neck, looking sheepish. "Yeah, I'm sorry about that."

"The details are a bit fuzzy, but I'm pretty sure I should be apologising. I threw myself at you," I say.

Another flashback hits. *Eddie enraged and pinning Paddy to the car.*

I groan as I slide in the front seat and Paddy shuts the door, before slipping in the back. "Eddie practically bit your head off. I'm so sorry."

On the drive home, I can't help but dwell on what an idiot I was last night. I drank myself into oblivion, threw myself at

Paddy and then finished the night off by throwing up in front of Eddie; all because my drunk of a mother turned up on Theo's doorstep sober. Maybe if she really is sober and seeing a therapist, she deserves a second chance. I think I owe a few apologies.

Jared turns off the engine, tearing me away from my inner musings. "Are you okay, Ruby? You were awfully quiet on the drive down here."

I turn to find him looking at me, his eyes full of concern. "Yeah, I'm good. I was just deciding who I should apologise to first; the list is endless."

"I don't need one and neither does Jared. So you're all square in here," Paddy says, exiting the car. Both Jared and I follow his lead and head for the house.

The front door bursts open before any of us are even close.

"Ruby, how are you?" I can hear the worry in my mother's voice as she runs down the steps. I glance at Jared next to me, searching for a way to dodge her. My thoughts from the car journey come back to me. *I need to give her a second chance.*

"I'm fine, Mum," I reply, trying not to flinch as she pulls me into a hug. I'm not used to her cuddling me. She's usually throwing punches in a drunken rage.

"Eddie came by earlier and told us you weren't feeling too good," she says, squeezing me so hard I can barely breathe.

"Mum, let her breathe. It was a hangover, she'll be fine," Theo commands, as he tugs her off me.

Marching to the house on a mission, she shouts over her shoulder, "I know how to deal with a hangover. Chips and lemonade will have you feeling right in no time."

"Mum, I've alread—"

Theo grabs my arm interrupting my words. "Let her do it. She wants to make things up to you. We had a long talk last night and she really does mean it. There was no lie behind her words. I took her into town to see her new therapist this morning."

I follow her into the house, with a sigh. If she's really trying, the least I can do is eat another bag of chips.

Before I can get too far away, Theo's arm falls over my shoulders. "Not so fast, missy. What the hell were you thinking trying to keep up with the boys last night?" He directs me into the house and through to the lounge.

"I wasn't thinking. I was drinking and I've been paying for it. What with vomiting and the flashbacks? I don't think you could give me anything worse as a punishment."

He grunts as though he appreciates my self-imposed punishment. "Don't do it again or I won't be able to trust you to go out in the future."

"I'm an adult, Theo, you can't treat me like a kid forever," I admonish, moving out from under his arm.

"You'll always be my kid sister. Even when you're fifty and look twice as old as I do," he says, planting a kiss on my temple before allowing me to step away. Another reason I wouldn't mind being a werewolf like my brother. I'm going to grow old as everyone around me stays looking like they're in their mid-twenties. Damn that werewolf gene and it prolonging their lives.

8

MEDDLING CHICKS

Concentrating on the vehicles I've been fixing has been hard. I haven't had any big jobs assigned to me today, just a few tyres and oil changes, both I can do with my eyes shut.

I've done nothing but think about Ruby's words all day long. *"I like you too!"*

My wolf isn't letting me forget them either. He doesn't seem to care about all the reasons Ruby and me wouldn't work. The fact that our alpha would never allow it is just a little obstacle we can easily jump over. He's clearly delusional.

My boss's voice pulls me away from my thoughts of Ruby for the tenth time today. "Ed, there's some Sheila asking for you at reception. Something about a bike service?"

"That'll be Bel," I say, wiping my hands on a rag and making my way through to the reception.

Bel pulls me into a hug not caring about the grease and oil I'm covered in, going on her leathers. "Hey Ed," she says, as I struggle to get away from her.

"I'm oily, I don't want to make a mess of your leathers."

She releases me and gives me a good once over. "No one seemed to know I was coming. I only saw you this morning, so I know I haven't got the wrong day. Why are you so distracted?" Her smile suddenly turns to a sad frown. "Oh…Ed, you're so…" Not bothering to finish her sentence, she pulls me into a hug once again.

"I'm fine."

"You do realise I can feel exactly how *fine* you are not?" Releasing me, she starts to play with the keys in her hand. My misery is no doubt rubbing off on her. I need to get my head off Ruby and into my work.

"Let me just pull this car out and you can ride her into my bay," I say, pointing to the bike parked outside. With a nod, Bel leaves the reception and I make my way back to the car I was working on so I can clear up space for Bel's bike.

In a matter of minutes, the car is out in the carpark and Bel's bike is in its place in my bay. Bel leans against the workbench at the end of the bay as she watches me drain the oil. "So…I guess it's a woman?"

Chicks! If it were a guy sitting there, he'd just leave me to my misery. Chicks always have to meddle. She'll just keep digging if I don't answer. *Fuck!* I can't tell her I'm in love with her mate's little sister. "A woman I can't have. I'll get over it."

"Why?"

I change the filter and start to refill the oil before answering, trying to give myself time to think of how to answer without telling her everything. "People who are important to her don't think I'm good enough for her." It's the truth.

Jumping down from the bench, Bel stands with her hands on her hips and a fierce look on her face. "You may be a flirt, but there's no one you aren't good enough for. Who are they? I'll tell them."

If only she knew she was mated to him.

"I appreciate the offer, Bel, but I'm not sure he'll take your word for it." I laugh.

"Aha, he? Is he an overprotective father?"

He sure acts like one.

"Yeah, although she has a few siblings who would probably feel the same. Honestly, I'll be okay. She'll probably hook up with someone and I'll move on."

"Or you'll want to tear him apart for touching your

woman," she says, with a frown. After the way I pinned Paddy to the car when I saw him kissing Ruby last night, I'm pretty sure she's onto something there.

Unable to deny it, I turn back to the bike without replying and carry on with the service. It doesn't take me long to swap out the spark plugs and have her fired up and growling nicely. I turn back to Bel and wave to the bike. "She's all yours, beautiful, it's not too late to ride off into the sunset with me." I flirt with a grin.

"I've got a couple of hours until sunset, I better go pack a bag," she says, playing along before throwing her arms around my neck and hugging me, without a care for the oil all over me. "Fine, I'll drop the subject, but if you don't get over her, I'm getting involved. Remember you can't fool me, Ed. I'm your alpha female and I'll make sure you're happy," she says, while squeezing the breath out of me. She's almost out the doors before she comes shooting back in. "I almost forgot, Theo needs you to pop in tonight, he's got a job for you tomorrow."

I nod in acknowledgement and she drives off, probably heading home to her mate.

9

TAKE ONE FOR
THE TEAM

I walk into the kitchen expecting to find Selena and Chloe waiting for me, for our weekly visit to the day spa. I'm surprised to find Theo and Eddie chatting over coffee instead.

"Morning Rubes, you're head feeling any better today?" Eddie greets me, as he takes a mouthful of his coffee.

I groan, embarrassed by the reminder of my idiocy from the night out. "Ed, did you have to remind me? I'd happily forgotten about my stupidity."

"You're not one of us until you've had a good ribbing about a bad night out." he laughs.

Knowing that no matter what he says, I'll never be one of them, I glance at my watch and quickly change the subject. "Where's Selena and Chloe?" I ask, looking at Theo for an answer. If they aren't here, he'll know exactly where they are. He knows where everyone is.

Theo walks over to the sink and rinses out his cup. "Selena has an ultrasound appointment, Mum and Chloe went with her. Ed can go with you to your appointment at the spa," he announces nonchalantly, bending to place his cup in the dishwasher.

As annoyed as I am at the fact that Selena didn't even think to invite me along to her ultrasound, I can't hold back the laugh at how out of place Ed will look at the day spa.

"I'm not participating, I'm on bodyguard duty." Ed's voice is full of authority, making the words I was about to say die on my tongue.

I'd love to talk him into getting a pedicure or even better, a wax. That will be my mission for the day. I'm not leaving the spa until I've put Ed through something uncomfortable. It can be payback for the ribbing he mentioned earlier.

We drive in comfortable silence until we pull into the day spa's carpark.

"How are things with your mum? Have you had a chance to chat some more?" Ed asks.

"I'm trying to give her a chance. She's seeing a therapist, and Theo says she isn't lying about her intentions. So I need to give her an opportunity, at least, to prove herself," I reply, feeling somewhat guilty because I just can't look past her previous indiscretions and give her the future she obviously wants.

He pulls into a parking space, removes the keys from the ignition and turns to look me in the eyes. "That's good. Trying is all you can do. If it doesn't work, it doesn't work. Sometimes your past can't be overlooked. You might come to forgive her in time, but unfortunately it's harder to forget."

Relief floods me, knowing that someone not only understands my side of things, but he doesn't expect me to forgive and forget. "Thanks Ed. You're the first person that hasn't expected me and Mum to be besties in a couple of months' time. You're pretty wise for a player."

A smile spreads across his face before he tries to wipe it off, and replace it with a look of horror. "Don't tell anyone. It will ruin my player reputation."

Reaching across the car and slapping his arm, I laugh. "As if anything could ruin that reputation of yours." I start to sing the

Britney Spears song *'Womanizer,'* as I exit the car and close the door behind me.

I don't get far before Eddie grabs me and starts to tickle my sides. I squeal and try to squirm away with no luck.

"Are you going to stop teasing me with that song? Or should I keep on tickling?" he asks, while still prodding away at my ribs.

I can't take any more. "Yes," I shout, between fits of laughter. "I'll...stop," I add.

His hands ease up on the tickles, but still grip my sides to hold me steady as I take a moment to catch my breath.

"Okay?" he queries, slowly releasing me. It's at that moment, I notice how close we actually are. I shiver at the loss of his body heat, even though it's a beautiful summer's day at thirty degrees Celsius.

"Yes," I say distractedly, as I head for the entrance humming the tune to *'Womanizer.'*

"Ruby," Eddie growls low in his throat; a sexy sound that's sending butterflies through my stomach. But it's too late for him to punish me, now that I'm already pulling the door open. To tease him more and to show him I know I've gotten away with it, I poke my tongue out at him over my shoulder as I make my way to the receptionist.

"Later, Rubes. Just you wait," he threatens playfully.

"Hi. Ruby Wilson. I have a waxing appointment with Gloria," I say to the woman behind the counter.

"Go straight through, Ms. Wilson. Your friend can take a seat out here," she informs us, with a pointed look at Eddie over my shoulder.

I nod, accepting her instructions until I feel Ed bristle behind me. "I'm going in with her," he says emphatically, leaving no room for argument.

It doesn't stop her. "I'm sorry, sir, but only paying customers can go back there, for health and safety reasons. If you would like to get a wax, you're more than welcome to join her," the woman announces smugly; confident he won't take her up on the offer.

"Are you good with your hands?" he asks. The big flirt. Having seen her blush, he quickly adds, "How about a massage?" in a suggestive tone.

I watch as she gulps, opens her mouth to speak, and closes it again without saying another word. With one sentence, he's rendered her speechless.

I quietly hum the tune to *'Womanizer'* again, as I turn my back to them both so I can hide the grin on my face. I feel his eyes trying to burn a hole in my back, but I don't stop humming.

"I'd be happy to offer you a…" She gulps once again. "A massage, but that's a waxing suite, so you'd need to book a wax," she informs him; making it clear that she'd happily give him more than a massage.

"Ed, looks like you'll have to man up and take one for the team," I tease.

"Fine. Book me in," he grumbles.

The woman behind the counter looks at Ed nervously. It's like she wants to say something but daren't. Finally plucking up the courage, she asks her question, "What kind of wax would you like? Back, chest, or crack and sack?"

The look on Ed's face, a picture, as he mouths the words *'crack and sack'* in disbelief.

Remembering the sprinkling of chest hair I'd seen when he was only wearing a towel the other day, I decide to save him from any more trauma. "He'll take the chest wax," I say with finality, as I pull him into the waxing suite.

Closing the door behind us and knowing how these things work, I prepare myself for Gloria's entrance by promptly dropping my jeans to the floor and jumping up on the table.

Ed clears his throat. "Rubes, you can't just drop your jeans in front of me," he says, sounding somewhat put out.

"Just be thankful I'm only getting my legs waxed. You'd be seeing a hell of a lot more, if it was time for my Brazilian," I say, only half-joking because I'm booked in for that in a fortnight.

Saving me from any smart remark he was thinking of embarrassing me with, Gloria, my beauty therapist, walks in silencing us both with her greeting. "Hello. I hear we have a new client today. I'll be gentle, I promise." The flirty tone coming from the grandmotherly-looking woman before me stuns me for a minute before I realise Ed has been surprisingly quiet since my Brazilian remark.

With a glance over at Ed, I see the hungry look on his face as he's watching me intently. So much so, I don't know if he's even noticed Gloria's entrance or greeting.

"Morning, Gloria. Eddie here is a little nervous." My words seem to snap Eddie out of his trance, but he doesn't get to speak before Gloria jumps straight into business. "Since you're ready and in the hot seat, I guess you've decided to go first."

I hadn't really thought about going first, I was just in routine mode. I usually come in alone; not that I'll be admitting that to anyone. Theo would not be happy with Chloe for dropping her duty so she could have a massage. Playing along with Gloria's suggestion, I quickly agree. "Yes, I figured this way Eddie can see that there's nothing to it."

"Eddie, there's a seat by the wall over there." She distractedly points over her shoulder in the direction of the chair as she gathers the things she'll need to do the procedure. "Sit back and relax for a few minutes." It sounded more like an order, even to my human ears.

Not making a move to follow her instructions he steps closer to my side, making sure to be out of her way. "I can see better over here," is all he says.

It doesn't take Gloria long to do my legs, I'm quickly

jumping down and pulling my jeans on. Gloria turns her attention to Eddie. "If you just take your shirt off and lie down, we can get started and it will be over in no time."

"You just want to see the goods under the shirt," he declares with a grin. I'm seriously starting to worry that he doesn't know how to communicate without flirting when it comes to the female species.

"Behave," Gloria chides, as he pulls his shirt over his head and does as he's told by laying on the table.

The sight of his washboard abs throws me as I fumble with the button on my jeans. I wouldn't mind being Gloria right now, getting paid to touch his chest. I quickly gather myself and pull my tongue back in my mouth before making my way to stand next to Eddie as he had me earlier. "Ready for the pain, Eddie?" I tease.

"It didn't look too bad when she did your legs," he says confidently.

Gloria smears some warm wax onto his chest covering the sprinkling of hair, placing a strip over it, she counts down from three. "Three, two…" Ripping it off before she even gets to one.

"*Fuck!*" Ed shouts, taking a breath as though he'd held it. "Holy shit, do I have any skin left?" he asks, as he lifts his head and stares down at the pink patch of skin on his chest.

Gloria doesn't bat an eye before she smears on more wax and places another strip over it. She doesn't bother with the countdown this time. She just rips it off.

Eddie manages to control himself, this time only giving a grunt of pain. "Where was my countdown?" his voice sounding strained.

"I thought it would be best to just get on with it," she proclaims, matter-of-factly. All while loading his chest with more wax and strips before ripping them off one by one.

She made quick work of it. After ripping off the last strip and ensuring she had all the hairs, I watch as she grabs an oiled up wipe and starts smoothing it over his chest, removing any remaining wax residue. My hands are itching to take over and rub their way all over that oiled up chest. I quickly fold my arms over my chest and trap my hands under my arms before they can follow through. Hanging around with these hot guys is sending me crazy. I've never fantasised over guys before, not even when I was surrounded by plenty of them back home. I'm here for a couple of months, and I'm having to physically trap my hands to stop from touching him. Maybe werewolves have stronger pheromones or something.

"Are you okay, Rubes?"

Eddie's voice pulls me out of my inner turmoil and I tear my eyes away from Gloria's hands on his chest. "Yeah. I can't wait to tell the other guys about this." I laugh.

"You're all done. If you want to get dressed and go see Donna at the front desk, she'll be happy to book you in for your next appointment," Gloria says, as she wipes her hands off and leaves the room, closing the door behind her. I'm suddenly aware of how small the room is and how close I'm standing to Eddie.

"You will not say a word of this to anyone," he demands. I take a step back giving him room to put his shirt on. "This shit stinks," he says, pointing to his oiled up chest. "They'll smell me coming a mile away, but as far as anyone else is concerned I had a massage. Okay?"

"What do I get for keeping my mouth shut?" I enquire.

"Ruby," he says in a warning tone, as he pulls his shirt over his head.

"Telling everyone would be so much fun. Watching them ribbing you about it for weeks would be *very* entertaining." I tease. It would be fun, I can hear them laughing and jesting already.

He glares at me menacingly as he walks towards me. My heart is beating so fast in my chest, he can probably hear it.

Supersonic wolf hearing. The look in his eyes makes me back up until I'm pressed against the very hard door. *I wonder what else is hard? Ruby. Don't.* I implore my brain to shut up.

Eddie's nostrils flare as he gets really close to me. "You said plenty of entertaining things when you were drunk the other night; you spill the beans on this, and I'll have to share a few things myself," he says, leaning in closer. His body is almost touching mine. My body sort of begs him to touch mine as panic flows through me. I thought I'd remembered everything I said the other night. *Is he going to kiss me? Did I come onto him when I was drunk?* His hand reaches around my hip and he opens the door. I stumble back slightly as the door moves behind me and I slip through.

"Fine, my lips are sealed…forever," I say, in defeat, not knowing what secrets he could spill if I don't.

10

BBQS AND
BACKYARD CRICKET

Walking out to the yard with a plate of bread rolls, I glance at the stack of sausages on the barbie and wonder if we're going to have anyone else turn up.

We have enough food to feed the whole pack, but it's only close members, or who I call *family*, that Theo and Bel invited. The guys are all gathered around the barbie; Eddie, Paddy, Jared, Billy, Wes, and Theo. I place the plate on the table and grab a beer from the Esky as I pass and head to the girls lounging on the grass. Mum pats the grass between her and Misty, inviting me to join her. Things are still strange between the two of us, I've been avoiding her at all costs, but unfortunately I can't do that today. I take the seat offered knowing it would only look vindictive if I tried to make a space between someone else.

"Thanks, Mum," I say, grateful for the seat.

The guys all make their way over to the table.

"Food's ready, ladies," Theo announces, as the guys all start making up their plates. "Before we eat, Bel and I have an announcement." Bel makes her way over to him and hugs into his side lovingly, as the rest of us all head for the table.

"When we mated it was a crazy time. We had the Controller running rampant and not to mention my ex-wife showing up out of the blue. So, we think it's about time we have our mating ceremony."

"Congratulations," Alyssa says, pulling Bel into a hug. "How much time do we have to pull this wedding together?" she asks, as she releases Bel.

"Congratulations, Ted, I'm so happy for you," I say, using his pet name and giving him a big hug. "Love you," I say, as I pull away and step back for Alyssa to grab him for a hug.

"Love you too, little sis," he says, before turning his attention to Alyssa.

"Three months isn't much time, but I think we can work with that," she says. I must have missed Bel's answer when I was hugging Theo.

"Pups..." Theo says, sounding stunned to match his wide eyes.

Alyssa having not seen his face wriggles free of his hold. "You never know what the future might bring. Of course, you guys can try for pups." She giggles nervously.

"No." He's starting to sound crazy, even to my ears and I know my brother pretty well. He's not looking far off it, either.

Bel strokes a hand down his forearm. "Babe?"

Ignoring his mate, Theo's eyes flit between Wes and Alyssa. "No. You're having pups," he says. The way his eyes are flitting between the two of them, I can see he's here, in the moment, and not having some crazy episode. "Alyssa, you're pregnant."

Suddenly each and every werewolf inhales all at once; no doubt trying to scent the hormones, or something. Mum and I, not knowing what else to do, look at each other and smile warily. It's somewhat comforting to know I'm not the only human around for once. I'm not alone with this feeling of being an outsider. Thinking back to my mum's reasoning for her turning to drugs, I can see how maybe her life with my father could have pushed her that way. Especially after her sons had been ripped from her life. Looking at my mother now, I can imagine the strength it must have taken to not only face me and my brother but to become the outsider in a pack once again. She did it for us.

A round of congratulations for both couples flows through the yard.

"You need another alpha to officiate the ceremony. Who are you going to ask?" I hear Wes question Theo, as I start to fill my plate with food.

"Who do I trust? Is a better question. Jesse O'Keefe from the Rossi Pack in WA is the only alpha I've ever felt at ease with, but he's not been the same since his mate went missing five years ago. I don't know if he'd be willing to do it considering his circumstances."

Wes nods his understanding as he takes a bite of a burger.

"You'll never know if you don't ask," Bel says, placing a kiss on his shoulder as she reaches past him for a bread roll on the table.

With my plate full, I look around the garden for somewhere to sit, spotting Paddy on a lounger on the deck. I head over deciding to bite the bullet and face the embarrassing things I did while I was drunk the other night. We've already discussed what happened when I first had the flashbacks, but I still feel sorry for throwing myself at him.

I grab an extra beer as I pass the Esky. Looking up at my arrival, he gives me a sheepish smile.

"Peace offering," I say, holding out the beer for him.

He takes the beer and places it at his feet next to his already half full bottle. "There's no need for that. Take a seat."

I shrug as I sit on the chair beside him. "I still feel bad about the other night." Not wanting to say something that makes me feel any dumber, I take a bite of my burger.

He reaches his hand out and places it on my arm halting me from taking my next bite. "Honestly, you didn't throw yourself at me. I wouldn't have danced with you if I didn't want something to happen."

I give a jerky nod, not knowing how else to reply. He removes his hand and starts back in on his food.

"Jared said you were doing an OUA course. What subject you taking?"

I swallow a mouthful of beer and tell him all about my criminology course, probably too much information. When I get talking about something I'm passionate about, I struggle to stop. He sits quietly taking in every word I say, smiling at all the right moments.

"It sounds like something you actually enjoy," he says, when I finally shut my mouth.

I grin at him and let the truth of my words show. "I love it."

"Do you want to join the police academy when you finish?" he asks, lifting his bottle to his lips and swallowing what's left in the bottle. He catches my eye as he sets the bottle down.

I can't help but blush at being caught getting distracted by his lips, lips I've had the pleasure of feeling on my own. Not that I can really remember what they felt like. "Yeah, that's the plan. Hopefully with the degree behind me, I can fast track into the field I'm interested in. I'll still have to do the initial training and I'll probably have to do the first couple of years on the job like everyone else, but I know where I essentially want to be in the end." I suddenly realise I don't know what he does. "What do you do?" I query.

"I'm doing a graphic design course. I only have this semester left and then I'll be let loose on the world. Well, that's if someone will give me a job."

"Doesn't anyone want to give you a go?"

"It turns out that everyone wants to design websites and things these days. Theo asked me to design a website for his carving business, and he said he was going to chat to the other alphas about setting up a communications network, so all the packs can stay in contact better. The degree won't be entirely useless. I just might have to look at other jobs in the long run."

"Oh, that network thing is a great idea. Theo was only talking about another alpha having a missing mate. I'm sure if there was a network set up we could spread her picture further and she might be found."

"Oh yes, Jesse. I don't know how he still goes on without Frankie, not knowing where she is." He shakes his head. "I've never experienced the mating bond myself, but I know it's strong. I don't think I'd be able to handle not knowing where she is or what's happened to her."

"Going by how Wes reacted when Alyssa was taken by the Controller, I can only imagine the strength Jesse must have, to have not lost control of his wolf or pack," I say, honestly stunned at the thought.

"Are you two up for some backyard cricket? Girls versus boys," Bel asks, as she passes by heading to the shed, no doubt to dig out the cricket set.

With a shrug, we both get up and follow her as she makes her way to the middle of the yard, cricket set in hand. "Girls bat first," she says, handing me the bat.

I take the bat and give it a wary look. "You've never seen me play cricket before have you, Bel? Maybe I shouldn't bat." I'm the worst cricket player, last time I played Theo banned me from ever playing again. I've got a habit of throwing the bat like in softball or baseball. If I wasn't playing with werewolves, I would have probably hospitalised half the fielders.

"Ruby's banned from backyard cricket," Theo orders. The other pack members nod their agreement, leaving Mum and Bel looking at me with caution.

"She can't be that bad," Bel declares, sticking up for me. Unfortunately, she's very wrong.

"I am," I admit unabashedly.

"Well, I don't care. It's a family game and we're all playing," Bel states, setting up the stumps behind me.

"You'll regret that decision later, baby," Theo mutters, as he takes the ball and swings his arm to stretch it ready for bowling.

Once everyone is in position Theo bowls the first ball. I'm expecting the ball to connect with the wickets behind me, but to my surprise it's the bat that connects with the ball. My internal chant of *'don't drop the bat, don't drop the bat,'* helps me manage to keep hold of the bat as I run to the safety of the stick where Theo bowled from. Bel runs from that side and stops where I'd started. I hadn't hit the ball hard enough to get any more than one run.

"Get ready for a good run, Rubes," Bel says, as she positions herself for Theo's bowl. I do as I'm told and brace myself to run and run hard. I don't even see the ball go past; the thunderous whack it makes with the bat is my starting gun. I bolt to the stumps and back, Bel waves me on so I run again. I feel the ball brush past me as I hit the ground at the base of the stumps with my bat. Calling my safety. It hits the wickets a second later and the guys all groan at the near miss.

I manage to hit the next ball Theo throws, and I hit it hard enough to do a double run. I stand ready for the next bowl, it sails right past the bat and hits the wicket behind me. The guys cheer and I hand the bat to Delly; a pack member who I would guess is around my age.

"Okay guys, the real game starts now," she says, insinuating they were only pretending to play while I was batting. Fucking bitch. Just wait until we're fielding, she'll be getting a ball to the back of her head once or twice, I'm certain of that.

I head over to the other girls waiting at the edge of the yard to bat. "You did well to hit anything Theo threw your way," Paddy compliments me, as I pass him in the field.

"Thanks." I blush, knowing he's only being kind. I know they were all holding back while I was playing, but there was no need for Delly to make me feel so inferior. I sit down, realising too late who I've sat next to. "Mum." I greet her with a smile.

"Ignore the bitch, she's only jealous because that cutie has his eye on you," Mum announces, nodding towards Paddy. I follow her nod with my eyes and catch the glare Delly throws my way. *Just great!*

"Mum, did you forget she's got werewolf hearing?" I question. Knowing everyone on the field just heard her comment.

"No, I wanted the bitch to hear," she claims. A few snickers from the field make me grin. I lean in and give my mum a side hug.

"Thanks, Mum," I whisper. Maybe we can fix things between us after all.

The girls won by five runs. So bragging rights are ours until the next game; which is amazing because I'm pretty sure the girls have never won before. Bel is like a pro, says she hasn't actually played before, but I'm sure she's telling porkies. I'll be grilling Jared later.

The doorbell rings through the house.

"That'll be the pizza," Bel shouts into the house from out back. Bel and Alyssa are still clearing the table from earlier.

"I'll get the door. Eddie, get everyone's money together," Jared announces, heading for the door.

"You heard the man, guys. Give me your money. Girls, you better enjoy this, because you won't win again," Eddie proclaims, as the guys dig into their pockets with muttered complaints about letting us win. After collecting all the money he heads to the front door. It's only a few seconds later when both Jared and Eddie enter loaded up with pizza boxes. I hear Eddie call my name out, but rather than fight through the hungry wolves, I wait back until everyone gets their pizzas.

Paddy barges through the crowd with two boxes in hand. "Here. I thought I'd save you the fight."

I take the box he offers. "Thanks!" The smell that hits me

when opening it is mouth-watering. I love Hawaiian pizzas; pineapple and ham. Yum.

"Pineapple? Oh, I don't think we can be friends anymore," he says, looking disturbed at my choice of pizza topping.

"That means you won't be stealing my leftovers like Eddie and Jared usually do. You can come more often," I say, before taking a huge bite out of the first slice.

"Your pizza is safe with me," he laughs, before tucking into his own.

I manage to eat three slices before I'm well and truly stuffed. "Okay, I'm done. Who wants it?" I ask, holding the closed box up. It practically flies out my hand as Jared takes it with a cheer. Eddie stops before me a second later.

"I thought you loved me, Ruby. I'm pack. You should have saved it for me. Not given it to the intruder," Eddie says glumly.

"Ha! You're too slow, Ed," Jared teases.

"She obviously has a new favourite. She's just teasing you all. She'll never put out," Delly insists in a snarky voice, catching everyone's attention.

I stand, ready to go on the defensive.

"Delly!" Theo's warning tone shows he's clearly not happy with her. As much as I love my brother, she'll never respect me if I sit back and hide behind him.

I take a step in her direction. "You clearly have a problem with me, Delly. What is it?"

She glances at Theo, as if she's seeking permission. "I've asked you the question. Don't look at him. I want an answer. I'm not living with this tension between us. I want to know what's bothering you."

With a huff, she lays it all out. "I've watched these guys paw all over you every summer and never batted an eyelash, knowing that once those eight weeks are over you'll be heading home and the females of the pack will get the attention back. These guys," she says, waving an arm around the room blindly, "they're the future of the pack. We've all been brought up together. Some of us will wait for our true mates, and others will choose a pack member to mate with. Every time you come home and flirt with them, you're taking the chance of a mate away from one of the females. Now you live here for good, it's not going to stop unless you date one of them. At least that way the others can focus their attention elsewhere." She stares at me with daggers in her eyes.

"Thank you, for being honest. But it's been known for werewolves to mate with humans, too. Hell, I came from one of those matings. In saying that, I don't think the guys give me any more attention than they do any other female, but I'll be more aware for future interaction," I say, and leave the room.

I was being honest. I don't think the guys focus on me when I'm home. Not unless Theo has set them on guard duty. It's not like we hang out in our free time except for family get-togethers, like today. The boys night out was a one off and after the state I was in, I don't think that will be happening again anytime soon. Deciding I've had enough, I head to my room.

I turn the door handle when I reach my room just as a hand on my shoulder spins me around.

I find myself face to face with Paddy. "Don't let her chase you away, Ruby. Did you mean what you said about mating? Would that be something you'd be interested in, if you met the right wolf, of course?"

I swallow the lump in my throat and nod. "The pack is part of my life. You know how overprotective my brothers are. Would you expect them to be happy if I married a human? I'm pretty sure they would want me protected by a werewolf mate."

Paddy nods with a smirk. "Yeah. I think you're onto something there. They aren't the only ones that wouldn't be happy with you marrying a human."

I move to turn towards my room. "I'm not letting Delly chase me away. It's late, so I'm going to call it a night."

His hand that's still resting on my shoulder halts me from turning. "Before you go, do you fancy going out somewhere with me tomorrow?"

"What, like a date?" I ask, feeling my cheeks blush. Jesus, if I can't handle him asking me out, how am I meant to handle a freaking date?

"Yeah, exactly. Like a date," he says, throwing me a wink.

"I'd love to," I answer honestly. I've had a thing for Paddy for a while now. He's a nice guy, not to mention gorgeous. What eighteen-year-old girl wouldn't have a thing for him? It would be stupid to say no.

"Great. Can you be ready for ten in the morning? We can make a day of it," he says, with an uncertain smile on his face, as though he's worried that I'd say no.

"I think I can manage that," I tease, with a wry grin, as I back away from him.

"See you tomorrow then," he says, as he turns and heads back downstairs. I stand with my hand on the door handle at my back, watching him make his way down the stairs, so I catch him as he turns to get one last look.

"Night," he says, somewhat shyly.

I can't wipe the huge grin off my face even as I close myself in my bedroom.

11

CONFESSIONS OF
A FIRST DATE

I head downstairs to warn Theo that Paddy will be picking me up for a date soon. I don't know if he'll be pissed that I'm dating a pack member, or if my guess the night before about him wanting me under a wolf's protection over a human's, would work in our favour. To be honest, I'm pretty sure he isn't ready for his little sister to be dating anyone.

I knock on his office door knowing he'll be there checking through his emails, with his morning coffee like he is at that time every day.

"Come on in, Rubes," he calls from behind the closed door. I know not to stress on how he knew it was me. I've been around the wolves long enough to know they have this strange sixth sense when it comes to someone being behind a closed door. Scent, the psychic bond that belongs to the wolves, which Theo insists I am part of, and even the sound of your knock are all tells.

I open the door and make my way to his side as he peers at the laptop screen before him. I plant a kiss on his cheek and give him a side hug before clearing a space on the edge of his desk and plant my butt on it.

Lifting his eyes from the screen, he focuses his attention on me as he sits back in his seat. "You went to bed pretty early last night. Is everything okay?"

"Yeah, I'm fine. I'd just had enough and thought an early night was a good idea," I reply, somewhat honestly. The look in his eye's telling me he can see there's more to it and he's right, but I don't want to get into it. I break the eye contact by glancing around the room to find anything I can use to distract him.

"I hope you didn't take anything Delly said to heart. She was out of order and I've spoken to her about it. You're pack, and she needs to treat you as she would any other female pack member. If she isn't willing to try and tear a guy's attention from you, she doesn't deserve that guy as a mate. It's as simple as that," he says, apparently not willing to drop the subject.

I look up quickly so I can see his face. Did he really mean that? Was he really okay with me being a pack member and dating as one?

I ask him, "Do you really mean that? You'd be happy with me dating a pack member, maybe eventually mating with one?"

"Let's get something straight, I won't be happy with you dating anyone, ever. But I know I'm going to have to deal with it, eventually, unless you have any interest in joining a convent. Have you ever been interested in becoming a nun? You did love that movie as a kid, you know, the one with the woman who makes dresses out of some ugly arse curtains?" We both laugh before he carries on, "Seriously, though, I'll hate it but I'll deal with it. The only consolation I get with it being a pack member is I'll know if he can protect you or not."

I guess now is as good as any to test that theory. "It's good you feel that way because Paddy will be picking me up in a minute," I say and watch as a number of emotions play over his face before he speaks.

"He did mention something about that last night."

"He asked for your permission?" The thought actually pisses me off.

"No, he was telling me not asking. It was after he'd followed you upstairs." He sounds angry at that thought, which makes me somewhat happy. "Although I'm a little concerned because I thought it was Ed you liked. I'm not complaining, I'm far happier that it's Paddy you're interested in. He's better suited to you," he adds. Making me lose the happy feeling I just had.

"You can like more than one person, Theo. I'd never have a chance with Eddie, he's completely out of my league. Paddy likes me back and has asked me out, so my interest in Paddy has taken over my interest in Eddie," I try to explain.

Why the hell am I babbling? I'm sure he's had crushes in his time.

"As long as he treats you right and keeps you happy, I won't interfere."

Jumping off the desk I pounce on my brother, engulfing him in a hug. "Thanks. I love you, Ted." My pet name for him sneaking out once again.

Hearing the doorbell ring, he pushes me off him. "Go have fun."

"I will," I say, as I run to the door. I don't need my mum answering and letting him in, if she finds out what's happening she'll give him the fifth degree now and me later.

"And for God's sake, behave," I hear Theo shout, as I run through the house.

Stopping in front of the door, I quickly straighten my clothes and check that I look presentable in the mirror on the wall, silently thanking my brother for being vain enough to need a mirror in the entry hall. Thinking on it, it was probably something Selena insisted on, back when they were married. Shaking the stupid thoughts out of my head, I pull the door open and greet Paddy with a smile.

"These are for you," he says pushing a bunch of sunflowers into my hands.

"Thanks, I...How did you know they were my favourites?" I ask, flicking a look down at the flowers.

"I do pay attention, you know. I've seen the little sunflower tattoo you have."

I swallow nervously, wondering when he's seen that tattoo.

It's extremely low on my hip. I didn't know anyone knew about it. I quickly manage to compose myself.

"Come in a minute, I'll put these in water and grab my purse." I turn and go straight to the kitchen. The sound of the door closing and heavy footsteps tells me Paddy is following behind.

I pause in the doorway, spotting Mum using the coffee machine. Taking a deep breath, I prepare myself for the Spanish Inquisition.

"Morning, sweetheart. Nice to see you again, Paddy," Mum says. "Let me put them in water," she adds, clocking the flowers. "You two get going. Have fun."

Surprised by her offer, I stay silent.

"Thanks, Mrs. Wilson," Paddy says, taking the flowers from my grasp and passing them to Mum.

"Please, call me, Trudy," she says, as she digs a vase out of the first cupboard she looks in. How did she know it was there? I've lived here for months at a time over the years and had no idea if Theo even owned a vase?

"Ruby?" Paddy's voice pulls me out of my head.

I quickly give Mum an appreciative hug. "Thanks, Mum." Taking Paddy's outstretched hand, I drag him towards the door. Snatching my purse and phone off the kitchen bench as we pass.

Once buckled in the car and moving down the drive, I turn to Paddy. "So, where are we going?"

"It's a surprise, but Theo assured me you'll like it," he says, as he takes his eyes off the road to throw me a wink.

"You tease! Stop winking and get your eyes back on the road."

As we pull onto the freeway, I have a guess at where we are heading. "Are we going to Sydney?"

"Yes, Miss Marple, we are going to Sydney. Choose some music and stop trying to guess things," he says, passing me his phone. I flick through his playlists and select the James Bay album I've been meaning to buy.

The album ends just as we enter the city. On driving through, I give up trying to guess where he's taking me, I sit back and enjoy his company. He tells me about his family who he hasn't seen for the last six years, not since the day he was attacked by a werewolf. The pack the werewolf belonged to was brutal. They didn't think they could do anything with a thirteen-year-old, newly changed pup, they'd planned to kill him, but luckily one of the females in the pack had a connection to Theo. She managed to get Paddy to Theo before they executed him. I had no idea where Paddy had come from. I remember one summer I turned up and there was a new wolf.

Theo spoke to his parents, he told them it wasn't safe for Paddy to live with them until he had a handle on his wolf. The wolves are secretive. I guess when someone is attacked they can't just leave the family in the dark, especially when it's a child that's been changed.

Paddy tells me how he was the baby of the family, his sisters being eight and ten years older than him.

"I miss them. They probably have kids of their own now," he admits, the sadness in his voice evident.

"Have you ever thought of going back?" I ask. "You aren't a danger to them anymore." I don't think I'd ever be able to stay away from my family. I can't imagine being so dangerous you have to be taken away, your life changed forever.

"I still have moments when my wolf doesn't listen. You heard about how I almost attacked Bel a few months back?" he questions. He pulls the car into a car park. Taking in my surroundings, I realise we are at the ice rink. Finding a space near the entry, he pulls in and stops the car.

"Bel's blood is different, even Theo had a moment, and it was a full moon. You've never attacked me and how many times have I bled in front of you over the years?"

"Yeah, you are pretty clumsy. You have a good point. Anyway, let's forget about all that. We're meant to be having fun," he says, getting out the car.

Taking my hand, he walks me to the entrance of the ice rink.

"We're skating," I say, stating the obvious. "I haven't been here in years. Theo used to bring me when he wasn't busy with pack stuff."

"He brought me once or twice when you weren't home. I'm pretty sure he had a thing for the chick in the café." he laughs.

"He was madly in love with Selena," I remind him.

"Okay. I think his wolf had a thing for the chick that worked in the café," he clarifies.

"Theo is the first to admit that his wolf wasn't a big fan of Selena's, but he'd never have cheated on her." I can't help but defend my brother, he was an idiot for many things he did in regards to Selena and their relationship—like not telling her he was a wolf. He still hasn't told her and she's living with a number of them under his roof. But he isn't a cheater.

"I didn't say he cheated, he just liked to look," Paddy says, giving my hand a little squeeze. "Come on. Let's get some skates so we can have a race."

"What's the prize?" I ask, hoping he can see the fun we could have with this.

He pays the man behind the counter our admission fee. "Winners choice," he says with a smirk, as he looks at me.

Pulling my hand out of his, I run for the skate stand. "Be prepared to lose," I throw over my shoulder.

"Oh. Those right there are fighting words, Miss Wilson."

12

BARBARIANS
AND DRAGONS

As I walk Ruby to her front door, I start to worry about whether any of my fellow pack members might be spying on us. The fact that there are no cars parked in the drive eases my concerns but only slightly.

"Thanks for today, I've had the best day," Ruby says, as she turns from the door to face me.

"Thank you for taking me up on the offer." A piece of her hair falls across her face and I can't stop my hand from reaching out and tucking it behind her ear. She leans into my hand welcoming the contact, making my wolf sit up and take notice. "You still haven't claimed your prize yet," I say, remembering her beating me at the rink.

Bloody hockey skates. How was I supposed to know they helped with speed?

She grins up at me mischievously as she lifts a hand and runs her fingers along my jaw. My wolf wants me to beg for more of that touch.

"I think I'll save it for a rainy day."

"You're a little minx." I laugh and decide to bite the bullet and lean in for a kiss.

Our lips touch and she doesn't push me away. Her lips part slightly offering me access and I take it. I kiss her, showing everything I feel, everything I've felt for a while now. Her little moan of appreciation almost does me in. I push my wolf back reminding him we can't take her, not on our first date. Thankfully he listens, not wanting to scare her away he allows me to end the kiss.

Releasing the grip she has on my shirt, Ruby takes a small step back and looks up at me with unfocused eyes. She's the most beautiful woman I've ever laid eyes on. An angel. *Our angel*, my wolf growls appreciatively.

"I best get going, if I kiss you again, Theo will have my head," I say, nodding toward the twitching blinds in the window beside us.

"He wouldn't dare..." she declares, probably knowing if he was spying he'd be able to hear everything with his wolf's hearing. The glint in her eyes screams trouble. "Fine," she says, grabbing my shirt in her fists and pulling me against her again.

I barely have time to steady myself with my hands on her hips, before she takes my mouth with hers. She releases my shirt and runs her hands up my chest and around the back of my neck, running her fingers through the tips of my hair. I dig my fingers into her hips, reminding myself too late she's only human and will bruise if I'm not careful.

The door behind Ruby bursts open and she's suddenly pulled from my grasp. "That's enough. She'll call you tomorrow," Theo says with finality, before slamming the door in my face. Knowing what he says goes, I head back to my car. Grinning at the protesting I can hear coming from Ruby.

I'm just pulling into my street as I hear my phone chime, alerting me that I have a text message. I pull into the drive and park behind Ed's Ford XR8 Ute before digging my phone from my jean's pocket to check the message.

Ruby: My brother is a barbarian. D=

Another message comes through before I have a chance to reply.

Ruby: I had a fab day, thank U. X

I quickly type out my reply as I unlock the front door.

Me: Just remember he could be worse. I had a great day too. So thank U. ;)

"About fucking time. It's Game of Thrones night. What kept

you out so late?" Ed shouts from the lounge.

In two minds about what to tell him, I delay by heading to the fridge for a beer first. "I'm grabbing a beer, do you want one?" I know he'll find out about my date sooner or later, but I have an inkling that he has his own feelings for Ruby. Not that he'll admit it. I've hung back for so long waiting for him to make a move on her but he hasn't. We're guys, we don't talk about feelings and shit, but at a guess, he thinks he's not worthy of her; which is stupid because if any guy is good enough for Ruby, it's him. He's as tough as nails, so he'd protect her fiercely, and he has a heart of gold that he'd worship her with. I'm not sure how he'll react to the details. He's my best mate and as much as he'll want to be happy for me, I think he'll be far from it.

"Okay, you're late in for Game of Thrones night and you *ask* me if I want a beer, something's definitely on your mind."

Grabbing two bottles, I close the fridge and sit on the other end of the sofa. I crack both bottles open and pass one across to Ed.

"Come on, tell Uncle Ed all about it." he jokes, before taking a sip of beer.

"Fucker!" Laughing, I punch him in the arm playfully, making him choke on the beer. "I was on a date—"

"And you didn't tell me about it beforehand," he interrupts playfully, holding a hand to his heart. "I'm wounded."

"A date with Ruby."

The smile drops off his face instantly, but he doesn't speak straightaway. I open my mouth to say something, anything, when he breaks his silence.

"Good, you both deserve to be loved up with someone." He doesn't sound even a bit convincing. I brace myself waiting for his rage, but instead he presses play on the remote. "We better not make the Mother of Dragons wait any longer," he adds, effectively ending the conversation.

13

SCARRED FOR LIFE

*P*addy and I have been dating for almost a month now. I had offered to cook a meal for everyone, but Alyssa and Wes wanted a quiet night in. Mum has taken the pregnant Selena under her wing and is having a girl's night at Chloe's apartment. Theo, Bel, Jared, Eddie, Paddy, and me manage to sit through a whole meal without too much tension. Eddie has been off with me for a while now. I don't know what I've done to piss him off, but it's got to be something because he's fine with everyone else. Paddy insists that I should just leave him be, but I miss him. I miss the Eddie that had become a close friend. I leave the table clearing all the plates into the dishwasher.

"Let's stick a movie in," Bel announces, dragging Theo into the lounge room.

I close the dishwasher, switch it on and move to follow Bel and Theo. Holding me back, Paddy pulls me into his warm embrace.

"The meal was lovely, angel, you did good," he says, before kissing me senseless. My heart would be a flutter at the term of endearment if the kiss weren't sending it into overdrive. Our lips part and once I have enough sense to breathe again, I register Eddie talking behind us.

"I need a fucking drink!" he snaps, pushing past us and heading for the front door. Long gone is the caring Eddie who nursed me through my drunken state. I step away from Paddy, ready to go after him and find out what the hell is going on when Jared places a hand on my shoulder to hold me back.

"I'll go. Wait up, Ed, I could do with a good drink myself," he shouts, as he follows in Ed's wake.

"What's his problem?" I grumble, not really expecting an answer. He's ruined the good feeling I had from Paddy's kiss.

Lifting my chin with a finger, Paddy gently presses his lips against mine before pulling back millimetres. "Stop worrying and kiss me!" he demands, before taking my lips once again.

Who am I to argue with a demand like that?

"Are you going to kiss all night or are you going to watch this movie?" Bel shouts from the lounge. *Movie or kiss?* We both pull away with a groan and head for the lounge.

"We chose '*Expendables 3*,'" Bel reports, as we take a seat on the sofa. With Bel and Theo cuddled up on the other sofa, it's a good job Eddie and Jared left, they would've looked funny cuddled up on the smaller two-seater sofa. Bel doesn't wait for us to get comfortable before she presses play.

The movie finishes in no time. Hearing an intimate giggle I glance over in my brother's direction, regretting it the instant my eyes land on the loved up couple with their hands happily roaming over each other's body, not caring that they aren't alone.

"Do you *have* to do that so publicly?" I complain, half-heartedly. You can't be too begrudging, not when you see how much they love each other.

"She's right, let's go to bed," Bel suggests.

Theo groans without moving. "I'm comfy here."

"We could be naked and comfortable in bed," Bel says, with a knowing smirk. Another visual I didn't need. Living with my brother is going to scar me for life.

"Well, if you put it that way," he says, as he gets up and throws Bel, who lets out a squeal, over his shoulder.

Both Paddy and I watch them leave, once they're out of sight and I can no longer hear them, Paddy turns to me with a smile. "I love seeing them like that."

Surprised by his comment, I joke, "Whatever floats your boat."

"No," he laughs. "It makes me look forward to being mated one day. Hopefully soon." I would say the look that crosses his face is almost a shy one.

I glance back at the door my brother and Bel left through and smile. "Me too," I say absently. To have that bond, that connection with someone, must be incredible. For a second, I hope that Paddy is thinking about us when he imagines himself with his mate because I am.

14

THE ONE

The look on Ruby's face, as she turns in the direction the loved-up couple went, gives me the confidence to throw a corny line at her. "Do you know, that sexy dress of yours will look fantastic on my bedroom floor?"

She swallows nervously. "Well, we might just have to test that theory out," she says playfully. The way she's blinking up at me all innocently, I can't help but pull her into my lap and kiss her deeply. She breaks the kiss and catches her breath. "What did I do to deserve that?"

"Nothing. Since when do I need a reason to kiss the woman I love?" I ask back. The shock on her face makes me go over my words again. I just told her I love her.

She recovers her composure quickly. "When you put it that way, you don't need one." Leaning into me she gives me a quick peck on the lips before jumping up and grabbing my hand. "Come on then, you better drive quickly because I need to show you how much I love you, and I can't do that with my brother and his freaky wolf hearing under the same roof." My wolf perks up at the admission. Grateful that she thought of her brother's hearing, I allow her to pull me up and lead me to the car.

The drive over to mine is a quiet one. It's a comfortable silence, though. I use the time to tell my wolf to hang back and allow Ruby to take the lead. We've refrained from being intimate up until now for various reasons; one being that Ruby hasn't had good experiences with sex in the past. There's no way I want to pressure her into anything she isn't ready for. In the heat of the moment, she's pushed for more a few times, but I know from some times, in the heat of the moment you'll agree to things you'll regret later.

We pull up in the drive and Ruby gives a little gasp at the sight of Ed's Ute parked before us.

"He's out for the night. You saw the mood he was in, he probably won't be back until the early hours of the morning," I reassure her.

"Sorry, I just panicked because of his hearing and everything," she explains.

We exit the car and I let us in the house. I barely have the door closed before she jumps in my arms, wrapping her arms and legs around my body, and kissing me thoroughly.

I stride through the house blindly, until we stumble into my bedroom. I break the heated kiss, placing her gently on the bed. She looks up at me with her dilated eyes and swollen lips.

"You're beautiful," I tell her, as I take a step back. I'm barely holding onto my wolf. He's never wanted someone so much before. *We can't claim her, not our first time.* My wolf throws himself at me in anger. I take another step back. "Are you sure you want this, Ruby? We can wait," I assure her.

She stands, and walks toward me with slow, sure steps. "I'm sure. I'm not a virgin, but my past experiences haven't exactly been consensual, I'm ready for it to be. And you're the one I want my first time to be with," she says, lifting her dress over her head. "Now get naked so I can show you how ready I am."

Her nakedness, the smell of her arousal, and her words ruin my resolve. I strip before she gets within touching distance, shredding my clothes from my body.

She bites her lip as her eyes roam my body hungrily.

Not able to keep my hands off her any longer, I pull her into my arms and pin her beneath me on the bed, ready to show her how good sex can be, when it's with someone who loves you.

15

FROM HEAVEN TO
HELL IN A SECOND

PADDY

Feeling a small body snuggle into me wakes me from my slumber. I glance down at Ruby as she uses my arm as a pillow and I can't help but wonder how comfortable that could really be?

I'm surprised to find I don't regret last night, not one bit. I'd been holding off on taking our relationship that step further because I wanted to make sure I was ready to take her as a mate. Looking at her now, I can't imagine waking up with anyone else again.

I watch as her green eyes pop open and she smiles up at me nervously. "Morning, beautiful," I state, trying to relieve her nerves.

"Hi. I can't believe I look very beautiful right now," she says with a giggle, trying to bury her face in my bicep.

"You always look beautiful," I announce truthfully.

She lifts her head and looks at me seriously. "Thank you." Leaning to me she places her lips against mine in a gentle kiss. I deepen the kiss before she can pull away, worrying about morning breath.

Ed's fist banging on the door as he passes causes us to break apart. "Wake up sleepyhead. We're going for a run, remember?" he says, as he closes the bathroom door.

"Do you have to go?" Ruby complains. "I'm sure we can come up with another form of exercise without even having to leave the bed."

"As tempting as that is, Ed will kill me if I stand him up," I say, kissing her on the head and pull my arm from under her. I hear Ed leave the bathroom. I quickly grab some clothes so I can jump in the shower and wash away the smell of all we'd been up to last night. I don't want Ed and other weres picking up on what we've been doing.

By the time I make it back into the bedroom Ruby is dressed in the sexy brown dress she'd been wearing yesterday; the one that got her into my bed in the first place. She pulls the covers tidy over the bed, leaning over to brush one stubborn corner. Sneaking up behind her, I grab the thigh she's unintentionally flashing, making her jump.

"You know, I really like this dress," I say, my hand working its way a little higher.

"Ah huh, you have a run to go on, remember? You lost all rights to touching when you turned down my offer of a day in bed," she says, giggling as she ducks under my arm and makes a run for through the door.

I follow her through the tiny house heading for the kitchen, taking slow and deliberate steps trying to keep my wolf calm because he likes the chase. I don't want him to start thinking of her as prey. One close call this year is enough, I don't need that embarrassment repeated. I'll never live it down. As soon as she reaches the doorway, I grab her around the waist and pull her back against my front. She squeals as I nuzzle at her neck.

"I've got you, now what shall I do with you?"

"I've told you, you gave up the chance of having me in bed all day. So get all those dirty ideas out of your head," Ruby says, as I reluctantly let her go; remembering too late we aren't the only ones in the room. I look up and catch Ed's nostrils flare before he storms out of the house, without saying a word to either of us. He'd be able to smell last night on Ruby. I shouldn't be surprised by his reaction, I know he wanted Ruby for himself. He hasn't said so, but I can see it in the way he watches her. It's the same way I watch her.

"Why does he hate me so much?" Ruby complains, watching the closed door Eddie stormed out of. "It's as if he can't even stand to be in the same room as me anymore. He was the first pack member that saw me as me, and not just Theo's kid sister."

I wish she didn't care what he thought about her, but it's something that's never going to change, they both care about each other too much and they can't even see it. I'm now kicking myself for taking it that step further last night. I'd be lying if I said that wanting to make sure I was ready for a mate was the only thing holding me back. The thought of Ed and his feelings for her are evident to me, no matter how well he tries to hide it. Plus, it was pretty common knowledge that Ruby had a crush on him a while back; they played a big part in my waiting. I should never have slept with her. I was kidding myself thinking it would work between Ruby and me.

"He doesn't hate you, that's the problem," I say, pacing across the small kitchen. My wolf is pulsing at my skin as he picks up on my agitation.

This isn't going to work; I'm not the one she loves.

If I don't stop this now we're all going to walk away with broken hearts, and that's with the hope I'm not already too late.

"I can't do this anymore, last night was a mistake," I blurt out, not giving myself time to back out of my decision.

"What…what are you talking about?" Ruby asks, clearly confused by my outburst.

I say the only thing that I know will send her running. "We can't stay together anymore. I need to wait for my true mate. I need what Theo has."

Ruby is barely out the door when I pull my phone out and hit call to the one person I know can comfort her.

16

PUSHING THE
WOLF DOWN

I wish I could be happy for them, but I just can't. My wolf believes Ruby should be our mate and he'd happily tear Paddy to shreds to make that point perfectly clear and I'm not allowing him to kill my best mate.

No fucking chance.

If that means I have to leave the room or even the house, every time they enter all lovey-dovey smelling of sex, then that's how it's going to be. I don't care how fucked up it is. It's better than the other option.

The vibration of my phone pulls my thoughts away from the argument I'm having with my wolf, and causes me to slow my pace to pull out my phone. Seeing Paddy's name on the screen I consider not answering for a second, but duty to the pack and my best mate forces me to answer. "This better be good, I already need a fucking drink and it's not even nine in the morning."

"You need to go find Ruby. She ran off and I can't go after her."

"Fix your own damn problems, Paddy. Whatever you've done she'll get over it soon enough. Just go after her," I offer, knowing she won't be mad at him for long, no matter what he's done. She was head over heels with him this morning.

"No, you don't understand. We're over. I was fooling myself from the start, she was always yours."

Hearing everything I need, I hang up and run back to the duplex hoping to catch her scent. It only takes me a couple of seconds to catch it and follow. It's leading out of town and in to the surrounding bush. Walking through some trees I spot her, looking beautiful in the middle of the field with the mountains in front of her and her golden ringlets blowing in the wind.

Once I reach her, I can hear her sobs. Turning Ruby around, I pull her into my chest. "Let it out, Rubes."

Time passes quietly as she lets all her tears out, with just the rustle of the wind in the trees and the grass, and the odd cockatoo calling its mate to be heard. "How could he do that? Why make love to me if he knew he wanted to find his true mate? Because no matter what he says now, he made love to me last night…" she pauses just long enough to take a breath before carrying on. "I thought he was going to take me as a mate, we'd talked about it."

A new wave of fresh tears start as she sobs into my chest once again. My heart tears in two at the thought of them making love. I should be the only one making love to her.

"I don't know why he'd do that, sweetheart, he's a stupid dick." My comment turns her sob into a giggle.

"Where have you been?" she asks, looking up at me with her big green eyes.

"I've been right here, waiting for you to need me," I say as I kiss her on the forehead, feeling stripped bare by the look in her eyes.

"I've always needed you, Eddie."

My breath catches with her words, and my wolf tries to take her as ours. Forcing him down, I squeeze her in our hug a little tighter not knowing how else to react without being inappropriate. She's not going to want more than a friend right now. I just wish my wolf would understand that.

We stand a while longer as she calms down. Her tears ease up, slowing their tracks down her cheeks. She pulls out of my hold and stands back from me, before silently walking over to a fallen tree and perching her arse on it. I follow her lead and do the same. Seeing I'm settled she turns her head to look at me, her whole demeanour changing.

I feel the anger coming off her before she opens her mouth. "What did I do to make you treat me like shit over the last few weeks?"

Her question causes my mind to run around in circles. *Do I tell her the truth?* No, I can't tell her the truth, not without coming across as a fucking creeper hitting on her when she's just been dumped. The truth is out of the question, but that doesn't help me work out what to actually tell her. I lift my head and look at the tree line opposite us hoping for some inspiration.

It's so peaceful here. How have I never noticed that before?

Making my mind up on what to say, I plaster on my most flirtatious smile, before opening my mouth, "You know me, Rubes, I don't know how to interact with a chick without flirting. I didn't want Paddy challenging me for it. I thought you'd miss him if I killed him." I throw her a wink and get a thump in the arm for my trouble.

"You're terrible, Eddie," she says, seemingly taking me at my word. The glint in her eye is telling me she's not entirely convinced, but her anger has dissipated so I'll take that as a win.

She leans her head against my shoulder and stares at the tree line I'd just been looking at. "I've missed you and your cheeky ways."

She'll never have a chance to miss my cheeky ways again because I'm not going anywhere. The last few weeks have been hell for me, and I can't do that again.

17

UNEXPECTED HEART
TO HEART

*A*fter Eddie let me cry on his shoulder for most of the day, he walked me back to Theo's. I had no idea there were tracks through the bush from their place to Theo's.

Although after he had explained about the many tracks leading from Theo's place to almost everywhere in town for the pack to use in emergencies, it made complete sense. I spent the rest of the day in bed; crying and wondering where I'd gone wrong in reading Paddy and his feelings, while dozing on and off.

I wake up to a dark room, reaching out I feel about on the bedside table blindly until I grip my phone, lifting it up glimpsing at the time. One in the morning, and I'm wide awake. *Brilliant.*

Knowing I won't fall straight back to sleep, I decide to go downstairs and make myself a chamomile tea. Walking through the house in the dark, I try to do everything as quietly as possible. Living in a house full of people is bad enough when three of those people are weres it's even worse. I hear footsteps padding on the carpet of the hall and curse myself for not just staying in bed. I'm really not in the mood for company right now. I don't even know if anyone but Eddie knows about what happened between me and Paddy.

I turn to see Selena enter the kitchen, giving me a small smile. "I'm sorry if I woke you up, I was trying to be quiet," I apologise, as I pour the boiled water over the tea bag in my cup.

"You didn't wake me up, this little mister likes to keep me awake, it's become our nightly ritual," she says, patting her swollen stomach lovingly as she shuffles towards the cupboard and pulls down a cup.

"Do you want chamomile?" I ask holding up a tea bag.

She nods. "Please."

I pour her tea and remove the tea bag from my cup, throwing the used tea bag in the rubbish bin under the counter, before giving the one in Selena's cup the same treatment. We silently walk over to the L-shaped sofa's and take a seat beside each other, both shuffling about to find comfortable positions. I sit back in the corner with my feet folded under me as Selena sits at the end turning herself slightly to face me while propping her feet on the coffee table.

"We've determined the cause of my lack of sleep. What's keeping you up?" she asks, as she takes a sip from the cup she's nursing between her hands.

"It's a long story." I brush her off, not knowing where to start or whether I even want to go into it. Especially with Selena, she doesn't even know about the wolves, so how would I start talking about mates and such things.

"Neither of us have anything better to do. I'm more than happy to listen, it'll make a nice change to the lonely nights I normally have," she offers.

Seeing the genuine look on her face I make a decision, I hope, I won't regret later.

"I broke up with my boyfriend this morning. Right after we slept together for the first time." Even I cringe at the bitterness in my voice.

"I'm sorry to hear that, Ruby. Any breakup is hard, but it's even harder after a night of loving."

I glance at her sharply. *How does she know it was lovingly?*

As if reading my mind, she answers the question that must be plastered on my face. "I've seen you and Paddy together over the last few weeks. I saw the way he looks at you. There's no way he wouldn't show you that love the first time you slept together."

"Yeah, well, he said he was waiting for his..." I manage to stop myself saying, true mate. "Waiting for the one," I correct myself.

"Finding the one is overrated. I learnt that the hard way. I had a good thing with Theo, it wasn't perfect, there were a lot of secrets between us, there still are, but you can live with secrets if they don't hurt you. I went and ruined all that finding my one. When he realised what we had, he couldn't destroy his brother's life, even though he knew we were meant to be."

Is she talking about Cain? She cheated on Theo with our brother Cain; who left straight after it happened. No one knows where he is, Theo has a number to contact him but I don't know if he'll ever use it. If what she's saying is true, and Cain left so he wouldn't destroy Theo's life; he was too late, sleeping with his wife already achieved that.

"Enough about me," she says, with a shake of her head. "What are you going to do to get him back?"

"That didn't work well for you," I say, before really thinking about my words. She takes in a sharp breath as though my words wounded her somehow. "I'm sorry, you didn't deserve that."

"No, you're right. It didn't matter how much love Theo and I had for each other, it wasn't enough. I couldn't get him to forgive me. I came back with the one thing he always wanted from me, hoping it would be sufficient for his forgiveness but I was too late, he'd met his true love." The sadness in her eyes gives me a whole new respect for her.

How can she live under the same roof as her ex-husband and his fiancée?

"How do you do it? How do you live with them?"

Taking a moment to have a sip from her cup, no doubt

giving herself time to think of how to answer such a loaded question, she slowly looks across at me ensuring eye contact while she answers. It's almost like she's laying herself out there for me to see everything she feels. "I'm not going to lie and say it doesn't hurt. But in saying that, anyone can see they're meant to be, that's why I gave him the divorce without a fight. I couldn't stand in the way of love like that. And if I'm being honest, my heart belongs to someone else. It always has." She reaches up and absently wipes a tear from her cheek. "We've ended up on me again." she laughs quietly.

"With Paddy's connection to Theo, he'll be around a lot. Can you handle that?" The way she said the word *connection* made me watch her with suspicion. She has never been told about the wolves, she always believed anyone he had over was a work colleague or friend. That every full moon when Theo was away for the night and sometimes the following day, he was on a business trip. We've always joked that she must be so dumb to fall for something like that, but looking at her now I'm starting to wonder if she's smarter than we've given her credit for. "He works at the gym doesn't he? Theo always treated his employees like family." With those words, I realise my mind is playing tricks on me. I was giving her way too much credit.

"I thought I heard voices," Mum says from behind us startling us both, so much so I slosh my now lukewarm tea all down my front.

"Shit!" I curse.

"Was it hot?" she asks, as she runs into the kitchen and grabs a tea-towel.

"No, it's fine, just wet. We didn't mean to wake anyone," I reassure her, as I dab at the wet patch with the tea-towel she hands over.

"The chamomile seems to have put the little mister to sleep, so I'm going to try and get a couple of hours sleep," Selena says, as she gets up with a groan. "This chair is too soft, if I get any bigger I'll never get up. Night ladies."

Mum takes the seat Selena left and reaching out she gives my hand a squeeze before dropping it again. "I'm sorry to hear about Paddy."

"How long were you listening?" I ask, shocked at the thought of her listening in to our conversation. I had thought the others in the house might overhear the conversation with their were-animal hearing, but I'd never considered my mum listening in.

"I'm sorry. I heard talking and when I came down you were both saying personal things and it didn't seem right to interrupt. It sounded like Selena needed to get some things off her chest as much as you did."

"What do you want, Mum?" I demand. Knowing there has to be a reason she's sitting here now, she could have just gone to back to bed and I'd be non-the-wiser about her eavesdropping.

"My therapist insists I be honest. Especially with you, since it's you I've harmed the most. I put you in so much danger over the years bringing home all those strangers. I don't blame you for hating me."

"The strangers that snuck into my room after you'd passed out. Those same strangers that I had to fight off night after night." I angrily wipe away the tear that runs down my cheek. "The one that caught me when I was weak with a fever, the one who stole away my virginity. Yeah, Mum, that's right, he stole the one thing I was meant to save for the one I love."

The tears are now streaming down my face, I don't bother trying to wipe at them. "Not that it really matters anymore, because the guy I loved enough to share myself with just dumped me after I had sex with him, so if I'd saved it for him it would've been wasted anyway." I stop talking to quickly catch my breath. "Who knows maybe you did me a favour after all."

She pulls me into her arms and I go, too broken to put up a fight.

The tears eventually ease and I pull away to sit back, only to realise I wasn't the only one crying all that time. "It looks like we both let out enough tears to fill a bathtub," I say with a sad smile.

"I know you had to guard your words with Selena. I just want you to know you have someone to talk to, who isn't going to instantly be on his side because they share the werewolf gene. I'm human just like you, and I understand them and the issues they can bring to a relationship."

"Thanks, Mum. I don't even know what to say about it anymore. I know I'm not his true mate, so I have to respect his decision. It just stings. Mainly because we spoke about it. He had said he didn't care about waiting for his true mate. Some wolves wait all their lives for their true mate and never find them. We held off being intimate for that reason. He wanted to make sure he was committed to me. Then we go there and he changes his mind." I feel like I'm talking myself in circles. My mind is running ninety miles an hour.

"I think it's for the best. There's nothing worse than him finding his true mate after he's mated with you. That's what happened between your father and me."

Stunned at her admission, I can't help but jump in. "I thought he was all for the pack?"

"Of all the werewolves you know, tell me, would any of them leave their mate in one town bringing up his kids, while he lived in another town surrounded by his pack. Remember, he was an alpha too. Would Theo do that?"

Thinking about what she was saying for a minute, I realise I've never really considered how he lived that far away from his mate. Of all the mated couples I know, not one of them would live like that. "He had his true mate with him in the pack," I say, stating the obvious.

Mum nods with a sad smile. "Her name was Margaret."

"You knew about her? True mates are notorious for killing the other mate, how did you survive?" The questions fall out of my mouth one after another.

"I only had Theodore when she arrived on the scene. She wasn't willing to bring him up as her own and your father wouldn't let her kill him. She couldn't hold a child to term so after a number of miscarriages he came back to me for more children. I don't know how he talked her into that, but somehow he did. I'm just grateful it didn't come down to a death match because I would've had no chance."

Seeing the light coming in through the windows, I realise it must be getting close to everyone's alarms going off. "I guess we should both try and squeeze in an hour's worth of sleep or we won't be up to much company today."

Mum glances down at her watch before slowly standing alongside me. "It's good that it's coming close to the end of spring and the sun is coming up earlier than normal. We might get a couple of hours sleep before we have to be up."

Before heading up the stairs, I give her a quick hug. "Thanks for the chat," I whisper in her ear. She squeezes me back tightly, before heading off to the front of the house where she's sleeping in one of the bedrooms, neighbouring both Selena and Jared.

18

SHOPPING MAKES
HUNGRY MEN

"Who's babysitting today, boys?" I enquire, walking into the lounge. After my heart to heart with my mum and Selena yesterday, I feel much better. I can't help noticing that Paddy is missing. *Does that mean he's miserable?* It may make me a bitch, but I hope he's hurting, even if it's just a little.

Ed shuffles over giving me room to sit next to him. "That all depends on what you have planned. I'm not doing a spa day ever again. I still have that stinky shit causing my nose problems," he says, referring to our previous spa visit.

I open my mouth before my brain kicks in. "But I bet the ladies like the smooth chest."

The stunned look on his face makes me realise what I've just said. I slip my hand up to cover my mouth too late.

The guys burst into laughter. "You…had a wax?" Jared asks, between his laughter.

"For fuck's sake, Ruby, that was supposed to be between us," Ed complains. He looks around at the boys; Jared, Wes, and Matthew. "They made me do it. They wouldn't let me stand guard if not. I took one for the team." They are all too busy laughing to even listen to his reasoning. *Poor Eddie.*

"You want to think yourselves lucky it wasn't you. I know each and every one of you would've done the same if you were in his shoes," Bel says, effectively silencing the guys as she enters the room. "You're all off the hook because we're dress shopping today. I've been told I can't get married in jeans and a T-shirt," she adds, with a roll of her eyes.

The guys all get up whooping at the thought of a free day. "Let's go shoot some pool," Matthew suggests. With nods of agreement, they all start to leave.

"Jared, can I have a quick word?" Bel asks.

I catch her eye and nod toward the other room, offering to leave them to have a private conversation, or as private a conversation one can get in a house full of werewolves. "Stay where you are, Rubes, it's nothing private."

Jared turns in the doorway and glances at the chair he'd just occupied. "Should I be sitting for this?" he asks sounding nervous. "You're going to tell me to go home, aren't you? My dad calls every day telling me the same thing, so don't waste your breath." I've never heard him sound so defeated. *What the hell is going on with him?*

Bel pulls him into a hug. "I don't want you to go. If I were selfish, I would demand you never leave. But I can't do that, the pride will need you one day but today isn't it."

"Really?" he asks leaning back to look her in the eyes, no doubt seeking the truth. Whatever he sees must be enough because with a short, sharp nod he releases her and steps back. "So, what did you want to talk to me about?"

"I don't know how to ask," Bel admits, as she fiddles with a strand of cotton hanging from the hem of her T-shirt.

"Just spit it out," he says playfully, as he reaches forward to tuck a stray piece of hair behind her ear. "Sorry, old habits," he apologises, realising what he's done.

"Be my man of honour," she blurts out.

He takes a step back, surprise written all over his face. "What?"

Bel turns away and paces across the room, before turning back to face Jared. "If you were a girl, you'd be my maid of honour. So be my man of honour, please?" she begs.

"Okay," he replies with a nod, before Bel throws herself at him.

"Thank you."

"I'm not wearing a dress," he scoffs, grinning at me over her shoulder. "I draw the line at that.

We spend all day traipsing around the bridal shops of Sydney. Rosabel has tried so many dresses on that I've lost count, and here we are back in the first shop we started in.

I never want to get married!

"Baby Bel, I love you. But I swear, if I have to go to one more shop I won't be held accountable for my actions," Jared complains once again. He said the same thing three shops ago.

Bel is standing in the middle of the room on the platform as she looks at herself in the mirrors wearing the beautiful lace covered dress. "This is the one."

Jared walks around her giving her a thorough once over. "You look stunning, Bel. Theo isn't going to know what hit him," he says, his voice full of pride.

I glance at Misty, who like me, has tears brimming in her eyes. I can only manage a nod in agreement. I don't think I can get any words out through the lump in my throat.

Misty and I chose dresses at this shop the first time around. They are a lovely purple colour with a sweetheart cut. So, thankfully, we don't have any more to worry about since the shopkeeper has the payment and fitting details.

Leaving Bel to undress, we head to the main sales room. "Who's opening the bar tonight, Misty?" I question, glancing the time on the clock. There's no chance we'll make it back in time.

"Lucy's opening up and Theo said he'd get a couple of the

lads to help her out until we get back," she answers. "It's mid-week so I'm sure they'll manage just fine."

"Eddie messaged me earlier asking how long we'd be. So I'm pretty sure he's one of the guys Theo is sending." His phone makes a noise and he pulls it out and laughs as he reads the screen. "Looks like Paddy drew the other short straw. Good, they need some time to sort their shit out. Let's grab dinner on the way home. All this shopping has made me hungry."

His comment about Paddy and Eddie catches my attention. "They're best mates. What shit have they got to sort out?" I haven't seen them having issues. Eddie was off with me for a while, but he explained all that when he let me fall apart on him the other day. I hope he isn't being pissy at Paddy for treating me like that. I don't want to be the cause of their problems.

Bel chooses that moment to come out of the fitting room and throw an arm over my shoulders. "Boy stuff. Where do you want to eat, Rubes?" She dismisses my question. *Fine.* I'll drop the issue for now, but if I sense any tension between them, I'll be putting an end to it.

"The Irish pub across the road looks like it could be good," I say, with a shrug as we exit the building. I'd been watching people leaving through the window for the last few minutes while Bel got changed, they all looked pretty happy. So the place can't be that bad. With nods of agreement, we all make our way across the road.

Jared holds open the door as we each enter. "You girls grab a table and some menus, and I'll get the drinks."

We choose a quiet booth at the back of the dining area, Bel and Misty slide into one side and I glide into the other. I glance across at the girls and it suddenly dawns on me, I've never had a drink with Misty and Bel before.

Jared places four glasses down and sits down next to me. "What does the menu look like?" he asks.

"So good. I can't decide what to have," Bel declares, not taking her eyes off the menu in her hands. "It was a good idea grabbing dinner on the way home."

Misty places hers on the table, sliding it across to Jared. "Have a look. I know what I'm having."

Taking the menu, Jared places it on the table between us so we can both see it clearly. Spotting the fish and chips, my decision is made and I push the menu so it's in front of Jared.

"I'm good."

While Jared and Bel make their decisions, I look over to Misty and ask her something I've often wondered. "How come you don't do food at Misty's? You'd make a killing with all the hungry werewolves you have in there."

"I can't cook," she says, like it's an obvious reason.

"What about hiring someone?"

She looks at me flabbergasted. "Do ya know how hard it is to find someone who knows about the supernatural creatures and can cook a decent meal? It's nigh-on impossible."

"I could do it. I'd need a bracelet to get in, but you made one for Benji easy enough," I offer on instinct. I've always liked to cook, I've never thought about making a career out of it, though. It's got to be better than cleaning up after my brother. Watching Misty think it over and feeling the butterflies in my stomach, makes me realise how much I really want this chance.

Bel looks at me, concern written in the furrow of her brow and pursing lips. "What about your criminology course?" Geez, it's like she's channeling Theo. If he were here that's exactly what he would say.

"It's an online course I can do it anytime. I'm not working." I can't hold back my defensive tone. "I know you're only saying what Theo would, but he has to accept that I'm not a little kid anymore. I'm a grown arse woman and I'm allowed to make my own decisions."

Bel glances down at the table, seemingly hurt. "I wasn't

implying anything by what I said. I just wanted to make sure you'd thought about it."

I pat her hand over the table. "I'm sorry, Bel. I shouldn't take my frustration at Theo out on you."

She smiles, grateful for my apology.

"Well, I think it's a great idea. Shall we give it a trial run, starting tomorrow?" Misty offers. "I'll make ya a bracelet when I get home tonight. I can't believe I haven't given ya one yet."

I can't hide the excitement from my voice. "I'd love that."

Bel bangs her hand on the table, making me jump. "Hey, we have a movie date tomorrow," she complains.

Misty waves her hand in at the table. "What did that table do to ya?" She laughs, before making an offer. "Go tonight. I'll get one of the guys to stick around when I get back, if need be."

Bel and I look at each other and nod our agreement.

"Thanks, Misty," Bel says, gratefully.

A pretty blonde waitress steps up to our table with a pen and pad. "Are you ready to order?" she asks, blatantly eyeing up Jared. You can't take these guys anywhere without them catching someone's eye.

Jared throws her a wink. "We certainly are, sweetheart."

I listen to them flirt with each other and can't help but smile. I suddenly realise I really I'm okay without Paddy, maybe we weren't meant to be after all. Blondie takes our orders without taking her eyes off Jared. It's going to be interesting to see what meals we actually receive.

19

BLACKNESS DESCENDS

*B*el and I walk out of the movies giggling at how I managed to trip up the stairs and face plant on the floor; while dashing back from a bathroom break. I can never get through a movie without having to go to the bathroom. I blame the coke.

"Ruby. One second…you were there, the next…you were gone," Bel manages to get out between fits of laughter. "I thought you'd turned vamp or gained a druid's power of teleporting in and out whenever and wherever they want. Until I heard the grunt as you got up." The laughter starts again.

"If only that was the case!" I say, hating the embarrassed feeling I have. I can't help but wish I was a werewolf like Bel. She is so graceful and has such good instincts, she would never have fallen so stupidly. It isn't the first time I've found myself dreaming of being a werewolf. With two werewolf brothers, I have yearned not to be the human of the family. The ugly duckling.

"I better get home before Theo sends someone after me," I say. "He's more like a prison guard than a brother," I add.

"He just worries about his baby sister, so don't be too hard on him."

"Fine. I'll try to be nice," I offer. "You're going to do more packing aren't you?"

Bel nods. "Yes. Tell him, I'll be home soon. I love that I've moved in with him, but I hate this packing business," Bel says, hugging me goodbye. I watch as she dematerialises before my eyes. That druid blood she recently discovered she has comes in pretty handy at times.

Having parked my car at the other end of the main road means I have a good ten minute walk ahead of me.

I start walking at a fast pace, hearing nothing but the click clack of my heels on the pavement.

Click clack...

Click clack...

Click clack...

The hairs on the back of my neck stand on end and a shiver runs down my back.

I freeze on the spot and dart my eyes around, having no idea what I expect to see. I don't have the sense of smell a werewolf has or the hearing of a vampire, but I do have gut instinct of a human and mine is speaking to me right now—telling me to get the hell out of there. I do just that.

I run across the road not even looking for passing traffic. Luckily, it's clear.

Once my feet touch the pavement, I notice all the feeling of worry has gone. I look around again and could have slapped myself upside the head. I'd been so distracted that I hadn't noticed during our giggles, we had crossed the road and ended up outside Misty's—a bar that caters only for Supes.

It's owned by a witch who puts wards on it that scare the bejesus out of humans; who also don't, won't, can't enter. It's impossible. What if a Supe carried them over the threshold kicking and screaming? I hear you ask. A human's heart would just stop. Dead. Misty has been known to drop it enough that a human could be carried in but only for a few special people.

I start walking again, laughing at my stupidity; letting a silly horror movie distract me enough to not notice Misty's. I know my car wasn't far up the road. Another five minutes at the most. I start listening to the click clack of my heels again.

Click clack....

Click clack....

Click click clack clack.

I hear double footsteps in quick succession. Knowing I'm not walking fast enough to warrant that means only one thing —someone is following me.

"You might as well come out. I know you're there," I say into the darkness, not bothering to raise my voice knowing which ever wolf my brother has sent would have no trouble hearing me even if I whispered. But I get no response.

I stop and turn to face behind me to where they must be hiding in a shadow or eave of a building because I can't see anyone, but I speak up anyway.

"I won't tell Theo you weren't covert enough." Werewolves can move without being heard. This one was obviously being sloppy for a human to have heard them following me.

I still get no response so I give up and turn around, starting for my car again, at a much quicker pace. I can see it across the road, when I'm suddenly grabbed from behind. An arm around my waist, the other hand over my mouth mutes my screams. The person holding me drags me into a dark alley between the shops.

I'm pinned against the wall face first. All I can see is red brick on the wall.

The hand over my mouth pulls my head to the side stretching my neck out, as the arm around my waist disappears.

I wriggle to get free but I'm still pinned in place by the body behind me, as hard and strong as the wall in front. I feel the hand that had been around my waist brush my long, blonde curls from my neck. He strokes over my thudding pulse with his rough fingers.

It's then I realise I'm not just trapped by a psycho; I'm trapped by a vampire.

That recognition hits a second before the fingers disappear

and sharp fangs pierce my neck. The pain's horrendous. I can feel my heartbeat rise with fear.

I bite down hard on the hand over my mouth, trying to distract the vampire at my neck. I try to fight with my body, but I don't have the room to move. The only thing I'm succeeding in is raising my pulse, therefore, giving the vampire a faster and easier meal.

My mind starts to become sluggish, listening to the vampire moan as he sucks my vein dry makes me push the fog back and try to think of a way out of this. If I don't do something quick, I won't survive this.

If I was a werewolf, I'd have the strength to get away, is the last thought that runs through my mind, before blackness descends…

20

GIFT FROM HELL

J forgo my standard mode of transportation, teleportation, and decide a brisk walk home from Misty's would do me good. I've needed to clear my head for a while. As much as I love my people, they don't give me much space to do such a thing. Being in no hurry to get home, a walk seems like a good idea.

Home. Home is a large compound where my vampires and me live together. A few handpicked humans live on the premises as well. They offer us blood in return for a home and protection. I often wonder if I should follow some of the other kings and live a more solitary life. I never wonder for long, I know solitary living isn't for me. I tried that a long time ago and it's a sure path to insanity. As much as I like some time to myself, I need to be surrounded by people. By family.

The smell of fresh blood pulls me out of my musings. As I take in my surroundings, I'm surprised to be in the alley leading to the compound. Taking uncertain steps into the shadows, I spot a body laid haphazardly across the doorstep.

The scent of werewolf hits me at full force and I can't help but panic. If this is one of Theo's werewolves, shit is going to hit the fan. The blonde is face down, so I reach out my hand and pull her over, I need to see her face and when I do I wish I could erase the sight of it. He's changed his MO. Her forehead has the word *'with'* etched into it, and her right cheek has the word *'love.'* It's the *JD x'* etched into her left cheek that throws me for a loop.

All this time I've thought he's just some random vampire bored with the rules. Never did I think it was JD, Jay Dawes. The same JD that was once my human lover. Once I look past the initials and see the face, a face I recognise as Theodore Wilson's sister, Ruby, I shake my head. *Focus dammit.*

She may still be alive. I don't bother trying to listen for her heartbeat, I probably wouldn't hear it over my own anyway. Instead, I pick up her wrist and pierce her flesh with my fangs, tasting her blood, hoping to feel the warm liquid flow down my throat. It isn't flowing, but her life force is there, her soul is hanging on. She's so close to death, there's no saving her from it completely, but I can save her from permanent death. I can sire her.

Make her one of us, one of mine.

I haven't sired anyone for centuries. I vouched that I would never sire anyone again. Not after I lost my one love. The thought of leaving her to die, lingers in my mind for a minute, before I tear at my own wrist and place it to her lips. My blood and life force flowing into her mouth.

I bang on the door beside me with my free fist, *"Niko!"* I shout.

The door opens and Niko is immediately by my side. "We need to get her inside and lying down."

He picks her up and cradles her in his arm as I tear at my wrist once again and place it back over her mouth before we awkwardly move into the lounge room closest to the entrance.

Ruby clamps her mouth on my wrist as Niko lays her on one of the sofas. That's a good sign, she's accepting the change. Her body is anyway. Deep down her soul or spirit is too, but when she wakes up, she'll have no idea what's happened.

OVER 2000 YEARS AGO

I opened my eyes to such brightness, I could only hiss in pain as I closed them tightly.

"Put out the fire, you idiot!" a female screamed.

I clamped a hand over my ears, it felt like she'd yelled directly into my eardrums, but I could feel that there was no one close enough to do that. I knew where people were in the room, it felt like nothing I'd ever experienced before, almost like ants crawling on my skin. I didn't understand how it told me where exactly they were positioned, but I just knew it did.

"Dominick? Feed!" The voice demanded and I couldn't do anything but follow the command. My mouth opened and I felt pain along my jaw but didn't have time to think about it, because soon the most divine tasting liquid was flowing over my tongue and down my gullet.

Whatever had been clamped in my mouth was suddenly torn away, for a moment I wanted to fight for it. I needed it back. But that voice poured over me once again commanding me to be calm. "That's enough for now, you'll get some more soon. I promise."

I opened my eyes once again and saw the beautiful monster before me. Taking stock of my body and my senses, I knew I wasn't the person I had once been. Somehow I'd been changed, changed into whatever this creature before me was.

I tear open my wrist for what feels like the millionth time, but before I can place it back over Ruby's mouth Niko grabs it and glares at me. "That's enough! If you give her any more of your blood, you won't see tomorrow."

Pulling my hand from his makes the world spin. I realise that he's right. I've almost drained myself dry. *Shit.*

I'd lost myself in my memories. I've lived for so long, I never allow myself to think of the past, there's too much pain to wallow there.

"Feed," a female voice commands, as a wrist presses against my lips. My fangs elongate but it's so close to my memories, I can't blindly sink my fangs in. Even though I know the voice is Sam, I need to see it's her. I look across the room to where the voice is coming from and see Sam before I turn my eyes to the person who the hand belongs to. Gerry. I flash back to a couple of nights ago when we shared a night of passion. My fangs ache, at the memory of his blood flowing over my tongue. If I don't feed soon, bloodlust may take over and that wouldn't be good.

His small smile of encouragement makes me pause, he's my lover, he deserves more intimacy than for me to draw from his wrist. I don't have the energy to take this somewhere else, but I change my position so I'm sitting on the floor with my back against the couch. I beckon for him to lay against my front between my legs, giving me access to his neck. The smile he gives me in return confirms I'm doing the right thing.

As he gets himself comfy and tilts his head giving me access to the vein in his neck, I command the others to leave the room. "Niko, ensure everyone knows not to enter for the rest of the night."

Everyone but Niko leaves the room without argument.

"Of course. What about the girl?" he asks, nodding his head toward her lifeless body.

"I've done all I can for her. We won't know if it's worked until she comes around tomorrow night. If she comes around." I don't want to think about her not coming around. Or the conversation I need to have with the alpha mutt. I might not like the guy, but I wouldn't wish this on him.

"Would you like me to move her?" he asks.

"If you could see to organising a room for her, I'll bring her when I'm done here," I say, dismissing him as I lean my head forward and lick at Gerry's neck; to make sure he's ready for my fangs, before sinking them in and taking my fill, while allowing my hands to roam over his body and feeling how much he's enjoying this.

21

CALLING THE ENEMY

I settle Ruby down on the bed that will be hers for as long as she needs or wants it. If she wakes. No, I'm not allowing that to be a possibility. *When* she wakes, she'll be a vampire and *my* vampires will always have a home at the compound.

I take a seat at the desk in the corner of the room and pull my phone out. Calling that furry mutt is the last thing I want to do. But he'll start worrying soon and I only have a short window to tell him what's happened before I'm out of action for the day. I find his name in my contacts list, press call and put the phone to my ear.

He answers immediately. "I don't have time for any shit, Drake. What do you want?"

"Let me guess, that beautiful little sister of yours hasn't made curfew? Do they still call it curfew these—"

"How the fuck do you know that?" he demands, cutting me off mid-sentence. "If you've done something to her, not even Bel can hold me back from killing you for it." He has every right to dish out the threats.

"You might want to listen to what I have to say before you start with the threats," I growl into the phone.

"I'm listening."

I take a breath I don't need and let it all out. "I came home to find another gift waiting on my doorstep. It...it was Ruby."

"*No!* You're wrong," he denies immediately, as though he won't even allow the idea in his mind.

"Theo, I'm sorry. I'm not mistaken. It's Ruby." I can't hide the sympathy in my voice.

"Is she…" Knowing all the others had been dead when they were found, I can understand him jumping to that conclusion.

I kick myself for not making him aware of her status sooner. "She was so close to death, Theo. Too close. I couldn't stop it…I…The only way I could save her was to turn her. She's currently going through the transition."

The silence on the end of the phone is unnerving. I'd thought he would've had some form of an outburst after I'd finished.

"Did you hear what I said?" I ask, the sound of his breathing is the only sign he's still on the other end of the phone.

"I heard you. She's dead," he says, his voice void of any emotion. He sounds…deadly. I've never been scared of the wolf but hearing him like that has me on edge.

"If it works, she'll be a vampire. She'll still be here on this earth. Hell. She can still live with you if she wants. Nothing has to change," I say, trying to get something out of him. I know he hates us, but surely he'd rather his sister be here, even as a vampire, than completely cease to exist?

"Everything has changed. She can never come here, it's a sanctuary for pack members. I can't let a vampire in here. Our scent will drive her crazy, I can't allow her to feed on pack members, just like I don't allow any of you bloodsuckers, too. I don't care if she *was* once my baby sister," he says flatly.

Fuck!

That's not going to help her transition, if she wakes up and has her brother and the pack waiting for her, she could fight the bloodlust. But if she wakes up and finds out she's been as good as disowned, she has nothing to fight for. I say as much to the furry mutt.

"Your sister is strong, she'll fight the bloodlust. She'll do it for you. For the pack."

"She isn't pack anymore. She's yours," he says. "She isn't mine," I hear him whisper before disconnecting the call. Those three words were full of the emotion his earlier words had been missing.

He's right. She is one of mine now. I'll make sure she has something to fight for. She'll prove how strong she can be to that furry mutt.

I watch the female for a moment hoping the unseen magic is doing all it can to change her body so it will stay forever young and beautiful. Knowing Ruby won't wake up until well into the night, I don't worry about leaving her alone throughout the day. I head to my room and allow myself the recuperation that vampires receive from dying for the day. Essentially that's what we do. We die with the sunrise and reanimate with the sunset. The older you are, the longer you can last between those hours. I open my door to find a small body curled in the sheets waiting for me, exactly where I'd left him after I'd had my fill earlier.

22

THE WORLD
SHATTERS

I'm standing in Theo's dining room-come-pack meeting room, with Billy, Jared, and Wes. They all look just as clueless as I feel. Our eyes are darting between each other. I received a phone call from Theo ten minutes ago. He muttered the word *'emergency'* before hanging up. Hearing the front door open we all turn and watch Paddy enter.

"What's happening?" Paddy asks.

"Your guess is as good as ours," Wes mutters flatly.

We all feel Theo's energy as he approaches the room. By the time he's in sight, we know this is serious.

The hackles rise on my wolf.

Our alpha isn't in a good place. He's on the edge of losing control; which makes our wolves testy.

Bel comes in chasing after him. "Theo! Take a second to calm down." She overtakes and stops in front of him, causing him to halt mid-stride. "Babe, please," she pleads, with a comforting hand pressed against his chest. "Once you tell them, they're all going to be struggling with control enough as it is. They don't need your wolf's anger pushed on them too."

In the silence of the room, I watch as Theo closes his eyes; eyes that are currently flashing wolf. He takes a deep breath and pushes his wolf down. It's a full sixty seconds before he opens his eyes and turns them on us. Human eyes.

I let out a breath I wasn't even aware I'd been holding, until just now.

Obviously satisfied with his change in temperament, Bel moves to the side allowing him to step closer to us all.

"Thanks for coming guys…" Theo pauses, and shakes his head as though he can't find the words to say. "There is no easy way to say this. So I'm just going spit it out, it'll be like ripping a Band-Aid off, painful but fast. The rogue vampire… he got Ruby. He killed my sister," his voice breaks with his last sentence. My heart shatters and I drop to my knees. I don't even realise I've hit the floor. Surely I didn't hear that right.

"Killed? Ruby? Are you saying Ruby is dead?" Paddy asks, sounding almost mechanical; yet confirming my ears aren't playing tricks on me.

"Yes." That one word hangs in the air. My wolf charges at me trying to get out. He wants to kill. He wants to tear everyone apart. He wants to tear me apart.

She was ours. We should have protected her.

He's right, but I push him back. I can't let him out now. I'll never regain control if I hand over the reins to him.

The room comes back into focus and I hear everyone talking at once. I can't even pick up on the individual words.

I stand up quickly. *"Enough!"* The order leaves my mouth before I can hold it back and the room falls silent. Theo takes a challenging step in my direction and I bow my head submissively. I should have never given an order like that. That's something the alpha should be doing. If she were my mate, it would be understandable, but I hadn't claimed her. Hell, no one even knows how I feel about her.

She died without knowing I love her.

I slump back against the wall before the weight of that thought tears me apart. I feel like I can't breathe.

"You love her," Bel whispers. "Loved her." Her correction tears at my heart even more.

I meet her eyes but don't need to say anything, I'm stripped bare. They'll all see it. On my face, in my eyes, in the way I'm being held up by the wall behind me. I can't hide it even if I try.

Both Theo and I choose that moment to ask each other completely different questions with the exact same word. "When?"

"Since…always," I reply honestly.

His eyes shift from me to Paddy and with a nod, I know he understands. He knows why Paddy ended things; he knows why two people who were once as close as brothers can no longer bear to be in the same room as each other. In fact, this is the longest we've been in the same room, without someone having to pull us off each other.

Theo addresses us all. "I received a call from Dominick, about thirty minutes ago."

"Domi—" Theo's raised hand causes the cursed name leaving Wes' mouth to stop.

"Dominick found her body outside his compound. She was left as a gift." He visibly swallows the lump in his throat and carries on, before any of us can argue. "The reason I called you all here tonight is because I need to know who was with her last? Who was meant to be guarding her?"

Bel waivers on her feet, her knees almost giving way beneath her. "Oh God." She slaps a hand to her throat.

Theo reaches out to steady her before her legs fall from under her. "Sweetheart? What is it?" he asks gently as he wraps her in his arms.

"No, don't." She pulls away from his reach. "I don't deserve it. It was me. I…I was the last one with her. We went to the movies and I left her to walk to her car alone. I was too wrapped up in myself, and grabbing my last things from Misty's. I just teleported without thinking." In a hasty move, she turns and leaves the room. "I need to go."

"*No!*" Theo shouts as he dives for Bel before she can teleport anywhere. We've seen them do it a number of times before. Bel is a werewolf with druid blood; one of her abilities is to tele-port at any time. Unfortunately, that means when she feels the need to escape she just dematerialises before your eyes and no one can stop her.

"You will not disappear on me again. Dammit! We've had this talk before, don't run. It was my fault, not yours. I should've had you both protected. You're my mate, and Ruby… my sister."

Bel stands stock still in Theo's arms as she takes in his words and no doubt feels his emotions through her empathy, another druid ability. Their mating bond will be telling her a number of things about his words and feelings too.

"The rogue will be hidden from the sun for the day, so we'll meet at sunset to hunt him down when he resurfaces," he says, as he comforts a silently sobbing Bel in his arms.

Unsure what else to do I mumble a reply, "Okay, boss." As much as I want to find the fucker and tear him apart right now, I know Theo's right. He'll be impossible to find before dark. Hunting him down now would be a waste of time and energy.

"Guys, you know the way out," Theo throws over his shoul-der, apparently dismissing us.

I leave the house feeling disconnected from reality. Surely this is some nightmare? Ruby can't just no longer exist. She was meant to be my mate. My back connects with the brick wall of the house painfully. I'd been so distracted I didn't even see Paddy set his sights on me.

"She'd be alive if you'd manned up and claimed her!" he yells in my face as he pins me to the wall with his body. His anger travelling over me feeds my own.

I shove him in the chest. "If you hadn't broken her heart, she'd have been with you," I spit back the lie, knowing he's right but not wanting to admit it.

"You're a coward. You won't even admit your guilt. You're going to leave your alpha pair in there," he points an angry finger to the house, "blaming themselves when it was you. I broke up with her because she was yours. You should have claimed her."

The truth of his words and the anger I have at myself forces me into action. My arm comes back and my fist flies forward connecting with his nose before he can block it.

Blood spurts everywhere. The sight of it doesn't make me feel any better, it makes me think of the blood Ruby would have lost in the moments before her death. Paddy's fist hits my cheekbone before I can dwell on that thought.

The pain takes my mind away from everything else. The ache in my chest eases and I stand there, ready to take anything he will throw at me just for a little peace from that ache. The punches come thick and fast and I soak up the pain, I deserve worse.

"For fuck's sake," I hear Billy shout, as Paddy's punches suddenly stop. "Can you not see he wants it? He's not even fighting back, Paddy."

Arms suddenly turn my body and through my swollen eyes I can just make out Wes' face peering at me, he prods at my face and I welcome the pain it causes. There's a click in my cheek as he manipulates the bones back in place before they heal. "You're lucky it wasn't shattered to pieces, it wouldn't do your lovely face any favours."

"I don't care," I mutter. "Ruby's dead and Paddy's right, it *was* my fault."

"Give yourself a break. If what Paddy is saying is the truth, I can see why you didn't claim her. She was still cut up over him. They broke up what, two days ago? She needed a friend, not someone dominating her by claiming her. You and your wolf did the right thing, you gave her what she needed."

I shake my head denying his words, even as the anger I had at myself dissipates. Without the anger, the ache in my heart intensifies and I raise my hand to clutch at my chest.

"Come on, come back to mine for a bit. You can get your head straight so we can get the bastard tonight," he offers.

I glance at the woods and know instantly what I need to do. "No. I need to run." I've denied my wolf to come forward even a little. He's calm enough to be allowed out now. He believes the only person to blame is the rogue vampire; even if I don't agree with him.

"Okay. You know where I am if you need me? Don't be alone too long." Accepting my nod as agreement, he turns his attention to Paddy and Billy. "Did you manage to straighten his nose before it set?"

Ignoring the rest of their conversation, I head into the woods. Once I'm out of sight, I strip off my clothes and place them over a tree branch for when I change back.

Crouching down, I release my wolf and welcome the freedom that comes with it. As soon as I transform, my wolf lets out a long, heartbreaking howl. Breaking my heart right along with it. *Ruby.*

23

REBORN

The noise wakes me. It's like someone's decided to take up the drums. But they have no rhythm. No, it's worse. It's like multiple people are having a drum off, and no one has any rhythm. It almost sounds like heartbeats, all beating at different times and paces.

It is heartbeats.

Concentrating on each individual one, tells me there are five of them. One of them is erratic. My breath comes in short, sharp gasps and I realise too late, that heartbeat belongs to me.

"She's waking up," a male voice shouts.

"Whisper. Remember how deafening every little noise seems when you first come around," another male says much quieter, not quite a whisper to my ears.

I open my eyes to a dark room. It scares me for a moment and I bolt upright. A hand rests on my shoulder holding me in place.

"Take it easy, Ruby. You're safe now," the second male says. I relax and he removes his hand. "What do you remember?"

My eyes are adjusting to the light and I can now see the silhouettes of four people, two are close to me and the other two are hovering by the door. He said I'm safe, but how do I know these people didn't cause whatever happened to me? I guess if they had meant me harm they wouldn't be hanging back from me. Wouldn't they have killed me instead of letting me come around?

I try to think about the question I'd just been asked. I

remember darkness and tell them as much. "Darkness," I reply. My voice sounds croaky, as if I haven't used it for some time. I cough trying to clear my throat.

"Can you remember what you had planned last night?" he asks.

I wrack my brain, trying to pin down anything. I have so many thoughts and worries going through it. I can't concentrate on just one. *My brother. Where the fuck is he?* I'd somehow been knocked unconscious, why isn't one of his wolves here? There is always one following me. Why am I in a room full of strangers? I was with Rosabel, she should be here. The thought pops into my head and I remember.

"I was at the movies with Bel," I say excitedly. "We left. She needed to pack some more things so she did her little trick of disappearing." I can't think of the word she calls it, hoping they know what I was meaning, I carry on with the memory. "I needed to get to my car down the road. I was jumpy, but I thought it was lingering from the movie we'd just seen. Until I heard footsteps behind me. I told them...told them Theo would be pissed because they weren't being covert enough."

The second male who seems to be in charge interrupts me, as I pause for a breath. "You told who?"

I think for a second trying to remember more. "Whoever was following me, Theo always has someone following me," I say, slightly confused at the question. Who else would I be talking about? I shake my head and allow the memory to flow. Not speaking, just reliving it.

The dark street.

The click, clack.

The vampire at my neck.

The terror.

My last wish of being a werewolf before nothing but blackness.

"It was a vampire. He was draining me. Killing me." Panic sets in and my stomach churns. *What happened to me? Am I dead?*

"Is this...is this heaven?" I ask in a whisper.

"Ha! Far from it sweetheart." A woman by the door laughs obnoxiously. The noise startles me and I jump back on the bed, pressing my back firmly against the headboard.

"Sam!" the leader admonishes.

"I'm sorry, Dominick, but you are babying her. I know you're trying to be gentle, but you're going to make it worse for her in the long run."

"Leave, before I say something I regret!" the male, *Dominick*, orders.

Dominick. I've heard my brother talk about him before. He's a vampire. The female leaves the room leaving the door slightly ajar, allowing a little light into the room.

"I know who you are. Did you kidnap me to piss my brother off?" I ask, stunned at the revelation. I carry on before he can get a word in. "Was draining me part of the order or did someone disobey the good king?"

The room becomes eerily quiet. I can feel a crackle in the air against my skin. I also hear Dominick take a deep breath in before I sense the power in the room dissipate.

I take a breath to question what that was, and the most delicious smell arouses my senses, making my taste buds salivate. My teeth start to ache and my stomach feels like it's on fire. I rub my tongue over the painful teeth and feel the points of fangs and I know in this instant that I'm a vampire.

A bloodsucking vampire.

"That smell?" I question. It's the only thing I care about at this moment; not what's happening to my body or why, but where that delicious smell is coming from?

"That would be me," the person near the door finally speaks. I watch as he steps closer.

"Wait!" Dominick stops him, stepping into his path. "We haven't explained things yet. She doesn't know when to stop."

"She knows what she is already, the look on her face says as much. None of the newbies know when to stop, but I trust that you will stop her before she comes close to killing me."

Dominick slowly moves out of the way, allowing the human to come closer to me.

I sit perfectly still, not wanting to scare my prey away. I don't want him to have doubts about what he's doing. I need his blood. I'm yearning for his blood.

"I guess I should introduce myself to you since you'll be feeding on me in a minute. I'm Jack, I volunteer for these first feeds because I'm good with pain, so don't worry about hurting me." He sits next to me on the bed and I can't hold myself back, I pounce on his neck. I pierce his skin and my fangs suck his blood into my body. It's heady and arousing. I moan against the human's neck.

The warm liquid running down my throat energises me, I've never felt anything like it. I need more. I pull more and more of the liquid. It's slowed its pace, but it's still coming.

"Ruby, stop!"

Someone pulls at me, effectively lifting me off my prey. I don't let go, but soon enough he's torn from my grasp.

"Take care of Jack. I'll deal with things here," Dominick informs someone.

I hiss at Dominick, I need the human back. I want the blood he has. I need the energy running through his veins.

"That's rather rude considering I'm the one that brought you the food in the first place. We wouldn't want to completely deplete our stock, now would we?"

His logic calms me considerably. Feeling me soften, he slowly releases me and I sit back on the bed. He walks across the room and using a dimmer switch on the wall, he slowly brightens a light on the ceiling.

"Did you do this to me?" I ask the question I'd asked earlier once again.

"No, not in the sense you are thinking." He pulls out the

chair; one of these office type chairs that swivel, from behind a desk in the corner of the room and rolls it so it sits facing me. He takes a seat before talking again. "Do you know why Theo has upped his security when it comes to you?"

I frown and think back. "Yes. There is some rogue vampire killing girls...who look a lot like me."

"Yes. Well, this rogue had been evading us for weeks. He's been leaving his kills for me, like a gift. Tonight, I came home to find you on my doorstep. You were so close to death, the only choices I had were to turn you or let you die completely. I chose the former."

"Did you get him?" I ask, not knowing what else to say. *Does he expect me to thank him?* How can I thank him when I don't know if he made the right decision for me, or not?

"No. But this time he left me a message. So I know who he is and his motives."

"A message?" I question.

"He etched his initials into your face," he says matter-of-factly, like it's a normal everyday occurrence.

I reach up to touch my face with a frown—feeling for these words.

"They're gone now. The transformation healed them, as it did any other wounds or scars you may have had."

I glance at the scar on the knuckles of my left hand, the one from a dog bite I had when I was ten, and see that he's right. It's gone.

"Who is he?" I ask, getting back to the monster who did this to me. *Monster...*I'm one of those now.

He stares at me in silence for a moment, presumably deciding what to tell me. "Since he took your life, I suppose you deserve to know, but to tell you his story, I need to tell you some of mine."

Hell yes, I deserve to know. I nod my agreement.

Having heard his name mentioned by Theo a few times, he

looks nothing like I had imagined. His tight, jet black curls were definitely not what I pictured. He's dressed immaculately in a slate grey suit with a waistcoat, but minus a jacket. It seems like he's been around for a long time; he comes across as old school in his voice, gestures, and appearance.

He settles back in the chair, getting comfortable. "I once had a lover, your brother would maybe call her my mate. We had a connection. I'd never believed in soul mates before but with Kathleen…I just knew it had to be. We were soul mates. I was already a vampire when we met, but that didn't matter to her. She wasn't scared of me. She was more than happy to live in the compound and be my feeder. You have to understand this was a lifetime ago, when I lived in Rome. I wasn't the king back then that came much later and is another story altogether.

"My beautiful Kathleen looked a lot like you, long blonde ringlets and green eyes. We were happy, but she started to notice her ageing, a wrinkle here, a grey hair there. None of it bothered me, she was as beautiful then as she was that first time I saw her. It bothered her though and she begged me to turn her. She wanted to be *Forever Young and Beautiful*. I put our request to the king, but he denied it. He said her spirit was weak and if she came through the transition she'd be lost to the bloodlust forever." His sadness seems to fill the room, I can feel it brushing against my skin.

"I didn't heed his warning, I turned her anyway and ended up having to rip her heart out of her chest; which in turn was as good as ripping out my own heart. That night I vowed never to sire anyone again."

I stare in rapt attention. It feels like this man is sharing a part of his soul with me. A soul that he doesn't share with many.

"I never fed from a woman again for a long time. I used men as my feeders and lovers. I didn't want to fall in love and if I stayed away from women, I naively thought I wouldn't. But what do you know, gender isn't really a selling point with me. It turns out I'm bisexual." He laughs and gives his head a shake; as though it's an amusing thought.

"One night I fed off the most beautiful man on earth, to this day I still haven't seen anyone who could compete. Jay Dawes. My loving JD. Ten years passed in the blink of an eye and the dreaded day came when JD noticed he had crow's feet beside his eyes. He begged me to change him, but with the memory of Kathleen and my vow, I denied him. I was king, I had no one's permission to seek, and yet I still denied him."

Dominick gets a soft, forlorn look on his face. That must have been heart-breaking. If I was in love, I don't know if I could deny my love…anything. *Eddie.* My heart aches at the thought of him. It is brief, as Dominick continues with the story.

"Even when I could feel how strong his spirit was, I still denied him. When he knew I wasn't going to change my mind, he stopped asking, until one night we'd made love and curled up in bed for the day. When night came and I rose once again, he was gone. Never to be seen again." He shrugs his shoulders.

"Well, we both know that's not the case and with the message and gifts of bodies who look a lot like Kathleen; whom I had told him about, well, we can only assume we'll meet again and soon."

24

PEEPING TOM

I find myself walking blindly through the hallways of Dominick's compound, thinking about his story hours after he told me. I have no idea where I am or where I'm going. I have a million thoughts running through my head. I try to focus on them all, hoping something will distract me from the burning in my stomach. I've been told it's the hunger and it will become more bearable as my body settles into this new form.

A vampire.

I've wished to be something more than human for most of my life. A vampire. That was never a thought. Never an option. My family are werewolves, they hate the bloodsuckers.

I hate the bloodsuckers.

And now I am one.

My life has forever changed.

My brothers. The pack. My friends. They'll never look at me the same again. Dominick told me of his phone call with Theo and his reaction to the news. I've lost them all.

I double over in pain as the burning intensifies. I could drain every human I come across and it wouldn't ease the intense pain. I'd just become a bloodthirsty monster that Dominick and his people would have to kill. I need to feed a little and often, as my body accepts the change. I need to learn how to control the hunger and only take what I need to survive.

I grit my teeth and straighten up, as I turn and start to head back to my room, a noise from further down the hall catches my attention. My stomach isn't the only thing that's changing, I can hear the slightest sound. I stand still and focus on that one sound distracting me, ignoring the footsteps and voices I can hear from various points throughout the compound. I hear it again—a woman's whispered moan. I find myself slowly making my way towards the noise.

As I reach the room the noise originates from, I come to a stop before the ajar door. As much as I know I shouldn't look, yet, I can't stop myself. My eyes fall on a beautiful naked blonde woman, who is laying back on a bed, as an equally naked guy pleasures her with his face positioned at the apex of her thighs. I can't tear my eyes away from the erotic sight.

"Stop teasing me with your fangs…fucking use them," the blonde says between pants.

Obviously having done as he was told and used his fangs, the woman screams a name in ecstasy. "Niko!"

"I love it when you scream my name like that, Sam," Niko says in a gruff voice. "Are you ready to do it again?" he adds, as he moves up the bed and lays over her.

The thought of him feeding from her makes my fangs elongate and pierce my lower lip, but before I can mutter a curse a hand clamps over my mouth and the voice whispers in my ear. "Shh…They won't appreciate knowing that you were getting off by watching their private moment."

I turn my head to glare at the jerk behind me.

Cas. Of course, it had to be Casanova, making a comment like that. Who else could it have been? His nickname says it all. He's one of Dominick's vampires; who I met just after Dominick told me JD's story. A good looking guy, the typical Mr Tall-Dark-and-Handsome, who looks to be in his late teens but could be any age. I wouldn't even want to hazard a guess.

He gives me a sexy smirk in return.

We silently make our way through the compound, and into

one of the lounge areas. Once I close the door behind us, I turn on him. "I was not getting off. And if they didn't want anyone watching them they should have closed the door."

"*The lady doth protest too much, methinks,*" the cocky bastard says, with a knowing smile.

"Don't fucking quote Shakespeare at me. It isn't cute. I was intrigued, but I wasn't getting off. Okay?" I don't even know why I care what he thinks. I should just shut my mouth already.

His smirk turns up another notch. "I wasn't aiming for cute." He pauses long enough for me to open my mouth, but before I can let a word out he carries on with his argument.

"Your fangs were out, that's a sure sign you were turned on. Sex and feeding come hand in hand."

I can't let him win. "I'm newly turned, so I'm constantly hungry. My fangs are always popping out."

He looks at me closely, before speaking. "You do look peaky. When did you last feed?"

I glance down at the watch on my left arm. It must have been a good four hours ago, maybe even five.

"By the look on your face, I'd say you are well overdue a feed. Especially for a newbie. Let's get you fed," he says, grabbing my arm and tugging me through the room and out into another corridor.

I try to pull my arm out of his grasp, but he's having none of it. So I let it be and allow myself to be led to God only knows where. If I get fed at the end, I'm not going to kick up a fuss. He knocks on a door and waits for an answer.

Within seconds the door opens and we are faced with a grandmotherly-looking woman. She reminds me of Gloria with her Greek looks. She's a human, I'm sure.

"Grandfather? I wasn't expecting you tonight."

I glance at Casanova. This woman must have him mixed up with someone else. How the hell can he be her grandfather? He releases me and pulls her into a hug. Catching the confusion that's clearly written on my face he reprimands her. "I've told you not to call me that, Elspeth, it only confuses people."

"I'm sorry, Cas, it's just habit." She glances at me and gives me a glorious smile. "Who is this gorgeous girl?"

Throwing his arm over my shoulder, he tugs me in close. "Newbie here is in need of a little top up."

"Well, you've come to the right place. Come on in and take a seat. I'll just go find someone for you," she says, welcoming us into a lounge room. After closing the door behind us, she wanders into what looks like another hallway.

"You heard the woman. Sit," Cas says, as he takes a seat and pats the spot next to him.

I choose to sit on the sofa opposite him and ask him the one question that's been running through my mind since the woman, Elspeth, he called her, opened the door. "Are you really her grandfather?"

"Yes," is all he says.

"How?" I probe, hoping for more information.

Ignoring my question, I watch as he tilts his head as though he's listening to something elsewhere in the compound. "You're getting a treat tonight," he says with a smile.

Elspeth comes back in the room with a male following behind her, chatting between themselves. He looks to be in his mid-twenties, blond hair, blue eyes. He reminds me a little of Jared; only he has a more of an oval face with a longer nose.

"Tyler, I haven't seen you in a while. Where have you been hiding?" Cas asks, sounding genuinely interested, as the others come to a stop before us.

"Dominick made me take a six-month break. You know how strict he is on overfeeding."

Cas nods. "Yeah, he doesn't want anymore Marys."

Elspeth tuts and shakes her head at the name. "Poor child."

Having no idea who or what they are talking about, I sit in silence watching this vampire before me casually making conversation with two humans; who smell ridiculously tasty. I never dreamt I would ever think anything along those lines.

I'm looking at these people and practically salivating over how good they're going to taste. I always thought vampires were monsters, who did nothing but drain people. Yet Cas isn't even hinting at wanting to eat them. There's no sign of his fangs. And Dominick sends them away for a six-month break from feeding?

My eyes fall on Tyler's pulse and I can't tear my eyes away. The sound of conversation drains away as I focus on the sound of his heartbeat, pumping his blood around his body. My fangs elongate and start to throb, giving the burning in my stomach some competition.

"Newbie!" Cas shouts, drawing my attention away.

Realising how awful I am for having my fangs out before we've even been introduced, I raise my hand to my mouth to hide them, while I try to concentrate on making them return to their hiding place. "I'm so sorry," I mumble around my fangs.

"Someone is hungry. Here." Tyler takes a seat next to me and offers me his wrist. "Let's get you fed before we worry about introductions." The look in his eyes, welcoming me. He's not emitting any fear, so he isn't afraid of me ripping his wrist to shreds, which is exactly why I'm not diving straight in. I quickly look to Cas for approval. He's not my sire so his orders won't affect me, but he's been a vampire a lot longer than I have so I feel like I need his agreement I'm doing what I should.

With his nod, I take Tyler's hand and raise his wrist to my lips. The sound of his pulse once again catches my attention and the impulse to feed takes over as I sink my fangs into his flesh and draw on his blood.

"Newbie, you aren't meant to be draining him." Cas' comment causes me to pause mid-draw. I look up at Tyler and take note of his pale complexion. I release his wrist immediately and jump back over the arm of the sofa and come to standing position about a foot away.

"I'm sorry. I..." I turn my eyes on Cas. "Why the fuck didn't you stop me sooner?" I snap, he should know better. *Why would he let me almost drain the poor guy?*

"Calm it, Kermit! You needed a good drink to tide you over through the day. I wasn't going to let you drain him, he hasn't fed anyone for six months, he'll be fine."

"I'm fine. A little...exhilarated," Tyler says as he puts a cushion over his crotch. The draw on a vein tends to leave humans sexually excited. Just as Cas said earlier, 'feeding and sex come hand in hand.'

"I'm usually more professional about feeding. The six-month break must've affected me more than I realised. You haven't harmed me, honest," he says, with a shake of his head; like he could shake the evidence of his embarrassment from his rosy cheeks. I notice that somewhere along the line he's placed a cotton pad over the puncture marks on his wrist, as he's cradling it tight against his chest.

"He'll be back to normal once he gets some sugar and fluids into him," Elspeth says, as she gets up and makes her way to a small fridge in the corner of the room. I watch as she removes a small bottle of orange juice and brings it back to Tyler.

"Cas said you're a newbie, but that can't be right? You seem to have a good handle on your bloodlust." I could hear the question in Tyler's statement.

"I was wondering the same thing. I've seen plenty of new vampires feed in my lifetime and not many of them are as neat at it as you were just then," Elspeth adds.

"She's sired by Dominick," Cas answers. As he pricks a fingertip on his fang, before leaning forward and pulling Tyler's wrist to him. "Here," he says as he rubs the droplet of blood over Tyler's still bleeding puncture marks.

I watch as the wounds close before our eyes.

Holy shit! How did I not know Vampire blood had healing properties for humans? Not wanting to look like an idiot I won't comment on it.

"Dominick doesn't sire people. The last time he did, it was centuries ago. You must be special to get him to break his own rules like that," Elspeth explains.

"My brother is the alpha of the Mount Roxby Pack, that probably has something to do with it," I admit.

"That explains it. He wouldn't have wanted a war between us and the pack, not now we've been working together. Theo and Dominick have been on the brink of war for years. It's only since the alpha's female came to town that peace looked somewhat possible."

"For the time being!" Dominick interjects as he enters the room.

25

HOT-TEMPERED PUP

"Master Dominick?" I only rose a matter of minutes before Elspeth's words accompany a gentle knock on the door.

Elspeth would not disturb me at this time of the day unless it were important. I dart to open the door not caring that I'm only wearing my underwear. "What's wrong?" I ask, the concern for my people bleeding out of me.

"I'm sorry to disturb you so early, but there's someone at the front door. He's furious. I'm not sure how much longer the door will hold against his strength." The door she's talking about is a reinforced door; it should hold up to almost anything.

I pat her arm to reassure her I'm not mad at her. "You did the right thing. I'll get dressed and go and see who it is. Go back to the human quarters. Make sure you lock the doors and don't let anyone in or out until I come and tell you it's all clear."

"Okay, I'll round everyone up," she says, before turning and leaving to fulfil her mission.

I throw some clothes on and materialise behind the closed door. I would like to keep this outside, but it's still early and the sun won't allow me to keep my people safe that way.

Bang. Bang. Bang.

"You better open this fucking door right now, bloodsucker, or I'll knock the fucker down." The person on the other side threatens. If he's going to throw threats he better be willing to stand up to me when he's before me.

I open the door as requested and find myself pinned to the

wall behind it. The door quickly slams shut, not giving the remnants of the sun a chance to touch me. At least he doesn't want me dead. Not yet, at least. The hands pinning me to the wall don't ease up on their grip.

"What the fuck have you done to my little sister?" the werewolf demands.

Sister? Is it really Cain? He always did have a hot temper; he killed his father after all. "I do believe it's in your best interest to unhand me immediately, pup."

Cain growls at the nickname but doesn't loosen his hold. "One of your bloodsuckers killed my sister. They need to pay, Dominick."

I glare at him, in silence, giving him time to think about what he's doing. Coming to his senses, Cain releases his hold. He's the polar opposite of his brother and sister, with jet black hair and deep cobalt eyes. He's the double of his father, leaving me to the assumption that Theo and Ruby take after their mother.

"Thank you," I say, straightening my shirt. "The vampire that attacked your sister was not one of my men. You should be grateful that I found her in time to turn her."

"You did what?" Cain growls, with a look of terror on his face.

"Cain?" Ruby's voice questions from down the corridor. We both turn to look in her direction as she races down the hall and into her brother's open arms. Her nostrils flare as she glances at her brother's pulse racing in his neck.

Seeing the look on her face, I rip her out of her brother's arms before she can sink her teeth in. *"No!"*

"What the fuck?" Cain questions, not having seen the look on his sister's face.

Tears roll down her cheeks. "You smell so good. I'm sorry."

Cain stares at me, helpless. I can tell he wants to pull her into his arms and comfort her. Easing my hold on her, I allow him to pull her to his side, making sure to stay in reach in case she loses control again.

"It's okay, Ruby, he understands," I say, hoping my words comfort her, if only slightly.

"But he's my brother, and I can't even hug him without wanting to drain him," she says miserably, pulling away from him.

"In time, you'll have the control you need. Trust me."

Looking up at me, she stretches on her tiptoes and kisses me on the cheek before walking away, leaving me standing with her brother in the corridor.

Cain sighs and leans casually with his back against the wall. "Theo didn't tell me you'd turned her. Why?"

"When I spoke to him, we were still uncertain whether she would transition or get through the bloodlust. He was adamant that she wasn't going to make it. I don't know what was going through his head." I pace back and forth, unable to relax with the wolf so close to my people.

"They won't hurt her will they, to get to us?" he asks, as he looks in the direction she'd gone a few moments ago; obviously referring to the rest of my vampires.

"No, I sired her myself. No one will dare touch her. She's one of the safest vampires in the town. You may not believe it, but we are a family here. A lot like your packs. Ruby is a vampire, she's one of us. A rogue may try to harm her, but she's stronger now, she isn't the weak human you once knew," I say, reminding him of her newly acquired vampire abilities.

He accepts my word with a nod and goes to open the door, pausing with his hand on the knob. "She may be a vampire, but she will *always* be my sister," Cain says adamantly, before leaving.

I stand, staring at the closed door for a moment. It looks like the Wilson pup that left town a lost little boy has come back a man.

26

CALMING THE STORM

While I was living the life of a lone wolf, I managed to find another wolf's missing mate. Frankie Rossi from the Rossi Pack in Western Australia. She'd been kidnapped and well hidden. My problem once finding Frankie, was convincing her to go back to her mate. We lived on the run for nine months, and then it was her mate's impatience that caused the reunion in the end.

As much as I had aimed to punish myself by living as a lone wolf for the rest of my life, after leaving Theo's life and marriage in a complete mess, I ended up finding myself a little pack of my own. I hadn't even realised it until I had to hand them over to their original pack. It hurt, so much more than it hurt to leave Theo and the Mount Roxby Pack over a year ago. Living together on the run gives you a connection like no other. When Theo called to tell me about Ruby, Frankie insisted on coming with me. Her mate and alpha somehow allowed her to leave his sight again, and I promised I would protect her as though she was mine.

When I went to see Dominick, my protective instincts kicked in, and I felt the need to keep Frankie well away from the vampire and his lair. Making my way back to where I'd left her at Misty's with Billy, one of Theo's wolves, I couldn't calm my temper down. Theo had made it sound like Ruby was dead, well and truly dead, when he gave me that nightmare of a phone call. To say I want to knock my brother's lights out is putting it lightly.

Storming into the bar, I let my eyes roam around the room looking for Frankie and Billy, ignoring the wolves that obviously recognise me with shock written all over their faces. Spotting Frankie's short spiky hair, I head over to the booth.

Sensing me, she turns before I even get halfway there. "Everything okay?" she asks. The worried look on her face says she already knows the answer to that question.

"Theo made it out as though she was dead! I'm gonna kill him," I snap as I pace beside the table; the energy flowing through me is too wild for me to sit.

"She's not dead?" Billy asks, apparently confused.

"Dominick managed to save her by turning her. She's a vampire," I state. "Why the fuck wouldn't he tell us there was a chance? Dominick said Theo knew she'd been turned, making it through the transition wasn't guaranteed, but there was hope. Hell, the King himself turned her."

"I need to tell Jared. He's been trying to talk some sense into Ed and Paddy; they both blame themselves. Bel is just as bad. She was the one that left her to walk to the car alone. The tension throughout the pack has doubled since last night's hunt for 'the Rogue' was a bust," Billy says as he stands, pulling his phone out of his pocket. He has the phone to his ear as he heads for the exit.

"You need to calm down before you see your brother," Frankie insists, tugging on my arm trying to force me to sit next to her.

With a shake of my head, I pull my hand out of hers. "If his mate is blaming herself, I need to go now."

After considering my words for a second, Frankie stands and follows me out of the bar.

"It was nice to meet ya, Frankie. Maybe ya could bring ya mate with ya next time ya're in town," Misty yells from where she's serving behind the bar.

The short drive to Theo's is a silent one. I use the time to calm my wolf down; he's pissed at Theo for not telling us the full story, but he's willing to hold back and allow me to take control of the situation. As much as I'd love to give Theo a beating, he probably has a valid reason for his actions. *I fucking hope he has a valid reason.* I park next to a blue Ford XR6 Ute and take the keys out of the ignition.

I don't make a move to exit the car.

Frankie reaches a hand out to stroke my forearm. Her wolf's omega energy does the trick at helping my wolf relax. Omega's are a special kind of wolf; there aren't many around and it can be dangerous for them to show what they are. "You shouldn't be doing that around a pack you don't know!" I remind her.

"He needed it," she observes matter-of-factly. She was right. My wolf needed it.

I give her hand a little squeeze in thanks. "Thank you. Are you ready to meet my brother?"

She nods in response and we both exit the hire car. We reach the door and I stare at it not sure what to do, this was my home at one point. I've never knocked on this door, but with the way things were when I left I contemplate knocking for a second until I remember why I'm here. I turn the handle and walk straight in. I'm immediately flooded with an onslaught of memories, I push them back. I'm not here to deal with the past, I'm here for what's happening in the present. Hearing raised voices Frankie and I glance at each other, and with a shrug, we follow the voices into the lounge.

"He's pissed and rightly so. Now fucking stand down, Theo," a beautiful brunette says, as she stands between Theo and Ed with a hand on each of their chests.

"That was a challenge, Bel! I can't just let it slide," Theo says, glaring at Ed over the brunette's shoulder. *Bel.* So that is my brother's true mate. She has to be made for him if she can stand between him and another dominant wolf like she is.

"He isn't going to be the only one challenging you before the day's end," I state, catching their attention like I'd intended; all three heads turn our way. "What are you going to do, duel the whole pack? I know how much they love our sister. Ed here isn't alone in that."

"What the fuck are you doing here?" Theo asks, as he moves out from under Bel's hand and strides my way. His intent apparent by his fists tight at his sides and the baring of his teeth.

"Do you really think you could drop a bombshell like that and I wouldn't turn up?" I growl, as we stand toe to toe. "Do you really want to do this? Our sister is alive. Do you want to duel and make sure one of us won't get to see her again? You didn't duel me when I slept with your wife because you worried about whether you'd make it out alive. Well, I haven't gotten any weaker since I've been away," I threaten.

Frankie pulls on my arm trying to pull me back from Theo. The feel of her Omega energy rolling over me, attempting to placate my wolf doesn't make me step back. No, it's the fact that my actions caused her to reveal what she is in front of a group of dominant wolves, that's what makes me back down.

I see the wonder on Theo's face for a second before it's replaced with recognition as his eyes fall on Frankie. "Oh fuck, Cain, what have you done? That's Frankie Rossi. I need to call O'Keefe." He pats his pockets no doubt looking for his phone.

"I assure you, my mate knows where I am and who I'm with," Frankie says, speaking for the first time.

"I sense the truth in your words. But..." I could tell he was torn, he wanted to call Jesse, but he didn't want to call Frankie a liar.

I pull out my phone and hit Jesse's number on my recent calls list making sure to hit speaker so he can hear me clearly. He answers almost immediately.

"Is Frankie okay?"

Frankie jumps at the worried tone of his voice. "I'm fine, Jesse. Theo just needed some confirmation that you know where I am."

"Good. Good. I'll be sure to send out a mass email, so it doesn't happen with anyone else," he says, sounding much more at ease. "Take care of her Cain."

"Always!" I reply, before ending the call and placing my phone back in my pocket.

"Something tells me you both have a long story to tell us. Who wants coffee?" Bel asks, as she makes her way into the kitchen.

Theo follows her into the kitchen and pulls out the mugs, as she fills the kettle. "Sweetheart, I know how much you believe coffee fixes everything, I just don't think it will even make a dent in this problem."

We all stand around the kitchen bench while Bel pours everyone a coffee.

"So, you're an Omega? I guess that explains the motive behind your kidnapping?" Theo says to Frankie, breaking the silence.

Frankie glances at me nervously and I stroke my hand down her back in a soothing gesture, before she has the courage to answer, "Yes."

"If I didn't know better, I'd say you two were mated," Theo says, with a sharp laugh. "Looks like you have a thing for taken women. I wonder if Jesse knows that?"

With his last sentence, I pounce over the bench top and knock Theo to the floor.

"For fuck's sake, when did this turn to the Theo and Cain show? Did you all forget about Ruby?" Ed yells, anger pouring off his body.

I feel Frankie's Omega energy fill the room and notice how it not only affects me as I release Theo and allow him to get up, but Ed calmly takes a cup off Bel and sits on the couch and relaxes into it, closing his eyes. "Darlin' I don't know what the hell you're doing to me, but please don't stop. It feels so fucking good."

He's right, when the Omega energy hits you hard like it obviously has Ed, it gives you a high. Very close to what a human would feel after smoking some good weed.

"What is all this noise? You guys know I haven't been sleeping well and I need to nap when I can." I turn at the sound of Selena's voice and feel my heart almost leap out my chest, as I find myself face to face with her and her obviously pregnant stomach.

"C...Cain? What...I..." Selena sounds just as tongue-tied as I feel. I left with the intention of never seeing her again. I'd heard she left not long after I did. I would never have come back if I knew she was here.

"Selena..." There's too much I want to say to her. I don't know where to start or even if I should. *What the hell am I thinking?* No. I shouldn't say any of it. I can't.

Frankie, obviously seeing something on my face saves me. "Selena, it's great to meet you at last. Cain has told me so much about you. Would you mind showing me where the bathroom is while Bel sorts these three out?"

Looking slightly stunned Selena allows Frankie to guide her through the house without argument.

I look to Theo, with no idea what to ask or even whether I want to know the answer to any of the questions running through my head right now.

He answers my unspoken questions regardless. "She arrived a few months ago. Her boyfriend had left her homeless and pregnant. Bel let her stay and as you can see, she's still free-loading."

Bel slaps his arm playfully. "Don't be mean. I don't person-ally like the woman but she's pregnant. She can't exactly get a job and earn the money to rent somewhere. Anyway, your mum has taken her under her wing. She'd kick up a fuss if you threw her out."

"Mum's here too?" I ask. Last I heard, Mum was a drug addict. I had planned to get Ruby away from her, but I stumbled upon Frankie and my plans changed. Being reminded of Ruby, I get back to the real reason we're all here. I shake my head to dismiss my last question. "Forget about that, Ed is right. We need to get back to Ruby. Why didn't you tell anyone Dominick had turned her?"

Theo sighs and picks up his mug.

Bel picks up her own mug. "I'd like to hear the answer to that question, too."

"I suggest we all take a seat," Theo says, pointing to the couches where Ed is snoring quietly. The three of us join him and Theo explains, "You both know how much I detest those bloodsuckers."

"Our sister is one of them," I growl in her defence.

"Are you going to listen, or not?" Theo snaps. I flick my hand in a gesture for him to carry on so he does. "When Dominick called me, his words made me believe she was dead, at first. When I finally understood what had happened, all I could think was that if she survives the transition, she'll be a blood-thirsty monster, craving our blood the minute she scents us. She'll be lost to us. I'd be lying if I didn't say part of me hoped she wouldn't make it. And I hate myself for thinking that way." I could see the anguish in his face and hear it in his voice. Bel squeezes his thigh gently, in a show of comfort.

"She's not lost to us, she fought the blood lust after scenting me, I saw it," I say, hoping to comfort him in my own way.

"You saw her?" Ed asks from beside me, having come around sometime while we were talking.

"Yes, she looked well, considering. We didn't talk long, she hugged me and once she caught my scent it was too much for her to stay and talk. Dominick believed she'll be able to handle it in time. She's only been dealing with the thirst for a day. We need to give her time."

"My baby's a Wilson. She's strong, she'll fight through it," Mum says, stepping off the bottom step. "Cain?"

"Hi, Mum," I say, as I stand and quickly stride across the room. I pull the sobbing woman in my arms and stroke her blonde hair softly. The woman I find myself holding together is far from the woman I'd once known as my mother.

BACK TO LIFE

I've been a vampire for almost a fortnight now and I've managed to get a good handle on the thirst. I still have some little lapses in judgement, but I haven't killed anyone and that's always a plus. Most newbies kill at least half a dozen people in their first month. Dominick says I'm a natural—I was born to be a vampire.

I was starting to go crazy being locked up in that compound. At least when I was under guard of the werewolves, I was allowed to leave the house. Cas came up with a way I can feel comfortably guarded and somewhat free at the same time, he organised a barista job for me in the small café at the cinema Dominick owns.

Dominick was grateful for the idea. He had been trying to talk me into getting out for days. So here I am behind the counter, wearing a little green apron over black trousers and a black T-shirt. I've been ignoring the scent of blood that's been tugging at me all shift without an issue.

I suddenly catch the delicious scent that belongs to a werewolf; alerting me one is nearby. Glancing up from the coffee I'm preparing, my eyes fall on Eddie. My stomach does a somersault that has nothing to do with the thirst and everything to do with the beat my heart just skipped.

"You're a sight for sore eyes, beautiful," he mutters, as he stops on the other side of the counter.

"It's good to see you too, Eddie," I say. My taste buds may be watering at his scent, but the need to talk to someone I care about outweighs the need to feed on him.

"Hearing my name roll off your tongue..." With a shake of his head, he lets his sentence fall short. Another scent fills the room, it's enticing, but Cas catches my attention.

"Who's your delicious friend, newbie?" he asks as he sidles up to Eddie, making a show of breathing in his scent.

"Someone you don't want to get any closer to, bloodsucker," Eddie says menacingly, before glancing up at me sharply; no doubt realising the elephant he just let in the room.

"Now that's not very nice," Cas complains.

"Cas, leave him alone. You can take over the counter, I'm taking my break." Ignoring the insult, I lift the counter and walk through, grabbing Eddie's arm as I pass before dragging him to one of the tables at the back of the café. Cas would still be able to hear our conversation, but I've learnt over the years that there isn't much privacy when it comes to supernatural hearing.

"How are you?" Eddie quizzes me before our butts even touch the seats.

"I'm doing good," I answer honestly. "How's Theo?" Cain's been to visit me a couple of times, but I haven't seen or heard from Theo. Cain says he's okay, but it's hard to believe that. *If he was okay, wouldn't he want to visit me?* If I accept that he's okay, I would have to accept that he hates what I've become.

"Theo is fine. Bel's keeping him busy with the wedding planning."

Now that, I believe.

"Are they looking after you in that compound? You can come and stay with me and Paddy, if they aren't?" he offers, sounding hopeful.

Panic runs through me, I wouldn't trust myself to live with two werewolves. Some nights when I don't feed just before I'm out for the day, I'll wake up ravenous, I'd want to drain them. I couldn't let that happen. Anyway, Paddy is my ex, I may accept that now, but I don't think I'd ever be able to live with him, no matter how much my life has changed. "I like it there, they have live-in feeders that are willing to feed you any time you need it. That comes in handy when you're a newbie like I am." I shrug shyly. It's strange talking about my feeding habits with him.

"Okay, but if anything changes, remember I'm always here waiting for you if you need me," Eddies says, before smiling at someone over my shoulder. "Looks like I'm not the only one that's missed you."

I turn looking for a familiar face in the crowded café, it takes me a second, but I finally spot Bel worming her way around the tables. As she reaches the table, Eddie stands to offer her his seat.

"I'll leave you girls to gossip," he says, with a wink.

Realising he's leaving, I quickly stand and give him no option but to catch me in a hug. I breathe in his unique scent; a mix of pine and engine oil.

"Hey, what's this for?" he breathes against my ear.

"To remind *you* that I always need you," I whisper back, as I loosen my hold on him. Something inside me shifts, almost like it's falling into place. Proving to me that just because I've become something entirely different, it doesn't mean my whole life needs to change.

This man is supposed to be in my life. I have a life I need to get back to, and seeing the smile on Bel's face as she sits at the table watching our exchange, I can see she agrees with the conclusion I've just come to. She isn't a mind reader, but her empathic abilities ensure she'll be able to feel my contentment and happiness as I reach the conclusion that I still have people who care for me.

"I'll see you again soon," Eddie says, before he gives me a kiss on the temple. "Make sure that dickhead looks out for you in that compound."

I hear Cas chuckle at the comment. I look up to see Eddie glaring in his direction on the other side of the room. "She can take care of herself pretty well these days, don't worry yourself fur-ball." He doesn't bother to raise his voice knowing our ears will pick it up.

Eddie growls menacingly, catching the attention of some of the surrounding customers. "Casanova is a wind-up merchant, ignore him. It'll piss him off," I say, hoping to calm him with that knowledge. With a nod, Eddie heads straight for the exit, without another glance in Cas' direction.

"Now I'm wondering. Were you worried for my well-being or his?" Cas asks in my head. All of the vampires tied to Dominick, be it because he sired them or because they have pledged their loyalty to him and in turn each other, can communicate tele-pathically. It was kind of strange at first, but it can come in handy when you don't want anyone overhearing your conversation.

"Fuck off, Cas. I'll tell Dominick you're causing tension with the wolves and he won't like that. He's the only one allowed to antagonise my brother and his pack," I threaten playfully; saying it out loud for Bel's sake, as I take my seat opposite her.

"Vampirism suits you," Bel says quietly, before pausing to laugh. "Well, that's something I never expected to say to anyone."

I laugh at her words. "It's funny you say that. Dominick keeps telling me I was born to be one," I say, with a roll of my eyes.

The smile on her face suddenly turns solemn. "I'm so sorry Ruby. If I hadn't been so wrapped up in myself this would never have happened. I should've walked you to the car. I—"

I cut her off as I reach for her hand. "Bel, it wasn't your fault. Please don't blame yourself, because I don't blame you." Her guilt is almost palpable in the air, swirling around her. "I was his MO. He'd spotted me and wouldn't have given up on getting me. He'd have done it some other time if you had walked me to the car that night," I add and receive a gentle smile and nod of acceptance in return.

"Have you got any special gifts?" she asks, sounding genuinely interested. It's known by all supernatural beings that vampires can have gifts. All vampires have compulsion; they can make people forget things or even make them feel things differently. That's how a vampire bite can feel so good.

Some vampires hand down gifts in their sire line; it's almost like how blue eyes or red hair gets passed down in a family. I take a quick glance around to ensure no one is watching, before holding my hand out, palm up, between us and concentrate on the trick I've been trying to master. A tiny flame forms in my palm before flickering out.

"I'm still working on it," I say, embarrassed at a weak performance. "Dominick assures me, I'll be able to form and throw fireballs eventually."

She frowns. "I thought fire was dangerous to vampires. I thought it turned them to ash if it touched them."

"It does, well, all except the rare ones that have the fire gift. We seem to be immune to fire. I'm the only one Dominick has known to have this gift since his own sire," I explain.

"Well. Theo will be happy to hear his baby sister is safer than most," Bel says and smiles as she says his name. The love between them is fierce.

I pick at the grain on the table, absentmindedly. "Ted won't care, he hates me. He hates what I've become."

Bel places her hand on mine stopping me from digging a hole in the table with my nail. I forgot my strength for a moment. "He doesn't hate you, Ruby. He misses you. You're his little sister, he loves you." I can sense the truth in her words. But his actions since my turning has shown the opposite.

"He hasn't done anything to show that. Hell, he hasn't even

visited me, not even once. Mum and Cain come every other day," I say, the anger evident in my raised voice.

"He hates *himself*, Ruby. When Dominick told him he'd turned you and there was a chance you'd make it, he couldn't see the hope in that, like everyone else did. He thought you'd be better off dead. And he feels so guilty for feeling like that. He can't believe he did, he hates himself for it." The pain of her words rip through me so quickly, I don't know whether it's because of how my brother must be feeling or the fact that he wished I was dead. Not knowing how to respond, I don't. "Please don't hate him for it, he hates himself enough for the both of you."

"He's my brother, I could never hate him. That doesn't mean I'm not disappointed, though. Not to mention hurt." Remembering back to the night I first rose, I didn't know if Dominick had done the right thing by turning me.

How can I expect Theo to think any differently?

"I can work with that." A satisfied smile graces her face. "Come back to the house with me. He needs to see you, he just doesn't think he deserves to."

Panic runs through me for the second time tonight. "I don't know if I can handle being in a house full of werewolves. Cas has been shadowing me, to ensure I don't lose control to bloodlust. Theo won't welcome him into the pack home," I explain.

Giving my hand a gentle squeeze, she reassures me. "We can handle one vampire, we won't let you hurt anyone. The wedding is next week, you need to be ready for that."

Cas appears beside us, no doubt having been listening to the whole conversation. "I think you can handle it. Rosabel here is the most tempting out of them all and you've been able to sit opposite her for the last twenty minutes without pouncing on her." It's his words that give me the confidence to agree to it.

"Okay. I'll meet you there. I can travel just like you now," I say shyly, referring to her ability to teleport.

"See you in a minute then," Bel says, as she walks out the exit. Heading for a quiet place to teleport. It's not that you need quiet to do it, but can you imagine the chaos it would cause if you just up and disappear in front of a room full of unsuspecting humans.

"Are you going to be okay here on your own?" I ask Cas, realising I'll be leaving him to deal with the shift I was meant to be working.

"I'll be fine. I'll call a couple of staff in and head home when you've left. I'm only here because you are." We both laugh at his honest admission.

"You're terrible," I announce as I give him a quick kiss on the cheek and dash out the exit, being careful to dash at human speed. Moving at vampire-speed can cause issues for humans watching, too.

I materialise on the front steps, not knowing how welcome I will actually be. Bel made me believe I would be welcome, but I won't believe it until I can see it on Ted's face. I reach out and knock on the door, only my knuckles don't connect as the door bursts open. I'm pulled into a strong set of arms I'd recognise anywhere.

"What the hell are you knocking for, this is your home, it always will be," Theo says, as he squeezes me harder than he's ever squeezed me before.

"I know I'm made of sturdier stuff now, but it still hurts when you squeeze that hard," I say, only half joking.

He releases me slightly before speaking, "I'm so sorry. Fuck, I'm such a dick. Everyone's told me as much." Letting me go, he slides his arm around my shoulder and leads me into the house.

"Come on. Everyone's here. We're just waiting on Wes to finish work."

Stepping into the lounge, I was happy to see that he really did mean everyone. It was like they'd thrown a pack barbecue in my honour. Who knows maybe we'll pull out the cricket set and I'll be able to whoop their arses with my vampire-speed.

HENS, PENISES, AND REVELATIONS

*I*t's the wedding tomorrow so the girls have taken over Theo's house, while the guys are running amok in town on Theo's stag night. I hadn't been back home since the impromptu barbecue a couple of nights ago, so I'm nervous as I materialise in the hallway by the front door. "Ahhhh." the scream behind me isn't a good sign.

I turn to see the one person that knows nothing about the supernatural beings of the world. Selena.

Great, just what I need.

"It's okay, it's just me. I didn't mean to creep in on you."

"You didn't creep in on me. You just appeared out of nowhere...like a magician, but without the smoke effects. How did you do that?" she asks, as she looks at me in wonder.

How the fuck am I going to get out of this? At least she isn't terrified.

"I...I..." I have no idea what to say. I wrack my brain to think of something that she'll accept, only to come up blank.

You're a vampire, you idiot. Use your compulsion and make her forget.

The thought runs through my mind and I could slap myself for being so stupid, not thinking of it straight away. I move closer to her, making sure to lock eyes with her, like Cas has been teaching me, and I pour out my power as I speak, "You watched as I walked in the front door, gave me a welcoming hug and forget the rest of this conversation." I watch as her glazed over eyes focus and she comes back from my compulsion.

"Ruby. It's so good to see you," she says, as she throws her arms around me and gives me as good a hug as she could with the massive baby bump she's carrying around. She's only at the seven-month mark, I don't think she has room for another two months if the baby keeps growing at this speed. "Everyone's in the lounge." She releases me and points me into the lounge as if I didn't know where it was.

The lounge is filled with half a dozen women. Misty and Lucy, who Bel works with, are both sitting on one of the red, L-shaped sofas next to Alyssa. As I pause in the doorway allowing myself to get used to the scent of werewolves, Selena walks past me and sits alongside my mum and Chloe, on the sofa opposite the others. I need to push down the hunger that comes as soon as I scent a werewolf; being in a room full of them takes a gentle approach.

Pulling a bottle of champagne out of the fridge, Bel shouts across the room, "Delly, grab some glasses, I'm pulling out the good stuff."

"Sure thing, Bel." With a spring in her step, Delly bounces in from the yard and over to the kitchen away from the group of girls she was talking to by the patio door. I'm surprised not to find any more pack members here. Bel is fairly new to town, she hasn't really had the chance to make any friends other than pack, so I thought most of the pack would be here. Misty and Lucy are both witches, so Selena is the only one here who's totally unaware of supernatural beings, as far as she's concerned monsters only exist in children's fairytales.

Bel pours the champagne while Delly carries the glasses around the kitchen bench. Once she reaches the sofas, she places four on the coffee table between them. Misty, Lucy, and Chloe all grab a glass. "I'll just go and get another couple," Delly says.

"There's no need, I don't drink," my mum announces, making me proud that she's still happily sober. "Being pregnant Alyssa and Selena both won't be drinking. So we have a spare as it is."

"I'll take the spare," I say, picking the glass up and taking a sip to calm my nerves. I'm a lethal vampire, you would think nothing could make me nervous. But put me in a room full of people; the majority being werewolves, and I can't help but think of draining them dry.

"Ruby, are you okay? You look a little peaky," Mum asks, as she weighs me up with her eyes, concern plastered all over her face. Last time I was here for the barbecue things got the better of me after a while. I had to leave without a word after my fangs popped out and I needed to feed. When I say leave, I mean I dematerialised on the spot, heading straight for the feeders wing at the compound.

Dominick found me a few minutes after I got my fill and threw his phone at me. Both he and Theo gave me a tongue-lashing about just disappearing. Once I told them it was that or drain everyone, they agreed I'd done the right thing. So I can understand the concern on my mum's face now.

"I'm all good, Mum. Surely I can't look as peaky as Alyssa does," I reassure her, giving Alyssa a concerned look of my own. She's an unhealthy shade of green.

"Morning sickness," Alyssa gripes grimly, before thinking about that assessment a little more. "More like all day sickness."

"Ginger ale will help with that, and a couple of ginger nut biscuits," Selena announces, as she makes a move to get up.

"Don't get up Selena, I know how hard that is for you. I'll get them," I offer, placing my glass on the table and heading into the kitchen.

Selena settles herself back into the cushions of the sofa. "Thanks Ruby."

I walk around the breakfast bar and into the kitchen. Seeing me, Bel pulls me into a hug still holding the half-empty champagne bottle in her hand. The cold bottle I feel through my tank top was a drastic difference in the heat coming off Bel.

"I'm so glad you came. If you need to leave at any time, I will completely understand," she says, giving me an out if I need it; no doubt remembering my speedy exit the other night.

"Thanks. I had a little wobble as I came in, but managed to push it down, should be fine," I say as I pull away. "Are you nervous about tomorrow?" I ask, leaning into the fridge and pull out a can of ginger ale.

Bel reaches a glass down out of the cupboard and slides it across the bench to me. "Not yet, I'm more worried about what the guys are doing to Theo right now. He better arrive in one piece," she confesses, taking some ginger nut biscuits out of the *'Cookie Monster'* cookie jar on the bench top. Its cry of *'cookies'* makes us both giggle.

Theo is a big cookie eater, he loves chocolate chip cookies, so I bought him the jar a couple Christmases ago when I saw it in a shop. Selena hated it, she used to hide it in the back of the pantry. It's nice to see it on show and holding Selena's biscuits. She probably grumbles every time she takes one out.

"He'll be fine. Knowing Theo he'll have ordered them all to behave," I say with a laugh, pouring the ginger ale into the glass.

"You're right. He won't make it easy for them to have fun." She places the ginger nut biscuits on a side plate. "Come on, let's go have enough fun for everyone."

We both make our way to the sofa and give a green-looking Alyssa our ginger goodies, hoping they do the trick as Selena promised. Alyssa takes a healthy sip of the ginger ale, as Bel and I both find a spot on the sofa to squeeze our butts in.

These people are family, I don't want to be on edge for the rest of my life when I'm around them. I'm immortal, for crying out loud. After I fled the last get together, Dominick assured me that in time I'd be fine. I do believe him since a number of vampires drink at Misty's without draining the werewolves there.

Although Misty probably has some form of ward or spell up to protect her customers. In saying, that if a vampire really needed to feed on a werewolf, they would do anything to get their fix. They'd probably attack before the unsuspecting werewolves even made it into the safety of Misty's. I know there are laws against feeding on a pack member, and serious consequences if we break those laws, but that doesn't seem to affect my fangs and feeding urges just yet.

"Don't get comfy, I think it's time we start some games," Alyssa says, around a mouthful of ginger nut biscuit, her voice pulling me out of my worries. "Okay girls, we need to go outside for the first game, *Pass the penis,*' we'll need plenty of space. Let's make two teams of four. Selena, you might have to just be a referee for this one."

"That sounds like a good idea to me," Selena says, as Chloe reaches down and tugs her up off the sofa. "I'm not sure this beast I'm carrying around with me is very game-friendly." She gives her ample stomach a loving stroke before waddling out to the yard.

As everyone makes their way outside, I take my empty glass to the kitchen and almost fall over Alyssa; who's on her hands and knees with the majority of her body in the fridge. "What the hell are you doing?"

She pulls out of the fridge just enough to look up at me. "I know they're in here somewhere," she says, before ducking back in. "If Theo's eaten them, I'll kill him. Ah huh! Looks like Theo lives to see another day." She rises to her feet with a joyful smile on her face and a cucumber in each hand.

I laugh and point at the cucumbers. "The penis for the game?"

With a nod and a grin, she confirms my suspicion. "We can't play *'Pass the penis'* without a couple of penises."

We join the others in the backyard and they have already assembled two teams, Bel, Misty, and Lucy are on one team; with Delly, Mum, and Chloe on the other.

"Ruby, come and join us," Mum shouts. Having no issue with being on their team, I join them in their little huddle as Alyssa explains the rules.

"Okay, ladies. This game is essentially a relay race with a cucumber as a baton. Only you can't touch it with your hands, it must be held between your legs and passed to your team members legs," she says, giving a cucumber to each team. "The first team to have all members complete their turn of the race wins."

Bel and Delly both get a cucumber in position.

"On your marks. Get set. Go!" Selena shouts from the lounger at the finish line. Bel and Delly both shoot off the line, they're holding back their were-speed to a degree. If clueless Selena weren't the only human here, I'd worry someone would notice. They reach the end of the yard and run back, Delly taking the lead by a stride. The cucumber Bel is holding is slowly working its way lower down her legs.

"I'm losing my penis," she shouts with a giggle.

"I'm sure Theo would be happy to offer you his," Alyssa shouts back, as we all burst into laughter.

The handover between Mum and Delly goes off without a hitch and Mum is halfway down the yard, when Bel and Alyssa have managed to get over their laughter enough to pass the *'penis'* between them. It doesn't take Alyssa long to make up ground. Mum makes her turn and drops her *'penis,'* the delay allows Alyssa to overtake her. The handover between Alyssa and Misty is quick and she makes it halfway back before Chloe manages to pass her.

We fumble our pass and I set off with the *'penis'* between my knees, which makes running harder, even with the grace being a vampire gives me. I cross the finish line with Lucy on my heels.

"Thank God, that's over. I need to pee," Selena says, getting up as quick as she can in her state and dashing inside.

"We had a disadvantage with two human teammates. It would've been a whole different race if we had been able to use our speed," Bel complains, as my team jumps up and down hooting about our win.

"The way I was running then, I could have done better than that when I was human," I state with a laugh. I'm not even kidding. I was abysmal.

"Fair enough. The next game isn't as strenuous, so even Selena can play. Let's head back inside," Alyssa orders.

Lucy and I both carry our cucumbers to the kitchen dumping them on the counter and join the others who are huddling around something on the wall, just as Selena reappears from her pee break. Once I get close enough, I realise there's a theme going on with these games. There is a large poster of a naked, good looking guy pinned to the wall. He has a target where his penis should be. The words *Pin the Junk on the Hunk'* are written across the top.

"Where the hell did you find these games? Did you do a Google search for penis-themed games or something?" I ask with a giggle, as I turn my attention to Alyssa; who chooses that moment to hand me a penis-shaped sticker.

"I've been to plenty of hen's parties, so I have a heap of penis games stored in this head of mine. No need for Google here." She winks.

As Alyssa passes Selena, she gives her huge baby bump a gentle rub. "I can't wait until I get to this size. To feel the baby moving must be an amazing feeling."

Selena holds Alyssa's hand firmly in place and smiles.

"Feeling it like this is fantastic, but feeling it from the inside is indescribable. There are just no words good enough."

I stand and watch the moment passing between them as I suddenly come to the realisation that I'll never experience that. I'll never feel a baby move inside me. I'll never have a baby of my own.

A tear escapes down my cheek and I quickly reach up to wipe it away. Not quickly enough, though. Mum grabs my wrist and pulls me through the house and into what used to be my bedroom. It hasn't changed one bit. I begin to wonder if anyone has been in here since that night.

Mum's voice snaps me out of my thoughts. "I'm sorry, honey. I was hoping you'd have longer before you thought about the things that won't be part of your new future."

"I can't have kids, Mum. I won't be able to give you grandkids," I say, as tears run freely down my face.

Mum pulls me into her arms and strokes my back soothingly. "Maybe you can't give me biological grandkids, but you can still give me grandkids. You can adopt or foster."

Her words run through my head on a loop.

Adopt or foster.

Adopt or foster.

I realise she's right, I can still be a parent one day. I just have to think and go about it a different way now. "You're right," I say, with a smile as I pull back out of her arms and wipe my face free of tears.

"Good," she says as she takes one last look at me before turning for the door. "We best get back downstairs, they'll be wondering where we got to."

With a quick glance in the mirror to check I don't have panda eyes, I follow Mum downstairs, determined to forget my worries and make sure my future sister-in-law has the best last night of freedom she can have.

I briefly wonder if Alyssa has a stripper booked.

29

THE ROMANCE OF
A WEDDING

*L*ooking at my brother standing in the fairy-lit garden, watching proudly as his beautiful bride and mate, walked down the aisle is a sight for sore eyes.

When things went wrong between him and Selena I never thought I'd see him happy again. I can see now that even in their happiest days he was never this happy. The love is pouring off him. Bel has been a gift to us all.

The wedding was meant to be during the day, but Theo wouldn't have it without his little sister attending, so the plans were changed and Alyssa went out and bought what looks like a million fairy lights. It's gorgeous. She's done such a good job, if she ever gets sick of being an accountant she should go into wedding planning.

Jesse O'Keefe, alpha of the Rossi Pack, has flown over from Western Australia so he could officiate the ceremony, bringing his mate, Frankie, with him. He's a big warrior of a man, built like a gladiator. Even with his suit on you can see he's all muscle, his blond hair is trimmed short on his head.

Frankie had arrived with Cain when news of my death had spread, but she flew back to Western Australia a few days later once Cain decided to stick around. Jesse had flown someone else out here to accompany Frankie on her journey back. Unfortunately, I hadn't been able to meet her before and even though everyone trusts me, I don't trust myself to speak to her now. I wouldn't want to have a mishap and anger one of the only alpha allies Theo has.

As Bel reaches us in her beautiful lace gown, with her brunette locks pinned up on her head in a fancy up-do, she hands Jared her bouquet before kissing him and her uncle on the cheek.

Bel's Uncle Jack, Aunt Lilian, and cousin Benji, arrived yesterday. The wolves are used to having Jared around, so they didn't seem to care about having an extra werelion on pack territory; which was good because Bel wouldn't have it any other way. It appears the lions come with Bel, like it or lump it. She turns her attention on Theo. The growl he releases in the back of his throat makes me think his wolf is pretty pleased with his mate's appearance, too.

"Behave," Bel says with a giggle, as she taps him playfully on the chest.

"I'll take that as my cue to start, shall I?" Jesse jests, before clearing his throat and addressing the crowd.

"Friends, family, and pack mates of Rosabel and Theodore, welcome and thank you for being here on this significant day.

"We are gathered together to celebrate the mating of Rosabel McGuiness and Theodore Wilson, alpha pair of the Mount Roxby pack."

He focuses his attention back to Bel and Theo.

"Rosabel and Theodore, you've already claimed one another and started the mating process. Your mental bond has formed and with today's ceremony, it will solidify."

Jesse reaches into his inside jacket pocket and pulls out a green cord and places it over Bel and Theo's joined hands.

"As this knot is tied, so are your wolves now bound."

So that is why Theo needed to trust the person who was officiating, he wouldn't allow just anyone to tie his and Bel's hands together.

"With the fashioning of this knot I do tie all the desires, dreams, love, and happiness wished between you, to your lives for eternity.

"As your hands are bound by this cord, may your mating be held by a symbol of this knot.

"May it be granted, what is done before this pack is not undone by man nor wolf."

I jump where I stand, as the wolves all stand in unison and howl to the couple.

Jared and Jack both join in with a roar before Bel and Theo howl, too. There aren't many humans here only Lucy, Misty, and those that are mated with other weres. The way Lucy and Misty are flinching at the sound is proof they don't frequent mating ceremonies.

Theo bought Selena a pregnancy spa weekend so she would have a chance to relax before the baby was born. The excitement of a full house of wedding guests would have been taxing on the mom-to-be. Selena pretty much agreed that she would love to stay but was really dying for some time to be pampered. It appealed to her selfish nature. It also gave the pack the chance to really be themselves for the wedding. It worked out for everyone.

Once the noise dies down, the happy couple makes their way hand in hand down the aisle. Being Bel's Man of Honour, Jared follows behind them with Bel's bouquet of flowers still in hand. Wes, Theo's Best Man, and Misty, Bel's Head Bridesmaid follow behind them. Leaving Ed and me to walk arm in arm after them.

"You look absolutely beautiful," he says, after a sharp intake of breath, before tucking my arm into his.

"Thanks," I mumble. I can feel the flush run over my face. "You look pretty dapper yourself." It isn't a lie, he looks amazing. But then, he always looks amazing.

I glance into the crowd and see my brother Cain grinning back at me, dressed in a smart suit and tie matching the purple of our dresses. His dark hair gelled back smoothly as opposed to his usual just out of bed look.

I hope he and Theo can sort things out between them. He was Theo's Best Man last time. It's going to be strange listening to Wes give the Best Man speech instead of Cain, but you can't sleep with your brother's wife and expect to be Best Man for him at his next wedding. I'm just glad Cain is here and they seem to be talking.

By the time we get to the end of the aisle, most of the guests are out of their seats and wandering around the yard. Bel and Theo are getting hugs and kisses from anyone that can get near them. Cain steps out in front of us and I release Eddie's arm.

"Thanks for being my date tonight. I'll see you on the dance floor." Eddie gives me a wink before making his way to a group of guys across the yard.

Cain throws his arm over my shoulder and pulls me into a side hug. "How are you doing little sis? Not wanting to sink your fangs into anyone yet, are you?"

"Now that you mention it, there *are* plenty of wolves here. I think I could take a few drops from a couple without anyone noticing." I make a show of looking around the yard at the unsuspecting wolves.

His arm tightens across my shoulder. I can't help but laugh at him for taking me serious.

"I'm kidding," I say, digging him in the ribs with my elbow. "I had a good feed before I left. I'm fine, honest."

"You little shit, you had me worried." He laughs and pushes me away from him playfully.

"I've missed you. Please tell me you're back for good," I say, as I hug into his side.

He gives a long sigh before speaking, "I don't know. I don't really belong here anymore. I ruined everything when I fell for Selena." Something in his voice makes me pull away and look at him. He fell for her? He doesn't give me time to dwell on that thought, before he carries on talking. "But I don't belong to the pack I made while I was away anymore either."

I follow his eyes and see them trained on Frankie. She's looking at her mate, Jesse, sheepishly. It's almost like she doesn't know him and they are on a first date, but they've been mates for years. There's got to be an interesting story behind that look.

The chairs were moved to the tables and the reception went without a hitch. Jesse brought Ben, one of his wolves with him, who happened to be a world-class chef. So needless-to-say the food was divine.

Well, it smelled divine and everyone else said it was. As a vampire I don't eat food anymore. It's not that I can't eat it, it's just that I don't have bodily functions like I used to as a human. I can still chew and swallow, but after that it won't do anything, it'll just sit in my stomach like a lead weight until it decomposes and breaks down on its own.

It wouldn't be a pleasant experience, no matter how good it may taste going down. Instead of looking odd watching everyone else eat, I'd offered to help Ben in the kitchen. I'm clearing the leftovers off plates as I feel a wolf's energy behind me, thinking I'm in Ben's way again, I start to apologise, "I'm sorry. I'm good at getting in the way," I say, as I hastily scrape the last plate.

"You're not in the way," Paddy says, causing me to drop the plate.

"Shit!" Even with my vampire reflexes, I don't manage to save it from connecting with the floor.

"I'm sorry, I didn't mean to startle you. I thought you knew I was here." He grabs the dustpan and brush from under the kitchen sink and crouches down to help me clear the mess I've made.

I pick out the big pieces as he sweeps up the smaller shards.

"I haven't quite figured out how to recognise each of your individual wolf energies and scents, yet," I explain, before taking a quick breath and carrying on, "I thought you were Ben. I came in here to help and I've done nothing but get in the way. I should've just left."

"It's your brother's wedding, you can't leave. They haven't even had the first dance yet," he argues.

I give him a grateful smile as I stand and lean back against the bench top. "Thanks. Anyway, what was it you're looking for? If it's more food, you'll have to speak to Ben about that."

He places the dustpan and brush back where it belongs with a shake of his head. "More food is always good, but no, I was looking for you," he says, leaning on the bench opposite me. "We haven't really spoken since…" he breaks off, not finishing.

"Since I became a vampire," I finish for him.

"No. I meant since…you know, me and you." He's referring to our night of lovemaking before dumping me the next day.

"Oh," I say sheepishly. "So much has happened since then, I didn't realise we haven't spoken in all that time…" I pause not sure what else to say. *What else is there to say?*

He steps forward and takes my hand in his. "I need to explain what happened. I—"

I cut him off. "You already explained Paddy, you're waiting for your true mate and I'm not her," I admit sadly. "I was devastated at first, but I understand now. I'd be a bitch to deny you what Bel and Theo have. We just weren't meant to be." I give his hand a squeeze before leaving him there and heading back into the yard.

It wouldn't do either of us any good to bring it all up again. What I said was the truth. I understand and I'm over it. We weren't meant to be and that's okay. He was my first love, but he's not my *for life* love—he's still out there somewhere and I have an eternity to find him.

30

FALLING INTO PLACE

The first dance song, 'I'll Be' by Edwin McCain, plays over the speakers that have been set up around the yard. Theo stands and offers his hand out to Bel. "May I have this dance, Mrs. Wilson?"

Bel makes a show of considering it. "I suppose it won't hurt," she says with a playful grin, before taking his hand and allowing him to lead her to the space that had been cleared for the dance floor.

He says something I can't hear over the music, as he pulls her into his arms causing her to swat at him with a laugh. He laughs back and elegantly sweeps her around the dance floor.

The song changes and out of the corner of my eye I see Wes offer Misty his hand, as Eddie offers me his. "Shall we?" Eddie asks.

I stand and take his hand, giving him permission to lead me to join the others, which I notice includes Jared, who's twirling Alyssa around the dance floor. "We shall."

Our eyes connect as he holds me against his body, swaying to Ed Sheeran's 'Thinking Out Loud.' I stumble, if not for his gentle grip, I'd be on the floor. I can't believe what I see in his eyes.

Love.

A look of love that strong can't be something new. *How have I not seen that before?*

Quickly sending me out in a twirl, we lose our eye contact.

The connection between us doesn't fade though, if anything, it feels stronger. I can feel it through the way he's pulling me back against his chest. I can hear it in the beat of his heart and the sigh that escapes his lips as I place my hand over his heart.

Sliding my hand up to his neck, I pause to feel his pulse behind my hand. I think about how he might taste for a split second before quickly moving my hand around the back of his neck and gliding my fingers into his short hair at the base of his skull. I pull his head down to me so I can taste his lips.

His hand holding my hip glides around my back, his fingers digging into my bare skin as he pulls me closer, it's almost as if he's trying to mold me into him. If I was still a human he'd be leaving bruises, but with my new vampire strength it does nothing but turn me on.

In our frenzied passion, the taste of blood breaks through my consciousness. It's the most delicious blood I've tasted, yet.

I freeze on the spot, but I can't make myself pull away from the magnificent taste.

Having no doubt he felt me stiffen, Ed pulls back breaking our kiss, taking the blood away from me.

"It was just a nick, it'll heal in a second," he says, probably in reaction to the horror that I feel, which is obviously written all over my face.

I make a move to leave his arms. "I'm sorry. I…" I can't believe I've ruined such a romantic moment.

His hold tightens, almost painfully. Not even giving me an inch to move away. "It was an accident. I got carried away and caught my tongue on one of your fangs."

I duck my head, so I don't have to face him. I don't want him to see the hunger in my eyes. With the taste of his blood fresh in my mouth, my struggle with not feeding on the werewolves has come back, double fold.

He kisses the top of my head. "Come on, beautiful. Let's get out of here. We need to find you something to tide you over."

I look up to see how serious he is. "We can't just leave. It's my brother's wedding reception," I argue.

"Sure we can. After that kiss people will just think we're going somewhere a little more private." He releases me and takes my hand in his, tugging me in the direction of the exit. "If you're worried about what Theo will say, he won't care. He snuck Bel out of here the minute everyone's attention was on the groomsmen and bridesmaids."

On the way out I give the yard a quick sweep with my eyes, I can see he's right, Theo and Bel are nowhere to be seen. Alyssa throws me a wink and nods her head in the direction of the exit, giving me permission to leave; the look on her face tells me she thinks *'I'm getting lucky,'* exactly like Eddie said they would.

Eddie quietly drives me into town and parks outside Misty's. "I don't know where you get your feeders from. Is there somewhere you need to go? Or do you just grab people off the street?"

There's no judgement in his voice, which surprises me. I know Theo hates that Vampires feed off people, with him being Eddie's alpha, I assumed Eddie would feel the same.

I turn slightly in my seat so I'm facing him. "I feed off the volunteer feeders at the compound. I've never fed from someone off the street."

Eddie starts the Ute and pulls away from the curb. "The compound it is then."

It's only a minute later that he's parking in the alley behind the compound. I sit here in the car staring at the compound door, not sure what to do next. Do I invite him in? Is he even allowed in? Maybe I should call Dominick?

Eddie breaks the silence. "I can sit here while you go in."

I nervously bite my lip, thinking of the kiss we shared not long ago. I want more of that. I can't have more if I make him sit out in the car.

"No. I want you to come in. I want you to see where I live. How I live." I quickly shut my mouth, realising I sound pushy and expectant. He might have only been lost in the moment when he kissed me. He might not want more. I open the Ute's door in a rush hoping to hide my embarrassment. By the time I'm out and closing the door, Eddie comes up behind me.

"I'd like to see it," he says, as he turns and sandwiches me between him and the Ute. Lifting his right hand off my arm, he runs it up my neck and into my hair, pulling it slightly to tilt my head enough to look at him. "That kiss back there, wasn't just some in the moment shit. I've wanted to do that for as long as I can remember. I want to do it every time I'm within arm's reach of you."

I don't need to hear anymore, I lean forward and take his mouth with mine, careful not to catch him with my fangs. I grab at his shirt pulling him closer to me, the sound of fabric tearing causes me to pull back. Shifting my eyes to the grip I have on his shirt, I see the fabric under my fingers is torn. I quickly release my grip. "Shit. I'm sorry. I…"

He laughs a big belly laugh. "It's a shirt, Rubes, don't worry about it. Anyway, the fact that you want to rip my clothes off me is hot!" He throws me a wink before laughing again.

"Oh, shut up," I say playfully. "It wasn't intentional. I just forgot my strength for a minute."

Putting his arm around my shoulder he tugs me toward the door. "I don't believe that for a second." He's such a big head, but he's right. I wouldn't mind ripping his clothes off. "Come on then, let's get you topped up."

"You make me sound like a phone that needs topping up with credit." I laugh, at how ridiculous it is that I need *topping up.* "I don't even know if they'll let you in," I say, suddenly sobering.

"Only one way to find out," he says, stepping up to the door and giving it a knock.

Casanova opens the door. "You live here, newbie, there's no need to knock." He catches sight of Eddie and his whole happy demeanour changes. "You, on the other hand, can take a run and jump. What's happening Ruby?"

I sigh, disappointed that my plans of showing Eddie all of me will be ruined. "I need to feed and I wanted to show Eddie where I live."

No doubt hearing the disappointment in my voice, Eddie kisses me on the temple and pushes me through the open door, as he takes a step away from the entrance. "Go. I'll be right here when you're done."

Taking him at his word, I enter the compound and head straight for the feeders quarters, just the anticipation of where I'm going makes my fangs ache.

I find Eddie, exactly where he said he'd be, waiting for me, leaning against the wall next to the compound's entrance. "All satisfied now?" he asks.

"Not completely. I still have a certain urge to satisfy," I say flirtatiously, as I run my hand down his chest. Feeding enhances your arousal and knowing that Eddie was waiting for me out here after things had been hot and heavy more than once tonight, has made me more sensitive than usual. I jump in the Ute and buckle my belt as Eddie gets in his side. He starts the engine and drives out of the alley, without a word. What I'd give to hear his thoughts right now.

He pulls to a stop in his drive but doesn't make a move to get out of the Ute. "If I take you in there tonight, I won't be able to help but take you as my mate. I've wanted you for too long, there'll be no holding my wolf back," he says, his eyes flash to wolf showing me exactly how close his wolf is to the surface.

Mate!

I scramble to get out of the Ute and take a few long strides up the drive. "You can't take me as a mate," I say, as I pace back down the drive.

"You don't want me as a mate?" he asks over the top of the Ute. The hurt in his voice evident. It makes me stop pacing and turn to face him.

"Of course I do. I love you." It's only as the words fall out of my mouth that everything falls into place.

I love him.

He's been there for me for as long as I can remember. He stood by and watched me date Paddy. He was a friend when that's what I needed after Paddy. He's given me space when I needed it as I got used to being a vampire. If what he's saying is true, none of that could have been easy.

He must have fought his wolf for a long time. But that doesn't mean I could let him choose me as a mate. He'd be sacrificing too much.

"There is nothing I'd want more than to be your mate. It's just...you can't choose me. I can't have children. I can't give you children, Eddie. I won't let you sacrifice that legacy, for me. Never have the chance to have pups of your own. I just can't..." I say, not able to mask the devastation in my voice.

Eddie is in front of me in a flash. "Plenty of people can't have kids, it doesn't mean they don't have kids," he say's logically. No doubt taking my silence as misunderstanding he clarifies. "There's surrogacy or adoption, or even fostering older kids that need a loving home for a while. There are plenty of options."

I fist my hands by my sides, angry at the world. "I'm as good as dead throughout the daylight hours. How can I ever be a mother, like that?"

He wipes a tear I didn't realise had fallen from under my eye and takes my hand before leading me into the house. "We'll figure it out. Together."

Closing the door on the world outside, he takes my lips with his in a gentle kiss. All the lust from earlier gone, only love and adoration in its place.

31

HEROES DON'T
ALWAYS WIN

My heart's first beat of the day startles me up and out of bed. It does it every day. I'm still not used to it. Maybe I will be eventually, but it is like being born, every morning. It's an incredible feeling.

Looking around the room I recognise it as Eddie's room; memories of last night flash through my mind. *My hands fumbling, pulling Eddie's shirt over his head. Our mouths breaking apart just long enough to strip each other naked.*

After we'd spent the night thoroughly mapping each other's bodies, Eddie ran around looking for a way to block out the windows before the sun rose. I told him I'd just teleport back to the compound, but he wasn't having any of it.

He didn't want us to be apart, not since we'd mated. He was right about not being able to hold his wolf back. I didn't even think a wolf would be able to mate with a vampire, but it happened. I mentally reach inside myself and feel for the strand —the bond—tethering us together. I smile when I find it, but that smile soon drops off my face. I can feel Eddie, he's anxious about something.

I quickly search for my phone, remembering too late that I didn't have it with me yesterday. I rummage through his chest of drawers and pull on a T-shirt and shorts, rolling them up at the waist so they don't bury me.

Just as I'm about to teleport, I spot a note on his pillow.

Sleeping beauty,

Theo rang while you slept. There's a lead on the rogue vamp. By the time you wake up, we'll have a plan. Come straight to Theo's.

Tonight we hunt. X

After a short detour to the compound to get changed, I materialise outside of Theo's house; not wanting to surprise Selena again. I don't know if compulsion would have any long-term effect on the baby. I open the door and follow the voices to the lounge.

"She's human, we can't use her as bait," Bel shouts.

"Bel, she's our only option. You want to catch him, don't you?" Theo argues back.

Jared, Jack, Wes, Ed, Misty, and Alyssa are all standing in the lounge looking at one another; probably hoping someone is brave enough to stop the alpha couple fighting.

"Looks like the honeymoon's over," I joke, hoping to ease the tension. Everyone turns to look at me in surprise; obviously not noticing me enter.

"The honeymoon hasn't even started yet," Bel grumbles.

Theo steps up to Bel and kisses her gently on the forehead. "The sooner we catch this bastard, the sooner we can go on our honeymoon."

Bel sighs. "She's my best friend. I don't want her to get hurt." She glances over his shoulder at Misty. "She isn't even blonde. How can she be bait when she doesn't fit his MO?"

"I can fix that," Misty says. She waves her hand over her head and mutters what must be an incantation, in seconds she's green eyed and blonde. She could almost pass as my twin. A collective "wow," goes around the room.

"I'm not completely helpless, I have a few tricks up my

sleeve and I'll be surrounded by all of you guys. Please, let me do this, Bel. Let me help stop this guy," Misty pleads.

Bel turns her attention to Theo. He wraps his arms around her. "Promise me you'll do everything you can to keep her safe."

He looks her straight in the eyes, unblinking. "I'll do everything I can."

"Okay," Bel says, as she steps out of Theo's arms and walks straight to Misty, stopping just in front of her. She tugs on a ringlet. "This is cute. If I'd known you could do that, I wouldn't have let Aunt Lil' torture me for hours yesterday," she says, referring to the time she spent getting her hair done for the wedding.

"It's not something I've practiced, and it's easier to do it on myself," Misty says, and shrugs.

"Just be careful tonight," Bel pleads. "It makes me nervous knowing we have to keep our numbers down, so as not to give him a heads up we're onto him. It means fewer people to protect you."

Misty gives Bel a friendly hug. "I will," she promises.

Following the lead that came from Dominick, we all gather in the alley he'd scented the rogue in last night. It was almost sunrise when Dominick caught the familiar scent, so we know he won't be far from here since the sun hasn't been down long. Misty walks down the alley purposefully, while we all sit back in the shadows hoping he takes the bait.

She passes a dark doorway and disappears with a blood-curdling scream. Forced into action, Dominick calls out to the vampire. "JD, you've been busy."

"I used to love hearing you call my name," JD says on a sigh. He steps out of the darkness with Misty in front of his body like a shield. He ducks his head and makes a show of licking at the blood trailing down her neck from the fresh puncture marks.

A growl echoes through the alley. I can't pinpoint which wolf it belongs to.

"Aww, you're no fun," he says releasing Misty and shoving her at Dominick. No doubt having caught our scents and realising he's surrounded.

The second I step out of my hiding spot I see the recognition on JD's face. "If only I'd thought of changing you. I could have been fucking you every day. Is it just like fucking Kathleen?" he questions Dominick.

Ed, Wes, and Theo all move to attack. "Fucker!"

I'm not certain, but I think the insult came from Ed. Wes reaches him first.

Seeing him coming, JD braces himself and punches his fist out, hitting Wes straight in the chest. Wes freezes on the spot and slowly drops his head to look down at his chest and the vampire's fist deep within it.

"Stop," he says, with a whimper as he gives Theo a dire look.

Everyone freezes and the alley turns eerily silent. You could probably hear a pin drop. I don't even think anyone is breathing. Even those that actually need to.

"Anyone moves and I'll rip his heart right out of his chest," JD warns. By the look of Wes' wince, he must be squeezing his heart in his fist to make a point. "I know you mutts can heal quickly, but I'm pretty sure you can't grow a new heart."

Theo's growl breaks our silence. "What do you want?"

"To let me go, of course. I've had my fun in your town torturing my old friend, and I guess it's time to move on."

The energy in the alley steps up a notch. I can feel the wolves' anger running along my skin, but theirs isn't the only energy I can feel. Dominick's vampire energy has a different feel to it because he sired me and I'm now part of his clan. His anger rushes through me, and makes my anger burn stronger. I feel my fangs elongate, making sure to part my lips, allowing room for them. I know from experience that it hurts when you forget and pierce your lips.

Feeling heat in my hands, I look down to see a ball of flame in each palm. It's the first time I've managed to control it like this. A fat lot of good it will do, I can't throw them without JD hurting Wes.

"You know we can't allow that to happen," Dominick proclaims.

"Dominick, think about it for a second. He has Wes, and he will kill him if we don't let him go. It doesn't look like we have much of a choice but to let him go," Bel counters, the panic clear in her voice.

"I can see that, but Wes is one life. If we agree to JD's terms how many innocent people will die?" Dominick asks adamantly. I understand what Dominick is saying, but it's *Wes*. We can't just let him die.

"But—"

Wes cuts Bel off. "He's right. Look after Alyssa. Don't let her lose the baby as well." Wes' courageous words spur everyone into action.

The vampire's arm pulls back.

Eddie and Jared both pounce for him.

"Go to Alyssa," Theo screams at Bel, before shifting in mid-jump for the vampire.

I drop the fireballs at my feet and dive forward catching Wes' body as he slumps to the ground. Patsy, one of the vampires, appears beside me as I bite at my wrist hoping my blood will be enough to heal him.

"Even our blood can't make his heart regrow." the sadness apparent in her voice.

"What about making him one of us?" I ask naively.

Dominick crouches beside me with a sobbing Misty tucked

into his side. "He'd need to have a spark of life for that, sweetheart."

The alley fills with the howling of Theo and Eddie.

Dominick, Misty, and Patsy stand slowly, stepping away from the body.

"Ruby, step away. Slowly," the command loud and clear in Dominick's voice.

"They won't hurt me. I'm Theo's sister," I say, with only half the confidence I would have had before I was a vampire.

"You are also a vampire. One of us just killed his beta. Theo isn't in charge. His wolf is. I wouldn't want to test his clarity right now." Dominick's warning tone tears my attention away from Wes' lifeless body.

I glance up to see Theo and Eddie stalking towards me, menacingly. Their fur is covered with a mixture of blood and ash from having slayed the vampire. Once a vampire has been ended their remains will turn to ash. There aren't many ways to end a vampire, fire or sunlight, decapitation, or a stake to the heart are the few things that work. Ripping the heart from the chest works just as well as a stake.

Realising Dominick may be right about Theo and Eddie, I move Wes' head out of my lap and place it gently on the ground. Not daring to reach up and wipe the tears from my eyes, any sudden movement could make them attack, I slowly back away from the body.

I watch as they start to lick at his wound. Understanding the dismissal, I gradually slip my phone out of my jeans pocket and call the only person I can think of that could help in this situation. He answers immediately.

"Where is he?" Cain asks, no doubt having felt the loss through the pack bonds, just as the rest of the pack will have.

"You need to bring a van, we're down Carver's Lane. Be quick. I'm not sure how safe the rest of us are." I glance at Jared, Dominick, Misty, Jack, and Patsy; who are all standing around quietly in the lane, trying not to catch the wolves' attention.

"Is Theo in control of his wolf?" Cain demands over the phone.

I consider his question as I watch the wolves with their pack mate. "I don't know," I answer honestly.

"He must be, you'd know if he wasn't." He hangs up after his words.

Looking away from the wolves at the others, I catch the moment Patsy teleports. "With more wolves coming we thought it would be safer if there were less of us," Dominick says.

I nod my agreement. "You should take Misty. Jared, Jack, maybe you should both go, too. I'll be fine with the wolves."

Glancing between the silently sobbing Misty and myself, Dominick nods, before whispering something in her ear and disappearing in front of me.

"I don't feel right leaving you," Jared admits. Jack soundlessly backs his way out of the alley, obviously not having the same fight with his conscience.

Eddie's rust-coloured wolf lifts his muzzle up and growls in Jared's direction. I can feel his annoyance through our mating bond. Probably annoyed that Jared thinks I'm not safe around my mate.

Jared backs away holding his hand up in surrender. "Okay mate, I'm going."

I hear howling in the distance before the sound of a van's engine reaches my ears. I stand for another minute until the van pulls up at the opening of the alley. Cain reverses to get the doors as close as he can. It's a narrow alley and the van is too wide to fit completely down it.

Turning off the engine, he jumps out. "What happened, Ruby?"

We both watch as Theo and Eddie howl to mourn the loss

of their pack brother, once they stop, they gaze in our direction.

"I'll watch him while you change, clothes are in the back," Cain says, pointing at the van over his shoulder.

They both pad over to the van and jump inside.

Knowing it will take a few minutes for the others to change and dress, I fill Cain in on what happened. By the time I finish and wipe at the fresh tears running down my cheeks, Theo and Eddie have both joined us.

"Come here, babe," Eddie says, and stretches his big, thick arms out and pulls me into his warm embrace. My body shivers at the temperature change from his body against mine. I snuggle against him tighter, needing him, needing his strength.

Ignoring us, Theo walks over to Wes and gently picks him up off the ground, cradling him in his arms and he places him in the van.

"Are you okay?" I ask Eddie as I lay my head against his chest.

"It's difficult to get a handle on my own pain when Alyssa's is being magnified through the pack bonds," he admits.

I can feel her anguish through our bond and my guilt bubbles over. Eddie pulls away from me, lifts my chin gently and stares at me, shaking his head. "No. This is not your fault. You know that. You just feel vulnerable right now but it is not your fault. Nobody thinks that way. Not even Alyssa," he says, right into my eyes. I feel it. But I don't want to believe it. I sigh as he wraps his arms around me tightly.

32

BROKEN HEARTED

Cain drives us to Theo's house. Theo choosing to spend the journey in the back of the van with Wes. The loss of such a good man is tearing everyone apart. I can't stop the steady stream of salty tears from escaping. I sit between Eddie and Cain, and sniffle the whole trip.

As soon as the door opens, I'm hit with a mass of emotions; fear, anger, sadness, terror, pain, so much pain, it causes me to cower away on instinct. I want to protect myself from that. Eddie gets out of the van and holds his hand up to help me down. It dawns on me that it is all Alyssa's emotions.

Is this what the guys have been feeling all along, through the bond?

I can't sit here ignoring it. I need to be there for her. Taking Eddie's hand, I jump out. We only manage a couple of steps across the gravel when the front door bursts opens and Alyssa comes running down the steps with Jared and Bel on her heels.

"I need to see him," she screams hysterically, bounding off the steps and onto the gravel before Jared catches her arm, pulling her to a halt.

"Alyssa, please. You don't need to see," Jared pleads, wrapping her in his strong arms.

"He's right, Lis. At least let Theo clean him up," Bel begs, coming to a stop beside them.

Cain walks round the back of the van and lets Theo out.

"I need to, Bel. I can feel it, but I need to see it. Please don't stop me." She stops struggling, but there's no stopping the tears rolling down her cheeks. I quickly wipe at my own tears.

Jared loosens his hold, allowing her to go. "We're all here for you, okay? You aren't alone."

She gives him a small grateful smile. "Thank you."

Steeling herself, she takes a breath and slowly makes her way to the back of the van. To the broken body of her mate. Jared follows a few steps behind, keeping the promise he just made.

From the side view of the van I have, I see the exact moment she sees him and drops to her knees on the gravel with a wail.

"Wes..." she sobs uncontrollably.

Theo crouches down and helps her to her feet. She climbs into the van and out of my sight.

Giving her some privacy I turn my attention to a weak-looking Bel. "Are you okay?"

She grimaces. "Too many emotions," she says, referring to her empathy. Seeing her knees give way, Eddie reaches out and catches her before she drops to the floor.

"Jesus, Bel. You need to get away from all this," he says.

"I can't, she needs us."

"You're no good to her like this," I say gently. "Let Eddie take you inside. I'll stay here with the others to make sure she's okay."

Bel gives a curt nod and Eddie guides her inside. I don't think she had much left in her to argue.

I turn back to see what the others are up to and find Cain taking sure strides in my direction. "I hear a congratulation is in order, Ed finally listened to his wolf."

My lips turn up into a smile for a second before I remember what happened tonight. "Thanks, but it's not really the right time to be celebrating."

Cain pulls me into a hug. "It's not every day you mate with a wolf. You're allowed to be happy." He gives me one last squeeze and heads into the house.

Alyssa emerges from the van and falls into Jared's open arms. "What am I going to do without him?"

"You're going to be strong for that little baby you're carrying. You're going to live a long life, so the part of Wes that is in you and in that baby can stay on this earth," Jared commands, while rubbing her back soothingly.

"I don't want a baby without Wes. I can't do this alone," she cries into his chest.

"You won't be alone, sweetheart. You have the pack, and you have me, too. I might not be a wolf but being taken by the Controller together a few months back, I look at you, Theo, and Paddy as a part of my pride. That's why I haven't left to go home to the rest of my pride; despite the incessant phone calls from my father."

She lifts her head from his chest to look at him. "So you're staying for a while?"

He nods. "Sure, I'll stay for as long as you need." They both head toward me as Theo joins them.

I walk to the house ahead of them and hold the door open so they can follow me in. Alyssa pauses at the door and grips at her chest, before backing away from the door and almost stumbling down the steps. Theo's grip stops her from falling.

"I can't go in there," she says, pain clear in her voice as she stares at the open door.

Theo turns Alyssa's body so she's no longer facing the house; I quickly step back outside and close the door. "Okay. You don't have to go in there." He sounds like he's trying to calm a wild animal. Just as the thought crosses my mind, I catch sight of her skin rippling along her arms. He is attempting to calm a wild animal. She's pregnant she can't change or she'll lose the baby. "Tell me why, and we'll sort something out?"

"I can't deal with the pain you're all feeling. He's my mate. I can't share the grief with you. He's *mine*. I...I just..." she suddenly stops making sense. Her skin rippling even more erratically.

"Alyssa, you can't shift. Do you hear me? You shift and you'll lose the one part of Wes you have left," Theo's commanding tone does nothing to stop her skin from moving. "Where do you want to go? I'll take you anywhere."

"It hurts so much. I don't want to live without him," she cries hysterically.

"Do you want me to take you somewhere?" I offer. Thinking that I'm not a wolf will mean she can't feel my pain.

She turns to face me with her wolf eyes, her face has even changed shape slightly along her nose and jaw. "You're pack. It's just the same," she mutters, with a shake of her head.

Jared steps up to her slowly. "I'm not pack or wolf. How about I take you somewhere?" He reaches his hand out and strokes the rippling skin on her forearm gently. I've seen the wolves try to comfort each other with touches like that over the years.

Her skin stops moving and she glances at him warily. "Your lion feels different to the wolves. It's comforting."

Glancing between the two of them, Theo nods his head as though he's come to a decision. "I'll be back in a minute." He moves past me and into the house, quickly opening and closing the door.

It's only a second later when he returns with a set of keys and a piece of paper. "This is a pack house, it's a small place but it's empty. You can stay there for as long as you need. Does that sound okay with you, Alyssa?"

She reaches out and takes the keys and piece of paper in

shaking hands. "Thank you," she says, her teary eyes trained on Theo.

"I wish I could do more for you." His sadness is evident in his voice.

She gives him a mournful smile before turning her attention on Jared. "Will you stay with me? Just for a little while?"

"I'll stay for as long as you need me." He reaches out and squeezes her shoulder gently before handing her his car keys. "Go let yourself in the car, I'll be there in a second." She gives him a nod before slowly walking down the steps to the car.

Waiting until she gets in the car and closes the door, he turns to Theo. "Are you okay with this? I don't want you to feel like I'm encroaching on your pack members."

"It's what she needs. Does it piss me off that I can't give her that? Hell yes! But I'm not going to let my ego get in the way of her healing. No matter how long it takes. Thank you, for offering to help her." Theo slaps Jared on the back, showing there are no hard feeling between them.

"There is one good thing that came out of the Controller taking us, and that's how close it made us. I don't think any alpha could invite another alpha into his territory, let alone his pack house for the length of time you've allowed me to stay. I have nothing but respect for you and I'll do anything I can to help Alyssa."

"You're right there! I don't think I can even handle Jesse staying in my territory for longer than forty-eight hours, and he's a werewolf alpha I actually trust," he says, peering at the house where the Rossi Pack Alpha is currently staying, after officiating his mating ceremony yesterday.

I can't believe it was only yesterday when we were all celebrating happily in the yard behind the house that's now full of sadness.

Theo suddenly turns his attention to me. "Rubes, if I give you the spare keys to Wes and Alyssa's, would you mind grabbing some clothes and things for Alyssa? Even though she said you're pack, with your mating bond being so new and not quite solidified yet, I think you're the best person to go."

"No worries," I reply, before turning my attention to Jared. "Do you want me to grab some of your things, too?"

"That would be great," he says, taking his eyes off a solemn Alyssa; who's staring blindly out the windscreen of the car for a second to give me a small smile. As his attention returns to Alyssa, he speaks again, "I best get her out of here."

Both Theo and I watch as Jared walks to the car, and gets in. It starts right away and he drives off down the long gravel driveway and out of sight.

Ted places his arm around my shoulders and leads me to the front door. "Let's go and comfort those we can. Ed is lucky to have you as a mate, that's going to give him comfort at least."

I stop with my hand on the door handle and look up at him with surprise. "You're not mad?"

"No. Don't get me wrong, I never wanted you to get with the *player* of the pack, but when he told me this morning, it explained everything. He was playing the *player* because he didn't think he deserved you. He wanted what was best for you and he thought that was Paddy. He's a fucking dickhead for thinking like that, but I can't be upset with him for wanting you to have what he thought was the best. No matter how wrong he was."

I throw my arms around his shoulders and squeeze him in a hug.

He laughs. "You might not need to breathe, Rubes, but I do."

I quickly let him go. "Sorry," I apologise bashfully.

"Don't be, kiddo, I'm just glad you're still here."

He opens the door and gestures for me to enter. The wall of sadness that hits me wipes the smile off my face, but it can't touch the small place in my heart filled with happiness from my brother loving me and being happy that I'm mated to a wolf in his pack.

My wolf.

My soul mate.

He was right there—under my nose, all along.

HE END

RECLAIMING THE ONE

MOUNT ROXBY SERIES: BOOK THREE

AIMIE JENNISON

DEDICATION

This story is for anyone who feels like they've let *The One* get away.

1.

INVITATION HOME

*L*eaving Ruby outside with Theo, Alyssa, and Jared, I enter the house.

Shock hits me to feel such an intense wave of emotion coming from the pack members. I don't know why I'm surprised. Wes was Theo's beta. He was well loved. Of course, the pack are going to be cut up about his death and are going to feel the loss for a long time.

Theo's been on edge ever since I turned up. He doesn't need to be stressing about the past while he's got this hole in his pack to worry about. I came home to see what happened to my little sister, Ruby. She's safe, happy, and mated to a wolf, who I have a hell of a lot of respect for.

Nothing is keeping me here anymore.

Selena's name runs through my mind, but I push it back into the crevice it had been hiding in. I ruined her life a long time ago. When I saw her the day I arrived, she seemed like she was in a good place, looking to the future with her soon-to-be-born baby. I'm not going to spoil that. The best thing for everyone is for me to pack my bag and leave, again.

I make my way upstairs and throw my stuff together. It doesn't take me long because I didn't bring much with me. I'm a metre away from the front door when it pops open. Theo waves Ruby in before him and closes the door.

I can pinpoint the exact moment the wall of sadness hits them: Ruby loses her smile, and Theo takes a deep breath and looks around. Probably looking for someone to comfort. That's when he spots me and my bag. Anger radiates from him.

"My office, now!" he orders, before marching off in the direction of his office.

I'm suddenly transported back in time to when Theo and I had been ordered into Dad's office as kids. We were always getting in trouble. Being as thick as thieves then, we'd both claim to be the one at fault. Dad would then punish us both, saying, "You both deserve it. One of you is lying and one of you did it." Sometimes he'd punish us for nothing, apparently to *"make us stronger."* He was a prick like that. It backfired on him in the end because it did make us stronger. Strong enough to kill him and take over the pack.

Theo is standing with his back to me as I walk in the room. He's staring out the window overlooking the backyard. I close the door and stand in silence watching him, wondering what he's thinking. What he's going to say.

"Were you going to say goodbye? Or were you going to leave another gaping hole? Do you not think the pack has lost enough tonight?" He sounds calm and collected, but I can tell by the fisted hands at his sides that he's pissed.

I join him at the window and sigh as I take in the view of the forest, remembering what it was like to run in those trees. The freedom I could find in there. "I didn't think you needed to be reminded of the past when you have enough of the present to worry about," I say honestly.

He sharply turns his head to look at me. His silence pushes me to say more.

"I know you hate me for what I did, and to be honest, I don't blame you. I don't expect you to forgive me," I admit.

"What is it with my siblings thinking I hate them? I must be one nasty bastard. I don't hate you, Cain. I never did." He rubs at his brows with his fingertips. "You hurt me. You slept with my wife and then you went AWOL. You pissed me off, but you're my brother. I'd never be able to hate you." He sighs. "I fucking love you, you moron," he declares. Catching me off guard, he manages to pull me into a headlock and knuckle my hair.

"Jesus, Theo, what are you? Fucking ten?" We both laugh, and for a second, I forget about the hand the pack was dealt tonight; forget the loss we all feel. We both fall silent, looking to the backyard once again, remembering tonight's events.

"Please stay, Cain. I need a beta who isn't so emotionally affected by the loss of Wes. Someone who can help glue the pack together while they come to terms with it. I need you, Cain."

I glance across at him not believing those words came from his mouth. "What about Ed or Billy? They're both dominant enough to be your beta. Ed seems stronger now he's mated. I haven't been around the pack for over a year. They'll never accept me as their beta."

I left Mount Roxby and became a lone wolf after being caught in bed with Selena, Theo's wife, knowing I wouldn't be accepted as part of the pack any longer. I roamed the country, drifting from pack to pack until I happened to find a mother and child being held captive by a nasty alpha. I managed to help them escape and keep them out of his clutches by moving on when his goons got close. After nine months of being one step ahead of the bad guys, she finally had enough of life on the run and told me who she really was, and I was able to reunite her with her mate, the alpha of the Rossi Pack.

"I'm not the only one who missed you when you left. I think you'll be surprised how many of them will be happy to have you back," he says, as he walks to his desk and pulls out a bottle of whisky and two short glasses. "I know things between the two of us are strained." He pours two glasses and hands me one. "But I trust you with the pack. It's your pack as much as it is mine."

Shock ripples through me at his words, and I down the liquid fire before I speak. "After everything I've done, you still feel like that?"

"I don't know why you did what you did, but I know it wasn't out of malice. That isn't you, never was." He grabs the bottle and tops up our glasses again.

"I need to tell you everything that lead to me sleeping with Selena, and if you still want me to be your beta after that, I'll do it."

He takes a seat on the sofa at the side of the room, places the whisky bottle by his feet, and gestures for me to join him. "Now's as good a time as any."

So I sit down and tell him everything, starting at the very beginning. The day *she* came into my life.

2.

DELECTABLE HONEYSUCKLE

CAIN - EIGHT YEARS AGO

I'm forever running errands for dad's mate, Margie. I hate the woman, and she's made it perfectly clear that the feeling is mutual. I walk out of the corner store with a carton of eggs in my hand when I smell the most alluring scent: honeysuckle. It invades my nostrils and makes my wolf try to jump out of my skin, wanting to roll himself in the delectable fragrance.

I pause in the doorway as I rein in the wolf and look for the female the scent belongs to, knowing she has to be my true mate. No other scent would affect my wolf this way. Excitement rolls through me at the notion. Some wolves can go a lifetime and never find their true mate; and here I am finding mine at the age of nineteen.

My eyes fall on the most beautiful female I've ever laid eyes on. Long dark-blonde hair with golden highlights flows over her shoulders and chest, covering the ample cleavage her low-cut top would be otherwise showing.

The carton of eggs slip through my fingers and I don't even glance down to see them smash on the pavement. I can't take my eyes off the beauty.

At the noise, she glances up from the ground where she'd been focusing as she walked. Her ice-blue eyes lock on mine and she gives me a shy smile.

I smile back, trying not to show the predator I am. Knowing it's my wolf's eyes that are showing, I pull out my shades and slip them over my eyes, hoping she doesn't catch them as he slinks back into his hiding place and they change back to my human eyes. Luckily, my cobalt eyes aren't too different a shade to my wolf's lighter blue ones. I know plenty of people whose eyes are completely different to their wolves'.

"You've made a right mess there, butterfingers." Her silky-smooth voice flows over me. I'm grateful for the shades as my wolf peers out, excited by her voice, yet a little insulted by the nickname.

I take a breath and ground myself, pushing the wolf back once again. I crouch down and try to clear up the mess as best I can, picking up the egg shells and placing them in the soggy carton. "Something caught my eye," I say, unable to think up a witty response with her scent surrounding me.

"I'll get a bucket of water to swill the pavement down. My dad won't be happy if we leave a mess right in the doorway of his shop." She disappears past me and into the building.

I glance in after her and catch sight of an Under New Management sign hanging on the door. I momentarily wonder what happened to Mr Thorpe, but the sight of my blonde beauty heading back towards me with a bucket in one hand and a plastic bag in the other, shoos any thoughts of Mr Thorpe right out of my head. She thrusts the bag in my direction, and I take it, ensuring my fingers brush hers. The contact makes me shiver, and my wolf lets out a content sigh. *Mate.*

"Are you going to step back or do you want the water over you, too?"

Her irritated tone makes me snap out of my trance. What the hell? It's like she's had a personality transplant in the time it took her to get a bucket of water. I stand up while placing the soggy carton containing the broken eggshells into the bag and then see my beauty's arm straining with the weight of the bucket. *That's why she snapped, unaware dick.*

I quickly reach out, taking the bucket's handle. "Here, let me do it. It's my mess after all," I offer, trying to tug the bucket out of her grasp.

She lets go with a shrug. "Give me the bag and I'll stick in the bin." She wiggles her empty hand at me.

Realising I'll be able to direct the water better with two hands, I pass the rubbish over to her. She disappears into the shop once again and I pour the water over the mess of my broken eggs.

Noticing one bucket of water isn't going to be enough to wash away the mess, I head into the shop to look for my beauty or the new manager, her father. "Hello," I call out as I make my way to the counter.

The small balding man, who served me not long ago, pops out a door behind the counter that must lead to a small staff room or office. "Hi, how can I help you?" I hold the bucket up and open my mouth to ask for more water, but recognition crosses his face and he doesn't let me get a word out. "Oh, you're the butterfingers Selena was complaining about. Did one bucket do the job or do you need more water?"

I glance from the bucket to the man before my mouth decides to engage. "It's going to need more water I'm afraid." *Selena.* He called my beauty Selena.

He takes the bucket and goes back through the door shouting over his shoulder, "Grab yourself another carton of eggs while I get us some more water." I stare after him, wondering where Selena's disappeared to and why she hasn't come back, until his words register. My errand for Margie is the reason I came here. If I return without her eggs, I'd be in a world of pain. She's the alpha's mate. My father's mate. If I don't return with her eggs, she'll say I was disobeying an order and demand I be punished for my disobedience. She's an evil bitch. I don't know what my father see's in her.

I walk to the aisle where the eggs are kept and open a carton, making sure to check for cracks and running my hand across them to check they're mobile. If they're stuck to the carton, they're likely to have a crack on the base of them. My mum taught me that before my father tore me away from her and my home.

"That's a neat trick to check for cracks," Selena's soft voice says from behind me.

I jump, clutching the eggs to my chest. The last thing we need is another mess of smashed eggs. How the hell had she crept up on me? My instincts wouldn't normally let that happen. Meeting her has thrown my wolf and me. "Jesus, where did you come from?"

She grins at me, and my heart skips a beat at the sight. I need to see her do that again. Hell, every day. "I didn't realise I looked like a man." She pouts, causing me to open and close my mouth, no doubt doing an awesome impression of a damn goldfish. She laughs, the sound sending shivers down my spine. Good shivers. "Don't hyperventilate. I was only joking. I'm Selena," she says, offering her hand.

I loosen the death grip I have on the eggs and take her hand in my free one. "Cain. Nice to meet you, Selena."

She gives my hand a firm shake and a small voice speaks from behind her. "I'm Maximus. Good to meet you."

I release Selena's hand as she steps aside, giving me a clear view of a boy who can't be much older than seven or eight. His blond mop of hair falling in his ice-blue eyes and his hand held out in my direction, just as Selena's had done a moment ago.

I clear my throat and straighten my shoulders as I take his hand. "It's nice to meet you too, Maximus." His face brightens with an enormous smile and an excited blush travels his cheeks. I release his hand and he looks at his sister as though he has no idea what to do next.

Selena opens her mouth to speak, but before anything escapes, the sound of splashing water takes our attention away from our moment. We all turn and head for the sound of water.

"I would have done that, sir," I say at the same time as Selena speaks.

"Dad. You shouldn't be doing that." She turns her eyes on me, giving me an icy glare. "Why didn't you ask me to refill it? Dad shouldn't be lifting anything."

"I'm sorry, I—" I start before her father cuts me off.

"Let the boy off. He wasn't to know. It's not like I have a sign hanging around my neck—" He swings his arms across his neck. "—saying 'don't let me lift a thing,'" he finishes as he walks through the door and back into the shop, causing us all to stop suddenly, so we don't crash into him.

Selena sighs and gives me an apologetic smile. "He's right. I'm sorry, Cain." Hearing my name roll off her tongue renders me speechless. The only response I can give her is a nod.

"Daddy…!" Maximus shouts as he runs into his father, wrapping his arms around his waist, effectively breaking the tension that had risen in the room.

"Hi, Maxie, did you have fun at Jimmy's this afternoon?" their father asks as he leads Max back towards the counter, leaving Selena and me standing in the doorway.

I glance at the eggs in my hand and back towards the counter. "I guess I should go and pay for these."

Selena shakes her head, making her long waves move across her chest drawing my eyes to her cleavage. "No, Dad won't charge you for them. They were broken on our property."

I glance out the door where I had dropped the eggs. "It was my fault and I was out the door. I should pay," I insist wide-eyed, knowing the eggs were all intact when I left the store.

"It will be a waste of your time and breath arguing with my

dad, but go ahead and give it a try," she offers with a wave of her hand in her father's direction.

I bite my lip wondering what to do. She obviously knows her father best, and if she says he won't take any money from me, she's probably right.

"Okay." I pull my wallet out and hand her a five-dollar note. "Here. Will you slip that into the till for me later?"

A broad smile crosses her face, making her eyes light up, and I feel like giving her all the notes in my wallet. "I can do that. Thank you."

"No worries, beautiful." The compliment slips out before I can stop it. I feel my cheeks heat up.

She drops her eyes to her feet as her face flushes. I want nothing more than to pull her into my arms and kiss her to make her blush more.

Walking home from the store, I can't wipe the smile off my face. I've found my true mate.

3

EXPLAINING THE PAST

My eyes come back into focus, the memories of the past fading back to where they belong—in the deep recesses of my mind.

Theo's eyes connect with mine, a frown creasing his brow. "Why didn't you ever tell me? I fucking married her." He runs a hand through his hair. "I married my brother's mate." The pain in his eyes infuriates me. This shouldn't be hurting him. I'm the one who's been separated from my mate for the last eight years.

"Fuck, Theo. Do you not think I wanted to?" Grabbing the bottle at Theo's feet, I fill both our glasses with the amber liquid. "I wanted to tell everyone. To scream it from the fucking rooftops." I take a sip as I pull my anger back. It's not Theo I'm mad at. "That day, when I got back, I'd barely stepped foot in the door when Dad decided I needed to go out of town on pack business. I tried to tell him, but you know Dad, he wouldn't listen to a nineteen-year-old. I was a kid."

"What about when you got back?" Theo runs his finger around the rim of his glass. "I would have listened."

I place my empty glass on the floor at my feet and settle back on the sofa. "By the time I got back into town, you'd been dating her for two months. You were happier than I'd ever seen you. I couldn't take that away from you. Neither of us had been happy since Dad took us away from Mum and Ruby. You'd been away from them longer than I had. You deserved that happiness."

"She is your fucking true mate, Cain. My happiness should never have come into it." The growl in his voice isn't backed up by anger in his wolf's energy.

I shrug. "What can I say? I'm a dick." My words elicit a short laugh from Theo. "It killed me to watch you two together. My wolf wanted to tear you apart. That's why I could never hunt with the pack. I couldn't trust him around you." I rub a hand over my chest, trying to ease the ache that's been there for the last eight years. "I've been torn in two ever since that fucking day."

Theo leans forward on the sofa, placing his head in his hands. "And I just thought you were a moody bastard. I guess that's why you left the pack?" I nod, even though I know he won't see me. "It kind of all makes sense now." He turns to me and places a hand on my knee. "You should have told me. When I found Bel, I knew she was my true mate, but I wasn't able to claim her for a few weeks. So I can only just begin to imagine how hard it must have been for you all those years."

"I fought the attraction as much as I could. Fuck, I dated Chloe on and off over the years, but she knew I would never commit and she started to resent me for it. My wolf just got more and more restless," I say with a sigh, remembering how he felt at the time. Not that he feels any different now. He's constantly pacing inside me, waiting for my defences to drop just enough for him to escape.

"But you slept with her in the end? How the hell did you walk away after that?" Theo asks, clearly curious... and sadly mistaken if he thinks that's the first time I'd slept with her.

"The time you caught us wasn't the only time I slept with her," I admit. The wounded look on his face makes guilt surge through me. "Believe me, I hate myself for that. More than you could imagine."

He nods. "Well then, I guess you should tell me the rest of your story."

Getting to my feet, I pace to the window and look at the forest before taking a deep breath and telling him the rest.

4

SORROW AND PAIN

CAIN - SEVEN YEARS AGO

A year has passed since I first met Selena. I've been successful in avoiding being alone with her, even for a minute, because I know that the first time I do, I won't be able to keep my mouth off hers. I've spent the last twelve months obsessing over how she'll taste and how her soft curves will feel under my hands.

The phone rings in its cradle on the counter, and I pick it up as I flick the switch on the kettle. I was meant to be making coffee. "Wilson residence."

"Mr Wilson?" a grandmotherly voice asks.

"Yes," I answer, even though I know she could easily be after Theo or our dad.

"I'm a nurse at Mount Roxby hospital. I have a Selena Graham here. She has you down as an emergency contact." She pauses, and my breath hitches in my chest. Selena's in the hospital? But before I can say anything aloud, the nurse speaks again. "Now, don't worry. She only has a few superficial cuts and bruises. Unfortunately, I can't say the same for her father and brother. They didn't make it. As you can imagine, she's not handling it very well. We had to sedate her, and I thought it might be good for a familiar face to be here when she wakes up."

I glance at the clock on the wall, my heart racing in my

chest. "I can be there in fifteen minutes. Will she be awake before then?"

"Don't rush. She'll be out for at least another hour. We don't need another accident on the road." She hangs up and I blindly place the phone back in its cradle. My mind races. Selena's lost her brother and father. Theo is all she has left. *Shit!* Theo. He's out of town.

Pulling my mobile out of my pocket, I quickly dial his number.

"Cain. The house is still standing, right?" I can hear the smile in his voice. Every time I call when he's out of town, he answers asking the same thing. He'll never let me forget the time I set fire to the kitchen when Dad left us both in charge.

"Theo, I just had the hospital on the phone. Selena's been in an accident." I rub my sweaty palms on my jeans, swapping the phone from one hand to the other. "She's uninjured," I go on, hoping to ease any panic he may be feeling. "But her father and brother didn't make it. They've sedated her and want a familiar face to be there when she wakes up. They said she'll be out for another hour." I hop from one foot to the other, eager to end this call and make my way to the hospital. I need to see Selena. I need to see she's safe.

"Fuck!" I hear something crunch in the background, leaving me thinking he's punched something, most probably a wall. "There's no way I can get home in time. Even if I manage to get on the next flight, it's a four-hour trip, and that's providing I don't have a stopover in Adelaide or Melbourne. She doesn't really have any friends I can call to go, and none of the pack girls like her."

"I'll go," I offer, planning on going anyway. Nothing's going to stop me.

"Thanks, bro. Take care of her until I get there. I'll text you my flight details as soon as I know them." He hangs up and I stare at the phone for a minute before slipping it back in my pocket and making my way to my car, not bothering to lock the door behind me. It's the pack house, and there's always someone coming and going. It's pointless locking a door when werewolves with supernatural strength are involved. Handles break too easily.

The nurse leads me through the ward and stops in front of a blue door. "Selena's in here." She glances down at her watch. "I'll be back before she wakes up. You've got time to go grab a coffee if you like?"

I shake my head. "No. I'd like to sit with her if that's okay?"

"Of course, dear. She's a lucky girl to have a partner like you." She gives me a smile and dashes off towards the nurses' station before I can correct her.

I stare at the door and can't help but think all my avoidance techniques will have been for nothing the second I set foot into the room beyond. Reaching out, I open the door. I pause in the doorway as I'm overwhelmed by Selena's honeysuckle scent.

The sight of her laid out on the bed has me moving, and I'm standing beside her in a second. I stroke her long locks with my hand. "My beauty…," I whisper as I allow my eyes to roam over her, checking for injuries. She has a cut on her forehead and another on her right cheekbone.

She lets out a small moan and my hand freezes on her head, not wanting to be the cause of any pain. "Shh… you're okay, Selena." I try to comfort her, not knowing if she can hear me.

Her eyes flicker open and shut again. "C…" She clears her throat. "Cain?"

"Yes. It's me, beautiful." The term of endearment leaves my mouth without even thinking about it. "Theo's trying to get a flight back from Perth. I'll stay with you until he gets back, if that's okay?"

"Dad? Maxie?" Her question hangs in the air, leaving me to wonder how the hell to break the news. Her eyes pop open and lock onto mine before she lets out a scream, no doubt seeing the answer in my eyes.

"I'm sorry…. We're going to look after you," I state, referring to my wolf and I, before quickly correcting myself. "Theo will look after you, okay? You won't be alone."

She falls into silent sobs, and sitting on the edge of the bed, I gently pull her into my arms, making sure not to hurt any injuries I can't see.

The door opens and the same nurse from earlier walks in. She lets out a surprised noise. "Oh, Miss Graham, you're awake. How are we feeling?"

Selena's sobs become louder as she cries into my chest.

"She's a little upset." I state the obvious.

"Understandably so," the nurse says, before walking over and holding a piece of paper out towards me. I reach for it with the hand that had been stroking large circles on Selena's back. "Selena's discharge papers," she explains.

"She doesn't need to stay… be observed?" I ask, disliking the idea of her not being near medical help if she may need it. The pack has our own doctors and nurses, but they specialise in weres, not humans. And Selena knows nothing about the pack or werewolves.

"She's been thoroughly checked over and has no injuries that require observation."

My wolf growls at the thought of her being checked over. Nobody but us should be checking her over. I quickly remind him that she's Theo's, not ours. In my mind's eye, he bares his teeth at me in a snarl, not happy with that prospect either.

Selena lifts her head and looks up at me with her red-rimmed eyes. "I can't go home. I don't want to be there without them…. I… I…."

I squeeze her gently. "It's okay, beautiful. I'll take you to my home."

The gratitude in her teary eyes cuts into me. "Thank you."

The drive home is quiet, but I hold her hand in mine the whole way, indicators be damned.

Once in the house, I lead her into the lounge as I call out. "Anyone home?" Receiving no reply and knowing any werewolf who may be here would have heard me regardless of what room they may be in, I come to the conclusion that we're home alone.

I focus my attention to Selena. "Here, beautiful. Sit down." I guide her down onto the sofa. Her dazed expression has me worried the doctors may have missed a concussion or something.

Leaving her on the sofa, I head into the kitchen to make her a hot chocolate. My phone vibrates in my pocket and I quickly pull it out. The caller ID telling me who it is. "Theo. When will you be in?"

"I won't be landing until four in the morning. By the time I make it through the traffic, it will be close to six when I get in. How's she doing?"

Opening the door, I peek out and see Selena staring into space, exactly where I'd left her. "She's... honestly, I have no idea. She seems overwhelmed and spaced out. I'm just making her a hot chocolate. I figure the sugar might help with the shock." I go back to mixing the hot chocolate.

"Thanks for looking out for her, Cain. What would I do without you?"

Guilt surges through me at his words. He'd be so much better off with me away from them both, because sooner or later, if I don't tear him to shreds, I'll be ravaging her. Damn the consequences.

"I'm sure you'd manage just fine. Hell, you'd be safer

without me ar—" I pause midsentence, realising I've spoken aloud and said too much.

"What the fuck do you mean by that?" The anger in Theo's voice is clear as a bell down the line.

"I'm going to have to go. Selena's crying," I lie, knowing he won't sense it over the phone.

He huffs. "I'm not going to forget about this. We'll pick this up later." He hangs up, and I know Theo well enough to believe what he says. I'll have to have the conversation with him eventually. Hopefully he'll be distracted with Selena long enough for me to come up with something that he won't sniff out as bullshit.

Grabbing the two mugs off the side, I head back into the lounge. I place a mug on the coffee table and crouch before Selena with the other. "Selena?" Placing a hand on her knee, I squeeze it gently, hoping to catch her attention more since my words got nothing. "Selena, I've got a hot chocolate for you here."

Her eyes drop down to the cup I'm holding and then up to my eyes, slowly seeming to focus. She smiles and my heart skips a beat. "Thanks." She reaches out with both hands and takes the mug from my one-handed hold.

I begrudgingly remove my hand from her knee and grab my mug off the coffee table as I take a seat beside her. "Do you want me to turn the TV on?" I reach for the remote in anticipation of her answer, not at all liking the silence between us. It makes me want to tell her things. Things I should never tell her.

I catch sight of her head shaking. "No, I can't bear to watch happy families at the minute." I pull my hand back without picking up the remote and sip my hot chocolate. I watch out the corner of my eye as Selena blows gently over hers.

"Tell me something… anything. Anything that will distract

me from thinking about…." She doesn't need to say the words. I know she means her family.

My wolf jumps forward wanting to comfort her. "I fell in love with you the first time I laid eyes on you." The words fall out of my mouth, catching me by surprise and her too, if her sharp turn of the head, wide eyes, and slack jaw are anything to go by.

I never meant to tell her that. *Ever.* She's fucking grieving. I can't say shit like that. "I shouldn't have said that. I'm sorry."

"Did you mean it?" She drops her eyes to the floor as her face flushes before flicking them back to me. "Did you mean what you just said, or is it some lame attempt at making me feel better?"

My mind races as I berate my wolf for coming to the surface and pushing me into breaking like that. Seeing the vulnerability in her eyes, I can't lie. Taking a deep breath to ground myself, I open my mouth and tell her the truth. "Every word."

I smile nervously, hoping she can see the truth in my eyes, the same truth I feel bone deep. "That day outside the shop, I saw the most beautiful woman on earth. You stole my heart and made me drop a carton of eggs." She giggles and the sound caresses my skin, causing goosebumps to rise on my arms. "I swear. I knew you were the one. Unfortunately, Theo stole your heart before I got the chance to." I shrug and take a long sip out of the mug in my hand in an effort to shut myself up.

She places her hand on top of mine. "I didn't know, Cain. Is… is that why you're always avoiding me?" She swallows and glances at her feet. "I thought you hated me."

Before I realise what I'm doing, my hand is running up her neck and her hair is falling through my fingers. "Never. I could never hate you."

My eyes lock onto her mouth, and I find myself inches away from her. Selena's tongue flicks out leaving a slight wetness behind, and I'm a goner. My lips crash onto hers, my tongue teasing at their seam. She parts her lips and I take that as an invitation. The sweet taste of hot chocolate and her honey-suckle scent explodes on my tongue.

I blindly place my mug on the table, wanting to run both my hands in her hair. My hands move to frame her face, her soft skin beneath my fingertips perfect.

She shifts, not breaking the kiss, and I hear a clunk as her mug connects with the table a second before her hands roam up my chest and lock around my neck. My wolf has practically melted, content to finally have our mate in our hands. Only she isn't our mate.

She's Theo's.

I break the kiss, jumping off the sofa and across the room, aiming to get some distance between us. "Shit! I'm sorry. You're my brother's girlfriend." I tug at my hair with my hands. "I shouldn't have done that." I pace in front of the French windows as I look out to the forest surrounding the house. I need to run. I should get as far away from her as possible.

Her hand on my back causes me to jump. I'd been so lost in my own head I hadn't even heard her move. "Cain. Please don't run."

Her choice of words has me turning. "Run?" I ask. Surely, she couldn't have meant—

She takes my hand in hers. "You look like you want to bolt. Please sit down again." Her pleading eyes have me moving towards the sofa and sitting down. "You're right. I'm with Theo and it's not fair to do this behind his back. I love him." Her words break my heart, but hearing the truth in them shatters it into a million pieces. A million pieces that will never be made into a whole again.

I nod, struggling to get words past the lump in my throat. "Let's put the TV on. Maybe we can find a good action movie or something."

Selena reaches for the remote and clicks through the TV channels, stopping on the first one that shows a screen full of explosions. A car crashes on screen and she flinches beside me before clearing her throat. "I think I'm going to go to bed. Will Theo mind if I sleep in his room?" She shuffles forward on the couch, readying herself to stand.

"Of course not." I grab the remote and turn off the TV. "I could do with an early night too. I'll show you up to his room." I run a hand through my hair as I stand, mentally berating myself at my idiotic offer—she's been dating him for over a year; she knows where his room is.

I hear the sofa crinkle as she stands. "Thanks."

I pause in front of Theo's room and open his door for her. "I'm just over there," I say, pointing to my door on the opposite wall up the hall. "If you need anything just give me a knock, okay?"

She smiles brightly and reaches out, taking the hand hanging at my side in hers. "Thank you for being there for me today, Cain. I appreciate it more than you'll know." She reaches up on her tiptoes to kiss me on the cheek. "When you meet 'the one' you're going to make her one happy girl." She drops my hand and walks into Theo's room, closing the door on me as I stare after her. I really hope she is a happy girl, or this last year of hell will have been for nothing.

The snick of my door opening rouses me from sleep. Sitting up, I tense, waiting to see if it's friend or foe. Selena's scent hits me and the tension in my body instantly floats away.

"Cain, are you awake?" she whispers, her voice barely audible.

"Yes. I'm awake." The shock of her arrival suddenly fades

and is replaced with worry as I wonder why she's coming to my room. "Are you okay?"

"Yes… no. Not really. Will you hold me? I feel so alone in there." Her voice breaks and I worry at my lip while considering her request. I'd love to hold her, but can I do it without taking it further? Without further murkying the water between us.

Taking a deep breath, I pat the bed beside me in invitation, forgetting that she can't see in the dark as well as I can. "Sure. Come and get in," I offer.

The door closes and I listen to her footsteps in the plush carpet as she makes her way towards me.

The bed dips and I hold the covers back as she slides in beside me. The T-shirt she's wearing goes down to her knees, and I know it must be Theo's. His scent wrapped around her helps me hold my wolf back. Yet another reminder that she isn't ours. *She's Theo's.*

Taking her into my arms, I pull her against me and settle down into the soft bed. Her breath becomes slow and steady, telling me she's drifted off to sleep.

I lie here, enjoying the feel of her body in my arms as the hours pass. I can't completely relax because I know if I do, my wolf may very well try to make the most of my unconscious state, and I can't allow that.

There's a loud crash on the stairs, and I gently release Selena, leaving her curled up in my bed as I head out of my room to see what's causing the noise. A glance at my watch tells me it's way too early to be Theo. It's only two in the morning.

I open the door and come face-to-face with my father. I see his nostrils flare as he takes in my half-dressed state. I'd gone to bed in just a pair of boxers and being a werewolf, you get used to being naked or half-naked around people. I'd not even considered pulling anything on when Selena had come in or just now when I'd gotten up.

"You fucker!" His fist flies at me, but I stop it in mine before it connects, his inebriated state having slowed his movements down. Some mean feat considering werewolves can't get drunk with alcohol. He's clearly had something. He's been known to get his hands on all kinds of drugs, ones that vets use on elephants. Even mixing the drugs together. He's always been a fucking dickhead, but since he lost his mate six months ago, he's been uncontrollable.

"It's not what you think, Dad." I shove him away from me as I pull the door behind me closed, not wanting him to disturb Selena. "You've got the wrong end of the fucking stick."

"She's been playing with your stick all right." His crude remark has him smirking. "It's okay, I won't tell Theo… as long as she gives my stick some attention too." He grabs at his crotch, emphasising his meaning

My fist flies at his vulgar display. The crunch as it connects with his jaw tells me something's broken. Pain surges through my hand, and I wonder if the crunch came from me or my father.

I glance at him on the floor as he shoves at his jaw, pushing it back into place with a grunt, unable to hide the pain. He gets to his feet slowly and steadily. The high he'd been riding will have been pushed away with the adrenaline now surging through him. My father glares at me in silence, his face turning red with anger as his energy pulses painfully against my skin.

My clenched fists shake at my sides. As much as I know I should never have attacked my father—my alpha—I can't help but feel I was in the right to do it. He's been a mess since Margie died, nothing but a burden on the pack. He shouldn't have said what he had about Selena, though. His own son's mate, or as good as. As these thoughts run through my mind, my back straightens and I lift my head, my eyes meeting his in a challenge.

"You better think long and hard for a second, Cain." His eyes bore into mine. "Back down now, because if you don't, I'll be forced to kill you and being my son won't save you from that. And that piece of skirt in there." He points to the door behind me. "She'll be fucking under me regardless of whether your brother takes her as a mate. I'm the alpha here." His lip turns up in a snarl. "Not him, and certainly not you."

I can see in his eyes he expects me to back down, but I can't. "You better go call in the pack. They all need to be here for an Alpha Duel." I stare him down until my eyes are stinging with the need to blink.

"So be it," he says, smirking as he pulls out his phone and walks away.

I head back into the bedroom and pace the room as my mind wanders. I have no fear for what tomorrow will bring. Tomorrow may be the end of my life, but I won't go out easily. I won't go out at all if I can help it.

It's been a long time since I last trained with Dad, just before he gave up training. *When you have a pack of werewolves to fight for you, what's the point in fighting for yourself?* He may even go into our duel tomorrow expecting one of his stronger wolves to stand in for him. Unfortunately, he's been a crap alpha lately, and I'm pretty sure he'll be sadly mistaken.

The only chance Dad has of beating me is if he draws on the power of the pack. Although he only has the ability to do that if the pack allows him to. I don't know if they would right now, so I could very well beat the old man tomorrow.

My wolf sits back, not caring about the fight ahead. It's going to happen and we can only deal with it at the time. There's no point worrying about it now. Liking this logic, I walk over to the bed and lay down beside Selena once again. I breathe in her scent knowing this will most likely be the last time I'll have her this close to me again.

———

The door clicks open and I jump up, alert, and ready to protect Selena from any advances my father may make. Unless he's here to kill me in my sleep having come to the conclusion he may actually have a tough fight on his hands when the duel comes.

The intruder's scent hits me and the tension leaves my body instantly. *Theo.*

"Hey. How's she doing?" He acknowledges Selena with a nod in her direction.

"She's…" I glance in her direction, memorising the sight of her on my bed. "She'll be glad you're back." I grab a pair of sweats off the chair by the wall and pull them on. "Go hug your girl. I'm done sleeping."

I consider telling him about Dad and the duel, but I can see his worry for Selena etched in the crease of his frown as he stares at her. I don't want to add to his stress or take away his attention from her. She needs him. Besides, there's nothing he can do to stop the duel.

5

ALPHA DUEL

CAIN - STILL SEVEN YEARS AGO

Theo catches me in the kitchen after lunch, finally having exited my bedroom and leaving Selena to shower. He claps a hand on my shoulder. "What have you done?" I start at the pressure of his hand, before he releases me. "Hey, I know it's something serious. I can feel it. The pack's energy through the bonds is beyond crazy, and yours isn't much better." He rubs at his forearms, no doubt rubbing my excess energy away as it brushes against his skin.

I hand him a coffee and pour another for myself. "I challenged Dad. He's calling in the pack and we'll be having an Alpha Duel tonight." I risk a look, flicking my eyes to his and see nothing but anger in his eyes.

"It should be me," he snaps, as he drives his fist into the countertop.

"You don't even know why I did it," I argue.

He takes a moment to sip his coffee, and I watch his eyes flicking from wolf to human as he pushes his wolf down. "It doesn't matter why. I should have done it a long time ago. He's been nothing but be a burden since Margie died."

Hearing his admission causes something deep inside me to settle. I know I'm doing the right thing, but hearing it from my big brother cements it inside me that little bit more.

"I can stand in for you. Challenge him myself," Theo offers.

"*No!* Don't you dare." I take a mouthful of coffee while I think carefully about my next words. "You take Selena away from here for a couple of hours. If I don't walk away from this, I don't want her to have to deal with the extra death on top of her family. Tell her… I've gone away." The thought of not making it causes my voice to break.

Theo pulls me into his arms, and I feel stupid hugging my brother. We're both fucking adults and we're hugging like babies. "I'm your big brother. I shouldn't let you do this."

I pull back and lock onto his eyes. "I need to do this for myself. I can't have you stand in for me. Promise me, Theo, look after that beautiful girl of yours."

He lets out a sigh, and after a moment's hesitation, he nods. "Fine. But you better beat the miserable old bastard." We break away, going back to our coffees.

I settle my arse against the countertop behind me. "I'll give it my all," I say, knowing I can't promise anything more.

"That's all I can ask." He weighs me up for minute, obviously thinking something over before nodding. "You'll make a good alpha if you do win."

I flinch, taken aback by his words. I wouldn't be alpha. I'd never take the pack. "No, Theo." I shake my head. "*You* would be a far better alpha than me, so I'd be handing the pack over to you." Winning an Alpha Duel would mean I'm entitled to the role of alpha, but Theo's older than me and far more deserving of the position. Not to mention he would be able to handle the stress of running a pack much easier than I would.

Theo's eyes widen, evidently surprised at my admission. "You mean that. I…." He releases a breath and gives me a heartwarming smile. "Thank you. It means a lot knowing you have so much faith in me."

Selena's scent fills the air a few seconds before she walks into sight behind Theo, effectively ending our conversation.

She wraps her arms around his waist, slipping by his side as Theo lifts his arm for her.

"Morning." She gives me a shy smile. "Thanks for last night."

"It was noth—"

She looks at me with a raised brow. "It *wasn't* nothing. Not to me," she snaps, cutting me off.

"Okay. Well… you're welcome then." I give Theo a pleading look and he quickly places a kiss on her temple.

"Dad's having a little get together later with some unsavoury characters." Theo throws me a wink she can't see. "I don't want them around you. So I was thinking, is there somewhere you'd like to go?"

"Actually, I'd like to go home. I don't know if I can stay there, but I will definitely need to pick some things up." She looks up at him with a solemn stare.

"Of course. Home it is." It's not like he'd deny her anything, let alone when she's looking at him like that. "I've just got to track Dad down to let him know our plans. He won't be happy we're leaving, but I honestly don't care what he thinks." He gives me one last look before walking out the room. Not knowing what the look was about, I grab a mug down and offer Selena a coffee.

"Yes, please. About last night… I…."

I shake my head. I really don't want to think about last night. I don't need thoughts of our kiss running through my mind. Not when I'm about to fight for my life. "Don't worry about last ni—"

She raises her voice over mine. "I heard you fighting with your dad. I didn't hear everything or even understand half of what I did hear, but I did hear what he said about me. Thank you for having my back. I know it must have caused trouble for you."

My face breaks into a smile. This beautiful woman always surprises me. "I'll always have your back. You're as good as my sister-in-law now." I throw her a wink and then almost bolt out of the room as I fight my wolf against releasing a growl. He did not like that statement one bit. I channel my anger, pushing it into my centre and hoping to hold onto it for later.

I glance at my watch for the fiftieth time—Nine fifteen. The pack started to arrive at seven in the evening, and they're still trickling in now.

My wolf has been pacing since my parting words to Selena at lunchtime. He isn't a patient soul, especially having to sit back and watch Theo with Selena most days.

Having her so close to me last night may have been a big mistake.

Unfortunately, I don't have the time to worry about that. I need to focus on the fight before me. *An Alpha Duel.*

Once my watch reads quarter to ten, I make my way to the clearing in the middle of the bush that surrounds the house. The fight is set for ten o'clock. Being tardy wouldn't really be an issue; it's not like there's any punishment he can give me. After all, he's going to try and kill me anyway.

As I walk through the last line of trees, all eyes fall upon me. It's hard to gauge in the bonds how everyone is feeling about our duel, but going by the occasional flat smile and nodding of heads I get as I pass, some of my pack mates must be happy with it. Let's just hope they'll get the outcome they want. I head to the centre and take off my shirt, throwing it to the ground as I wait for my opponent.

Chloe strides out of the crowd and stops before me. "Good luck, Cain." She lowers her voice to a whisper, obviously in the hope I'm the only one who can hear her next words. "The pack has needed a shake-up like this for a while."

I nod in agreement, and thank her for the luck she'd

offered. After giving me a quick peck on the cheek, she walks back to the crowd as Billy and Wes take her place beside me.

Wes claps a hand on my shoulder. "I don't know what provoked you to do this, but it's the right thing for the pack. You'll be a young alpha, but you have it in you to be a great one."

I let out a laugh. "I have to beat him first, Wes."

Billy looks at me with a raised brow. "You're a lot fitter than he is. You train every spare minute you get. I haven't seen your father train in years."

Pack members around us stir and we turn to see Dad strut through the parted crowd. A couple of the older wolves pat him on the back as he passes, offering him good wishes. It surprises me not more members follow with the action. I guess that in itself tells me just how much of the pack are wanting me to win today. He stops before us.

Billy and Wes both make a move to join the spectators, but Dad calls out. "Wes, we need a referee. I would've liked Theo to have the job but unfortunately, he's otherwise engaged." He looks at Wes with a raised brow. "Are you up for it?"

Wes's back stiffens at the request. "Of course. Are we ready?" he asks, looking between the two of us.

I grunt in answer.

"Let's get this over with," Dad says. There's no empathy in his voice. If he wins, he'll be killing his youngest son, and he doesn't seem to give a toss. *Bastard.*

Wes takes a moment to clear his throat before acknowledging the crowd. "Thank you for your patience tonight. We've been called here to play witness to an Alpha Duel. Cain Wilson has challenged the current alpha, his father, Marcus Wilson." He turns his attention to me. "Does the challenge still stand?"

"Yes." My words come out confident and clear. No one would know I'm worried about not making it through this fight. I've had duels before, but there's something in the air tonight. Some underlying current that makes me feel that this isn't anything like those regular duels.

The crowd stirs at my words and Wes turns his attention back to them. "Does anyone contest this duel?" Usually this line gives someone else the opportunity to fight me first. Either in hopes to weaken me for the fight with my real opponent or if not, kill me before I even get to fight my intended opponent. Most duels are to the death, but one can submit anytime during the fight if they wish to. That isn't the case in an Alpha Duel. This is to the death.

Everyone stands stock still. Even those that had wished Dad luck on his way in.

Dad stands taller than he had been before Wes's question, not showing any disappointment. Maybe he's happy to be fighting for himself.

"Marcus, will you be fighting as human or wolf?" Wes asks his voice bellows.

I tense as I wait for my dad's answer. It's well known that fighting in human form is more technical, and the winner would usually be more worthy of the win. Fighting in wolf form is dangerous, a stray claw caught in the wrong place could mean a quick death. It could go either way, and that seems too risky for my liking. I'd much rather a longer fight knowing I have the stamina to outlast my dad as well as the fighting skills to outmanoeuvre him.

"Wolf." That one word causes the crowd to go wild, because that means it will most likely be a bloody fight, and we are bloodthirsty creatures after all.

Wes gives me a worried glance. I guess we'd both been hoping Dad's answer would've been different.

I channel my wolf, allowing him to come to the forefront as I strip out of my remaining clothes. I can see my father already in his wolf form as I crouch down to all fours and feel my wolf take over my body completely.

Dad will have pulled on the powers of the pack to make his change instant, not even bothering to remove his clothes first.

I clench my teeth through the pain, not wanting to whimper and allow my father to consider it a weakness. After shaking off the last tingles of the change paw by paw, I look across to Wes.

"Ready?" he asks, turning from me to my father, trying to gauge how we may be feeling. He wouldn't be able to feel through the pack as clearly as an alpha would—it's usually the alpha who referees a duel for that reason.

We both snarl and turn to face each other.

"May the best man win," Wes announces as he steps back to the line of the crowd.

Dad pounces as soon as the words leave Wes's mouth, not giving me a chance to think about my movements.

I jump back out of reach and circle behind him. I'm not allowing him to win with a lucky shot. Everyone knows it's why he chose to fight in wolf form. I'll make him work for it.

He spins to face me, obviously not wanting me at his back, and snarls. His anger causes my fur to rise, but I don't let it distract me.

Pouncing on him and aiming for his neck, I end up with a mouthful of ear as he drops his head. His yelp of pain spurs me on to tear at it until it comes free, and I drop the piece of flesh to the ground.

He recovers quickly and throws out an identical manoeuvre.

Seeing it coming, I drop to my stomach, protecting my neck from his teeth, and then twist as he lands on top of me. My change in position throws him off target, and he scrambles for purchase as I flip onto my back and slide out from under him, ripping at his stomach with my claws as I go. Straightening up onto all fours, I jump back to get away from him in case he tries to attack.

I focus on my enemy to find him wavering on unsteady legs, blood dripping from underneath him, my claws having caused more damage than I'd thought. He howls, striking out for me sluggishly, seemingly using his last remnants of strength. I pounce sideways, hoping to get away before he hits. My side is suddenly searing in pain as his sharp teeth sink into my flesh. I bite back a whimper not wanting to give my opponent the confidence to keep fighting. His teeth connect with my ribs, and I brace myself, knowing he'll snap them to clear the way to my organs.

An excruciating burning sensation rolls over me, and I can't hold in the yelp this time. His jaws release me and I stumble back in a fog of pain, wanting to get as far away as possible, to give my head time to clear enough for me to focus on my next move.

I circle around him as he spins with me, not taking his eyes off me. I feign a lunge for his side. My teeth make contact, sinking into his throat. Coppery blood fills my mouth; his artery is pumping out his blood faster than he can heal. He slackens beneath me and I drop him to the ground, finally relaxing in the knowledge that I've won.

Wes appears before me, hands stretched out, showing he means me no harm. It throws me for a second. *I know he wouldn't hurt me, so why gesture?*

Hearing a fierce snarling, I glance around the crowd to look for the wolf it belongs to, only to find the pack members on their knees with their heads dropped in submission—every single one of them.

I suddenly realise it's me who's snarling. I immediately rein in my wolf, persuading him to retreat as I shift back to my human form, which comes easier than usual. It still hurts, but it takes a fraction of the time, quite unusual when you counter in the fact that I'm injured, which would usually slow the process down even more. I shake the thought off along with the tingles running over my skin from the change and turn to Wes, who's now bent over my dad.

"Is he…?" I start to ask as I reach through the bonds to feel for my father. He's no longer there. Just an empty space where he used to be.

Wes turns at my words, staying low to the ground in submission. "I pledge my loyalty to you, Cain Wilson. The new Alpha of the Mount Roxby Pack."

With his words, something stirs through the pack bonds. They alter as each pack member around me mutters the same words, and I suddenly become the centre of the pack, filling the space my father had vacated.

"I, Cain Wilson, live to protect the Mount Roxby Pack and its members." The words leave my mouth before I can even register them. In the silence that follows, I wonder if I've done the right thing. Theo should be alpha. He's older, wiser, not to mention stronger.

Theo's not here, my wolf reminds me, and I understand why he jumped in and claimed the pack, taking the choice out of my hands.

The pack needs an alpha in this moment, and I'm the rightful one to fill the hole.

6

SIN BEFORE MARRIAGE

CAIN - SIX YEARS AGO

A year after fighting my father and handing the pack over to Theo, it's the eve of his wedding, and I find myself in the worst place I could possibly be—standing before his blushing bride-to-be in an empty house.

"Where is everyone?" I glance behind Selena at the large open-space living area, hoping to see someone, yet knowing I won't because I can only feel her energy. Meaning we're the only two people in the house. "I thought some of the girls were staying over?"

She laughs whilst walking over to the sofa. "I told Alyssa to go to Wes. You know what those two are like, forever on each other's minds." She pulls a blanket over her lap as she settles herself into her spot. "Chloe had a date." Selena glances at me and winces. "I'm sorry. I know you two have been on and off lately. I...."

I shake my head. "Hey, it's fine. We were never anything serious." Telling her the only woman I've ever wanted to be serious about is her, is on the tip of my tongue, but I swallow it down.

The tension leaves her shoulders and she pats the spot next to her in invitation. "So, we've discovered why I'm a loner. What about you? Why aren't you at the hotel boozing it up with Theo?" She turns her body to face me, giving me her undivided attention.

Unsure what to say, I bide my time, glancing around the room at the TV. Seeing Ian Somerhalder on the screen, I know she's watching her favourite show, *The Vampire Diaries*, and missing it since it's on mute. "Hey, you're missing sexy Damon. I'm certainly not as interesting as him."

Her laugh sends chills over my body. "Damon may be mighty sexy, but I care about you and why you're not having fun like you should be," she says, as she playfully nudges me with her blanket-covered foot.

To be honest, I don't really know why I came. I just needed to be here. I open my mouth to tell her as much when something completely different comes out. "I need to show you something."

I look to the door sharply, expecting to see someone there speaking instead of myself. The words register in my mind and I instantly know why I came tonight. She has no idea about the existence of werewolves, yet by this time tomorrow, she'll be tied to one for the rest of her life. Married to Theo, an alpha werewolf. The danger that brings her way… she deserves to know it beforehand.

"This sounds serious." The concern in her voice has me kicking myself before I've even started. What if I scare her and she runs away from Theo? She doesn't have anyone but us.

I debate internally on how to tell her. Where to start. Deciding against an immediate show and tell, I take a deep breath and jump in at the deep end.

"Have you ever noticed anything strange about us? Theo, me, some of our friends?"

She frowns, her cute little nose crinkling slightly as she thinks about my question. "Not that I can think of. There are a lot of you and you're all really close. But… nothing strange. No."

"I don't know how to tell you this." I rub the back of my neck with a hand. "Jesus, who'd have thought this would be so hard?" I joke before trying a new tact, having gotten an idea from her favourite show flicking across the TV screen. "Have you ever wondered where those stories come from?" I point to the screen which now has a werewolf character on it, front and centre. "Werewolves and vampires," I clarify.

Her brow creases once again, and I can see the deep thought on her face. "Well, I guess some people have good imaginations?" She ends the sentence high as though it's a question.

"What if I tell you they aren't just some creative peoples' made-up story? What if I tell you they're real?" I stare at her intently, wishing for her to believe me.

Her eyes widen in surprise. "If you weren't the most serious person I've ever met, I'd be worried you're playing some kind of trick on me. But you don't do pranks." She's right in the fact that I don't do pranks, not since meeting and losing her anyway. She takes a deep breath and levels me with a soul-searching stare. "Let's say I believe you. I guess they could exist. Why is that so important on the night before my wedding?"

After taking a quick, grounding breath, I blurt it out. "You're marrying one, Selena. Theo's a werewolf. We all are."

She scoots back on the sofa, giving me as much distance as she possibly can. Her fear is palpable against my skin.

"Please don't be scared. You've known us for a long time and we haven't harmed you," I beg, my heart hurting at the thought of scaring her.

"I'm not scared of you, Cain. I'm scared that the only people I care about in the world have lied to me for the last two years." The sadness in her voice cuts me in two, and I suddenly think I'd rather her be scared of me.

I reach out, taking her hand in mine, not bothering to slow my supernatural movement now the cat's out of the bag. "Selena… please don't hate me. Or at least don't hate Theo for it." I snatch my hand back, angry at myself. It shouldn't matter if she hates me, but it does. She picks up my hand and gives it a reassuring squeeze. "Our existence is a big secret. We're ordered by our alphas to never tell anyone."

"Alphas?" she asks tentatively.

"An alpha is the leader, the boss of the wolf pack, or family. He keeps the pack members in line, making sure nobody endangers the pack or humans." I greedily take in her features with my eyes, trying to gauge how well she's following.

"Are you all related? The pack." The word rolls off her tongue without confidence, like she's unsure of the word.

I shake my head, no. "We're made up of lots of different families. Like a tight-knit community."

She nods her acceptance, and before I can carry on, she asks another question. "So, if Theo couldn't tell me because of his alpha's order, how come you can?"

I'd wondered how long it would take her to get to the tricky questions. I stand up and start to pace the room, taking the moment of silence to think my words over before I speak them. "There's a loophole, so to speak. Do you believe in soul mates?" I stop my pacing and pin her with a stare, needing to see the truth in her answer.

She swallows and nods. "Yes, I did, but now I'm wondering if I was being a fool."

"Every wolf has a mate who belongs to them. Their true mate. Some wolves are lucky enough to grow up with their mate knowing them for their whole lives. Others find them somewhere down the track." I take a calming breath before speaking my next words. "Unfortunately, that means there are the unlucky ones who never find them, too. There comes a time in a wolf's life when he needs to decide whether he should persevere to find his true mate or to choose a suitable mate for himself." I catch sight of Selena watching me intently as I pace. "Theo decided to choose you over searching."

Her gasp of hurt causes me to want to slap myself. I should have handled that better. Of course, she thought she was his mate. "I'm not…."

"No, I'm sorry." I run my hands through my hair and tug at it, trying to free my frustration.

Her hand rests on top of mine, and she eases the grip I have on my hair. "Don't harm yourself, Cain. I know you didn't mean to upset me."

The fact that my words caused her pain, hurts me so much more than any tugging on my hair could have done. If only I could show her that. *We can.* My wolf's words run through my head, and I contemplate them for a second. *What good would telling her do?*

If I say the words out loud, claim her out loud, it will only cause pain for me and most probably her too.

She'll know she's someone's mate. She'll know she is so much more than unimportant.

I frame her face in my hands and beg, "Tell me you feel it."

"Feel it?" Her furrowed brow tells me it's all one-sided.

Needing to spell it out, I go on. "The attraction between us. Tell me you fucking feel it too." My wolf paces inside me, waiting for her answer, lacking his usual confidence in the matter.

She smiles, but it doesn't reach her eyes, causing my heart to plummet. She's going to let me down. "Of course, I feel it." Her sadness is palpable. "Ever since that first day we met. But… I'm with Theo, and I…."

I search her eyes and finish the sentence for her. "Love him." We sigh in unison. "I love him too. That's why I've never claimed you, even though I know you're my true mate."

Her eyes widen in surprise. "Your true mate?" She whispers so quietly I can only just hear it, even with my supernatural hearing. "Me?" she asks a little louder.

"Yes." A weight seems to lift off my shoulders as I say the

word. I can breathe again, having finally spilt the beans. I've been so weighed down hiding my secret and I hadn't even realised, until now. I point to the couch. "Shall we sit again? I guess I have a lot to explain."

She nods, and we both take our seats. Selena shuffles back into the corner once again to face me better.

Taking a calming breath, I go on. "That first day I saw you, I knew you were meant for me. Your scent does things to me." I inhale, breathing her scent in, allowing my eyes to close as a smile crosses my face, not at all conscious of showing her the reaction I'm talking about. "I left that day with a plan to come back in the morning and woo you."

Selena frowns. "But you didn't."

I sigh. "No, I didn't. When I got home, Dad sent me to do business with another pack. I arrived back to find Theo had a new girlfriend. *You.*" I let out a sad laugh as I look at my fisted hands. "My mate was no longer mine to claim." I can't help but be mad at my father for sending me away at such a pivotal moment in my life. If only he'd listened to me that night, my life could be so different now.

Selena's hand brushes mine. My eyes come back to watch her flatten my fists as she takes my hands in hers, pulling them into her lap and shuffling closer towards me. "Cain, I don't understand the whole werewolf and true mate thing but, if the pain and sadness I can see in your face and body are anything to go by, I know it's taken a lot for you to live like this. Why didn't you tell me or Theo earlier?"

I turn her hand over in mine and trace her lifeline with my index finger. "Because Theo was happy. For the first time that I could remember, he was fucking happy. He made you happy too. I couldn't take that away from you both." I slide my hand up her arm and edge closer to her on the sofa. "I wish I could be selfish and take you. Claim you. But I can't. It's too late for that now." I feel my wolf at the surface. He wants to claim her regardless of the consequences.

Selena's widening eyes tell me she can see him in my eyes before the change in my eyesight registers with me. "You're not Cain," she states, surprising me by not cowering from us as I'd imagined she would if she ever saw my wolf.

"No." Selena flinches at the change in my voice as my wolf talks to her. "I won't hurt you," he says. Both of us wait on tender hooks to see how she'll react.

Her shy smile and relaxing posture go a long way to calm both my wolf and me down. I find myself leaning closer to her as her tongue pokes out and licks her bottom lip. Still in control, my wolf takes advantage of this moment, taking her mouth with mine in a fierce kiss. She melts into me willingly as my wolf slips back into his hiding place, handing me control of myself once again. Addicted to the taste of her honeysuckle scent, I take as much as she is willing to give me. It's been such a long time since I've tasted her lips, it invigorates me. I feel like I haven't been living all this time I haven't been tasting her. Selena's hand roaming up my chest spurs me on, and I sink my hands in to her hair as I pull her closer towards me. There's no turning back now. Not for me. I need to have my fill while I can.

Selena pulls back, breaking our kiss and I let her go—this isn't a good idea anyway. It will only lead to pain and heartbreak for us all. She reaches her hand down to her waist and pulls the tie on her silk robe, revealing her hourglass figure and erasing any thoughts I had of ending this.

I brush my hands over her shoulder as I push her robe off, leaving it to drop to the sofa. "You're absolutely stunning." She looks even more magnificent than I'd imagined in all of my fantasies.

A blush runs across her face, but she doesn't try to cover up. She kneels on the sofa before me, allowing me to take her in with my eyes. I trail my hand down over her chest and caress a circle around her nipple.

"Your touch feels so good." She tilts her head back and closes her eyes, seemingly basking in the feel of my touch. "It's almost like electricity running over my skin." She's feeling the mate connection between us as I touch her.

Part of me knows I should stop my ministrations and explain it to her, but I also know if I do, I would never start again. Leaning forward, I take the pink bud into my mouth as I allow my finger to trace circles around the other one. The needy moan that leaves her throat tells me I did the right thing. I lower her back so she's lying on the sofa without breaking the seal between my mouth and her breast. She opens her legs to give me room between them, and my attention shifts to her other nipple.

Her hands roam over my shoulders. "Take it off, Cain." She tugs at my cotton tee. "Please. I need to feel your skin."

Needing to give her exactly what she wants, I grab the material at the back of my neck and I pull it over my head, throwing it across the room as she runs her hands over my chest and abs. My wolf growls his appreciation. Her wide eyes tell me I allowed the sound to escape my mouth, and I give her a sheepish smile before crushing my mouth against hers whilst her hands make quick work of my button-up jeans.

7

TOO MUCH INFORMATION

CAIN - PRESENT DAY

"Fucking hell, Cain. I don't need to hear the gory details." Theo's voice pulls me back to the present. "I may be married to someone else now, but I don't need to hear the ins and outs of you cheating with my ex-wife the night before our wedding." He shakes his head as though to jiggle away the thoughts.

Sometime during my story, I'd perched on the edge of Theo's desk. I glance down at the ball of rubber bands I've been nervously rolling between my fingers. "Sorry, I didn't think about TMI. I just wanted to tell you everything at last."

Theo releases a short sigh. "Well, one mystery is solved at last." I frown at him, unsure what mystery he's talking about. "I know why we suddenly had a new sofa after the wedding. What the hell did you do with the old one?"

I laugh at the memory of that night and the realisation of the task before me—in keeping our betrayal a secret. After the night's events, if a wolf had walked into the house, they would've smelt what we'd been up to. Selena's scent and mine would be mixed together along with the tell-tale scent of sex. It was all over the sofa. "After…" I pause. Knowing he doesn't want to hear the details, I hold back on spelling the situation out. "Selena told me that it changed nothing. She loved you with everything she had and wanted to marry you the next day." My heart aches at the memory, even with the time that has passed. "She didn't want anyone to find out, so I had to do everything I could to make sure it stayed between us. That meant the sofa had to go."

"Is that why you didn't turn up for your best man duties?" Theo asks. His sadness fills the room, becoming so thick in the air it feels like I'm choking. I cough, trying to once again breathe.

The guilt that runs through me reminds me of my reasons for missing my brother's wedding. "I couldn't face you, and to be honest, I didn't know if my wolf would sit back and allow the wedding to go ahead if I were there. I needed to stay away for everyone's sake." I rub a hand over my face, trying to wipe away the tiredness that I've been collecting over the years. I've never fully been able to drop the guilt I've been carrying.

Theo's arms wrap around me in a hug. "It's okay, little brother. You don't need to feel guilty anymore," he says, having clearly sensed it through the pack bonds. I give him a quick pat on the back and he pulls away. "I can't believe Selena has known about us all this time and just played along pretending she didn't." He shakes his head in disbelief. "Why didn't she tell me? There were so many times she could have used it as ammo against me. Especially towards the end when we constantly argued."

"Most probably because I told her how dangerous it was for her to know." Thinking back on it, maybe I shouldn't have told her. If she'd used that ammo in the heat of an argument like Theo had suggested, she could have been killed.

Just the thought has my wolf on edge, has him wanting to break free and fight off anyone who may harm our mate. I close my eyes and take a deep breath.

Theo's hand rests on my shoulder, his energy giving me the power to push my wolf back.

"Thank you," I say, opening my eyes and locking them with his.

He drops his hand from my shoulder. "You've been a lone wolf for far too long. I think you need us as much as we need you." He pours us both another drink.

Taking the glass, I swirl the drink around as I contemplate his words. "So, you still want me to stay?"

"Of course, I do. Hell, I want you to stay more than I did before you started talking." He laughs. "Who would have thought, telling me about how you slept with my wife could have such a happy outcome?" I laugh along with him. It is kind of crazy when you put it that way. "The only issue now is how are you going to claim your mate?"

I shake my head in disbelief at how this is all turning out. "Selena's a runner. She isn't going to welcome me with open arms." I sigh. It's going to take time. But if I'm taking Theo up on his offer, I'll have plenty of time and we'll be under the same roof, so there'll be plenty of opportunities to win her trust.

I guess I owe thanks to Theo and Bel for not slamming the door in her face when she turned up on their doorstep, pregnant and homeless. From what I've heard, she'd returned hoping he would take her back and be willing to raise another man's child. Which knowing Theo and the fact he's always wanted to start a family, he would have done just that… if he hadn't already found Bel.

Theo spins his glass in his hand, his eyes pinned to the amber liquid swirling around it. "How do you feel about the bringing up another man's baby?"

Lifting my eyes, I lock them on his, hoping he can see my certainty. "A stranger may have brought the baby into existence, but it will be mine and my mate's baby in all the ways that matter.

Theo downs his drink and pats me on the back. "Drink up.

We've got a grieving pack to deal with, and you've got a woman's heart to win."

With a smile, I salute him with my glass before downing it. As I grab my bag from the floor, I revel in the settled feeling that flows through me. I have a pack. I instantly realise Theo was right: I've been a lone wolf for far too long.

8.

CAT'S DON'T LIKE BAGS

SELENA

I stop in my tracks as I face my biggest mistake. To this day, my heart and head can't decide whether the mistake was sleeping with him or letting him go.

I've been avoiding him since he first arrived back in town. The day I came face-to-face with him after all this time… my God, I felt like running for the hills. Most of me still feels like running, but that little piece of me, the tiny bit that thinks letting him go was the mistake, keeps me here. Well that, and the life growing inside me. I need to stay here for him or her. I've got friends and support here in Mount Roxby. Even if they did come from a failed marriage. As soon as I'm able to work and get some money behind me, I'll find my own place. I'm just grateful that Theo and his new wife, Bel, are willing to let me stay under their roof for the time being. I'm not sure I'd be as understanding if I were in their shoes.

"Selena." My name rolling off his tongue makes my legs turn to jelly. I've missed him saying my name.

"Cain," I breathe his name. It's barely a whisper but I know he'll hear it with his wolf's hearing. He's the only one who knows I'm aware of their secret. After all, he told it to me years ago, but he also told me we'd both be in danger if anyone found out. So I never let on that I knew, not even after I was married to Theo.

Cain's eyes drop to the hand resting on my growing stomach. "How far along are you?"

I look down at the bump in question and stroke it lovingly. I've found myself doing it more and more as it's grown. "Seven months. I already look like a beached whale. I dread to think how I'll look nearer my due date."

"You couldn't look anything but beautiful." The words seem to leave his mouth before he realises what he's saying. He clears his throat and drops his eyes to his feet.

My eyes follow his. Spotting the bag at his feet, my heart sinks. *He's leaving again?*

"No. Not anymore." His answer has me snapping my eyes back to his. I register I must have said the question out loud. "I'm needed here. Wes…." He doesn't finish the sentence, but I was here when it happened. Wes has been killed and somehow, they all knew without even receiving a phone call. It was as if they were psychic. Obviously, it has to be a wolf thing, and it's not like I couldn't question it. In fact, I have a feeling they've forgotten I'm still here.

But Cain knows.

"So, he is… dead." I struggle to say the word. The last time I had to think about that word, I'd lost my baby brother and father.

The grim look on his face is answer enough, but he still gives me a quick nod.

"I'm sorry. He was…." Glancing around, I spot people looking at us, clearly eavesdropping, and I let my sentence fade off. I don't want to say anything that could alert them to me knowing their secret.

"Pack. Yes. He was beta, which is a huge part of the pack. Theo's…." The horror must show on my face because he reaches out and takes my arm as my legs wobble threatening to give way. I've kept this secret for so long. Now he's going to get us both killed. He pulls me towards the window seat. "Sit down before you fall down. Then tell me what made you look so terrified."

I glance around the large formal dining room again and notice one of the guys glaring at Cain. "You said…" I lower my voice. "Pack."

"Oh." He laughs. "That cats out the bag now, beautiful. I've just spent the last hour telling Theo everything."

My eyes well with tears. "Everything?" I repeat, as dread fills me. He's in a world of trouble and it's all my fault.

He crouches before me and brushes away a tear as his hands frame my face. "Don't look so worried. Everything is going to be fine. No one will be upset with you. Okay?" He clearly has the wrong end of the stick. I'm not worried about me.

I pin him with a stern look. "It's not me I'm worried about. What's going to happen to you?" I bite my lip in concern, part of me not wanting to hear his answer.

"I told you a long time ago, I was the only person who *could* tell you. You're my true mate, and whether I've claimed you or not, I'm allowed to tell you." He pops my lip from between my teeth with his forefinger. "So, stop chewing on that poor lip."

I lift my hands and wipe at my eyes, feeling marginally better. "He'll hate me. Oh God… the night before the wedding. And I've lied all this time, pretending not to know." I hide my face in my hands as thoughts of Theo kicking me out of his home and running me out of town run through my mind.

"I don't hate you, Selena. In fact, it helps me forgive you." Theo's voice has me peeking out from between my fingers. He's crouched before me where Cain had been only moments ago.

"Really?" I ask. Seeing him smiling at me genuinely helps me relax. I slowly drop my hands from my face.

"Yes. I understand why you and Cain did what you did. Neither of you had a choice in the matter. You were meant for each other. It's as simple as that."

Meant for each other. Is it really that easy? If we were meant for each other, wouldn't we be together now? The thought makes my heart ache.

Part of me wants to look around for Cain, to see if Theo's words hurt him as much as they do me, but I don't. Instead, I give Theo a smile that I'm not really feeling. "Thank you."

Looking in his emerald eyes makes me remember how much I loved him. He is the one person who made me believe the saying "one's eyes are the window to one's soul." His eyes say so much.

"I did love you… so much. I hope you don't question that." I feel the need to make him understand. I wipe a tear from my eye and look away. Seeing a number of people looking at us, my stomach sinks as I'm suddenly aware we aren't the only ones in the room. *How could I have forgotten?*

"I don't, Lena." The nickname he used to call me has me snapping my attention back to him. He really doesn't hate me. "You wouldn't have stuck around if you didn't love me."

I give him a genuine smile as a weight I didn't realise I was carrying lifts from my shoulders.

Feeling freer than I have for as long as I can remember, I glance around the room, and for the first time tonight, I really see the people here. See the solemn expressions on everyone's faces. And I realise it doesn't take a werewolf to feel the sadness in the room. The loss of Wes has hit everyone hard. "How's Alyssa?" I ask, knowing what the answer will be before the words leave my mouth.

Theo sighs as he stands and then sits beside me in the window seat. "She's a mess. She can't bear to be near any of us. It just makes her miss him more."

I nod, conscious of what it's like to grieve someone. "She needs to deal with her own grief before she can deal with all of yours."

"How did you know that?" The surprise I hear in the high pitch of his voice has me turning to look at him.

I shrug. "My dad went through the same thing when we lost Mum. It was a hard couple of years."

He nods. "Of course. I'm sorry."

I place my hand on his forearm. He always seemed to be comforted by touch. "It was a long time ago." A throat clears, and I glance up to see Bel step up beside Theo, causing me to remove my hand quickly. I don't want her to get the wrong idea. I give her a quick smile before speaking again. "If Alyssa can't handle being around the pack, she's not going to be able to go home. Where will she be staying?"

"As much as that statement has me wanting to ask a number of questions, the main one being the fact that Selena seems to know about the pack, I'm going to let that slide because I want to know the answer to Selena's question more." Bel prods Theo in the arm. "But you better fill me in later."

Theo pulls Bel into his lap, enticing a laugh from her. Watching them like this, I can't help but think they really are made for each other.

"I wouldn't dream of keeping you out of the loop," he says, giving her a quick peck on the cheek before turning his attention back to me. "I've sent her to a safe house. It's one we haven't used before, so there will be no wolf scents inside."

"Is she on her own?" Bel asks frantically. "She shouldn't be on her own."

Theo rubs a hand down Bel's bicep. "Hey. You know I wouldn't leave her alone. Jared's with her. He's going to stay for as long as she needs." Bel relaxes in Theo's arms and hearing his words, I relax too. Having lived in the same house as Jared for a while now, I know Alyssa will be well looked after. He's a protector, not unlike Theo.

"I'd like to go and visit her. Maybe give her another shoulder if she needs one." Theo looks at me with distant eyes, making me think he must be weighing up my plan. "We were close once, and I'm not part of the pack."

He nods. "You might be right. Give me your phone and I'll put the address in."

I glance around, feeling somewhat stupid. "I don't have a phone." Theo and Bel glance at each other, both frowning. "I don't have anyone to keep in contact with." I swallow and lower my voice, feeling vulnerable and somewhat ashamed. "I don't have any friends."

"Here." A phone is held out across me, towards Theo. "Put it in mine. I'll take her," Cain says as Theo takes the phone and starts tapping at the screen. Cain's fingers brush my shoulder and I look up.

"I'm perfectly fine getting myself there if you have things to do." I glance around the room at the people filling it. The room has a sorrowful feel to it, although people are chatting whilst giving small touches here and there—comforting each other.

"I'm sorry, Selena, but I don't think you'll get that bump behind the steering wheel." Theo's words have me snapping my attention his way. He might as well have said I was a beached whale. Although, he's right. The last time I drove it wasn't exactly comfortable being squeezed behind the wheel, not that I'll let him know that.

Bel smacks him in the chest. "I can't believe you just said that." She turns to me, a blush on her cheeks as she smiles, obviously embarrassed by her husband's comment. "Don't listen to him, Selena. He can be so insensitive sometimes."

Cain holds his hand out to me. "Shall we?" Taking his hand, I use everything I have not to groan as I stand. I may feel and look like a beached whale, but I don't need someone else to point it out. I do have some dignity.

We barely make it two steps before we're stopped by Frankie and Jesse. From what I've read between the lines, they're from Western Australia. I'm assuming another pack, since Jesse has the same intense feeling that Theo and Cain both give off. Frankie is different. She has a warmth to her the others don't. Not even the women in Theo's pack. Frankie had been missing, and somehow Cain ended up finding her. She's timid around everyone except Cain, even her husband, Jesse. I can't help but feel jealous of the connection she has with Cain. *Have they slept together?* It's irrational; it's not as if Cain's mine. Hell, I'm his brother's ex-wife. I have no right at all to be turning all hulk over thoughts like that.

"Cain," Frankie says quietly as she edges forward towards his already open arms. It's like he knew she wanted a hug without her even suggesting it. Like I said, they have a unique connection.

"Hey, darling." Cain greets her as she settles in his arms, her head tucked nicely under his chin.

I watch her husband and can't help but wonder if he's feeling jealous, too. The tightness of his jaw and clenching of his fists at his sides confirms my thoughts. Jesse closes his eyes and takes a deep breath. Upon opening them, he looks behind me, and I can only guess he's looking at Theo. With a sharp nod, he walks past me.

"We're leaving," Frankie says, lifting her chin to look up at Cain. "Theo needs to focus on the pack and I don't think he can, not with another alpha in his territory." She lets out a small sigh. "And to be honest, Jesse's struggling having me around all these wolves we don't know." She rests her head back on his chest and he gently rubs her back.

"I'm going to miss you and Angel. Give her a kiss from me." He smiles the sweetest smile as he talks about Angel. I can't help but wonder who she is? The green-eyed monster comes through even stronger than before.

"We'll miss you, too. You could always come back with us." I can hear the eagerness in her voice, but it seems to make Cain stiffen.

"You don't need me anymore, darling. You've got Jesse and his whole pack." He pulls her off his chest and holds her at arm's-length leaning down to get to her eye level.

I look around the room, wondering whether I should leave? I feel like I'm intruding on something intimate.

"You've got to let him in, Frankie. It's the only way you can both heal," Cain's says, his tone soft yet insistent.

She nods. "I know." I watch entranced as a tear runs down her cheek. Cain's quick to wipe it away before giving her a kiss on the forehead.

I feel a hand brush my back and I jump, my hands going straight to my stomach, protecting my baby. "Sorry. It's Selena, isn't it?" Jesse asks as he steps around me holding his hands up in an "I'm not going to harm you" gesture. I nod. "There's just a lot of people in here. It's hard not to touch people as you pass."

I smile and relax, lowering my hands to my sides. "That's okay. I was away with the fairies," I say, offering an excuse for me jumping. I can't exactly say I was spying on his wife and Cain.

"Hey, mate." Cain offers Jesse his hand, and they pull each other into one of those one-armed slap-on-the-back man hugs. "Have a safe trip back."

"Thanks… for everything, Cain." Jesse looks in the direction of Frankie. "I don't know…" He looks back at Cain, piercing him with his solid stare. "…what I would have done if you ha—"

"We've had this conversation already." Cain cuts him off as they release each other's hands.

Jesse holds his hand out towards Frankie. Watching through the gap between Cain and Jesse, I see her look at his hand for a second before taking it loosely in hers. He offers her a warm smile before turning his attention back to Cain. "You'll always be welcome in my territory. And if things don't work out here, there's a place for you in my pack."

Cain steps back. "Thank you, Jesse. I really appreciate your offer, but I've got things I need to do here," he says, the pitch of his voice tells me he must be surprised at the offer. "In saying that, when you find that bastard, I'll be more than happy to jump on the next plane to help you out."

Frankie tenses and Jesse strokes her arm with his spare hand. "Thanks. Theo gave us the same offer."

Cain laughs. "I'm pretty sure the whole pack would be ready to hightail it to Perth."

With one last handshake, Jesse turns to leave, his hand on the small of Frankie's back gently guiding her ahead of him. Frankie suddenly stops, and I think she's going to give Cain one last hug as she turns, but her arms are suddenly around my neck. "Look after him, Selena." With those four whispered words, she releases me and is out of sight before I can question what she meant by them.

9

PRECIOUS CARGO

*S*tanding at the gate, I watch as Selena knocks on the door. She turns to look at me, and I wonder if she can feel my eyes on her. "I'm okay, you know. You can wait in the car."

I sigh. She might be okay, but I can't bear to let her out of my sight.

The door opens and I hear Jared's deep voice. "Selena." He glances at me, then back at Selena. "What can I do for you?"

"I was hoping to see Alyssa. To let her know she isn't alone."

Jared lets out a rumble deep in his chest. "She isn't alone." The force of his anger prickling against my skin has me stepping up beside Selena.

Selena's hand reaches out to stop me stepping in front of her. "Don't, Cain. He isn't going to hurt me." Jared steps back, his jaw slack and eyes wide in what I can only assume to be shock.

"My b— Wait…." He looks at Selena, an eyebrow raised in question.

"Oh. Yes, I know. It's a long story. I've known about your secrets for a long time." She frowns. "Well, not yours, but his." She points a thumb in my direction.

Jared glances at me, and I give him a quick nod in agreement. "Well, in that case, I'll be straight with you both. My beast is close to the surface. It's the only way I'm managing to keep Alyssa from shifting. Her wolf keeps trying to make her shift in her sleep." My gaze drifts over him. The stiffness of his body and his golden lion eyes on his face tells me how truthful his words are.

I grab Selena's hand in mine. "I think we should go. We can come back another day when things are a little calmer." *Mainly Jared.*

Jared's head tilts as though he's listening to something inside the house. "It sounds like she's waking up. Come in. I'll go see if she's up for visitors." He glances at me sharply. "Are you part of the pack still?"

"Faintly," I admit, wondering if Alyssa would be able to feel me through whatever is left of the bonds. I can barely feel them myself.

He bites at the inside of his cheek whilst he thinks. "Come in. I'll let her know who's here."

We follow him in, stopping in the small lounge as he walks further into the house. There's a mustard-coloured sofa facing a large TV, which is hanging on the pristine white wall. The faint smell of paint leaves me wondering whether it's a recent refurbishment. I'll have to ask Theo about it. If he's still doing refurb's, I could probably help him out and make myself some money at the same time.

"Sit! Your feet will thank you for it," I suggest, catching Selena's longing look at the sofa.

She opens her mouth speak, but Jared comes back in the room causing her to quickly snap it shut again. "Cain, she doesn't feel comfortable seeing you, but she said you could go into the bedroom to see her, Selena." He points in the direction he'd just come back from. "It's the last door on the right."

She looks at him sheepishly through her lashes. "Is there a bathroom I can dash in on the way?" She points to her bulging belly. "This little monster is right on my bladder."

"Of course. First door on the left." Jared walks over to the sofa and takes a seat. Following his lead, I lower myself into the armchair to the side of the sofa, angled to face the side of the coffee table.

"She'll be safe? Alyssa won't shift without you there?" I hear the worry in my voice and cough to try and cover it. Surely Alyssa wouldn't hurt Selena—a human.

He closes his eyes and takes a deep breath. "She's in control for now. I'll sense it and will be able to send my energy to her before Selena is in any danger." He opens his eyes, showing me the golden orbs of his lion once again. "I wouldn't have let you in the house if I thought Selena or the baby would be in any danger." I nod, taking him at his word. "Alyssa looked panicked at the thought of being close to another wolf. She might not be able to sense you through the pack bonds, but she'd be able to feel your wolf against her skin and she wouldn't be able to handle that right now."

I raise a brow at him. "But she's okay with your lion?"

His energy flares and brushes against my skin making my wolf stand to attention. He grins. "He feels nothing like a wolf."

"I guess you're right." I glance up the hallway once again, wondering how things are going in there. "Theo will appreciate all you're doing for her. The whole pack will."

Jared sighs. "I'm not doing it for Theo or his pack. I'm doing it for Alyssa." He frowns. "She needs someone, and if I can fill that position, I'll do it for as long as I'm needed to."

I finally relax in his company, realising he's a bona fide good guy. "I can see why Theo lets you stay around even though you're Bel's ex." I give him a genuine smile. "You're a good guy."

"That he is," Selena says as she shuffles back into the room. "Alyssa asked for you. She can't sleep in the empty bed. She thought…" She glances at me and then back to Jared before finishing her sentence. "She thought she might be able to sleep next to your beast."

Jared nods. "I was planning on offering to do that anyway."

We both stand. "We'll let ourselves out," Selena offers, glancing at the door. "We can lock the door behind us."

Jared leans in and gives her a gentle hug. "Thank you, Selena. You take care of yourself." His eyes drop to her belly. "And the little one."

Selena laughs. "Little… it's far from little. But I will. I'm sure Cain and the pack will be keeping an eye on me." She glances shyly at me, and I give her a wink. Of course I'll be watching over her. I'm aiming to win her heart this time. Jared nods and heads towards the hallway and Alyssa.

We walk out the door and Selena pauses just as I'm about to close it. "Do you have Jared's number?"

I frown, wondering why she'd want his number. Jealousy raises its ugly head for a second, but I quickly snuff it out as I tell myself to stop being stupid. "No, but Theo or Bel will. Why?" I can't stop myself from asking. Maybe I haven't managed to shove the jealousy away completely.

"Of course they will." She starts towards the car and I finally allow the door to shut before following her. "I want to be able to call and check on Alyssa between now and Monday."

Pushing the button on my key fob, I unlock the car before she reaches for the handle. "Monday?"

"I told her I'd come back and see her on Monday, when the buses are running." She says buses like there's more than one. Mount Roxby has one bus that drives through the town over and over again. The driver's name is Simon. He does a good job, driving through most of the streets and not just the main ones on the route. But in saying that, it means the schedule never runs on time due to the detours.

"I'll drive you. No buses for you and your precious cargo." I nod towards her stomach. My hand itches to reach out and touch it, but I know some women hate random people touching their pregnant bellies and I'd rather not make her feel uncomfortable.

"Cain Wilson! Are you insinuating I'm as big as an aeroplane?" I flick my eyes off the road to see if she's joking with me. Her slack jaw and wide eyes have me anxious before she laughs. "Don't look so worried."

Fuck it. Biting the bullet, I reach out blindly—my eyes back on the road—and place my outspread palm on her beautiful bump. "This does not resemble an aeroplane in the slightest." I move my hand in a circular motion. The soft cotton of her summer dress is so thin I can feel the warmth of her skin through it. "I meant it earlier when I said you're beautiful. No one is as beautiful as you." I flick my eyes to her and catch her watching me.

She shakes her head. "I've seen plenty of women who are prettier than me. Frankie is for a start." Taking my hand off her stomach, I grab her hand in mine, entwining our fingers.

"Nobody holds a candle to you." Lifting her hand to my lips, I press a gentle kiss to her fingers.

I can see her observing me out the corner of my eye. "Did you two… date?" Before I get a chance to answer her question, she snatches her hand out of mine and speaks, once again. "Forget I asked. I have no right to ask that." She groans and rubs her face with her hands, obviously distressed about either her question or having asked it.

Flicking the indicator on, I pull to the side of the road. After putting the car in park, I unclip my seatbelt and turn my body to face her, as much as the seat and steering wheel allow me to.

Reaching out, I cup her cheek with one hand, feeling reassured as she leans into my touch. "You have every right to ask me." I take her hand in mine again and kiss it, needing to taste her. "I'm yours and I always will be, whether you want me or not."

She swallows what I can only assume is a lump in her throat. "Cain... I...."

I place a finger over her lips to stop her talking. "Don't. You don't have to say anything. Just know that I'm here for you, even if all you ever want is friendship. Okay?" I don't remove my finger to allow her to speak, so she nods in agreement.

Satisfied, I straighten in my seat, put the car in gear, and then pull out onto the empty street. "It was never like that between me and Frankie. I saved her from a living hell and kept her safe until she felt ready to tell me who she was. It took her a long time so we became close, but it was purely platonic." I push down my rising anger. It's anger that always rushes to the surface when I think of that hellhole she was in. "In any case, she was already mated. And so am I... technically." I shrug nonchalantly as I give her a quick smile. I don't want her to feel pressured into feeling things she may not be ready for.

10

PART OF THE PACK

SELENA

*B*eing with Alyssa was hard. She's always been such a happy person, so seeing her so withdrawn really pulled on my heartstrings. She acknowledged my words with a nod, though whether she actually heard what I was saying is another thing entirely. I will go back though. She needs people, and considering she only wants to be with Jared because he's not pack, he's going to need a break every now and then. Having made the decision to go back, I let thoughts about Alyssa and Jared leave my mind as I watch the scenery fly by through the windscreen.

"I'm yours and I always will be, whether you want me or not." Cain's words are on repeat in my head as he drives us through the dark empty streets. Of course I want him. I just don't know if I can handle the heartbreak if it all goes wrong again. What if he's wrong about me being his mate and it all falls apart? Would he just turn around and say, "Sorry I was mistaken?" That would kill me now, let alone if I'd fallen for him even more. My stomach is in knots just thinking about it.

"Hey." Cain's hand brushes my knee. "Are you okay? You're really quiet and seem to have come over a little sad."

I look at the scenery out the window, seeing we're just turning into the large drive. "Yeah. I'm just thinking how cruel the world is. Wes was a nice guy, you know? He didn't deserve to die."

Cain pulls the car into a space beside Billy's bike and turns off the engine. "Good people never deserve to die, beautiful. Unfortunately, sometimes there's nothing that can be done to stop it."

Knowing he's right, I nod. "At least Alyssa and the baby have everyone here." I wave at the house as we walk up to the door. "You'll all help her through it, just like you did for me." Turning the handle, I walk into what's fast become my home once again. The house is still brimming with people. It seems like maybe even more have arrived since we left.

Wanting to get out of the way, I edge my way towards the corridor leading to my room. Billy stops in front of us, blocking my escape.

"How is she?" he asks. I frown, wondering how he even knows where we've been. "Theo told us you went to see her," he explains.

"She's pretty out of it, but Jared is taking good care of her." I try to give him a reassuring smile, but I know I fail. I just can't seem to smile after seeing her so broken.

He nods. "He's a good guy." He weighs me up with his eyes and grins. "Theo told us you know our secret too. Welcome to the pack." He pulls me into a hug and I come out of it feeling dazed. *Part of the pack?*

"I'm not part of the pack," I say, glancing at Cain. Do people know about what went on between me and Cain all those years ago? Surely Theo won't have announced that.

"You've always been part of the pack, sweetheart," Billy informs me, giving me a warm smile. "Ever since Theo brought you home." He shrugs. "You just know about it now."

"Oh." I let out a nervous giggle as my stomach settles. "Thank you. Although I'm pretty sure most people have hated me for most of that time, and especially since I left."

He waves a hand dismissing my words. "Not the important people." He throws me a wink before looking at Cain over my shoulder. "I also hear you're staying with us? Welcome back, buddy." I step aside as they have a manly hug. Making the most of their distraction, I slip off down the corridor and head to bed, wanting to get away from the grief that fills the room before it dredges up old memories.

Lying in the dark, I listen to the gentle chatter of the people below. Hearing the sound of car doors, I gather people must be finally heading to their own homes.

A knock on my bedroom door startles me into a sitting position.

"Mum. What are you doing?" I hear Cain's voice question Trudy through the door.

"I wanted to let Selena know she isn't the only one around here who isn't a werewolf," Trudy says, sounding somewhat excited at the prospect.

"I'm sure she'll be happy to hear that, but I'm fairly sure she's asleep. She looked pretty drained when we got back from Alyssa's. Why don't you tell her tomorrow?" Cain sounds anxious, and I can't help but wonder if I did look as drained as I felt. *God, I hope not.*

"Good idea." I hear a shuffling sound and assume they're walking away. "Wait a minute. Your room's at the other side of the house. Why were you up here?" Hearing Trudy's question has my heart pounding in anticipation of Cain's answer. I hold my breath to hear better.

"Like I said, she was drained. I just wanted to check she was okay. I can't hear her moving and the lights off, so she must be sleeping."

I release my breath, filled with disappointment at his explanation. *What was I expecting him to say?* I shake my head at my own stupidity.

"Come on. I'll make you a cuppa. I have a feeling you have a lot to fill me in on." Trudy's voice sounds quieter as their footfalls pad away.

Closing my eyes, it doesn't take me long to drift off into a dreamland that has Cain walking in and doing wicked things to me.

11.

IT'S THE HORMONES

SELENA

As usual I barely slept last night. I thought you lost out on sleep once the baby arrived and needed feeding through the night, not before. Looking at the bed after getting washed and dressed, I feel like I could just fall back into it and sleep for a week, but instead, I lean over and tug the covers straight. I know if I start napping throughout the day, I won't even get the couple of hours sleep at night that I'm currently getting. Plus, I'd planned on going to see Alyssa again today, even if it's just to give Jared a moment to catch his breath. There must be a lot of pressure on his shoulders. Yesterday I'd told him I'd return on Monday, but having thought about it overnight, I'm pretty certain he won't have had the time to go grocery shopping yet, and I want to give him the opportunity to do that because I don't think the idea has crossed anyone else's mind either.

Losing my father and brother would have killed me too if I hadn't had Cain. Theo may have gotten me through the months following the loss of my family, but Cain, he got me through those important first few hours. Even thinking back on it now, it's a fuzzy blur. I was so disconnected from everything, but his presence was like a warm blanket when I'd felt numb with cold.

Knocking on the door pulls me out of my memories. "One

sec," I call out as I grab my empty glass off the bedside cupboard, not wanting to have to come back up for it later—waddling up and down the stairs takes energy I don't seem to have these days.

Pulling the door open, the peppermint aroma of a steaming tea hits me as a cup is thrust in my face.

"Tea?" Trudy asks, seemingly full of energy if her dancing feet are anything to go by.

I sidestep her and place my hands around hers on the cup, aiming to calm her movements before the hot liquid can burn either of us. "Sure, thanks. Let me take that before you spill it." I glance at my watch to double-check the time. "How many coffees have you had this morning, Trudy?" Seven o'clock is way too early for her to be this jittery from coffee. Knowing she used to have a problem with drugs and alcohol causes worry to surge through me as I wonder if she's fallen off the wagon, again. I can't imagine what would have caused her to do such a thing. As far as I know, she wasn't close to Wes.

She waves me to lead the way downstairs, and I do just that, hoping once I have my back turned, she'll feel more comfortable to talk. I've barely taken three steps when words tumble out of her mouth.

"I've had a couple. I couldn't sleep last night." She pauses, taking a deep breath. "I had hoped that you'd maybe be in the same boat. Actually no… I didn't want you not to be sleeping, but I really wanted to catch you down there like we often do during the night."

I stop at the bottom of the stairs and turn to face her. "Trudy, you're worrying me. Are you okay?" I peer at her, taking in her clean blouse and jeans. She doesn't look like she's been on a bender. Leaning forward slightly, I breathe in, aiming to get a discreet whiff of her breath.

"I haven't been drinking if that's what you're sniffing for," she says, making it perfectly clear I wasn't as discreet as I'd been aiming. "I didn't mean to worry you." She pats at her blonde bob. "Shall we go sit on the deck? You can drink your tea and I'll explain what's gotten me so excited."

I look at her full of surprise; my eyebrows must almost be in my hairline. "This is you excited?" She laughs and gives me a sheepish nod. "Okay, but I'll have to sit at the garden table because I won't get out of the lounger if I try to sit on that." I head through the French doors and pull a chair out at the table sitting on the edge of the grass.

As I wait for Trudy to be seated and tell me what's going on in that crazy head of hers, I glance around the yard, taking in the tables and chairs that had all been part of a wedding only a couple of days ago. All that happiness has been wiped away with death. Theo and Bel should be having a honeymoon, not planning the burial of a friend. A family member, that's what he was. Wes was as good as Theo's brother. I could see that, even before I knew about the pack connection.

"The wedding feels like weeks ago, but the flowers aren't even wilted." Trudy sighs, and I watch her finger the centre-piece between us. She shakes her head as if to clear it of whatever thoughts are present before grabbing my hand on the table and giving it a squeeze. "That's not what I wanted to talk about."

I wipe at a tear with my spare hand, my hormones clearly getting the better of me.

"I had a long chat with Cain last night. I want you to know you aren't the only human around here. I've always been an outsider of sorts." I frown, unsure where she's going with this, but I allow her to finish without interrupting with questions. "Don't get me wrong, you'd never be an outsider. Not if you mated with Cain."

I cough. "*Trudy!* I… we… I think you have the wrong end of the stick. Cain and I aren't—"

She cuts me off with a wave of her hand. "Oh, I know

exactly what's happening, but don't worry about that for now. What I'm trying to say is, I'm here if you need to talk to someone without the pack bonds and stuff, if they get pushy." She looks at me with raised eyebrows. "Because werewolves can be pushy bastards."

"*Mum!*" Cain's voice coming from the trees at the other side of the yard has me jumping in my seat. "I told you to leave her alone. Jesus, are you trying to scare her off?"

"I'll have you know I'm offering her support." The indignation in her voice makes me laugh.

Closing my eyes, I soak in the warmth of the sun as I listen to them bickering.

"You were calling us pushy bastards, Mum." Cain's voice sounds much closer than it had been a moment ago. The sound of a chair knocking the table alerts me to the fact he must be joining us.

Opening my eyes, I take a sip of the rapidly cooling peppermint tea whilst watching Cain over the top of the mug. He's giving his mother a stern look. I can tell he's only joking by the slight lift at the corner of his mouth. He has a slight shadow over his jaw, making me aware that he probably hasn't shaved this morning. I lift my hand, wanting to run my fingers over the scrub only to catch myself, tucking my own hair behind my ear in hopes of disguising my hand's initial intentions.

"You can be pushy," Trudy argues gently. "And you were born out of wedlock, so technically...." She grins, clearly thinking he won't argue with her reasoning.

"Well played, Mum." He laughs. The sound caresses my skin as I watch him pull her into a one-armed hug.

I'm surprised by her words. I knew she hadn't always been with Marcus, Cain's dad, because when I first started dating Theo, Marcus was with another woman, Margie. I had no idea they hadn't actually been married beforehand. Margie hated Cain and Theo and made it perfectly clear whenever she had the chance. Come to think of it, she hated me too. Thinking back on it now, I wonder if it was because I wasn't a werewolf.

"So, what do you ladies have planned for today?" He releases Trudy and flicks his eyes between the two of us. I look to Trudy.

She shrugs. "Nothing yet."

Both their eyes fall to me. "I was planning on visiting Alyssa again."

Cain glances at his watch. "If you give me twenty minutes, I can drop you off on my way to work and then I'll pick you up again when I finish around lunch."

"You're working?" I ask, my voice high with surprise.

"My brother owns a gym, which conveniently has a vacancy since Paddy left town," Cain says, before throwing me a wink. "You didn't think I was planning to be a slacker, did you?" Pushing his chair back, he stands.

"No, it's just… it was only yesterday you decided to stay in town." My heart beats erratically in my chest at the thought of him staying. We caused such a mess all those years ago, and here we are back in the same town. Hell, we're in the same house. "It was quick," I add.

"I, for one, am glad you're staying," Trudy exclaims with a gentle squeeze of his arm.

"Thanks, Mum." He leans and gives her a kiss on the cheek. "Now, I really do have to get ready for work. I'll meet you by the car in twenty?" He looks at me, his eyebrow raised in question.

I nod and watch as he runs into the house. His sweats and T-shirt cling to his muscles. Muscles that will have water running over them any second now. I lick my lips and shake my thoughts of him naked in the shower out of my head, before turning my attention back to Trudy, who is sporting the biggest, knowing grin. "Oh, shut up. It's the hormones," I admit guiltily.

Trudy purses her lips and a frown creases her brow. "Have you seen him in his other form?"

"Wolf?" I ask stupidly, as if there's another form of his.

She nods.

"No." I shake my head. "I didn't think they'd be allowed to change in front of us. I remember he said their existence is a big secret and it's dangerous for us to even know about it."

She reaches across the table and squeezes my hand. "You'll see them soon enough. It's magnificent." Without any more explanation, she heads off towards the house, leaving me wondering why they'd risk showing me if it's so dangerous.

Glancing at my own watch, I figure I have enough time to have a quick bathroom break before heading to the car.

I knock on the door before me as I listen to the car idling at the kerb. Cain's waiting to see that I get in safely. It's not like I'm a grown woman or anything.

Jared opens the door, looking somewhat bedraggled in a T-shirt and loose-fitting shorts. His hair's sticking out in all directions having seemingly just woken up. "Se—" He clears his throat before trying again. "Selena, I wasn't expecting you until Monday."

I grimace. I should have called. "I—"

"I'm being rude, forgive me." He rubs a hand over his face. "I just stumbled out of bed. Come in." He waves me in, and I have a quick glance out the door before he closes it, catching sight of Cain pulling onto the road. I step into the lounge and Jared follows. "Alyssa's still asleep. Do you want a coffee? Actually, I'm not sure if we have decaf."

"I'm assuming you haven't really had a chance to do any shopping. That's kind of why I came today." I frown, hoping he doesn't think I'm butting into their business. "I figured since

Alyssa was okay with me yesterday, you might like to pop out and grab what you want. Or if you don't fancy leaving, I can go pick some stuff up for you. Although I'd probably have to borrow your car." Sure I'm babbling, I press my lips together to stop myself from going on.

Jared strokes a hand down my arm, like I've seen the werewolves do a thousand times. "Hey, it's okay. It's really nice that you thought of doing that for me. I'd actually like to quickly pop to the shop for a few bits." He turns his head to the side as though he's listening to something before focusing back on me. "Come into the kitchen with me. We can get a list together while we wait for Alyssa to wake up. I don't want to leave without telling her first."

I smile. "Sure. That sounds like a good plan."

12.

DIE TRYING

As I make my way to the kitchen for my afternoon peppermint tea, there's a knock on the front door just as I'm passing. Reaching out, I open it and turn to let them in without much thought. It's a pack house after all; there are people coming and going all the time.

The face of the person standing at the door registers with my brain and my heart starts to race. "Stu," I whisper. I never thought I'd see him again, not after he all but booted me out the door when I told him I was pregnant. My hands drop to my stomach in a protective gesture, and his eyes follow their movement. I fell into Stu's lap—quite literally—within hours of leaving Mount Roxby. I'd stopped off in a tavern in the next town over and drank myself into a stupor, before falling over my feet and landing in his lap. Stu took me home with him. Even though over time, I felt he was keeping secrets from me just like Theo had, I ignored the little supernatural warning signs that should have had me running a mile, and I settled into life with Stu. It was amazing. He was a caring boyfriend, and I thought I could see us lasting the long haul. Until I told him I was pregnant. That's when he became a whole other person. *Violent*. Terrifyingly violent. I ran to Theo hoping for a second chance, but I also ran to Theo because I knew he'd protect me and my child. No matter what had happened between us in the past, he'd never put a child in danger.

"You haven't popped it out yet then." His stating of the obvious makes me glare at him, belatedly remembering how much he hated me glaring at him. He steps forward menacingly and pulls me out the door with a harsh grip on my arm that causes pain to radiate along the limb. "If you want to live long enough to have that baby, you better wipe that look off your face."

Falling back into old habits, I cower before him, dropping my eyes to the floor and slouching my shoulders. "I'm sorry."

"You better let go of her and leave." Cain's demanding voice behind me has me relaxing instantly. Stu can't do anything to harm me or my baby, not while Cain's here. "Right. The. Fuck. Now!" The growl behind Cain's words has the hairs on the back of my neck standing on end. Cain steps up beside me, and I glance at him gratefully as he brushes a reassuring hand over my back.

Stu releases my hand as he locks eyes with Cain. "I'll be going as soon as I've collected what belongs to me." The set of Stu's shoulders and his feet planted firmly where he stands shows how determined he is as he points to my stomach.

"I think you might be mistaken, mate, because she's *mine!*" The growl in that one word makes the hairs rise on the back of my neck.

"That baby she's carrying is *mine*. So, I'm taking her with me." Stu takes a step towards me, making his intentions perfectly clear.

Cain gently ushers me behind him. "You're not taking my mate anywhere, but you are more than welcome to die trying." Hearing Cain call me his mate has my heart skipping a beat. I rub a hand over my belly wondering if he really meant it and, if he did, has he considered that another man's baby comes with me?

"Mate? If I'd have known you knew about us, we could have had some real fun in the bedroom." He winks at me over

Cain's shoulder, making bile rise in my throat at his insinuation.

Cain lets out a furious growl and charges forward.

Suddenly overwhelmed with the need to protect Cain from getting hurt because of me, I jump forward, grabbing his arm. "Please," I plead. He turns his head to look at me. His eyes are glowing an ice-blue, reminding me of the wolf's eyes he once showed me.

Knowing I need to get Stu to leave, I turn my attention to him and I speak up. "You kicked me out the minute you found out I was pregnant. Why do you want it now?" I can feel Cain's skin beneath my fingers rippling, and I slide my hand down, taking his hand in mine, hoping to calm him. I've lived with wolves long enough to know touch like this is something that calms them.

"Honestly, I'd rather kill you both right now, but my alpha feels differently." Cain's hand tightens painfully on mine, causing me to grit my teeth.

"I'll tell you what." Cain words seem forced, as though it's taking all his energy to fight something else. "Go tell your alpha if he really wants my mate's child, he can come back when it hits puberty." He loosens his hold on my hand, and I quickly cradle it in my other hand, massaging it and hoping to get the blood flowing again. Stu grins seemingly satisfied. "Don't get me wrong, he won't be leaving with the child, but I'll be more than happy to end his life for him when he does come knocking."

Stu stares at Cain, indecision written in the crease of his brow. "Fucking rock and hard place, every fucking time," he mutters to himself.

"Now, if you don't want me to show you what being between a rock and a hard place really feels like, you might wanna get off my property... *NOW!*"

Turning without a word, Stu hightails it down the drive.

The speed he moves tells anyone watching that he's something other than human. I've never seen anyone move so fast

"Fucking arrogant fox, moving like that. Humans could be around for all he knows." Cain stares at the drive as if he can see through the trees Stu ran into.

"He's a fox?" My voice rises in surprise. Cain spins to face me and nods in answer. "I had no idea there were more than just werewolves."

"Any animal could be a were-animal or shifter as some prefer to be called. In fact…" He glances around as though looking for something, before training his eyes back on me. "Jared isn't a wolf. He's a lion."

My eyebrows almost pop out of my head with surprise, or so it feels anyway. "A lion? Like a big, roaring, golden-maned, lion?"

He nods and grins. "I haven't seen him in his lion form, so I can't say whether he's big or not. But considering he's meant to be his pride's next alpha, I'd assume he's pretty big."

"Oh wow, I'd love to see it. His lion. I bet he's so majestic." I wave my hands in excitement at the thought and hiss as pain soars through the one Cain had squeezed the life out of.

Cain's eyes drop to the offending appendage and his smile is wiped from his face. I pull the hand behind my back, trying to hide it from his view. "Selena, let me see it."

Not wanting him to see the bruise I'd caught sight of a second ago, I try to placate him. "It's nothing, just a little bruise."

"Please, Selena." The pleading and his solemn eyes have me moving my hand out from behind my back and placing it into his outstretched palm. I avert my eyes from his face, not quick enough to miss the anguish in his pained stare. "That was me, wasn't it?" His grim look tells me he already knows the answer. "I'm sorry… I.… *Fuck!* There's no excuse for something like this. I know you're human. How could I have done this?"

Taking my hand out of his, I fight not to show the discomfort the movement causes as I cup his face. "Cain. Listen to me. It wasn't your fault." He opens his mouth to argue, but I rush to keep talking, not giving him the chance to jump in. "I knew your wolf was close to the surface. I saw him in your eyes and felt your skin rippling under my fingers. *I* put my hand in yours anyway. It was my fault. Not yours."

He turns his face to kiss the bruised hand. "You need an X-ray."

I sigh as I give him a short, sharp nod. I'd come to the same conclusion the second it happened.

He pulls his phone out of his pocket as I drop my hands from his face and cradle them over my stomach. "Zainab," he says, holding the phone out in front of him, having put it on speaker. "I need your expertise."

"Okay," Zainab's voice answers warily through the speakers.

"Is there still an X-ray machine in the big shed?"

"Yes. Why? What have you done?" Her voice sounds anxious, no doubt at the thought of someone hurt.

"Selena has hurt her hand. It's bruised up pretty quickly, so it looks like there could be a fracture or two." He grimaces with the words, and I offer him a reassuring smile, trying to show him I'm okay.

"Selena? No, the baby… we don't have a lead apron, so she can't have an X-ray in the shed."

"*Fuck.*"

"Cain, it's probably just a bruise. Don't worry about it. A bit of ice and a couple of days and it'll be on the mend." I reach out, trying to soothe him with touch again, but he steps back before our skin connects.

"I am worried about it, Selena. You're in pain. I can sense it. And It's my fucking fault."

"*Cain!*" Zainab's voice shouts through the phone's speakers, reminding us both that she's still present and listening to every word. "Are you listening to me now?" He lets out a rumble "I'll take that as a yes." My eyes widen in surprise as I realise Zainab heard the sound. "My shift is nearly over. I can borrow an apron from work and do the X-ray when I get there. Is that okay with you both?"

"Thanks, Zainab." The defeat in Cain's voice pulls at my heart.

"It's what I'm here for. I'll see you both soon," she says before hanging up.

Cain shoves his phone back in his pocket, and I do the only thing I can that will pull him out of his own head.

I kiss him.

Kiss him with everything I have.

Kiss him like I've imagined kissing him for the longest time.

Fisting my hands in his shirt, I tug him down towards me so I don't have to balance on my tiptoes.

It doesn't take him long to reciprocate. One of his hands slips around my waist as the other slides across my neck and grips the hair at my nape. His mouth moves on mine ferociously, like he's drinking me in.

We finally break apart, both breathing heavily, staying wrapped up in each other as close as my gigantic belly will allow. "Selena, does that mean—"

I answer before he even finishes his sentence. "Yes, Cain. You said it yourself." I dive in for a quick peck on his lips, just because I can. "I'm yours… your mate."

He drops to his knees and holds my enormous belly between his hands. "Did you hear that in there? Your mummy just said she's mine." Like magic the baby gives a kick in answer, causing Cain to look up at me in awe. "You like the sound of that, too, don't you?" he says, once again focusing his attention on my belly.

"Of course, it does. Because that means it's going get the most wonderful daddy by default." I laugh at the warmth of his breath as he kisses my bump through the thin fabric of my top.

He reluctantly gets to his feet, his movements slow. "Let's go get you some ice and wait for Zainab in the shed. Once you've had the X-ray, I can spend the rest of the day revelling in your body." It feels like a swarm of butterflies are floating around in my stomach as I take in his words. It's been such a long time since we've been together like he's suggesting. As much as I want nothing more than for us both to take pleasure in each other's nakedness, what if he's disappointed in what he finds beneath my clothes? My body isn't what it once was.

e walk into the shed, and I marvel at the sight before me. The floor is covered in those foam mats that you'd find in a martial arts place, not that I've seen any real-life martial arts places. I've seen them in the movies though, so I'm sure that's what they must look like.

Along the back wall of the shed, there are what look like hospital beds—three of them all lined up. *Do these guys get that many injuries that they'd need three all at once?* I ask as much. "Do you really need three hospital beds?" I glance at Cain over my shoulder, wanting to see his face as he answers.

"Being a werewolf has its dangers." He shrugs. "And it's not like we can go down to the hospital. We heal too quickly, so we'd draw unwanted attention."

I nod, understanding his reasoning.

A woman of Indian decent walks into the shed, something black with maroon piping hanging over her arm. "Selena, it's nice to finally meet you. I've been in the pack since before you and Theo, but I don't think we've ever met." She looks at me, an eyebrow raised quizzically.

She doesn't look familiar at all. "I don't think we've met

before." I shrug, unsure. "But my memory is rubbish, so I could be wrong."

She laughs. "That will be the baby brain. It only gets worse once the baby arrives."

"You've got kids?" I ask, surprised. I hadn't noticed any kids in the time I've been around Theo and the pack, except Alyssa. I assumed they struggled to have children.

"I was bitten and had my first shift after I had kids," she states with a knowing nod, before wheeling a stool over to one of the beds. She positions a plastic board with grid type markings on top of the bed, before motioning for us to join her. She hands me the apron, which is far heavier than she made it look. "If you just put your arms in here." I do as instructed and glance at Cain, who's leaning against the wall beside the bed. His leg's bent at the knee, his foot flat against the wall.

He gives me a reassuring smile, before I look back to Zainab as she tells me how to position my hand for the X-ray.

"That's perfect," she says, once she has me sat on the stool with my hand outspread on the plastic board. She pushes a button on the machine and repositions my hand before doing it again, my hand at a slightly different angle. "That should be enough."

We head over to a computer in the corner of the room, which I'd not noticed on entering the shed. After Zainab clicks the mouse a few times, an X-ray of a hand pops onto the screen. My hand.

I squint at the screen, trying to see a break of some kind jumping out at me. Deciding there's nothing obvious to me, I turn to watch Zainab's face. She is the qualified doctor after all.

Zainab's lips are pressed together as she frowns at the screen, clicking through the different shots of my hand. "Okay. Do you see here?" She points at the screen. "That mark there is a fracture." She points elsewhere on the screen. "As is that."

Cain stiffens beside me and I grab his hand with my good

one, praying to whatever god wants to listen. *Please let that be it.*

Zainab changes the screen to one of the other images and points at the screen again, making my heart sink. "There is another."

Cain growls, and I squeeze his hand, trying to comfort him. He snatches his hand back and paces behind us. I don't know what he's doing, but whatever it is has the hairs on the back of my neck standing to attention, and a shiver runs down my spine.

Zainab takes a deep breath before speaking again, sounding somewhat pained. "Luckily, they're just fractures so you won't need surgery, just a cast."

I nod, before turning my attention back to Cain. I take a tentative step towards him until Zainab reaches out, halting my steps with a hand on my arm.

"Give him a minute," she says, her tone demanding.

"He's blaming himself," I say, my voice high-pitched, unable to keep a lid on my anxiety. I need to help him.

"He *can* hear you, you know?" The deepness of his voice tells me he's anything but calm.

I pull my arm out of Zainab's hold.

"Be careful, Selena. His wolf is riding him right now. I can feel it," Zainab warns, whilst rubbing her hands over her forearms.

I take slow, sure steps towards him, wanting to show them both that I'm not scared of Cain, or his wolf. I know neither of them will do anything to harm me again. He's punishing himself too much for his earlier mistake.

"Cain," I say as I approach him, not wanting to startle him. I place my hand firmly on his broad back as I step around him, sliding my hand over his shoulder and down his arm as I go.

He stands stock still, and I worry he might shrug me off. I stop before him and look up into his eyes.

Ice-blue eyes.

Not Cain's eyes.

His wolf's.

"Mate." The word leaves my mouth before it even registers in my head. I have no idea what it means—the fact that I've said it—but I know it's momentous.

Zainab makes a noise behind me, but I'm too focused on Cain and his wolf to pay attention to her.

Cain swallows. "Mate." His voice is deeper and gruffer than usual. It's the voice of his wolf. His hand snakes out and slides roughly around the back of my neck. Pulling me close to him, forceful, but without hurting me.

My eyes are locked on his wolf's eyes.

He leans forward and I think he's going to kiss me, but his mouth brushes past my jaw before he bites at my neck.

I gasp in shock at his move and the slight pain it causes.

He licks and kisses the spot, like he's caressing it, causing me to giggle as I grip at his bicep with my good hand. My knees start to give and my body floods with my arousal as he slowly kisses his way back up my jaw, to my lips.

I close my eyes, luxuriating in the feel of his warm mouth on me, imagining it being in other places. Places that are now tingling with need.

His mouth disappears, and I take a few seconds to compose myself before I open my eyes. I'm greeted with happiness beaming out of Cain's deep blue eyes, his smile wide across his face.

"Hey," he says, his voice sounding like his once again.

"Hey," I say with a grin of my own. "Mate," I add, letting him know, I understand the depth of what just happened between us.

We claimed each other. *Permanently.* Whether there are more steps to the claiming—if that's even what it's called—or not, there's no going back from what we've just done.

And I for one, wouldn't want there to be.

13

MINE AT LAST

*M*y wolf settles down, content in finally having our mate accept us. We've been waiting for it for such a long time. I search her blue eyes, wondering if really understands what just happened between us. The confidence I see tells me she does.

Unable to wipe the smile off my face, I crush my lips on hers as I hold her body against mine. Running my hands over her curves, excitement fills me as I think about being able to trace these curves with my mouth.

A throat clears behind us, and I get pulled back to reality and the shed.

"If you'd like to be left alone to…" Zainab clears her throat again. "Finish what you've started, you need to let me put a cast on that hand."

Her hand. My euphoria comes crashing down. I fractured Selena's hand in numerous places. I broke my mate. How could I have been so rough?

A finger caresses my temple, and lips press a gentle kiss on the tip of my nose. "Please don't blame yourself, Cain. Watching you blame yourself hurts me more than the damn hand does."

Taking a deep breath, I'm almost floored by the scent of our arousal being so thick in the air. I immediately understand why

Zainab may have felt uncomfortable. I give Selena a reassuring smile as I try to push my self-blame back. "Let's get you patched up."

It doesn't take Zainab long to fix a cast up. I don't know how she had all the equipment since we very rarely need casts due to our exceptionally quick healing abilities. Usually, we'll just strap anything broken in place whilst it fuses together.

"Six weeks? I need to keep this thing on for six weeks?" Selena glares at the stark white cast that covers her hand and most of her forearm. "I'm due in six weeks. What if the baby comes early? I won't be able to change nappies or anything." She shakes her head defiantly as she pulls at the opening around her fingertips. "Nope. Take it off. I can't have a cast."

I step up to her and place a calming hand on hers, hoping to still it. "Hey, calm down, beautiful. You don't want to cause more damage and have to have it on longer." I glance across at Zainab, pleading with my eyes for her to back me up.

"Yes." Zainab nods. "How about we play it by ear. We'll give you a weekly X-ray and reassess the situation as we see how it's healing. You could have it off in as soon as four weeks."

Zainab's words cause Selena to pause her ministrations. "Really?" She looks at Zainab, her eyes wary. "Four weeks?"

"Four weeks," Zainab reassures her with a wide smile, causing Selena to flash a smile back. I suddenly have the urge to hug the woman. She managed to talk Selena down from her panic, something I couldn't do. Part of me feels put out by that thought, but I brush it aside.

I pull Selena into my arms and press a kiss to her forehead. "How about we call for some takeaway and watch a movie or two?" I offer, wanting to take her mind off her worries. As much as I want to get her naked in my bed, I want it to happen for the right reasons, and as a distraction from her injury wouldn't be it.

She nods against my chest. "That sounds perfect."

I release my hold on her and pat her behind gently. "You go pick the food and the movie, and I'll help Zainab clean up here. I'll be with you in five."

Zainab waves me off. "Don't worry about it. I know exactly where everything belongs. It will take me twice as long to clean up if I'm telling you where to put everything. Go, enjoy your night."

Selena steps forward and says thank you to Zainab, giving her a quick hug before heading back to the house.

Bending slightly, I place a gentle kiss on Zainab's cheek. "Thanks. For everything."

She waves me off once again. "Go, enjoy your mate, before I change my mind and make you clean up the mess."

I laugh and back out of the shed with my arms raised in surrender.

I find Selena in the kitchen, flicking through a handful of takeaway menus. Picking two out of the pile, she holds them up, fanned out in her good hand. "Chinese or Indian?"

The thought of honey chicken and sweet and sour pork has my taste buds singing. "Chinese," I answer instantly.

As Selena states her choice. "Indian."

I laugh and surrender the choice to her. "Indian sounds great. Pick what you want and I'll give them a call."

She hands me the menu without looking at it. "Butter chicken and garlic naan bread."

I shake my head in disbelief. "You'd already decided before you even gave me the option." I laugh. "Did you just want to torture me with the thought of Chinese food?" I take the menu and pretend to pout.

She lets out a chuckle, clearly amused with my silly pouting face. "I didn't, honestly. I always have the same thing when I have a curry." She frowns and I want to rub away the crease between her eyes. "In fact, I'm pretty boring. I have one set meal from each of the takeaways. I never really have to look at a menu."

Taking note of the phone number, I throw the menu on the counter behind her before pulling her into my arms and taking her lips with mine. I want to wipe the frown off her face. She's anything but boring. Her body relaxes into mine within seconds of our lips connecting, and I contemplate ignoring the whole idea of food, to just sweep her up and take her to have my wicked way with her. The grumbling sound coming from her stomach has me pulling away with a laugh. "And on that note..." I release her and grab the phone out of the cradle on the side. "I better order some food."

In no time, I'm throwing the phone on to the counter and pulling Selena back into my arms. I can't seem to keep my hands off her. "Food should be here in twenty minutes. How do you want to pass the time?" I slide my hands down her back and over her perfect butt, giving it a gentle squeeze in the hope of hinting at what I'd like to do with the time we have.

She grins, raising a brow in a knowing look. "If we pass the time how you're thinking, we won't get fed at all because you won't be ready to stop at twenty minutes."

I roll my eyes playfully. "Fiiiine," I concede, knowing she's right. It'll take me all night to worship her how I want to. Twenty minutes just won't cut it. I tap her butt gently as I step away from her. "You go choose a movie and I'll grab us some drinks and plates for the food."

I potter around in the kitchen, keeping myself away from the temptation of Selena. The sound of a car on the gravel drive alerts me to the arrival of our takeaway. It reminds me of old times when I was avoiding her so I wasn't tempted to sleep with my brother's wife. Thank fuck those days are over and I only have to wait for another couple of hours.

I promised her food and a movie, and that's what she'll get —until I can finally make her mine.

It doesn't take me long to have everything served up. Placing Selena's glass of apple juice on the coffee table, I hand her the plate of food and watch as she balances it slightly on her stomach, causing me to let out a laugh.

"What?" She looks at me with wide, innocent eyes. "I have to reap some benefits from being this huge." Grabbing a piece of naan bread and popping it in her mouth, effectively stops her from explaining any further.

After collecting my own meal, I sit beside her, placing my beer on the coffee table before tucking into my lamb rogan josh. "What movie did you pick?" I ask between mouthfuls. She grins at me, and I wonder if she's going to torture me with a chick flick. "It's not *Bridget Jones*, is it?"

She laughs heartily, the sound causing my jeans to get tighter over my growing erection. "No, although I'm sure you enjoyed Bridget when I picked it for movie night once."

I purse my lips as I make a show of thinking. "Nope, I never paid attention to any of those movies. All I could think about was the feel of your feet pressing into the side of my thigh." Her wide-eyed expression makes me lose the joke in my voice and keeps me talking. "The three of us would share the couch, and although you'd be leaning against Theo, your feet would be encroaching into my seat. I loved it, and hated it in the same breath because even though I could feel the heat of your skin against mine, it reminded me I was never going to hold you in my arms like Theo did." Feeling raw and exposed, I swallow the lump rising in my throat.

"You were wrong, Cain. I'm yours. You can hold me whenever you want and nothing will ever change that." Her words sound like a promise.

I force myself to keep eating as I push my wolf down. He's trying to rush forward to claim her here and now.

Her eyes flick to mine, and I know she can see him in them. "*Yours.*" That one word has him retreating without a fight.

Sitting on the couch with one leg across the back of it, I direct Selena to sit in the V of my legs. Her back against my chest.

"I'm heavy. I might crush you," she says with a wary look.

I give her a raised brow. "Get your mighty fine butt on this seat, or I'll have to skip the movie and carry you to bed to show you how heavy you aren't."

She lets out a sweet giggle before sitting exactly where I'd suggested. "Don't say I didn't warn you." She leans back without any hesitation, resting her head against my shoulder as I wrap my arms around her waist, placing them on her beautiful bump.

I give the top of her head a quick kiss before pressing Play on the remote and once again settling my hands across her bump. I mindlessly caress it as the movie starts, letting out a loud laugh as I realise what movie it is. "I should have guessed. You always loved Sandra Bullock movies." She would watch *Miss Congeniality* over and over again. The pack hated it. In fact, I think someone even went as far as throwing the DVD out after the fifteenth viewing.

"I couldn't find *Miss Congeniality*. So I chose the next best thing. *Heat.*" Hearing the smile in her voice has one creeping across my own face as I settle back to enjoy the movie with my mate in my arms.

14

CLAIM ME

SELENA

*C*ain's breath hitches against my ear as the baby wakes up and performs a somersault against Cain's hand, which has been resting on my bump rubbing circles here and there throughout the movie. The menu comes on the screen having run through the credits. I ignore it as I place my good hand over Cain's.

"Holy shit… it felt like she just rolled right over."

I laugh at the excitement in his voice. "*He* did." Butterflies flutter in my stomach at the thought of whether it could be a boy or a girl. There's a kick against the tip of Cain's finger, and he slides his palm over the spot.

"I can't imagine there'd be enough room for that. Wow." The awe in his voice keeps me lying there and allowing his hands to chase the baby's limbs as it moves around in it's little home.

The minutes pass and the movements start to become further apart and much gentler. "I think it's worn itself out. Or at least gotten comfortable," I say.

"Hmm. Well, I wonder what I should do with my hands now?" Cain asks, his voice gruff in my ear as one hand roams lower. Fingers brush under the edge of my underwear.

I let out a moan as I slip my hands behind his neck, awkwardly pulling him towards me with my casted arm so I can nuzzle at his throat.

His fingers rub over my sex and my core clenches. "Fuck, you're so responsive." He dips a finger inside as he rubs at my clit. The fingers on his other hand pinch at my nipple. His mouth descends on mine before he kisses his way down my jaw. The sensation of him being everywhere causes an orgasm to crash over me. He removes his hand from my underwear and I capture it in mine, tugging it back, greedy for more.

"*Please*, Cain."

"Shh. I'm not finished with you yet." His lips brush over my temple. "I just want to get you somewhere more comfortable." He manages to sit me up and eases out from behind me. He stands, and I move to slide my legs around so I can join him, only to be blocked as he bends and effortlessly scoops me into his arms.

"Cain, put me down." I push at his shoulders, trying not to be too hard with the heavy cast. "I'm too heavy for you to carry me."

Picking up his pace, he takes sure strides to his bedroom. "It's not my strength that will be in question if I drop you. It's your wriggling, so stop it."

Realising he's probably right, I pause my fidgeting and make the most of my position as I kiss my way up his jaw. My nibbling at his earlobe entices a growl from him.

"That's not exactly helpful either." He picks up his pace, and I struggle to track the things we pass, which tells me he's most probably tapping into his supernatural power. I'd seen Stu run this fast, but I'd never imagined I'd be able to experience it like this.

His door makes a loud bang as it hits the wall with force. It doesn't have the chance to hit us as it rebounds because I'm suddenly laid out on the bed with Cain standing over me. The heat in his eyes has me squirming in anticipation.

Remembering how he'd made me feel downstairs, I pull at

my stretchy maternity pants as I try to get naked. "Cain, I need you."

Cain stills my hands with his. "Let me." His hands taking over the job and he deftly removes my underwear and pants all in one gentle tug. Moving onto my top, he starts undoing the buttons one by one, and I curse myself for choosing to wear something so hard to take off. Having worked his way through the buttons, he peels the two sides open and runs a finger over the edge of my bra. I cringe internally as I picture the unflattering maternity bra I put on this morning. But the way Cain is looking at me wipes my thoughts away. He's looking at me as if I'm wearing the sexiest lace money could buy. He licks his lips before his head dips, and the feel of his warm, wet tongue traces the same path his finger had just been on. My eyes close in ecstasy. "Honeysuckle... mmm... I've missed the taste of you."

I arch my back to get closer to Cain just as his hands snake underneath me. The pressure of my bra releases and his fingers brush over my chest as he lifts the bra before finding a nipple with his mouth.

"I need you, Cain," I beg once again. "My hormones have made me so sensitive. *Please....*" I sit up as he helps me out of my bra and top.

Reaching for his jeans, I work on freeing him from their confines with the zipper and button.

"Selena." He breathes my name like a caress, sending goosebumps down my arms. "I—"

I kiss the rest of his sentence away as I shove his jeans and boxers down his legs. I wasn't kidding when I said I needed him.

The warmth of Cain's body follows me as I lie back on the bed. I wrap my legs around his waist, making our bodies come together where I need him most. "Cain...." I rub myself against him wantonly, hoping he catches on to what I'm aiming for because words are failing me.

He pauses and pulls back enough that our groins are no longer touching. I lock my legs around his waist to stop him from leaving completely. "Honey, I can't... the baby."

I frown as I lock eyes with him, seeing the concern etched into his face. My mind tries to make sense of his words. *The baby... what about the baby?*

"The baby won't care," I say, tugging at his arms as I try to pull us together again, but he's like a statue, solid and unrelenting. "It will be fine. Pregnant women have sex all the time."

I slide my hand between us and try to direct him to where he needs to be, only for him to pull away another inch.

"I swear to God, if you don't fuck me…." I let the sentence fall short, the threat to find someone else is on the tip of my tongue, but I daren't say it. If I say it and he can't follow through, I wouldn't want to find someone else. I open my mouth and say the only thing that I know will get him to past his irrational thoughts of harming the baby.

"Claim me, Cain."

15.

PACK MAGIC

CAIN

I twirl a strand of blonde hair around my finger, watching the sun shimmer through it. It looks like spun gold.

"Look, that one looks like a wolf." Selena's excited voice tears my eyes away from her hair and up at the sky.

We'd woken up at dawn—Selena unable to sleep because of the baby tap dancing on her bladder, and I wasn't willing to sleep when she couldn't—and decided to lay in the garden, to watch the stars go to bed as the sun rose through the trees surrounding the property.

A good hour passes by and Selena's guessing shapes of the clouds. I look where her finger is pointing and laugh.

"That looks more like an elephant. The ears are massive. Do you even know what a wolf looks like?" Her sudden silence makes me run over my words in my head. What the hell did I say that would take away her excitement so suddenly? All the other clouds we'd disagreed over, she'd laugh and insist she was right before moving onto the next one.

She turns her head to look at me as I change my position to lie on my side. Our new mate bonds tell me she's nervous, but I'm so used to reading her face I need to watch it now. "Actually, I've never seen a wolf. Well, only on TV." The look in her eyes is demanding. Does she really want what I think she does?

"Do you want to see one?" I ask tentatively. All the while, running names through my head of who I would be able to have change before her. It would have to be a submissive wolf. I wouldn't want a dominant wolf changing around her in case she spooks them or makes them see her as prey.

She shakes her head. "Not just any wolf, Cain. I want to meet your wolf."

I swallow as my wolf perks his ears, jumping to attention in that deeply hidden place he lives when I'm not in his form. "I... I'd never forgive myself if he hurt you."

She lifts her good hand and caresses my jaw with her palm. "He would never hurt his mate." Her hand slides down my neck and rests over my heart.

I place my hand over hers and feel my wolf come forward, knowing the eyes she can see in my face are his ice-blue ones. *"Never,"* my wolf says.

She rewards us with a heart-warming smile before pushing herself up and taking my lips with hers. Conscious of the strain it must cause her to be in that position, without breaking the kiss, I lower myself, so her head is once again resting on the ground.

I pull away, leaving us both panting for breath. I'd love to worship her body like I had last night, but not here in the garden where anyone could walk up on us.

Theo and Bel had stayed at a hotel last night, wanting some privacy from the pack, so we'd been lucky to have the privacy ourselves. Mum had stayed at Chloe's to give us space, and I'm assuming someone must have spoken to the rest of the pack because it's not often a night will go by without a pack member dropping by. Someone is bound to arrive home soon.

"Well then, I guess we should give our mate what she wants," I say, not quite sure whether I'm addressing her or my wolf. Maybe both. Standing, I start undressing, discarding my shirt on the floor as I bend slightly to tug down my jeans.

"Do you have to be naked to change?" she asks, her curiosity showing in the higher than normal pitch of her voice.

Fully naked, I throw my jeans on my shirt and glance down at her, my hands on my hips. "We don't have to be naked, but it's much more uncomfortable with clothes on. Not to mention, you ruin a lot of clothes if you shift in them."

Her gaze moving to my groin has it suddenly springing to attention under her scrutiny. Her tongue sneaks out to lick her lips, and I clear my throat, causing a blush to flow over her face at being caught ogling my dick. The sight makes me throw my head back and groan as I cover myself with my hand. "If you don't stop looking at me like that, you won't get to meet my wolf today. He'll force me to take you right here and now."

Her eyes suddenly pop up to meet mine. "How do you all manage to be naked in front of each other without, you know?" She nods in the direction of my dick while fighting to keep her eyes on mine.

"What, without jumping each other?" She nods, and I let out a laugh. "Nakedness isn't sexual for us. Not when we're doing it to shift. It's a necessity."

Selena frowns, and I feel like bending down to rub the cute crease between her brows away. I can't though, because I'll be too close to her and I'll want to do other things.

"So, you don't get turned on seeing the female wolves naked?" she asks.

Suddenly realising she may be feeling insecure about the female wolves, I grab my boxers and slide them back on. "I want to sit with you while we talk about this and I need clothes on to do that," I say, answering her questioning look.

Once beside her, I rub a hand over her beautiful bump as I let the words form on my tongue. "Like I said, being naked is a necessity to shift. It's just natural. Over time my eyes have learnt to avert themselves and I barely even notice they're naked. Obviously teenage guys are constantly getting wood, so seeing the females naked was a definite an issue during puberty." She nods, but I can tell she still has reservations by the sharpness of it and absence of even a small smile. "We try not to be naked in front of each other out of respect for mates, but sometimes it can't be avoided. I promise you, I have never had a female wolf look at me full of lust like you just did."

"Really?" she asks, her eyes wide in disbelief. "They must be blind... or crazy." She presses her lips against mine before pulling away all too quickly. Missing her mouth on mine, I try to connect our lips again only to have her lean back out of reach. "Nope. No more kissing until I've met your wolf."

With a roll of my eyes, I stand up and remove my boxers once again. "You are such a fun spoiler."

"Fun spoiler?" She lets out a giggle. "I'm not spoiling. I'm just postponing."

Silence falls over us as I crouch and allow my wolf to come forward. My shift doesn't take long. Ever since I defeated my dad—my alpha—my shift has been quick. It's still painful, but it's something I can handle. I'd expected my shift speed to revert to a slower pace once I handed the pack to Theo, since most alphas can use the power of the pack to speed up their shift, but it never did. Maybe it was a perk of defeating my alpha. Who knows? I guess it's just another mystery of the werewolf to add to the list of mysteries we seem to carry.

I shake out the last tingles of the change and let out a sneeze as my nose deals with the assault of all the extra scents it's picking up. I say *I*, but I can't help but wonder whether I should say my wolf since he's the one at the forefront. He never has complete control of my body, even when I'm in his form. It would be too dangerous; he's a predator and wouldn't think twice about taking someone down if he felt threatened. He needs my humanity to hold him back from running on instinct. If I left it to him, I'd probably end up lost in his form forever because he feels weak as a human, without his claws and teeth, so he'd never shift back.

Selena's gasp catches his attention. Lifting his head marginally, he takes the sight of her in. We both see the awe shining in her eyes, but he only knows what it is because I do. She looks different as I look out of his eyes, but her scent is the same. If not more intoxicating. He growls appreciatively as we breathe it in, before slowly padding towards her.

She doesn't move.

If it wasn't for the fact that I can't scent any fear, I'd guess her to be scared. I nudge my snout against her hand, hoping to ease any anxiety she may be feeling.

"You're beautiful," she states as she runs her fingers up my snout and over my head. I lay beside her, allowing her to play her fingers through my fur as she wishes, closing my eyes and basking the sensation. "You like that, huh?" She eases back down, still trailing her hand through my fur, and I'm aware we're resting just as we had been before I shifted.

———

*T*he sound of an engine nearing has my eyes popping open and my muscles tensing, ready to attack if the visitor is an unwelcome one.

Selena's breathing beside me is steady and as I glance at her, I see she's fallen asleep. Going by the sun's position in the sky, it doesn't look to have moved a great deal, so not much time could have passed since we'd lain down.

The patio door slides open and I wait for our visitor to announce himself. Two distinct sets of footsteps on the decking tells me it's not one person like I'd thought. My wolf releases a warning growl before I can even try to use my other senses to identify them.

"Hey, that's no way to welcome us back from our extremely

short honeymoon." Theo's voice has us relaxing. There's no threat; it's just my idiot brother. I had been expecting him back today, so I don't know why we'd been on edge in the first place. My wolf growls at my thoughts. Making me grasp exactly why I was on edge. My pregnant mate is beside us, and all his protective instincts are kicking in full force, for her and our young.

Selena stirs beside us as I reposition myself to get a clear view of Theo and Bel. "Cain?" Her hand sinks into my fur. "You're still... I thought I heard voices."

"You did," Bel says, causing Selena to suddenly push up into a sitting position. I glare at Bel for making Selena jump, and Theo returns my growl.

"Don't growl at my mate."

"I wouldn't need to growl if she didn't scare my *mate."* I think towards him, forgetting not all wolves can communicate telepathically and especially out of wolf form. I'd hung around Frankie for too long. She was wolf born and had the gift of communicating telepathically with wolves, regardless of her form.

"That wasn't her intention. And besides, you know as well as I do that she isn't scared. There's no scent of fear." I lift my head, surprised he'd heard my thoughts. An amused grin spreads across his face. "What good is it to have a beta if I can't communicate with his wolf?"

"It's not official."

"You would have been my beta a long time ago if shit hadn't gone pear-shaped. Maybe being official in our hearts is enough for the pack magic." Bel takes Theo's hand in hers before giving it a comforting squeeze, obviously hearing something in his voice that I didn't. All alphas can communicate with their pack mates in wolf form, and their betas can communicate back. Some alphas have enough power that their whole packs can communicate in wolf form. Unfortunately, we aren't one of those packs. The only one I'm aware of is the Rossi Pack over in Western Australia.

Feeling the need to communicate properly, I stretch as I stand, readying myself to shift again. Grabbing my clothes between my teeth, I head for the trees at the edge of the garden. "What's happening?" I hear Selena ask as I trot through enough trees to give myself some cover as I change.

"He's shifting back," Theo explains.

"But why is he going away to do it?" Selena's confusion comes clear through our new mate bond, and I pause, ready to shift now to explain my reasons.

Theo takes over, obviously reading my mind again. "He didn't want you to feel uncomfortable about him being naked in front of Bel." The love that pours through our bond tells me I did the right thing. I push my love back through to her, hoping she can feel it as well as I can, even though she's human. We haven't had the chance to really learn what she can and can't feel through the bond. I don't know many mated humans. I should have asked Kelly when I was with the Rossi Pack. His mate was human. Although, she's no longer with him and I'm sure my mentioning her loss would only cause pain for him.

The shift comes over me as quickly, as it had earlier, and I'm pulling my clothes on in no time. I grit my teeth at the sensitivity of my skin as the material brushes against it, feeling like sandpaper.

I walk through the line of trees, my eyes falling immediately on Selena. She's struggling to stand, a hand on the floor and her belly almost up in the air. I run over. "Let me help," I offer, placing a hand under her armpits and lifting her with ease.

Once on two feet, she throws her arms around my neck, her baby bump pushing into me adorably. "Thank you."

I place a kiss on her temple. "I'm sure Theo or Bel would have helped you up if I hadn't got here first."

"Not for that, silly." She gives me a knowing look; she's

talking about my shifting under the cover of the trees. Maybe she didn't feel me through the bond after all.

"As much as this was nice and all"—Theo ruins our moment —"we need to chat business for a bit."

I give Selena an apologetic smile. "It looks like I need to earn my beta badge."

Bel clears her throat. "I was planning on going to spend some time with Misty. Would you like to come?" she offers, referring to her boss and friend. I can tell by the way Selena stiffens in my arms, she's going to decline the offer. "I'd love to get to know you better, Selena."

Selena snaps her head around to face Bel, probably in the hopes of trying to see if there's any truth to her words. I don't know what she sees, but she relaxes in my arms and nods. "I'd like that. Thank you."

"Great," Bel sounds genuinely happy about Selena's reply and even though I hadn't felt a lie, I realise she really meant what she'd said. I watch as she pulls my brother towards her, his shirt fisted in her hands.

His appreciative growl has me laughing. "Come on, guys. You do have an audience you know?"

Selena taps my arm gently. "Leave them alone. They're newlyweds."

I lean into her and let my arms slide down her sides. "We're newly mated. Does that mean I can get carried away with you not caring about our audience?"

"Mated?" Bel appears at my elbow and tugs Selena away from me. "You'll have to tell me all about that, but right now we need to leave or they'll never get to discussing pack business."

The sound of Selena's laughter is music to my ears as it fades away with every step she takes. I'm thankful for the effort Bel is making to get to know Selena. Having your true mate's estranged wife turn up acting like a mighty bitch and wanting him back, can't have been easy for her. Selena's personality change and willingness to sign the divorce papers probably went a long way to help though. As they round the side of the house, heading towards the car, Theo claps me on the back. "Come on then, brother. Let's deal with our responsibilities for a bit." He leads the way to the house, and I follow, planning to grab a beer on the way. "If we do it quickly, we might be able to meet the girls at the bar."

I pause midstride. "Misty's? Will Selena even be able to go in? Surely it's not safe for the baby." I shake my head with the words, unable to keep the panic out of my voice.

Theo grabs two beers out of the fridge on his way past and offers one to me over the counter. "I'm sure Misty will keep that in mind as she makes one of those bracelets of hers. Anyway, she's your mate. Pack magic may even negate Misty's wards."

My eyes widen as I place the bottle on the side before I squeeze it too hard in my tightening fist. "I wasn't thinking about the wards. It was the customers I was more concerned about." I pull my phone out of my pocket and before even unlocking the screen, I place it back in my pocket. "I need to buy her a phone," I mutter to myself. "You need to call Bel and tell her not to take Selena to the bar. I thought they'd be going to Misty's apartment, not the bar."

Theo pulls out his phone, glancing at the locked screen but doesn't bother to put his pin in. Maybe he has one of those thumbprint things set up. "It's only lunch. They'll go to Misty's apartment for a couple of hours first." He places his phone back in his pocket and grabs my beer off the side before marching towards his office. "If we get through business quickly, you can get to her before they even leave Misty's apartment."

I grunt, not entirely happy with his decision. But not having any of the Pack's contacts in my phone, it's not like I can do anything else about the situation.

16

WE BELONG

I give the bracelet a nervous glance as Bel ties it around my left wrist. It looks like an ordinary leather bracelet, but it's supposed to counteract the magical wards on Misty's bar, the ones meant to repel humans. "Are you sure this is going to work?"

Bel runs her hand over it. "I know it looks like any other bracelet to you, but I can sense the magic." She closes her eyes, and it looks as if she's really feeling something out of the ordinary.

I glance across to Misty as she walks in the room with her work uniform on. "The baby will be safe?" I ask cautiously. I've always wanted to go to Misty's, but I won't put my baby's life at risk. I've heard how powerful the wards are, how a human could have a heart attack if they were somehow forced to go in. Living around a pack of werewolves who think you're a ditz, means they sometimes forget what they say in front of you.

After I lost my father and brother, I wasn't the carefree girl I'd been before, but Theo helped me slowly find her again. The day Cain told me about their secret, that's when I became a nasty bitch, and played up to the ditzy image everyone seemed to be treating me as. I thought Theo would eventually tell me himself, but with every day he didn't, I completely lost myself.

A hand rubs against my bump, pulling me back to the

present to find Misty giving me a serene smile. "I wouldn't put ya baby in danger. I adjusted the spell to cover ya both. It's much stronger than the one I gave Ruby when she was a human."

"When she *was* a human?" I ask, my eyes widening in surprise.

They both snap their eyes towards me. "You don't know?" Bel asks, before shaking her head. "Of course, you don't know. We thought you were in the dark when all that happened."

"Is it something to do with her being mated to Eddie? I've put two and two together and worked that much out."

Misty looks at her watch. "I've gotta get to work. We can fill ya in on the way." She reaches out to hook onto my casted arm before thinking better of it and walking a few steps in front. "I can't believe Cain did that."

"Guilt must be eating him up." Bel glances across at me from where she's walking beside me, her arm hooked in my good arm. "His wolf will be having a hard time. We protect our mates. We don't hurt them."

I sigh. "We weren't mated at the time."

"Maybe not, but his wolf has thought of you as his mate for a long time. Technicalities like that won't make a difference."

We walk out of the apartment complex, Misty giving the guard a polite "Catch ya later" on her way past. As we slip into Misty's purple VW Beetle, I change the subject.

"What did you mean about Ruby when you said she *was* human?"

Bel turns in the passenger seat to look at me through the gap between the two front seats. "Do you remember when Cain turned up and everyone was pretty much yelling at everyone?"

I nod, of course I remember that day. That's the day I saw the man I never thought I'd lay eyes on again.

"Well, she was attacked by a vampire, and Dominic, the king of the local vampire coven turned her in order to save her life."

My heart picks up speed. Surely, I didn't hear that right. "Vampire? Did you just say vampire?"

"Yes. Just remember they've existed all the time you haven't known, and you weren't killed," Bel states, before giggling at my raised brow. "That probably isn't as comforting as it sounded in my head."

"No kidding." I shake my head. Unbelievable. I'd never imagined vampires were real. But then again, if you'd ask me all those years ago, before Cain shared his secret, I wouldn't have thought werewolves were real either. "So, Ruby's a vampire." I raise a hand to my mouth as I think of all the adjustments a change like that must take. "How is she coping with all the change?"

Misty pulls into an abandoned alley and stops beside some large bins at the back of a building. Bel jumps out the car. "She struggled at first but seems to be doing well now. She'll be here once the sun goes down. She'll be more than happy to chat to you about it," Bel states as I heave myself out of the car. "Do you need a hand?"

After a bit of effort, I straighten beside the car. "Thanks, but it looks like I've got it. Although I might need to take you up on that in the next couple of weeks."

Misty lets us in and goes about opening up. I pause before the doorway, taking stock of my body, searching for any reaction to the wards that are supposed to be here. I feel… nothing. Well, nothing unusual.

"All good?" Bel asks, giving me a curious glance.

Smiling, I step over the threshold and release a breath as again, nothing happens.

"Fabulous," Bel says, before getting me seated on a stool at the side of the bar. It has no back support so I know I'm not going to last long on it, but before I can say anything, Bel tells me we'll move to a table once it starts getting busy.

An hour passes and customers have been slowly filing in. My back is aching on the stool, and I'm desperate to move but Bel is distracted, chatting to someone at the other side of the bar and I feel that if I try to slide off the stool, I'm likely to fall off the damn thing.

Warm hands glide around my back and rest on hips, causing me to jump. The stool wobbles on the spot, but the strong hands hold me steady.

"Hey, I didn't mean to startle you." Cain's breath falls over my neck in a caress, causing goosebumps to rise.

I lean into him, and my back screams out at the movement. I let out a grunt of pain as I try to reach around to rub my lower back.

Cain pushes my hands away and takes over. "I can take you home if you want?"

"No, I want to hang around for a while and see what you guys have been getting up to all these years." I let out a moan of pleasure as his hands ease away my aches.

He leans in, and I can feel a familiar hardness pressed to my back. "If you keep making noises like that, we'll have to make use of Misty's office." He presses a kiss to my shoulder before I hear him breathing in my scent. "Let's get you sat somewhere more comfortable."

"I don't think I'll ever get used to you doing that." I let him help me off the stool and lead me towards a round table near the dance floor.

He pulls out a chair and I take a seat. "And what might that be?" he asks, sitting beside me. I let out a squeal as he tugs my chair closer to him. Once next to him, he runs a finger over my shoulder and inhales in again.

"That. Sniffing me." I laugh. "It's weird."

"I can't help it. It's a were thing. You'll just have to get used to it."

Theo takes a seat opposite us and glares over at the bar. "It's her night off, yet she'll spend most of it behind the bar."

I glance over at the bar for a second and watch Bel serve a customer before I give Theo a sympathetic smile. "She did say once Lucy turns up for her shift, she'll join us. If you sit at the bar, she'll probably talk to you between customers."

He stares me down with a raised brow. "Are you trying to get rid of me." He drops his eyes to follow Cain's hand caressing the skin at the edge of my top, dropping dangerously close to my breast. "I know you're newly mated, but you're in a bar full of people. People who can smell arousal."

I slap Cain's hand away, earning a laugh from the pair of them. "Aw, beautiful, I can't help it. You bring the sex beast out of me."

"Oh my God." I lift my hands to cover my flaming cheeks. "Maybe I should have gone home."

"And miss out on all the fun to come? No way," Bel states as she drops into Theo's lap. He thoroughly ravishes her mouth, making me feel the need to avert my eyes.

"I thought you were waiting for Lucy to arrive." Theo's voice makes it clear it's safe to look back in their direction, and I do in time to catch him breathing in her scent, just like Cain seems to love doing. I can't help but grin at the sight.

"You were staring daggers at the customers. Misty said I should come over here before you scared them all away." Bel leans in and gives Theo a gentle kiss on the lips, which he instantly deepens.

"Oh, come on!" Ruby shouts from behind us. "I thought moving out meant I wouldn't have to witness you two playing tonsil tennis anymore." I glance across to Cain as Ruby kisses his cheek. I can't help but look for vampire signs, but she doesn't look any different to any other time I've seen her. She's got the same long wavy blonde hair and green eyes, which are a sage rather than emerald like Theo's. "I hear congratulations is in order." She looks at Cain with raised eyebrows, and I feel like shrinking into my seat. When it became clear that Theo was never going to tell me about his secret, I started to resent him. I never cared what the pack or the Wilson family thought of me. Now, I do. I love Cain, and I want everyone he loves to like me. I don't want them to think I'm the evil bitch I once was. I was only that person because the resentment was eating me up.

Cain slides his hand down my arm and takes my hand in his, making me wonder if he's sensing my anxiety somehow. He did say there may be some weird feelings that may come through to me, like a side effect of our mating, but I haven't felt any different. So I hadn't thought it would have affected him either. I'll have to remember to ask him later when we are alone. "Thanks, Rubes. It's been a long time in the making."

Ruby gives him smile and a nod before turning her smile on me. "Welcome to the family again, Selena. I'd love to have a chat and compare our mate bonds. The one between me and Eddie seems to be normal. Although when I'm dead for the day, it's completely severed. Like I'm really dead…" She frowns, before carrying on. "Which I am, so that makes sense… I guess."

"The first time that happened I freaked out. I shifted and tore up the bedroom." Eddie sidles up to Ruby, who spins around and throws her arms around him before planting a kiss on his lips. "Hey, baby. I missed you too," he says as he pulls away.

"Weren't you just telling me off for playing tonsil tennis?" Theo laughs. "Hypocrite," he jokes, with a shake of his head.

"There was absolutely no tongue action. I do know how to behave in public, unlike some," Ruby snaps back while peeling herself off Eddie and taking a seat next to Cain.

Eddie pulls a short stool up beside Ruby and straddles it. "I can attest to that. I'm disappointed to say there was absolutely no tongue action." He looks genuinely disappointed.

I can't help but laugh.

Cain slides into my space, my laugh having obviously caught his attention. "I think we should show them what a proper kiss looks like."

Before I can argue, his lips are on mine and I'm melting into his arms. A shrill wolf whistle has me pulling away, remembering we have an audience. "It's looking like couples' corner over here. Maybe I should take these drinks and drown my sorrows elsewhere."

Eddie stands and reaches for one of the drink-laden trays Billy's holding. "Don't even think about it, buddy."

"Ginger ale for the beautiful Selena," Billy says, giving me a wink as he places a glass on the table before me. My eyes widen in surprise as I wonder how he knows what I drink. "I've seen you drinking the stuff by the gallon at the house," he says with a shrug, correctly guessing my thoughts.

"Thanks, Billy." I give him a grateful smile. "It's one of the only things that kept my stomach settled in the beginning. Now I think I've become addicted to the stuff." I laugh.

Billy pulls a chair over from the next table and sits to my right. *"Holy shit!* What happened to your arm?" His eyes are focused on my cast.

Cain stiffens on my other side, no doubt dwelling in the guilt once again. I give him a quick glance and seeing his jaw tight with tension, I give his hand a comforting squeeze. "My ex turned up yesterday. Things got a little heated."

"*I* got a little heated," Cain snaps, pulling his hand from mine to run it through his dark hair.

I ignore the numerous gasps around the table and turn to him. "Cain," I plead. He's staring across the room and I don't want to use my cast-covered arm to turn his head so I squeeze his knee. "Look at me, Cain. Please." He turns his head stiffly.

"You didn't do it intentionally."

I let my eyes roam around everyone at the table, pinning each one of them with a glacial stare, daring them to disagree with me. "He was fuming at my ex, who tried to drag me away."

I turn back to Cain, demanding with every fibre of my body that he listens to me. "*I* put my hand in yours, even though I knew you were in a rage and on the edge of shifting. *I* did that Cain. Do you hear me?"

I hold my breath, waiting for him to reply or even show any sign of listening.

His eyes close and I slowly lean back in my seat, thinking he's come to his senses. "You sound like a domestic abuse victim, blaming yourself." His words are whispered, but at a quick glance around the table, I can see the others heard him too. And by the pitying looks on all their faces, they agree with him.

Anger surges through me. "For fuck's sake, it was *me!*" I slam my cast on the table, regretting it the second my hand starts to throb. I school my features, not wanting anyone to know about the extra pain. My drink topples over and I scoot my chair back before the liquid pours off the edge of the table and soaks into my floor length maxi dress. Cain storms off towards the bar, leaving me watching him and wishing he would just think about this rationally.

Billy places a firm had on my shoulder as I move to follow him. "He'll be back. He just needs a breather."

Cain might not be listening to reason, but I sure as hell want everyone else to take my word for it. I turn away from Cain and look at Theo. He's the leader. If he understands, everyone else will. "It wasn't like he's making it sound." Tears fill my eyes. I don't want them to think badly of him. He's hating himself enough for everyone.

"Selena. Sweetheart." The term of endearment startles me to glance in Bel's direction, hoping it didn't upset her. She gives me a reassuring smile as she traces a finger over the back of Theo's hand. "We don't blame him. Hell, if I were in his shoes, I would have probably done the same thing. You're human. You break easily."

Billy strokes my forearm comfortingly.

"But it doesn't mean he has to like what he did," Theo finishes. His eyes flick behind me and I know Cain is there.

I can feel him.

A gentle caress over my skin, like static electricity—only it's Cain. It's the first time I've felt something like this. Closing my eyes to focus better, I feel a tugging in my mind's eye and become overwhelmed with love.

I turn my head and pop open my eyes to find Cain looking down at me with the same love in his eyes. Sensing a pang of guilt, I know it's coming from Cain. Excitement pours through me as I realise we really do have a mate bond. Cain's smile grows, and I can only assume he's feeling my excitement. I let my love pour through the bond.

Cain places a glass of ginger ale on the table over my shoulder and slides into his chair before leaning into me, his hand wrapping around my neck and his fingers gripping the hair at the base of my skull as he kisses me senseless.

"*Fuck!* It's getting hot in here. What the hell did we just miss?" Billy picks up his pint of beer and drains the glass. "I need another fucking drink."

Cain doesn't take his eyes off mine as he pulls away. "Our mate bond just kicked in, didn't it, beautiful?" At a loss for words after that kiss, I nod my agreement as his hand snakes around my neck and he runs his thumb over my bottom lip.

"Did I hear ya say ya needed a drink?" Misty catches our attention, and we all seem to look towards her in unison as she places a pint in front of Billy before giving him a wink. "Hi, guys. I figured I'd come and visit you while I have my break."

"Thanks, doll, you're a mind reader," Billy says as he takes a gulp of the amber liquid.

Misty glances around, seeming to look for a spare chair. "Nope, ya just shouted loud enough for everyone to hear ya," she states before leaning a hip on the back of his chair.

Billy sticks his leg to the side a little. "Here." He pats his knee. "You can't spend your break on your feet."

Misty takes him up on the offer and I catch sight of Billy's hand slide along her back. I can't help but wonder if there may be something happening between the two of them that nobody knows about. I glance around the table and see a questioning look on Theo's face, confirming my suspicions.

"Well, if it isn't my favourite people, all at one table," a well-spoken male voice states.

Theo growls, eliciting a playful smack from Bel. "Behave."

Theo sighs. "Dominick," he greets with a slight nod. *Dominick.* The name rings a bell and it takes me a second to remember where from. Dominick is the king of vampires here in Mount Roxby. Misty and Bel were only talking about him earlier.

I lean into Cain's side a little more as I try to hide a shudder. I'm not sure I like the thought of him being a king of people who suck blood. Jesus, my sister-in-law is one of those people. I flick my eyes to Ruby before flicking them to Dominick to try and find any similarities, some sign of vampirism, but I see nothing that screams vampire. Ruby looks just as she always has and Dominick looks like a regular guy. Quite possibly a little arrogant, but there are a lot of regular guys who have that trait.

Dominick comes to a stop behind Billy, placing his hand on Billy's shoulder. Cain stiffens beside me, and I wonder if it's some supernatural creature political stand, but Dominick suddenly gives the shoulder a gentle, almost intimate, squeeze before letting go. "Ruby, I haven't seen you at the compound lately. Are you keeping well fed?"

"I haven't seen *you* at the compound lately, and considering I've been feeding there most days, that's somewhat strange." The curiosity in Ruby's voice seems to interest everyone around the table. Theo sits forward slightly in his seat, and Bel squints at Dominick as if she's trying to read his mind. Although she's more likely to be trying to sense his emotions, since she's an empath. That was something else she managed to fill me in on today. I actually learnt a world of information in just those few hours I spent with her and Misty.

"I guess I've been otherwise engaged." Dominick glances across at Bel and frowns, no doubt at her scrutiny.

"You're seeing someone. You actually care about them," Bel states, sounding shocked at her discovery.

Dominick waves a hand dismissively. "I do have the ability to care for another person. I'm not a complete monster." He shakes his head. "Anyway, I do believe you wanted to ask me something, Theo?"

Theo clears his throat before speaking. "Yes. Have you given permission to a fox or a skulk of them to enter my territory?"

"*Our* territory," Dominick corrects. "No, the lion was the last shifter I allowed in, and I believe after that, we agreed you would deal with shifter request from then onwards."

"We did, but we had a fox turn up at the pack house, and I wanted to make sure they didn't have permission before I retaliated." I shiver at Theo's threat of retaliation. Stu is a dangerous man, and although I know Theo and Cain aren't weak, the thought of them fighting with him has me scared.

Cain's arm around my shoulder rubs up and down my bicep. "Hey, everyone will be fine. It's what we do," he says, clearly catching onto to my feelings through the bond and putting two and two together.

Misty jumps off Billy's knee. "Well, it's been entertaining, but my break's up. I'll try and catch ya'll later."

"I'll walk you back to the bar," Dominick says, offering Misty the crook of his arm, but not before running a finger over the back of Billy's neck. Glancing around the table, I don't see anyone else react to the discreet move.

Misty takes his arm and hugs it to her body. "Well, thank you, kind sir."

"Misty! We have a lot to talk about, girl," Bel calls across the table as Misty and Dominick walk away. It seems she's come to some conclusion I haven't.

"Sure thing," Misty shouts.

Eddie turns to Bel after watching Misty and Dominick walk away. "What do you know that we don't?"

Bel tucks a strand of her hair behind her ear and flicks her eyes away from Misty, letting them fall on Eddie, but not before they drift over Billy a second too long. "I'm sure we'll all find out soon enough. When it's set in stone."

I lay my head against Cain's shoulder and close my eyes as I listen to the chatter around the table. I haven't felt like part of a family for a long time. It's so nice to finally feel like I belong. I place my hand over my bump as the baby kicks and I correct my thought.

We belong.

SURPRISES SUCK

As the weeks pass, I realise I need to get out of the pack house. Having people around constantly is too much for someone who's been a lone wolf for such a long time. Plus I want some privacy with my mate—which is nigh-on impossible in such a busy house. With this in mind, I've made arrangements to take Selena to view an apartment in town. I'm hoping she'll like it.

"Okay. Let's escape before I get another foot to the bladder. This baby seems to be enjoying making me suffer today." Selena comes into view and I push off from the wall I was leaning on. "What's this surprise you have anyway?"

Sliding my arm around her, I lead her out the door. "You'll find out when we get there."

Selena buckles herself in the passenger seat with a huff. "Surprises suck. Every time."

I lean over the centre console and place a kiss on the tip of her nose. "Not mine. Everyone loves my surprises."

She pins me with a serious look. "Don't say I didn't warn you."

*T*he lift doors close and I push the number eight, making the lift start its incline. Turning to face Selena, I catch sight of her wince. "Are you okay?"

Selena takes a few shallow breaths. "Yeah. The beast was pushing on a nerve. It's all good now." She gives me a reassuring smile.

The lift suddenly jerks to a stop, and I reach out to steady Selena as she jolts forward. *"Fuck!"*

"Cain, tell me this lift is going to go again." Her eyes, wide with panic, lock on mine. "I don't want to be stuck in here."

I push the Emergency Call button before pulling her into my arms. "Someone will answer our call, and they'll have it up and running in no time, beautiful." She stiffens in my arms as her tension doubles the longer we listen to the ringing through the speaker. The speaker falls silent and I push the button once again.

After another round of unanswered ringing, I pry my phone out of my pocket and dial the estate agent. "Hi, David. It's Cain. You showed me round number sixteen in Sanori House."

"Yes, did your wife like it?" he asks, his voice high in excitement at the prospect.

I flick a glance to Selena as she steps out of my hold and paces the confines of the lift. "She hasn't had a chance to see it yet. We're currently stuck in the lift, and no one is answering the emergency call. I was hoping you'd know who to call?"

"I'll get on with the building manager and make sure someone gets to you ASAP." His voice is sharp and to the point, which makes me feel comforted in the fact that he'll do all he can to get someone to us. He wants a sale after all.

"Tha—"

"Cain!" Selena's panicked voice cuts me off.

I drop the phone from my ear and focus my attention on

Selena, who's looking at me through wide eyes on a dangerously pale face.

"I think my water just broke." Her words send a wave of terror through me.

I shake my head. "Maybe it was a bladder kick and you didn't realise."

"I haven't fucking pissed myself, Cain," she snaps angrily, her hands fisting at her sides.

My eyes drop the puddle beneath her feet. "Shit. Shit. Shit," I chant. Pushing the Emergency Call button once again.

Selena grabs hold of the handrail on the wall, her cast making a clanging noise as it hits the metal. She bends at the waist, all the while groaning. "Please let this be Braxton Hicks," she pleads. The terror in her voice makes my heart sink. *Focus, dammit! She needs me.*

Remembering my phone, I call the only person I know who's been through childbirth.

"Hello." Mum answers on the second ring and I relax marginally at the sound of her voice.

"Mum, Selena's in labour." A million questions run through my mind, but I ask the most important one. "What do I do?"

"She's not due for another couple of weeks. You need to get her to the hospital to be safe."

I rub a hand over Selena's stiff back as she lets out another groan. "I would, Mum, but we're currently stuck in a fucking lift." I take a deep breath and realise Selena should be doing the same. "Breathe, Selena. Do you recall what you learnt in those birthing classes?"

"I took her to most of them. Put me on speaker," Mum demands, and I place the phone on the floor. "Selena, remember how they taught you to pant?" The sound of Mum panting comes through the phone and Selena joins in.

"That's it, beautiful. You're doing great."

"Cain, you need to keep her calm and breathing, just like

she is. I'm going to hang up now so you can call an ambulance. Tell them what's happening and they'll get a midwife on the line. Okay?"

"Okay," I reply to the silent phone as the line goes dead.

Selena whimpers into the empty lift. "I can't have this baby in a lift."

I turn her so she's facing me, ducking slightly to catch her eyes with mine. "You can do this, Selena. I know you c—" My sentence is cut short as she leans into me, gripping my shoulders with fingers that feel like talons and letting out a pain-filled cry.

I rub circles on her back until her hold loosens and I assume whatever caused the pain has passed. Picking up my phone off the floor I quickly dial 000. The call is connected immediately.

"This is emergency services, what service do you require?"

"Ambulance… and fire brigade," I add, thinking about our predicament. "We're stuck in a lift."

"What is the address and location of the lift?"

I reel off the address hoping the estate agent already has someone working on getting us out. Selena lets out another pain-filled cry that tears my attention from the phone. I place it onto the floor after ensuring its once again on speakerphone.

"Can you tell me who's injured, sir?" asks the female on the other side of the call.

"My wife's in labour." Remembering the midwife Mum mentioned, I bring it up. "She needs a midwife."

"Okay, sir. I have a midwife coming on the line. While we wait, let me get your names and a few details about your wife's pregnancy."

"Cain and Selena. She's—"

"Thirty-eight weeks," Selena says through gritted teeth.

"I'm just going to relay your information to the midwife and then she'll take over the call."

Selena slides down to the floor and reaches out for my hand with her cast-covered one. "I'm scared, Cain. What if something goes wrong?"

I sit down beside her and brush some loose hair from her sweat-coated brow. "I won't let it."

"This isn't an enemy you can just cut down," she snaps. Her fear is thick in the air causing my wolf to stir. He wants to protect her, but there's nothing he can protect her from. I tell him as much as I push him back down.

"Hello, Cain. Are you still there?" A new voice speaks over the phone.

"Yes." I jump forward, ready to do anything the midwife directs me to.

"Selena, I hear your baby has decided to surprise you with an early appearance." Her voice has a calming quality to it, which I guess is good for situations like this. "My name is Katie, and I'm going to talk you through this until the paramedics arrive."

I take a deep breath to centre myself, knowing I need to stay as calm as possible for Selena's sake.

"Cain, the first thing I need you to do is take a look and see how things are coming along."

I steal myself. Mentally preparing myself for what I may see. I've seen the videos of men fainting during childbirth, and I know I can't do that. I'm all she's got right now. I reach for her skirt as she lets out another cry.

"She shouldn't be in this much pain." I wish I could take her place. I reach through our bond hoping to pull some of the pain from her, having heard it's something mated couples can do. Unfortunately, nothing happens. Our bond is probably too new or maybe Selena's humanity gives it limitations.

"Cain." The voice pulls me out of my head. "Women have babies every day. You're both doing great."

Selena quietens down once again, so I decide now is the

best time to take a quick look. "Beautiful, you're doing amazing." I rub her knee comfortingly. "I'm going to take a quick look. Okay?"

"Hurry up, Cain. I think I need to push."

"Don't push just yet, Selena. Cain needs to make sure everything is okay with baby first." Katie says, her voice sounding higher pitched than it had been a moment ago. The sound makes my wolf stir, once again.

Lifting the hem of Selena's skirt, I fold it up and over her bump. I rip the edges of her underwear and part Selena's legs to get a clear view. "Holy shit, I can see the head." I shake my head at the sight. "It's too fucking big. It'll get stuck."

"*Shut up!*" Selena yells.

"Women's bodies are made for this. It'll fit just fine," Katie insists. "Can you just see the head or is it protruding?"

I give Selena's knee another squeeze. "Protruding. Is that what we want?"

"Yes. Selena, when the next contraction comes, I want you to push. Okay?"

Selena nods. "Yes."

"Isn't this all too quick? I thought labour lasted hours." My concerns are out of my mouth before I even have time to think about asking them.

"Every woman is different, Cain. Some could have been in labour for hours and not even realise it. They could just put the pain down to indigestion," Katie says calmly.

Selena licks her lips and looks at me guiltily. "I've been having cramps all morning. I thought it was just be Braxton Hicks. It's too early to be in labour. I was told most first-time mums have to be induced."

Taking a deep breath, I turn my focus back to the matter at hand. "Okay, Katie, what do I have to do next?"

"Cain, you need to hold your hands around the head and guide it out. As the neck comes into view, you need to make sure the cord isn't around the baby's neck. Okay? That's really important."

Selena's fear presses down on me with Katie's words. I lift myself up and place a kiss on her lips, hoping to ease her worry. She shoves me away before I can say any comforting words.

"I need to push."

I drop back on my heels and place my hands where they need to be.

Selena bares down with a feral sound. The baby's head moves out fractionally, and my hands itch to be wiped on my jeans. *What if they're too slippery to catch the baby?*

"You drop my baby and I'll kill you, Cain." Selena lets out a growl any werewolf would be proud of. "I don't care if you have fangs and claws." Her last words are barely recognisable behind the growl, but I heard them loud and clear, suddenly realising I must have spoken my worries aloud.

The little head pops out before my eyes, and I instantly slide a finger around its neck, looking for the cord. "The neck's free of a cord."

"That's good," Katie says, the relief evident in her voice. "Selena, one more big push and baby will be out."

"Ready, beautiful?" I ask.

She grits her teeth once more, determination written on her features. "Now!"

I cradle the baby's head, and the body seems to slip out once the shoulders make it through. The lift is filled with the sound of a baby's wail, and I release the breath I didn't realise I've been holding.

"That sounds like a healthy cry. I've just been told the paramedics are outside. They're going to be coming through the lift doors any second now." Katie says.

"Hey, sweetie," I coo to the baby in my arms. "Come and meet your mamma." Crawling up beside Selena, I place the baby on her chest. Not moving my hands away until I'm certain Selena has a secure grip. "We have a daughter. She's just as beautiful as her mamma."

I place a soft kiss on Selena's head.

The gaze on her tear-streaked face doesn't leave our baby's. "She's gorgeous."

The doors creak open and two guys dressed in green drop in from about waist height, the lift having evidently stopped between floors. "Hi, I'm Marcus and this is Eric. You must be Selena and Cain. Congratulations," one of the guys says, placing his bag on the floor.

I step aside giving them room to get to Selena and the baby. Picking up my phone, I pocket it before anyone steps on it.

He digs around in his bag, coming out with a couple of clips and a pair of scissors. "Dad, I've got one more job for you" He holds the scissors out towards me, and I take them warily.

Eric crouches beside Selena, reaching towards the baby. "Can I have a quick look at baby? I'll get her back to you in no time."

Selena nods and I watch her loosen her hold as he lifts the baby. Marcus places a clip on the cord near the baby's tummy and another clip a couple of inches away. "Just cut right there," he says, pointing to the space between the clips.

Taking the scissors, I make the cut, surprised at how much force it takes. It's tougher than I'd imagined. I smile feeling like I've taken the last step in making her birth official. Eric steps away, handing the baby to a fireman—who's crouching on the floor in the corridor—before lifting himself up and taking the baby away. "Where's he taking her?" I ask, torn between following him and staying with Selena.

"He's just taking her into a better light. He needs to check her colour looks good." Marcus places a blood pressure cuff on Selena's arm.

I raise my eyes to her pale face and watch as her eyes roll

back. My stomach sinks and I watch Marcus work feeling helpless.

"*Fuck!*" Marcus places a finger on Selena's pulse. "*Eric. I need you back here, STAT!*" he shouts.

I try to listen to the pulse he's feeling for, but I can't hear anything over my own blood rushing through my ears.

Eric joins us immediately, handing the freshly swaddled baby off to me. "Your baby is perfectly healthy." He turns his attention to Marcus and Selena, crouching down beside them. "How's mum doing?"

"Her blood pressure's low. We need to transport her immediately…" Marcus's words fade off as fear grips me.

18.

VISITORS

SELENA

My eyes flicker open and roam the room until they fall on Cain. He's sitting beside the bed, his head thrown back against the wall and his hand resting in a plastic cot. The baby's hand is wrapped around his index finger. Seeing the man who holds my heart in his hands, with my beautiful baby has me smiling from ear to ear. I didn't think I could love anyone as much as I love the two people in front of me.

I reach out and stroke my baby's cheek. "Hi, gorgeous. It looks like you already have Daddy wrapped around your little finger."

Cain jumps in his seat, pulling his hand out of the baby's grip causing her to cry at the loss of his finger. "You're awake. I should call a nurse." He pushes a button beside the bed as his eyes roam over my face. "How are you feeling? It was touch and go for a while." He places a gentle kiss on my lips, leaving them to linger for just a moment. "You scared me to death." He brushes back my hair before cradling my face in his hands. His face is pale and the bags under his eyes tell me he's barely slept, so I know what he's saying must be true.

"I told you, surprises suck," I say, trying to lighten his mood.

He smiles and lifts the baby out of the cot. He looks comfortable with her, as if he's done it a number of times already. "This little surprise didn't suck."

"She's an anomaly," I agree. "She needs a name."

"Well, it's good to see you awake. Baby can have some mummy cuddles now," a nurse announces as she rushes into the room. She pushes a button on the machine beside me, and the cuff I hadn't noticed around my bicep tightens uncomfortably. "Perfect," she says, reading the numbers on the screen. "Let's get rid of this and you can try breastfeeding." She pulls the cuff off my arm and undoes the tie on the gown around my neck.

Cain places the baby in my arms, carefully wedging her in against my cast. I look at the nurse dumbfound. "I don't know how to do this."

"It's instinct. Just place her little mouth near your nipple and she'll do the rest." She nods towards the baby. "Give it a try."

After pulling the gown down to expose my right breast, I guide the baby's mouth towards my nipple, just as the nurse suggested. Her little mouth roots around for a minute searching, and I start to think she isn't going to do it until she latches on with an uncomfortable suction. I look between Cain and the nurse, excited. "I did it."

"You did." Cain gives me a proud smile before standing and stretching. "I'm going to give Mum a call and let her know you're okay," he says, pulling out his phone.

"I'll hang around until you get back, make sure Mum's feeling well enough to keep holding baby," the nurse offers as she takes a seat at the side of the bed with all the equipment.

"Thank you. I won't be long." Cain leans down and places a kiss on my head and then the baby's before leaving the room.

The door has barely closed behind Cain when there's a knock on the door and Bel's head pops in the opening. "Hey, a little bird told me you were awake."

I turn my body slightly, hoping to hide my breast from Bel's view.

She strolls in as though she hasn't even noticed I have my boobs out.

The nurse glances between the two of us before standing. "Maybe we should give Selena some privacy while she feeds the baby." She tries to tuck and arm around Bel to guide her out the room.

Bel easily dodges her. "Privacy? We're like sisters. There are no secrets between the two of us." She lets out a short chuckle. I can't help but grin at Bel's words. Secrets are one thing that aren't between us any longer. I wish she really did feel like we were sisters. Unfortunately, I'm pretty sure she'll never be able to feel like that, not with the history I have with Theo. "If you have other patients you need to attend to, feel free to go. We'll be sure to ring the button if we need anything."

The nurse hesitates at the door, and I give the her a reassuring smile as she weighs me up. "Make sure you do that," she orders as she strides off.

"I wasn't expecting any visitors," I say, closing my mouth quickly, trying to get over the shock of her being here.

Bel makes herself comfortable in the seat by all the machines. "You're pack. Of course we're here. We arrived a little while ago. The nurses wouldn't let us in until you woke up."

The baby's suckling suddenly stops and I glance down to find her asleep. I lift her up and gently pat her back as she rests against my shoulder.

"We?" I ask, as Bel's words suddenly register.

"Theo, Trudy, Billy, and Misty. Cain's talking to them now. He was trying to get them to go home before I snuck in. He didn't think you'd want the fuss."

I glance at the door wondering whether I do actually want the fuss. I've not had any real friends for such a long time. My heart swells at the thought of these people wanting to visit me.

"I think I'd like a fuss." My cheeks burn in embarrassment at the admission.

The door opens and Bel stands, reaching over the bed for the baby. "I'll take the baby while you fix up your gown."

Remembering I have my boobs on show, I willingly let my daughter go, and pull up the gown. I feel Cain's energy enter the room and look up to find him holding up a bag. "They brought your bag. Do you want to freshen up before I let them in?"

"Yes, please." I glance at the baby in Bel's arms as she coos at her and knowing she'll be safe, I slide my legs out the bed and place them gingerly on the floor. I wobble slightly and lurch for Cain's arm to steady myself as he dumps the bag on the bed and reaches out to me.

"I've got you." He tucks me under his arm and slowly walks me to the bathroom. Lowering me down into the plastic chair placed under the shower, he orders, "Don't move. I'm just going to get your bag. I'll be right back." He dashes back towards the bed.

He's back within seconds. After hanging my clean clothes on the back of the door, he places a towel on the rail. "Do you want me to help or should I just stand by?"

I stand and feeling steady enough, I start to strip out of my hospital gown. I'd feel embarrassed under his scrutiny if I'd thought it was sexual, especially since I feel like a complete mess, but the tension in his shoulders tells me it's worry that's making him watch me so closely. "I'm good, I think. Just stay close, in case."

The tension in his shoulders eases with my words, and a smile spreads across his face. "I'm not going anywhere, beautiful." His words send my heart soaring as I feel more loved than ever.

I turn on the shower and step under the spray. The thought of our baby in the other room and people waiting to see us has me making quick work of it. I turn off the taps and Cain steps up behind me, wrapping me in a fluffy towel that smells of our washing powder. "Is this from home?"

"Yeah, I put it in your bag a few days ago. I didn't think hospital towels would be soft enough for you, not when you probably feel like you've just been put through the wringer." How did I manage to get myself such a thoughtful mate? I must be luckiest woman alive.

Turning in his arms, I give him a quick kiss. "Thank you for thinking of me."

"Always." He places a kiss on my forehead before stepping away and handing me my clothes, one by one as I pull them on.

I run a brush through my hair and quickly plait it to keep it out of my way before opening the bathroom door and entering the room once again.

Bel looks up from cooing at the baby and nods towards the door. "You better tell them they can come in. Theo's impatience is suffocating me through the closed door."

Feeling a little weak and hoping Bel can't pick it up with her empathic abilities, especially not while she's being bombarded with Theo's impatience, I sit on the bed and keep my smile plastered on my face. "Go put him out of his misery, Cain."

Cain gives me a long stare before striding towards the door. He pauses with his grip on the handle. "You need to remember we have a bond. I'll tell them it'll have to be a quick visit." Not giving me a chance to argue, he opens the door and tells them exactly that.

Theo playfully slaps him in the chest as he passes. "Stop being so overprotective." Theo walks up to me and places a kiss on the top of my head. "Congratulations, Lena. Now let me have a look at our precious new pack member." He makes quick work of crossing the room and taking the baby out of his mate's arms.

"How are you doing, sweetie?" Trudy's question catches my

attention, and I flick my eyes towards her. "You look shattered. We won't stay long." She rubs my hand with hers and calls over to Theo. "Stop being a hog, Theo. I want to hold my grandbaby."

Her words make my heart flutter. Part of me can't believe that this wonderful family is accepting my baby as if she is their own blood. Seeing Cain hovering over Theo ready to jump in the second he can, makes me certain Cain will be the best father this baby could ever wish for. My heart is full to bursting with the amount of love I feel for Cain.

Trudy carefully slips her hands under the baby and Theo releases his hold. All the while Cain's hands hover underneath the transfer; clearly he's concerned that the baby may fall.

"Support the head," he orders.

Trudy gives him a glare as she steps out of his reach. "I have held a baby before, Cain." She rolls her eyes before turning her attention on me. "Does this little beauty have a name yet?"

I glance at Cain. We haven't exactly had a chance to talk about a name yet. After doing all the silly things I could try, to predict the baby's sex I'd been certain I was expecting a boy so I only had boy's names picked out. "Do you have any favourites?"

A small smile crosses his face and he lifts a hand to his chest. "Me? You want me to name her?"

"I can't think of anyone better than her daddy to give her, her name," I say, hoping he can feel my honesty through our mating bond.

He makes it across the room in two strides. His hand sliding around my neck in a possessive gesture as he crushes his lips on mine. "I fucking love you," he says, pulling back and resting his forehead against mine. "I love Olivia too. With my whole damn heart."

"Olivia?" I lean back and raise a brow in question.

"Olivia. Our daughter." Releasing me, he steps over to Trudy and takes our little girl out of her arms, settling her small body against his broad chest. "She's beautiful. She needed a beautiful name too."

I smile as he brings her towards me. "Olivia." I test the name on my lips and as I watch her in his arms, I decide the name fits her perfectly. "It's perfect."

Trudy leans over Cain's shoulder and strokes Olivia's hair. "The question is does my grandbaby like her name?"

Olivia releases a loud tommy gun-sounding fart, causing us all to laugh.

Theo looks at Cain and doubles over. After a few moments, he catches his breath enough to get a few words out. "On that note, we'll leave you to it." He waves a goodbye as he places his arm over Bel's shoulder and leads her towards the door, wrapping his spare arm around Trudy as he passes her.

"Maybe I should stay, at last to help change the nappy. I'm pretty sure that's more than air." She tries to fight against Theo but has no luck whatsoever as he tugs her out the room.

"I'll be fine, Mum. It's not the first dirty diaper I've changed, and it certainly won't be the last," he says, digging one-handed through the bag on the end of the bed. He changes the diaper like a pro, making it clear to me that he actually has done it before. Many times.

After popping the last stud on the baby grow, he lifts our complaining baby and holds her out to me. "I think this little princess wants her mummy."

I happily take her, glad to have her back in my arms. "Hey, Olivia, are you a little hungry again?" I ask as she searches with her mouth when I pull her against me. I glance up at Cain. "What do you think? She did fall asleep when I was feeding earlier."

"That looks like a hungry baby to me." He gives me a warm smile as he sits on the seat beside the bed. I'll have to ask him about his baby experience when I'm not concentrating so hard on feeding Olivia properly.

19.

HOPE AT LAST

CAIN

I glance back at the baby seat in the rear-view mirror for the fifth time since driving away from the hospital.

Selena lets out an amused giggle. "We haven't even left the car park yet. Seriously, Cain, you need to calm down." She glances at the seat over her shoulder. "She's sound asleep and perfectly fine."

I sigh. Knowing she's right, I focus my attention onto the road before me. I just want to get us home in one piece. Because of Selena's recovery from her postpartum haemorrhage, and Olivia having some weight loss, they've been in the hospital for ten days. It's been the longest ten days of my life. Having caught Olivia's biological father's scent at the hospital once or twice, I want to get them away from here and to the safety of our new home. I've been spending all the time I wasn't at the hospital decorating. The best thing is, Selena knows nothing about it. I fucking hope this secret doesn't turn out to suck.

Out the corner of my eye, I catch sight of Selena straightening in her seat as I pass the turnoff to the pack house. "Where are we going?"

"We're going home," I announce.

"You just missed the turnoff." She laughs. "Are you still focusing on the baby?"

I let part of the secret drop. "I said we're going home. Not to the pack house."

She turns her head sharply to look at me. "What?" The word comes out loud, and she grimaces, flicking her eyes to the baby to check she didn't wake at the sound. Selena's shoulders relax, clearly satisfied at what she can see.

She lowers her voice. "Have we got somewhere of our own?"

I smile at her before focusing back on the road, making sure to take the correct turn.

I pull to a stop outside of a family home that will be perfect for us, even as we grow as a family. I didn't like the idea of Selena and Olivia getting stuck in a lift, so an apartment was out of the question. "Home sweet home," I announce as I slide out the car.

Stepping out of the car, Selena looks at the house with wide eyes. The amazement on her face makes all my work this last week worth it. "Is this really our home?"

I nod. "I signed the papers the day after Olivia was born. It's all ours." After Theo heard about our disaster in the apartment, he offered to sell me one of the pack's safe houses. Once I saw it, I knew it was the perfect home for our little family.

Selena carefully rounds the car and wraps her arms around my middle. "I love you, Cain Wilson. We are the luckiest girls alive."

Leaving my car door open, I lift her into my arms and dash to the front door, fumbling with the key as I unlock it. "I love you too," I say, carrying Selena over the threshold and then placing her gently on her feet in the entranceway before heading back to the car to collect our daughter.

Once we settle Olivia in her Moses basket, I finally get some alone time with my beautiful mate. I slide my arm over her shoulder as she cuddles into my side on the plush sofa. "Do you really like the house?" I ask, conscious of the fact that I chose all the paint and furnishings. "If you don't like how I decorated, you can change it. Just tell me what you want and I'll do it."

Selena runs her fingers over the back of my hand. "Cain, I love it. There's nothing that I would change." She lifts her head and our eyes meet. Tears well in hers. "You even had a canvas of my father and Maxie made. No one else would have thought of doing that."

I wipe away an escaped tear, and she turns her face to place a kiss on my palm. "Thank you."

"I love you, sweetheart. I'll do everything I can to make you happy." I place a gentle kiss on the top of her head before listening to the car I can hear pulling up on our drive. "I think we have visitors."

Selena lets out a small sigh before she shifts in her seat, making to move away. I tighten my arm around her. "Where do you think you're going?"

"To get our guests some drinks," she admits, still trying to wriggle out from out of my hold.

I jump out of my seat and head for the kitchen myself. "No chance. You've just had a baby. I think you deserve to be waited on."

Footsteps approach the door and feeling the pack energy coming from them, I quickly invite them in without raising my voice, knowing they'll hear me and saving them from waking Olivia up with a knock on the door. I go about making some tea and coffee while listening to Theo greeting Selena. His footsteps then get louder as they head in my direction.

"You did a great job of decorating this place."

I turn to see his eyes roaming around the room as he leans back against the counter opposite me.

"Does Bel want tea or coffee?" I ask, feeling a little bad not knowing what my alpha's female drinks.

"She's a coffee girl." Theo rubs at the back of his neck.

I tilt my head, listening to the voices coming from the other room. "Who else is here? I can hear Eddie and…"

"Chloe and Mum. Ruby will be arriving as soon as the sun goes down." He gives me a guilty look as I pull more cups out of the cupboard. "I did try to talk them out of visiting, but once they heard I was coming, they all had to jump in the car."

I pour the drinks, coffee for everyone, except Selena. I take what I can carry, making sure to pick up Selena's tea, before nodding at the rest sat on the side. "You might as well make yourself useful and hand those out. They're all the same."

After giving everyone their drinks, I sit down on the arm of the sofa next to Selena, since Mum seems to have stolen the seat I'd vacated. Olivia's bellowing cry comes loud and clear through the baby monitor on the coffee table.

Selena eases up from her seat. "She'll need feeding." She glances around the room. "I won't be long," she announces.

She takes a few steps towards the hall before turning her eyes on me. "Any chance you could come help set things up?" She solemnly raises her cast-covered arm in answer to the question that she must have seen in my eyes. She can't lift the baby out of the cot with the cast, not safely anyway. She had an X-ray whilst in hospital, which unfortunately showed it wasn't healed enough to be removed. I have a feeling Selena will be ringing Zainab in the next couple of days and begging to have it cut off regardless of the consequences. I see the frustration in her eyes every time she can't do these things on her own.

I stand and stride towards her. "Anything you need, beautiful."

Taking my hand in hers, she gives me a small smile.

It only takes a couple of minutes to settle the two of them in on the rocking chair in the corner of the bedroom. "Give me a shout when you're ready to come back through to the lounge." I place a kiss on Olivia's head and then one on Selena's before heading back to our guests.

They're all talking between themselves as I walk back in the room. The mention of foxes catches my attention and I focus on what Theo is saying to Eddie as I sit in Selena's empty space.

"...foxes in town?"

Eddie shakes his head. "No, Ruby said Dominick and his vampires haven't seen any evidence of a skulk of foxes living in town. Which makes sense since neither have we. I'm thinking they must be just outside the territory to be able to come and go with so much ease."

Theo looks to me. "Are you sure it was his scent at the hospital?"

I nod. "Without a doubt." I wouldn't ever forget his scent. "I've been checking around here every time I come home from the hospital, but I haven't caught it. I'm hoping he doesn't know we aren't at the pack house."

"You might be right. He's definitely been snooping around the pack house. I picked up the scent from the hospital in the surrounding bush this morning," Eddie admits, before adding more. "He's getting around in a car though because it just disappears at the roadside."

"I'm going to put a couple of wolves on patrol tonight. Hopefully we can catch him snooping and interrogate him," Theo says before draining his cup.

Bel stands, taking Theo's empty cup and grabbing Eddie's too. She walks off into the kitchen, Mum and Chloe following closely behind.

A gentle knock sounds on the front door before it instantly opens and Ruby walks in. I glance behind her and notice it's dark and we're all sitting in just the light of the TV. Realising Selena must be in the dark, I give Ruby a brief hug and head back into the bedroom.

"Hey! Are you okay?"

"I think we're done. I was just about to give you a shout." I can hear the smile in her voice, and as I get close to her, I can even see it with my wolf's eyes. I scoop Olivia out of her arms while Selena straightens her clothes.

With Olivia tucked safely in my right arm, I offer Selena my other hand and pull her out the rocker. As we step into the brightness of the lounge, I squint against the light. Flicking my eyes towards Olivia, I watch her little baby blues squinting too.

"Hey, princess. That nasty light is bright, isn't it?"

Mum jumps up off the sofa. "I didn't think. Should I put the lamp on instead?" She steps towards the light switch.

"It's fine, Mum. She's getting used to it now." I turn my attention back to Olivia whose wide eyes are looking up at me, seemingly enraptured.

"He enthrals me too, baby," Selena says, looking at Olivia over my bicep.

Ruby pulls Selena into her arms. "Congratulations." Quickly releasing Selena, she looks over my arm at Olivia. "She's so beautiful."

"Do you want a cuddle?" I offer Olivia across to Ruby.

Ruby gulps and flicks her eyes from me to Olivia. They finally fall on Selena. "You trust me?" The astonishment in her voice causes my heart to hurt.

"Of course," Selena says, her voice full of certainty. She gives Ruby a gentle squeeze on her upper arm as she passes her, heading back towards the sofa.

Ruby reaches out and gingerly takes Olivia out of my arms, settling her against her own chest as she walks towards Eddie, who stands, offering her his armchair. Once she's seated, he rests on the arm of the chair, leaning over her and talking nonsense to Olivia. *They'll never have that with their own children.*

My heart lurches in my chest at the thought, taking my breath away for a split second. Selena reaches out and takes my hand as I sit on the arm beside her, giving it a comforting squeeze, probably having caught on to my thought through the mating bond. Taking my eyes off Ruby and Eddie, I catch the warm smile she gives me as we lock eyes. "It's back," she says in confirmation.

Leaning in, I give her a quick kiss on the top of the head. "I love you."

"Oh, I was meant to tell you…" Ruby lifts her gaze from Olivia and locks them on Theo's. "Dominick's sending Casanova out to hunt for the fox tonight."

His eyes widen in surprise. "I didn't think he wanted to dirty his hands with *mutt* business?" The word mutt drips with disdain.

Ruby smiles down at Olivia, who is gripping her finger in her little fist. "Dominick hasn't used that word in a while. I think he's warming to the pack."

Theo lets out a laugh. "Or just a certain pack member."

I glance up at him in surprise and catch Eddie's sharp turn of the head in the corner of my eye. So, I'm not the only one surprised to hear that. "He's dating a pack member?"

He grunts and focuses back on Ruby, seeming to dismiss my question. It leaves me to wonder if Ruby is the pack member Theo is talking about, since she is one of Dominick's now, too. "He's mine to interrogate, so if Casanova finds him, he brings him to me."

Ruby nods. "Dominick understands and respects that."

A growl rumbles up my chest and escapes my mouth. *"Mine!"* my wolf demands. I clear my throat whilst pushing my wolf down. "I need to be there, Theo." My words sound like a beg to my own ears, and seeing the sadness reflected in Theo's eyes, he heard the same.

Selena's hand tightens on mine. "Stu's still in town? I thought he'd left." The tremble in her voice has me kneeling in front of her.

Cupping her face in my palms, I stare into her eyes, making sure she sees I mean every word I'm about to say. "He's not coming anywhere near you. He doesn't even know we're here. Okay?"

The terror is clear on her unnaturally pale face. She nods, but not at all convincingly.

Holding her eyes with mine, I push all the love I have for her through our mate bond in the hopes of her feeling how much I'm willing to protect her. "You heard Ruby and Theo. Everyone is on high alert, even Dominick and his vampires. You and Olivia are safe."

20

OURS

I glance at my watch and hope Cain returns from his pack business soon. He's been gone longer than I expected and I don't want Olivia to wake up before he returns. I wouldn't be able to pick her up with this stupid cast on my arm. At least after tonight I should be able to look after my daughter alone. Cain has promised to take me to see Zainab, and I've already decided that I don't care what the X-ray shows. I want this damn cast removed.

A clanging noise catches my attention. I reach for the remote and mute the TV as I glance around the room, straining to hear the noise again. The hairs on my body stand on end and a sudden sinking feeling hits my gut. My instincts scream at me.

Something isn't right.

Another thud comes from the direction of the bedrooms. I rise from my seat and head that way. We'd only put Olivia down a short while ago, and she's not big enough to be making noises like that.

I push the door open and catch sight of someone climbing out of the broken window. My heart races and my eyes immediately fall to the cot. My stomach plummets at the sight of it empty, as the world around me seems to slow down.

"Olivia!" I scream like a banshee. *"My baby. Give me my baby."*

Climbing out the window after them, I ignore the glass cutting into my feet. Someone has my baby and I need get to her back. *"Cain!"* I scream, needing him here. I know he's got no chance of hearing me from Theo's though.

Chasing the person through the yard as fast as my legs will carry me, they get further and further ahead. Reaching the line of trees, I fall against one, gasping for breath as I frantically search the bushes, hoping to see some sign of the person who has my baby. There's nothing. They can't be human.

Helplessness overcomes me, and I fall to my knees with a wail.

As heavy hands fall on my shoulders. I don't even turn to see who my attacker is. If they're going to take me too, I won't even fight. I'd go willingly to be with my baby.

Cain's concerned eyes lock on mine as he drops to his knees, coming face-to-face with me. "Selena, baby. Shh… I'm here."

It's only with his words that I realise I'm still screaming his name. I close my mouth and swallow past the soreness of my raw throat.

"What's happened? Where's Olivia?" He looks over my shoulder at the house, and his eyes widen.

Turning, I see Theo looking out the broken bedroom window, a grim look plastered on his face.

"Someone took her." Sobs wrack my body and I try to fight them, knowing they need any information I can give them. But all I can think about is my missing baby. "I just want her back." The sobs take over and I can't do anything to fight it.

"I've picked up a scent. I'll follow it. You look after your mate. Her feet are all cut up." Theo's words flow past me, and I barely take them in.

"We're going to get her back, beautiful. I promise," he says, his words ending on a growl.

I focus on his wolf's eyes and know he'll follow through

with that promise. He loves her as much as I do. I fall into his arms as fresh tears run down my cheeks. My helplessness eases with the comfort of knowing we have a whole pack of were-wolves ready to lay down their lives to get Olivia back.

Lifting me into his arms, Cain carries me around to the front of the house. I stiffen as I spot a couple of neighbours. *What do they think happened?*

"The police are on their way, but it's okay. Mike's a pack member. He'll smooth it all over," Cain whispers in my ear, having most probably picked up on my concerns through the bond.

I reach down to the bond to feel the comfort I know will be there only to find an empty space. "Our bond?" My voice quivers and panic flows through me. *I can't handle losing that too.*

Placing me on the kitchen bench, he rubs his hands down my arms and presses a gentle kiss to my head. "It's just a little burnt out. It'll be back."

My brows crease as I frown. "How did you know I was worried about the neighbours?"

"You stiffened the second they came into view." His explanation brings a small smile to my face. I love how he pays attention to those little things. It's like he understands me on a level that no one else has.

Leaving me on the side, he fills a bowl full of warm water and adds a little disinfectant. He then reaches into the medicine cupboard and pulls out a large first aid kit.

"They'll find her?" My question hangs in the air as I wait with baited breath for his answer.

"Yes." That one word has so much certainty behind it, it's indisputable.

I take a deep, calming breath before nodding. "Let's get my feet cleaned up. I need to be walking when she gets back." The stupid cast on my arm has interfered with everyday stuff, I don't want cuts on my feet to do the same. Thoughts of the cast have me glaring at it.

Cain lets out a chuckle. "It's not going to run off if you glare at it enough. You'll just give yourself wrinkles from frowning." He presses a kiss to my forehead.

I can tell with his joking that he's trying to make me smile and ease my worry, but I can't bring myself to do it. "I love you, Cain," I tell him as I lift my feet so we can both assess the damage.

Grimacing at the sight, he picks up the tweezers. "You just keep remembering that as I pull out all this glass, because I'm afraid it might hurt a bit."

I grit my teeth against the pain as he digs around, pulling piece after piece of glass out of my feet. Just as I'm about to tell him I can't take anymore, he places the tweezers down.

"I think that was the last of it," he announces.

Throwing my head back in relief, I take a calming breath. "Thank God for that."

A knock at the door pauses my next thought, and a familiar voice calls through the house. "Hello? Anybody there?"

"In the kitchen, Mike. Come on through," Cain replies, as he dabs at my feet with a cotton bud soaked in antiseptic liquid.

"*Fuuuck!*" I curse, batting at his arm away. "You could have bloody well warned me."

He presses a kiss to my lips. "I thought you were watching me." The anxiety on his face makes me think he must be having a hard time, being the cause of my pain. "I'm going to wrap them and then you are as good as you'll get until your body starts to heal on its own."

Giving him a small smile, I brush a wayward strand of hair off his forehead. "Thank you," I say, before turning my attention to Mike, who's walked in with a phone to his ear.

"I'll let them know." He pulls the phone from his ear and

places it in his pocket before giving Cain a grim look. My stomach plummets.

Reaching out, I take Cain's hand in mine, needing it to centre me. I squeeze it tightly as I wait for Mike to speak.

"That was Theo. The scent stopped at a road just past the bushland." His eyes drop to the floor as soon as my eyes connect with his. It's almost as if he can't bear to look at me.

My eyes drift from Mike to Cain and back again. "What does that mean?" I ask, not wanting to believe what my mind is telling me.

Cain sighs, and Mike lifts his eyes, looking from Cain's to mine in quick succession. "It means they got into a vehicle. I'm going to go back to the station and access the traffic cameras and see what I can pick up."

"Wh… what if there aren't any traffic cameras on that road?" I ask, even though I don't want to hear the answer.

Mike takes a step backwards before turning towards the front door, completely ignoring my question. "I'll be back as soon as I've got something. Eddie's on his way to Theo. He's been known to track vehicles before."

Cain gives Mike's back an absent nod, his eyes glazed as he's obviously lost in his thoughts.

I glance around the room, unsure what to do for the best. I can't give him comforting words because I don't have them. My eyes roam his body, taking in the strain of his shoulders and clenched fists at his sides. I know he needs to be out there.

"Give me your phone," I demand, my hand outstretched, waiting for him to give me it.

His head snaps in my direction, confusion etched on his face.

I wiggle my fingers. "Your phone… give me it."

He frowns, but places it in my palm without question.

Quickly scrolling through his contacts and finding Bel's

number, I press Call. My brows rise in surprise as the sound of a ringing phone comes from the front of our house.

Bel's voice calls through the fly screen on the front door as the phone call gets rejected. "Hey! Are you after me, Cain?"

"No, it was me. Come on in. We're in the kitchen." I hand the phone back to Cain and he gives me a questioning look. I want nothing more than to fall apart in his arms, but I know I need to be calm just for a little while longer because he needs to leave, and he never will if I break. Seeing his eyes flicker as his wolf comes forward, I place my good hand on his shoulder. "You need to be out there. Hunting." I give him a knowing look. "I might not be a wolf and our bond may be a little burned out right now, but I can see it in your posture and your eyes. *You* need to find our baby."

He closes his eyes and his shoulders relax before he speaks in a guttural voice. "*Ours.*" His eyes open and I know it's his wolf talking to me. He strides past Bel and out the house without another word.

Fresh tears stream down my face with the bang of the fly screen closing behind him, and I can finally fall apart.

Bel jumps up beside me and wraps an arm around my shoulders. "You did the right thing, Selena. He won't come back without her." Reaching behind her, she tears off some kitchen roll and passes it to me.

I dab at my cheeks, wincing at the roughness of it. "That's what I'm worried about," I say through the tears that don't want to stop. My thoughts run wild with what he may be about to face, and it kills me that there's nothing I can do to help.

21

FIERCE FEMALE

CAIN

Seeing Selena broken on the ground caused my wolf to jump to the forefront. He pushed me to let him take over. Her terror-filled scream of my name was the only thing that allowed me to hold him back. I was the one she needed in that moment, not my wolf.

The moment she told me to find "our baby" there was no holding him back. I managed to get out the door and under the cover of the vast bush behind our property before he burst free from my skin.

He doesn't give me the chance to shake away the last tingles of pain before racing through the bushland, following the now familiar scent of the fox. As the scent dies off by the road, I skid to halt and lower my snout, trying to find it again.

Picking up Theo and Eddie's scent, I turn to see Eddie approach in his wolf form. He drops his snout in submission, releasing a small whine. My wolf recognises the compassion.

"Eddie, see what you can pick up." Theo's voice pulls my attention from Eddie. Theo is stepping out of his clothes, folding them and placing them under some thick shrub just off the road. "Time is precious. We need to catch up with that fucking vehicle." I take a deep breath and try to catch a scent that shouldn't be here. Walking in a circle, I smell diesel and rubber, making me think he must have left with a skid of tyres in his hurry.

Eddie lets out a howl and runs off down the road, having detected up on something and considering it a lead.

I hesitate, giving Theo a quick glance.

"*Go!* I'll catch up." His shift starts to take over before the last word is out of his mouth, making it sound somewhat garbled.

Chasing down the road after Eddie, Theo's energy closes in behind me. Eddie slows his pace, and I follow suit as I search our surroundings, spotting a vehicle parked at the side of the road. The hushed sound of a baby crying has my wolf wanting to race forward instantly.

"*Cain!*" Theo's commanding tone sounds in my head, stopping me on the spot.

"*Olivia,*" I say, half explanation, half beg.

Theo steps up in front of Eddie. "*We can't just rush in. We need to be smart.*" He stalks towards the van, ears perked up on high alert. Eddie and I flank him, silently following his lead.

"For fuck's sake. Stop crying." The fox's voice comes from the open side door of the transit van. I know Selena told me his name but I can't remember it right now. Steve…Sam…It was definitely an S name. "I don't have anything to feed you. You'll have to wait until Bert and Rachel arrive."

"*He's alone.*" Theo's words run through my head telling me what I'd already deduced.

Theo slinks up to the opening as Eddie and I stay back. "*Olivia's in a car seat. Let's draw him out.*"

Stalking around the other side of the van, I barge into the side of it hard enough to make it shake.

"What the fuck?" the fox cries out. His feet hit the dirt and I hear his footsteps around the van.

As he steps into view, I pounce, not giving him time to see me. He screams as I sink my teeth into his shoulder. I curse having made the mistake of missing his neck as we both hit the floor.

"He needs to be alive for us to get information from him," Theo reminds me.

I'm grateful for my silly mistake, when only moments ago I was cursing myself for it. Releasing him, I step away, poising myself and ready to take him down if he runs or starts to shift.

Theo rounds the van on two feet. "You might as well just accept defeat. You're outnumbered and your pack mates are nowhere in sight."

The fox's shoulders slump and his head drops in submission as he gets to his feet, turning his body just enough to have a view of Theo whilst keeping sight of me, too. Clever fox, not to have a wolf at his back.

Eddie steps out from behind the van in a pair of sweats, cradling a swaddled Olivia in his arms. I let out a whimper at the sight of her, and he hooks a thumb over his shoulder. "There's a pile of sweats in the back of there. It's a shifter's van after all."

Not caring to hear another word and knowing Theo has it in hand if the fox tries anything, I dash around the van and force my shift to be as quick as possible, ignoring the extra pain it brings.

Once in human form, I duck into the van and grab some sweats, pulling them on as I walk back, the hot gravel burning the soles my feet.

Eddie holds Olivia out to me as soon as he catches sight of me.

"Hello, princess. It's good to have you in my arms again." I fight back tears as I hug her against my chest. I would never have guessed I could love a baby so much.

A scuffing sound draws my eyes from Olivia, and I watch as Eddie cable-ties the fox's arms behind his back. "Found these in the van too, so thanks for that, buddy." Heavy duty cable ties are another thing shifters tend to keep handy in their vehicle—you never know when you'll need to restrain an enemy. The largest and buffest cable ties you can buy are strong and won't break even with the force of a supernatural being behind them.

Theo steps up to them and starts patting the fox down. "Aha! Just what I'm looking for," he says as he straightens, a phone held in his hand. After tapping the screen a couple of times, he raises the phone to his ear and strides to the other side of the van.

"Billy… yeah, I borrowed a phone. We're on the road that runs parallel with Cain's, behind the bushland, and we're in need of a lift…" He pauses obviously listening as Billy replies. "You'll need to floor it. We've got a couple of foxes incoming and I want to be away before they arrive."

Theo steps back around the truck wearing a borrowed pair of grey sweats, identical to the ones Eddie and I have on and throws the phone to Eddie. "See if there's anything useful on there."

"So, you're the loser who kicked my ex-wife out on the street… pregnant?" The growl behind that last word is unmissable. My skin ripples as Theo's anger brushes against it.

The fox glances between me and Theo. "What… y-your… ex—?" he stutters.

"Jesus, mate, there's no need to stutter." Theo sighs. "My ex-wife. My brother's mate. Yes, we keep it in the family. Now we've cleared that up… what's your name?"

"Selena didn't tell you my name?"

My laughter at the outrage on the fox's face causes Olivia to let out a little wail.

"Shh, it's all right, princess. Daddy has you," I soothe, watching her little eyes stare straight at me.

Theo's growl catches my attention, and I lift my eyes to see him shoving the fox on the ground. "Don't even think about it."

"He ain't her daddy. I am," he says, venom practically dripping from his words.

Theo's fist snaps out and connects with his jaw. I smirk at the sickening crunch I hear from across the road and can't help but wonder if Theo's fist is as damaged as the fox's face seems to be? If the scream of pain the fox is letting out is anything to go by.

"Well, he can't say you didn't fucking warn him." Eddie pelts the phone through the vans open window as he heads my way. "The dude's name is Stu. That's the name he signs at the end of his texts anyway. I emailed myself the addresses in his maps history so we can check them out later."

"Good wor—" Theo stops midsentence as the sound of a vehicle approaching reaches our ears.

We all spin to look in the direction of the incoming 4x4 as it screams towards us.

I tense, ready to flee with Olivia if it's Stu's pack mates.

I catch sight of Eddie's shoulders relaxing as his eyes fall back on our prisoner. "I'd recognise that Pajero anywhere. I've been telling Billy he needs a new exhaust for months."

Grabbing the car seat out of the van, I strap Olivia in as the others bundle our prisoner into the back.

"I'll sit here." Eddie gestures to one of the folded-up seats in the rear of the car. "I can make sure Stu doesn't try anything silly."

As we drive in the opposite direction of our house, I straighten in the back seat as I lean forward to peer through the windscreen. "Where the hell are we going?"

"My place. It's the safest place for Olivia. Stu's pack—"

"It's a fucking skulk not a pack," Stu interrupts. There's a thud from the back and a grunt, which leaves me to assume Eddie kicked him or something equally as painful.

"Fine. Stu's *skulk* won't attack the pack house," Theo

announces. "Not without knowing how many of us could be there."

I stroke Olivia's little hand and she grips onto my fingers. "Selena…."

"Will be at the house when we get there. I called Bel on my way to picking you guys up," Billy says, as we turn down the private road that leads to Theo's.

I'm just lifting Olivia out of the car seat as the front door bangs open. Turning, I tense ready for impact as I see Selena running at us full pelt.

"Livie… is she okay?" Selena asks, coming to a steady stop beside me and peering at Olivia as she worries at her lip.

"She's perfectly fine. Just had a little adventure."

A commotion at the back of the 4x4 breaks out, catching Selena's attention before I get the chance to offer Olivia over.

"Is that them? The person who took her?" Evidently deciding she's correct in her assumption, she marches to the culprit.

I follow behind and spot Stu on the floor, clearly having been rolled out the back by Eddie, who is now jumping down himself and not caring about the dust cloud he kicks up in Stu's face as he lands.

"Stu?" she screeches.

Seeing her good hand fisted at her side has me quickly passing the baby off to Eddie. "Take Liv."

"You fucking son of a bitch." She gives him a swift kick in the side. Stu lets out a grunt, and she kicks him again. "*You* took my baby. You don't even fucking want her, yet you have the audacity to take her from me."

Stu lets out a pained cough. "I told you last time, my alpha wants her." He flicks his eyes to me as I step in beside Selena, ready to protect her if she needs me. "You know what it's like. If your alpha orders you to do something, you have no choice."

Selena steps closer to him, trying to block his view of me as she stares him down. "Don't expect him to be on your side. He loves her just as much as I do." My heart jumps in my chest and my back straightens as I stand proud… and somewhat turned on by my mate's ferocity.

Olivia lets out a wail and Selena turns away from Stu, heading for a flustered Eddie, who's failing to calm Olivia down.

"You're lucky my daughter's needs come first," she says, giving Stu one last filthy look.

Eddie happily hands Olivia over to Selena, ensuring she has a secure hold before stepping away. "He won't be thinking himself lucky when we've finished with him. I promise you that, Selena."

Eddie may be a couple of years younger than me, but he sure does have a good head on his shoulders. Olivia is pack and Stu has done wrong by taking her.

He's going to pay.

22.

FACE OFF

CAIN

*P*ushing myself forward to follow Selena into the house, my wolf and I argue with every deliberately slow step I take. He wants to be in on the interrogation of Stu, but I know if I go in there straight away, we won't get any information out of him because he wants to tear Stu apart. *Hell, we both do.* Olivia is ours, and Stu should never have touched her.

Mum runs into the hall. "Is she okay? He didn't hurt her, did he?"

I close the door behind me as I listen to Selena trying to placate my mum. "Olivia's fine, Trudy. If she was hurt, they would've taken her straight to the hospital."

The door handle snaps off in my hand at the thought of Olivia needing to go to the hospital. Turning around, I find two-sets of stunned eyes on me.

"Are you okay?" Selena asks as she brushes her fingers over my forearm.

I open my mouth to speak, but only a growl leaves my parted lips. I clear my throat and try again. "Sorry. I didn't realise…." I shake my head, not knowing what to say. I'm not okay, and the only thing that would make me okay isn't going to help us put a stop to the danger our daughter is in.

"I get it," Selena says with a nod. "Come on. Let's go feed our baby."

Giving her a grateful smile, I allow her lead me to the lounge as I silently thank the heavens I found her. *Both of them.*

*T*wenty minutes later I'm burping Olivia over my shoulder, with Selena sipping a mint tea beside me, when Theo strides into the room through the French doors.

"I've gotta make some calls." The growl beneath Theo's words has my wolf on edge as his eyes meet mine. "Meet me in my office in five minutes." I nod my agreement as I continue to pat Olivia's back.

Bel watches Theo walk by and out of sight before jumping up off the sofa opposite us and rushing after him.

Selena's hand squeezes my knee. "Will you place her in her bassinet before you go? Trudy can help me get her out if she cries."

"Sure," I say as I stand. I gently place Olivia in the bassinet beside the sofa and wipe at the dribble of milk escaping her puckering lips with a muslin cloth. Leaning over, I press my lips to her forehead, silently promising her that I won't come back until every threat to her is gone.

A hand slides around my waist as Selena's energy wraps around me. Turning, I pull her into my arms, tucking her head under my chin.

"Thank you." The wobble in her voice squeezes at my heart.

I kiss the top of her head. "You don't need to thank me for anything," I tell her, meaning every word.

"You brought her back." She lifts a hand and wipes at her eyes, making me squeeze her a little tighter as I rub her back.

"I'm her father. I wouldn't have returned without her. She needed to be brought home… where she belongs."

The French doors slide open and Eddie walks in, a wide grin on his face. "I never thought I'd hear a fox squeal like a pig."

I give Selena one last kiss on the head before releasing my hold on her. "We best go and see what Theo has planned."

Eddie rubs his hands together in glee. "We haven't had a good pack fight in ages."

Rolling my eyes at his immaturity, I lead the way to Theo's office, pausing to rap on the closed door before entering.

"It's safe," he calls out. Bel's giggle makes me smile as we step into the room, spotting her curled up on his knee before she jumps off to stand beside his chair.

"I've had too many close calls with you two. I wasn't taking any risks," I say with a wry grin.

"Amen to that," Eddie agrees, whilst taking a seat on the sofa against the wall. "So, what's the plan, boss?"

Theo sighs and runs a hand through his short blond hair. "Stu said there were only six of them staying in the next town over." Bel strokes her fingers over his shoulders. He leans into her touch, and I watch as the tension seems to leave his shoulders. "I'm inclined to say we should take double that figure in case he's bullshitting us. We don't want to go in there too confident and have it backfire."

"I'm going." Bel's determined tone leaves no room for argument, and I look to Eddie in surprise—wondering if we should leave before things kick off between the alpha couple—and find him watching them with rapt attention.

Theo takes a deep, calming breath, seeming to steel himself before speaking. "It's too dangerous." He shakes his head.

"I'm the alpha-female, Theo. I'm going."

Theo turns his seat to face Bel, before taking her hand in his. "If you go, it'll make things more dangerous. I'll be distracted and so will most of the men. They won't like seeing their alpha-female in danger."

"If Selena was a wolf, you wouldn't stop her going—even if she was a distraction to her mate," Bel argues. "I need to go for her. I need to go for the females in our pack, those too submissive to fight. They need to know any future kids they may have will be protected and fought for by their alpha pair. Not just you, Theo. You have a mate now and that changes things." Leaning in, she gives him a gentle kiss before dropping his hand and stepping away. "I'm going to check on Selena while you guys make a plan. I'll gather the pack mates in the meeting room as they turn up, so we can all be in on the briefing."

We watch in silence as she leaves the room.

Theo takes his time turning his chair around to face us once again. "*Fuck!* She's right."

I nod in agreement. "Sadly, she is." I'm impressed with my sister-in-law. She's smart enough and strong enough to step into the role of alpha female. Bel knew exactly what the submissive wolves—who are always extremely timid and too scared to fight—would need compared to the more dominant wolves, who would jump in on their own and never need someone else to protect what's theirs.

"What's the plan, then?" Ed asks, once again sounding eager for action.

"There are five foxes at the house, one of them is the alpha. They'll have found the empty van by now and are probably making their next plan. We'll go in quietly and end it quickly. It's a built-up area, and we don't want any innocents getting hurt." Theo glances at his phone on the desk, and I give him a questioning look.

"Billy's doing a drive by on the address we got from Stu. There better not be any surprises." He rubs a hand over his face.

Seeing how stressed times like this make Theo, I'm still glad I handed the pack over to him. Despite his stress, he's handling it well. Plus he has the perfect woman for him by his side, and that thought warms my heart. "We're not going to rush in without thinking. Who'd you call in?"

"Mike, Dave, Stefan, Pete, Karl, and Trevor. Do you think I made the right call?" He raises a brow as though he's doubting his decision, which isn't like Theo.

"Add the four of us and Bel. We'll be a force to be reckoned with," I say confidently. It's not a lie. Everyone named are great fighters, and putting us together will make us a dream team. Excitement rolls through me at the thought of a fight. I can't stop wondering why the fox alpha wanted Olivia so soon. It's not like she'll show any signs of being a shifter until puberty anyway. "Who are we leaving here? We don't want to leave and have them attacking our home."

Theo grunts and nods his agreement. "I'll make that decision when Billy reports back."

Eddie glances out the window before checking his watch. "You realise Ruby is going to be gutted when she wakes up and discovers she's missed all the fun."

"It's not like we can hold off for the sun to set." I step over to the window and take in the view of the yard as I try to calm my wolf down at the thought of waiting. He's eager to get out there and fight for what is ours and, to be honest, so am I. "We need to hit them before they can arrange for more members of their skulk to arrive."

———

*O*nce Billy arrived and verified Stu's confession, we came up with a solid plan and jumped into three separate cars. Trevor and Chloe were left at the pack house to protect Selena, Olivia, and Mum. Stu is still locked up and left under the supervision of another pack member. Knowing he was only following orders means he'll be released once we've dealt with his alpha. Although, the thought of him getting off scot free does grate on me. Eddie did ensure me the interrogation he received wasn't a stroll in the park.

I watch out the windscreen, memorising the route in case anything goes wrong and I need to make my way home on foot. The silence is almost deafening, and I can only assume the others in the car are doing the same. Maybe even looking for shadows that will hide our wolves if we have to flee in our wolf forms.

As our surroundings become more built up, I catch sight of Theo sitting straighter in his seat.

Billy, in the lead car, pulls over down a quiet side street and as planned, Theo drives past, parking in a vacant space on the next street along.

As we exit the car, Pete drives past in the third car, heading for the street behind the Skulk's house. Their group will be jumping over the back fence as we join Billy's group at the front of the house.

Theo throws an arm over Bel's shoulder as was walk through the street. They'd look like a regular couple on a stroll if anyone was to look out of their windows. Unfortunately, Ed and I don't look as inconspicuous.

Tension in my body builds with each step, taking us closer to our destination. A glance in Ed's direction tells me he's feeling the same from the stiffness in his shoulders.

"Guys, you need tone it down. They're going to feel you two coming and it'll blow the surprise attack," Bel states, her tone light and airy, just like her energy. I don't know how she can be so calm knowing we'll be walking into a fight. My wolf is chomping at the bit to get out and deal with our enemy.

I take a deep breath, hoping to bring my energy down a notch or two. "Sorry. My wolf's riding me hard right now."

Ed pats me on the shoulder. "I feel ya, buddy. The adrenaline is making my wolf practically impossible to calm, too."

As we get closer to Billy's car, he steps out alone—Mike and Dave having already slinked off into the street as planned.

Theo glances at his watch, causing me to look down at my own. "Everyone ready?" Bel slips out from under Theo's arm and rolls her shoulders in answer as Billy, Ed, and I all give grunts of our own agreement. He drops his arm and stares up at the house. "*Now!*"

Being the father of the kidnapped child, I lead our party up the pavement and to the front door. Without pausing, I send out a solid kick and can't hold back the smirk as the door gives under the pressure of my foot.

The sound of glass shattering throughout the building confirms the other teams are making their way in via their planned entry points.

I'm instantly met with a female, who cowers at the sight of me. The energy playing along my skin makes me wonder why the alpha would have brought such a submissive fox on this kind of a mission.

"We're here for your alpha. Point us in his direction and you won't be hurt," I inform her, trying to tamp down the growl behind my words—my wolf close to the surface. The sudden shaking throughout her body tells me I've failed.

Stepping to the side, she plasters her back against the wall, giving us access to pass by her, eyes cast down to the floor. Raising her left hand a couple of inches, she points in the direction of the back of the house.

Bypassing the lounge to my right, I follow her direction. Feeling Eddie's energy drop back behind me, I expect he's checking the lounge for skulk members.

Alpha energy presses against my skin with every step I take, confirming the female was pointing me in the right direction. Allowing my wolf closer to the surface, I push out my own energy. I may not be the alpha of my pack, but that is out of choice, not strength, or power.

I step into the kitchen and catch a fist as it slams towards my face from my left side. The fucker had tried to hide beside the door. With a twist of my wrist, I wrench him around until he's standing before me.

"Bastard!" He spits the words out angrily, spittle hitting me in the face.

Releasing his fist, I wipe my face clean with my hand. "That's not how you should be welcoming guests."

He steps back, leaving enough space between us to ensure I can't reach him without him seeing it coming.

Theo's energy presses against me, and I step aside, giving him room to enter. "I'm wondering... are we the guests or is he? He's in my territory after all."

I stroke at my chin in thought. "Huh... you have a good point there. It was still rude either way."

Our guys walk into the kitchen through the numerous entries, having round up the other foxes. The foxes gather in the middle of the room, their eyes flit to their alpha, clearly looking to him for instruction. .

"You have what's mine. I have every right to be here." The determination in his voice along with the straightness of his spine tells me he's not going to back down. He's not going to leave without Olivia, and that means he won't be leaving this building alive.

"You lost any rights to claim her when you allowed Stu to kick her mother out on the street." A growl rumbles up my chest, and I fist my hands at my sides, trying not to attack before Theo gives me the okay. He's my alpha after all. How this goes down is his call.

A whistle fills the air as a knife flies right for my head. Raising my hands, I clap them together, managing to trap it between them before it hits its target. I drop it to the floor and see the blood on my palms before I feel the sting of the slices it's caused. *Fucker!*

"Fucker," Eddie calls from across the room, seemingly reading my thoughts. He starts towards the alpha, only to be held back by Billy's arm across his chest.

"No. This isn't your fight," Theo states from beside me. His words sound guttural, causing me to suddenly swallow.

I turn to Theo, needing to see his face to understand what he wants to do next. Catching sight of Bel standing behind me, leaves me feeling suddenly grateful. If I had just ducked away from the knife instead of catching it, it would've most likely found a target in her.

Theo gives me a nod, and I take that as my permission to attack. Before I can move to attack him like I'd planned, my wolf jumps forward taking control of my body. Within seconds, I'm stalking towards him on all fours. Teeth bared, a menacing growl escapes my snout.

The female I'd met in the hall earlier cowers as I pass, eyes on the floor as she plays with the hem of her shirt in her hands.

"You've made it perfectly clear you aren't leaving without his daughter so there's no chance he's going to let you leave." Theo's nonchalant comment comes from where I'd left him by the door.

The alpha fox takes a step back and looks at me with wide eyes, no doubt belatedly realising he just made a grave mistake.

My wolf snarls at the sight of his prey trying to escape.

I gnash my jaws at him, feeding on his fear that I can taste in the air. Deciding I've played with my food enough, I pounce, jaws wide to allow my teeth to sink into his neck when I make contact. As his blood fills my mouth and I rip at his neck, I start to relax for the first time since hearing Selena's earlier screams.

As the alpha fox's heartbeat diminishes, so does the threat to what's mine.

23.

SAFE AT LAST

It's been a week since Cain and the others came back from chasing the foxes out of town. It didn't slip my attention that Cain had come back wearing a completely different outfit to the one he'd left the pack house in. I didn't question him about it at the time. He came back to me in one piece and that's all that matters, regardless of what he had to do to ensure Olivia's safety. But it's been playing on my mind and I know I'll have to ask at some point. I've been to visit Alyssa a few times and even took Olivia with me once, which seemed to help bring Alyssa out of her deep sombre mood, even if it was for only a few minutes. I'm hoping it's a sign that when her baby arrives—which Cain informed me could be as soon as next week, due to werewolves having a similar duration of pregnancy as normal wolves— it'll help her heal by giving her a new focus for her life and future.

We're driving towards yet another surprise. I don't know how many sucky surprises it's going to take for him to realise they aren't worth doing.

I bite my lip as I contemplate asking about the foxes.

Cain flicks his eyes to me having taken them off the road for only a second. "Ask. I can see something's eating away at you." He blindly reaches out and gives my knee a gentle squeeze. "You might as well ask or it'll ruin the whole day."

I release a deep breath and relax into the seat at the comfort of his touch. "What happened to the foxes? Did you kill them all?"

"*What?*" His high-pitched question causes Livie to stir in her car seat. We both stare in her direction, and I silently pray she doesn't wake up until we've finished this conversation.

A second passes without her crying and Cain lets out a breath. "Do you really think we killed them all?"

Guilt runs through me for thinking such a thing, but he's spot on: I had thought that. "I didn't know what to think," I admit, feeling the need to explain more. I press on before he can react. "I know what you are and how dangerous you can be even though I haven't seen it first-hand. You came home in a different set of clothes. It was obvious your wolf had been out and I'm betting it wasn't to play."

Cain shakes his head. Seeing the unhappiness in his down-turned facial features, I grab his hand, locking my fingers in his as I feel the need to touch him. To comfort him. "I shouldn't have left you thinking like that. You've been with the pack for so long, I forget you'd been left in the dark for most of that time." Cain lets out a sigh.

I rub the back of his hand with my thumb. "Cain, it's not your fault. I should have asked sooner. Part of me didn't care… *doesn't* care what you had to do. Whatever it is, you did it to protect Olivia, and that's all that matters. I just wondered if anyone else was going to come and try to get her later… or heaven forbid take you away from me as payback for what you and Theo did to the other foxes." I swallow past the scratchy feeling in my throat, suddenly overwhelmed by the heaviness in my chest.

Cain pulls the car off the road sharply, and once the engine's switched off, he turns in his seat. "Hey, shh." He cups my cheek, lifting my gaze to meet his as he wipes a tear on my cheek with his thumb. "Nobody is coming for Olivia or me. I can promise you that. Okay?"

Seeing the truth in his sparkling blue eyes, my fear dissipates. I swallow away the lump in my throat and nod.

"Only one fox died, and that was the alpha. He wouldn't leave without Olivia, which meant I couldn't allow him to live." His piercing gaze searches my face, and for a moment, I wonder what he's looking for. A smile crosses his face, and he sits back, seemingly satisfied with whatever he sees.

"The beta fox took charge, becoming the new alpha. He gave his word that his skulk would never come back for Olivia. If I had any doubt, I wouldn't have let them leave, but they didn't even want to be there in the first place, like Stu, they were just following orders."

I slide my hand over his cheek, feeling the slight stubble under my palm. Leaning forward, I place a searing kiss on his lips, heat floods my body and I suddenly wish we were anywhere but parked up on the side of the road. I pull back before I end up climbing into his lap and taking what I need from him. "I trust your judgement. If you say we're safe, we *are* safe at last."

Tempted to lean in for another kiss, I lick my lips. Cain rubs his thumb over the wetness on my bottom lip. I can see the temptation in his eyes and the way he licks his own lips.

"Let's get back on the road, or we'll never get to our destination," he says, starting the car and pulling into a gap in the traffic as he leads us once again to our surprise destination.

As Cain's pulling down a dirt track road, I get a familiar sensation, like I've been here before. Once the fields beside us start to fill with sunflowers, I know I've been here before.

"Cain," I say, my voice breaking on the one word, unable to keep the emotion hidden.

He stops at the side of the road beside the fourth field on the right. "I thought it was about time we introduced Olivia to your father and Maxie."

The thought about bringing Olivia here hadn't even crossed my mind yet, but the fact that Cain knew it's something I'd want, makes my heart almost explode with love for him. Tears well in my eyes, overwhelmed with emotions.

Cain wipes at my escaping tears. "This wasn't meant to make you sad. We don't have to get out. I can turn the car around and go home," he offers, putting his hand back on the keys still hanging in the ignition.

I place my hand on his arm. "No. I'm not sad. I'm happy. So happy that you thought of what I needed before I even knew I needed it."

Pulling the keys from the ignition, he relaxes back into the seat. "I'm your mate. It's what I'm here for."

I slide over the centre console and sit in his lap, facing him. "I love you."

He crushes his lips to mine and causing my somewhat rounder bottom—since having Olivia—to press against the steering wheel, setting off the horn. Olivia lets out a wail, and I press my forehead against Cain's as I try to contain my laughter.

He taps the side of my thigh. "Get that bubble butt out the car and I'll grab Livie."

24.

OUR FAMILY

CAIN

I let out a hearty laugh as Selena climbs out of the car, knocking the horn twice more on her way out. "Shh… it's all right, Livie. It's only Mummy and her big bubble butt," I call back to Olivia in her car seat.

Selena swats at my arm. "I swear, Cain, if you refer to my butt as a bubble butt one more time I won't be held accountable for my actions."

Holding my hands up, I give in. She shakes her head—clearly not believing my offer one iota—before walking off into the field where a few years ago we'd scattered her father and brother's ashes.

After getting out the car, I open the back and unhook Olivia from the car seat. Turning to face the field, I watch Selena, her head thrown back as she looks up to the sky, her blonde waves hanging loose as her mint green dress flutters between the flowers in the wind.

I tilt Olivia in my arms so she's looking in Selena's direction. "You see that beautiful goddess, Livie? She's your mummy. And my mate. I think that makes us both the luckiest people on the planet."

I walk through the field and come to a stop beside Selena, slipping my free arm around her waist. "Have you told them why we're here?"

She looks down from the sky, and I catch sight of the blush crossing her cheeks before she drops her eyes to her feet. "I must look like an idiot."

"Far from it, beautiful. In fact, we were just saying how you looked like a goddess. Isn't that right, Livie?" I glance at Olivia for confirmation and get a smile in return, which I take as a win. "See? She just agreed," I say, nudging Selena in the side.

Selena chuckles. "I'm pretty sure that was wind, but I'll believe you." She presses a kiss to my shoulder, and I kiss her on the top of the head before offering Olivia over to her. She takes her without question, and I slip my keys into my back pocket before taking another item out of my front pocket.

I drop to one knee at her feet.

She gasps and lifts a hand to her mouth.

Taking a deep, calming breath, I swallow the panic running through me at the thought of her possibly rejecting me. "Selena. I knew you were my mate from the first time I laid eyes on you. We've had some obstacles in our way but we finally found our way back to each other." Having seemingly forgotten how to breathe and talk, I take a quick breath. "Even though we're officially mated, for my wolf and the pack to be happy, I'd like to make things right for you and Olivia. Selena, will you marry me?" I hold out the ring I'd picked a few days ago, the one I've been dying to see on her finger.

Selena drops to her knees before me. If I wasn't so concerned about her answer, I would probably be worried about the mess her dress will be in. "Of course I'll marry you…. Oh, Cain." She presses her soft lips against mine in a quick kiss before pulling back and looking at me with wide eyes surrounded by wet lashes. "You didn't have to do this, you know? I was perfectly happy being mated, without the ceremony."

"Maybe I'm selfish, but I want to stand in front of everyone and make us a family. My family."

"Our family," Selena corrects me before I sink my hands in to her hair and kiss her senseless, while being careful not to crush Olivia between the two of us. I'm filled with euphoria in the perfectness of the moment. I can imagine us coming here for years to come—chasing Olivia between the sunflowers while Selena cradles another child of ours in her arms.

We may have hurdles to face in our future, but I know *together* we can get through anything that comes to try us.

The End.

EXCERPT

Please turn the page for an excerpt of

Love of Three
Mount Roxby Series, #4
A Novella.

Previously published as a short story in *Haunted by Love Anthology*.

Coming soon with extra content.

NEVER
UNDERESTIMATE
A WITCH

Clearing the tables at the end of the night can be therapeutic—all the mess disappearing and the bar being ready for opening up the next day. Unfortunately, there are times when it isn't so good. Like tonight, when that last customer hangs around, moving with every table you clear.

I place the chairs upside down on the last table and glance around the room to make sure I haven't missed anything. All the tables leading to the dance floor are clean, and the chairs are upside down how I like them. The row of booths along the right-hand wall all have chairs upside down on the edges of the table so people know they're no longer to be used.

I turn to the bar with my cloth, preparing for my last job of the night. Well, that and nonchalantly getting the vampire who's leaning against the bar to leave.

"Look, buddy, it's time for ya to go home." I collect a handful of glasses along the bar, taking them around the other side to put them in the little dishwasher. "I wanna get home before the sun rises and I'm pretty sure you do too," I state, making it clear I know exactly what he is. I don't share his reasons for getting home before sunrise, though. I'm a witch, not a vampire.

In a flash, he's behind the bar and crowding my space.

"We could have a pretty good time between now and

sunrise." He glances around the room. "Besides, it's not like this place has any windows. We could keep going until the sun puts me to sleep."

I shudder at the thought of being stuck with his lifeless body. I take a step back, and he follows. "Look, ya need to get outta my space or I won't be held responsible for my actions."

He throws his head back and lets out a heavy laugh. These other supes always underestimate us witches. Vampires and shifters are the worst culprits. Demons seem to be the only ones who remember how dangerous we can be. "You won't be held respon—"

I cut his sentence short by throwing a spell at him with a clench of my fist. He drops his head into his hand as I squeeze his brain in my fist.

"Shiit," he groans. The pain is clearly too much for him to handle.

The front door opens and I glance that way as I step around the bar and away from the vampire.

"Is everything all right in here?" Billy, one of the local were-wolves, asks from the doorway, his eyes flicking from me to the vamp.

I loosen my fist, effectively releasing my grip on the vamp's brain, but only enough for him to hear my words through the pain.

"Would ya mind giving Dominick a call?" The vamp whimpers at his king's name. "Let him know we've got a misbehaving vamp for him to pick up."

By the time I've finished my sentence, Billy already has his phone out and up to his ear. He takes a couple of seconds to relay my message before hanging up and sliding the phone into his back pocket.

"There are a couple of wolves outside who I'm going to send home. Then I'll show Dominick in when he arrives. Are you okay with him?" He nods towards the vampire who's still holding his head in his hands.

I wipe my nose with the back of my hand and see the blood as I lift my arm away. Magic always takes a toll, and it usually demands payment in blood or power.

"We'll be fine." I give my wrist a sudden flick, effectively breaking the vamp's neck.

The vampire's body slumps to the floor and Billy gives me an appraising look. "Jesus, sugar." He clears his throat. "I need to get some air before I do something to embarrass myself," he says, walking back out the door. I catch sight of him adjusting himself in his pants before the door closes and I realise what he meant with his parting words. Could seeing me snapping a neck really have turned him on? Werewolves are known for being violent. I guess that could float his boat.

I step over the vamp as I go about cleaning the bar. He isn't dead, just incapacitated until his body heals. I'm sure Dominick will be here to deal with him long before he comes to.

There are only a couple of ways to kill a vampire: staking and beheading. Not everyone knows that there are a few other tricks, like the one I just shared with Billy. Dominick will probably be pissed at me for that, but I'll deal with those consequences later.

I slam the dishwasher closed and stand up to find Billy and Dominick strolling in the front door. They're like polar opposites. Dominick is tall, dark, and handsome, always impeccable in a suit with his wiry frame and dark curls hanging around his face, whereas Billy looks rough and dangerous in his jeans and biker leathers, with his shaved head and large muscular body.

I shake my head as I rake my eyes over their bodies, trying to kill the thoughts of having them in my bed. *Jesus!* I'd sworn I would never date another supernatural creature. Not after my ex. He was an angel, except he acted more like a demon. He was so controlling and, after seeing how the werewolves act around their mates, I can only imagine Billy would be the same. Not to mention Dominick; he likes to control anything that breathes in his territory. The alpha of the Mount Roxby pack, Theo, has had to push for equal pegging in their joint ownership of the area.

"Like something you see?" Billy smirks, catching me ogling.

Dominick straightens the cuffs of his jacket. "She was clearly looking at me. This suit is fitted to perfection, after all."

I roll my eyes. "I was deciding, if I took ya both to bed with me, who'd bottom for who?" I say with a smirk. It wasn't exactly a lie. The question *had* crossed my mind when I pictured them naked in my bed.

It's well known that Dominick doesn't care about gender when he chooses his lovers. His ex-boyfriend recently turned up and caused havoc in the town. Not only did his actions make Dominick sire the alpha's sister, turning her into a vampire, but he also murdered Theo's beta wolf, his second. He did it all as a punishment because Dominick wouldn't make him a vampire, so I'm not surprised to see Dominick step aside and give Billy a thorough eyeing from head to foot.

"I don't bottom for anyone, but I'd definitely be happy to..." He raises a brow and a smirk crosses his face. "...*wrestle* with him over the position."

Billy steps up close so their chests are touching. "For me you will." He places a kiss on Dominick's lips, biting his bottom lip between his teeth before pulling away. "And you'll be begging to do it again." My mouth goes dry at the sight before me. *Holy shit.* I blink, unable to believe what I'm seeing.

The groans of the vamp at my feet break the heated moment.

"Bitch!" he calls as he grips my ankles, digging his nails in and drawing blood. His fangs descend at the smell of my blood, but I don't worry about him trying to feed from me. My wards won't allow such severe violence in the building. Well, unless

I'm the one inflicting the violence. Dominick suddenly appears on this side of the bar, dragging the vampire up by his throat. He apparently doesn't care about the pain my wards are causing him. I throw out a hand and mutter a few words, disabling them.

"That wasn't necessary, but thank you." He walks around the bar, pausing as he reaches the door. "This—" He points his finger between Billy, me, and back to himself. "—we'll deal with this another night when the sun isn't so close to rising." He smiles. "I have a feeling we'll need plenty of time to explore things thoroughly." He disappears out the door, and I struggle to tear my eyes away from the purple painted wood.

Billy clears his throat and I watch him lock the door. "Well, that was… interesting."

I laugh. "That's not the word I'd use to describe it." I take a deep, calming breath and pull my shoulder-length hair back into a loose ponytail with an elastic band I always keep around my wrist. "Jesus, I never would've guessed ya swung that way. It was just a fantasy that popped into my head and I couldn't keep my damn mouth shut," I say while walking around the bar and straightening the stools.

I feel Billy step up behind me. "Have I ever told you how much I like your British accent?" Placing a hand on my hip, he spins me around before sliding his other hand over my shoulder and around my neck. I grip his biceps and shake my head. "Dominick intrigues me. Someone needs to take his control away, and I wouldn't mind that being me."

He crushes his lips against mine, as if he's trying to prove he doesn't only like guys. "I'd certainly swing for you, sugar," he says, brushing his lips against mine before capturing them in another kiss. I slide my hands up his arms and around his neck as I lose myself in the moment.

ALSO BY
AIMIE JENNISON

Mount Roxby Series

Pride to Pack

Forever Young and Beautiful

Reclaiming the One

Love of Three - Coming late March, 2018

Losing Pride - Coming late 2018

Rossi Pack Series

Releasing the Wolf

ACKNOWLEDGEMENTS

I want to thank *my family* for supporting me unconditionally. For not getting stressed when the simple stuff slips my mind. I love you all to pieces.

Sam Destiny, My Parabatai, You are my rock, forever and always. Love ya, girl.

Sloan, from Sloan J Designs, Thank you for the amazing cover. You always seem to hit the spot with exactly what I imagine.

Finally, I'd like to thank you guys, the readers. Without your love and support, this journey wouldn't be as fun. I love my stories and characters but knowing that you guys love them too means the world to me. Thank YOU.

ABOUT THE AUTHOR

Aimie is a Yorkshire lass calling Queensland, Australia, home. She is a mother to three boys.

Aimie loves to people watch, it's her favourite way to come up with new characters and stories. So next time a stranger is staring at you in the street don't panic, they could be an author basing a character on you.

Aimie has always loved to read and write. Her favourite place to listen to her characters is at the beach.

Aimie would love to hear from you. Comments and questions are always welcome.

For more information:
www.aimiejennison.com
aimiejennison@gmail.com

facebook.com/AuthorAimieJennison

twitter.com/Aim4theNeck

instagram.com/aim4theneck

bookbub.com/authors/aimie-jennison

goodreads.com/Aim4theNeck

www.ingramcontent.com/pod-product-compliance
Lightning Source LLC
Chambersburg PA
CBHW070728120726
47910CB00001B/20